IN THE SHADOWS

BY THE AUTHOR OF

The Red Floor (2011)
The Courier Wore Shorts (2013)
Where Bodies Fall (2015)

IN

THE

SHADOWS

SHEILA KINDELLAN-SHEEHAN

Véhicule Press

Published with the generous assistance of the Canada Council for the Arts, the
Canada Book Fund of the Department of Canadian Heritage, and the
Société de développement des entreprises culturelles du Québec (SODEC).

SODEC
Québec ✚ ✚

Funded by the Government of Canada
Financé par le gouvernement du Canada | Canadä

Cover design: David Drummond
Cover and back cover photos: Robert Idsinga
Typeset in Minion by Simon Garamond
Printed by Marquis Printing Inc.

LIBRARY AND ARCHIVES CANADA CATALOGUING IN PUBLICATION

Sheehan, Sheila Kindellan, 1944-, author
In the shadows / Sheila Kindellan-Sheehan.

Issued in print and electronic formats.
ISBN 978-1-55065-481-3 (softcover).– ISBN 978-1-55065-489-9 (EPUB)

I. Title.

PS8637.H44I58 2017   C813'.6   C2017-903138-4
C2017-903139-2

Published by Véhicule Press, Montréal, Québec, Canada
www.vehiculepress.com

Distributed in Canada by LitDistCo
www.litdistco.ca

Distributed in the U.S. by Independent Publishers Group
www.ipgbook.com

Printed in Canada on FSC certified paper

Forever remembered, always loved—

Irene Pingitore,
the vivacious team member
with the sparkle of a young girl.

Louise Morin,
what a joy for me to say
you were a friend of mine,
a touchstone of every day.

In memory of
Heike Emma Hanna,
a gentle friend with
the heart of a lion.

Yet each man kills the thing he loves
By each let this be heard
Some do it with a bitter look
Some with a flattering word
The coward does it with a kiss
The brave man with a sword.

—OSCAR WILDE, "The Ballad of Reading Gaol"

Before you embark on a journey of revenge,
dig two graves.

—CONFUCIUS

Characters

Major Crimes: The Team

TONI DAMIANO: 44, new acting chief of the Crémazie Division, working alone, trying to maintain her focus on a new investigation while assuming the responsibilities of the division

PIERRE MATTE: 43, detective, partner to Damiano who finds himself embroiled in a murder investigation that threatens his job and his person

RICHARD DONAT: 58, Chief of the Crémazie Division who enjoys a long-awaited anniversary Cajun dinner that goes horribly wrong with dire consequences

MARIE DUMONT: 43, a meticulous Crime detective who pursues all leads when the chain of custody is broken in a first-degree murder inquiry

MICHEL BELMONT: senior pathologist at Parthenais, the Montreal city morgue. When this pathologist plays detective, he proves his skills and insight to Major Crimes

DANIEL BOUCHER: a decent cop who decides to play vigilante and loses his badge, his livelihood and his freedom.

GEORGES PICHETTE: a high-priced mouthpiece hired to help Officer Boucher avoid prison time

CARMEN DIMAGGIO: 34, business woman, leaves a late-night party and inadvertently ventures into a nightmare as a witness to a shooting

CAITLIN DONOVAN: 36, university professor, the steadying influence of a long-lasting friendship with Carmen DiMaggio

MATTHEW ALLEN: an intelligent, quirky storyteller with dangerous skills

VELMA: the flamboyant producer of shows staged at Café Cleopatra confronts a real-life drama

PETER HENLEY: a university professor who 'plays' dangerously and pays the price

NATHANIEL GOLDBERG: a Montreal surgeon with new-found freedom that he uses to full advantage

RACHEL MEYER: Goldberg's wife and mother of his two children, drawn into the spill of a tragedy

PAMELA MULALLY: the strength, the match and the love of the cantankerous Chief Donat

DYLAN KANE: the beautiful young man who finds more than shelter from middle-aged men

Chapter One

[June 17]
West Island

Saturday night began with a promise almost kept.

Chief Richard Donat and his wife Pamela, chic in a pale yellow dress and sporting a spring tan, celebrated their thirty-fourth wedding anniversary at Bistro Nolah, a little gem Pamela had discovered online in Montreal's 'burbs – the West Island. The closest Pamela might come to her dream of ambling down Bourbon Street in New Orleans and listening to signature jazz into the wee hours at Preservation Hall on Peter Street, was their dinner that night. Her friends took vacations – she planned, and then often cancelled hers.

Bistro Nolah had a New Orleans atmosphere and earned raves for its Louisiana cuisine. Modern and refined, the bistro offered impeccable service, subtle lighting and the glow of intimacy. Richard had chosen a Chablis les Clos Grand Cru and had eaten his and Pamela's "home-cooked" hushpuppies. When the bouchées arrived, Cajun Arancini, Pamela raised a hand to Richard. "No, you don't! I want that. I left the hushpuppy because I'm saving myself for the bread pudding with its 'boozy' Bourbon sauce, as advertised."

"Well, you've done your research, Pamela."

"Of course I have! I'm ordering the shrimp Creole with Jambalaya. You said you wanted the blackened catfish, the house special." The waiter stood a few feet from the table and approached to take their orders when the Chief gave him the nod.

Richard was a second away from placing his cell phone on the table when Pamela's green eyes turned dark. "You're not …" Richard didn't have time to comment.

"Your detectives can hold down the fort for tonight. You've trained them, so I know the team is capable of handling the weekend shift. We need this time, Richard. I want you with me on our anniversary. That cell phone of yours is an addiction, worse than another woman. At least she'd have her own place. It's become a barrier between us and I hate it!"

Chief Donat could argue with the best and have big men sweating.

Every ounce of his body was wired and angular. Stress came with the job and he'd begun a cop's life at nineteen. Donat was a career man. Yet, he wasn't above guilt for his many absences, late nights, and the loneliness his work had brought into their lives. He was no match for Pamela Mulally. He loved his Irish wife. Always had. He turned off his phone and stuck it in his pocket. Since the main course was freshly prepared at the bistro, the couple had time to talk.

Donat looked at his wife and still puzzled at times how Pamela had managed to handle him through the years. He wasn't bothered by her skillful MO; it was a comfort and a consistency he relied on. Pamela appeared to be reading the timbre of his thoughts.

"If you're wondering if I still love you, Richard, the answer is, I do. All in all, the years have been good to us. We have two beautiful sons and a grandchild on the way, and we have each other. We have been lucky. When I think of our many friends whose marriages just dissolved, I'm happy we've stuck it out. You're part of me and I like that. Since I've gone back to work, I'm energized again and I have new challenges."

Richard owned a decent smile he rarely used, but he used it then. Still he had to add, "You knew what you were getting into, Pamela. And I'm speaking English tonight for you." Both languages were spoken at home, and at times, a blending of both. Pamela was fluent and for that she credited Richard.

"I appreciate your English tonight. Your other point is hogwash! I was twenty-three. Who understands anything at that age?"

"Hmm, that's probably true. I thought I'd be doing good when I joined the force, protecting Montrealers and putting bad guys in jail. I certainly never foresaw that political games, bureaucracy and stress go with the job. I suppose, I can add, who knows anything about the years ahead?"

"The present is what matters, Richard. You're still doing good. You've remained a principled man, and I admire you for that."

Donat rubbed his forearm and forced another smile. "I love you, Pamela. Know something? It was your name that caught my attention. I've always liked it. Classy."

Pamela rarely missed anything. "What's wrong with your arm?" There was a hint of alarm in her voice. There were times Pamela feared a phone call telling her Richard had collapsed at the office. She almost expected it. She worried about him. He was never able to turn the job off. Too many nights Richard came home stiff with anxiety and stayed awake for hours, staring at the ceiling and whispering to himself. Sometimes, he struck out in the night, narrowly missing her. Pamela tried to ease the anxiety by telling Richard she might need a helmet in bed. Richard began propping two pillows around his shoulders.

"The only problem with my arm is that I sleep on it at night. Getting too old for that, I guess. Everything wears out. I'll have to find another sleeping position, and I'm already on my second one."

Donat rested both his hands on the table. "Pamela, I make this promise tonight. For our thirty-fifth, we *will* drive to New Orleans and stay there until you've heard all the music you love and you've eaten so many beignets that your lips are white from the icing. Deal?"

"Don't forget the cemetery. I'll need a whole day, Richard. It's a trove of history and lore, and I don't want to miss anything. I intend to hold you to that promise."

"I'll keep this pledge, you'll see."

When their steaming entrées arrived, they didn't disappoint. Nolah boasted of its presentation, and the boast was merited. Pamela took the first bite and began waving her hand in front of her mouth. "Whew, hot!" The waiter headed to their table with a pitcher of water, smiling. *First-timers.* Pamela grabbed a glass and drank.

"Are you alright?" Richard asked.

"I wanted authentic Cajun. Well, it's that, and fire! I'll take smaller bites with water."

Donat doubted the catfish was as hot and dug into the daub of caviar and the fish. He too grabbed a water glass, not as desperately as Pamela. He took a second bite of fish including the generous bed of sweet potato under the fish. Richard tried to swallow, but he couldn't – he didn't reach for more water. His fork fell to the floor. He clawed at his upper arm and crashed to the floor. Pamela knocked her chair aside, rushed over to her husband and fell to her knees beside him. "Call 9-1-1! Hurry!" Their waiter ran over as concerned diners around their table looked on. Even the chef emerged from the kitchen because he could see his guests as he prepared the meals. Pamela undid Richard's tie, unbuttoned his gray jacket and screamed his name.

"Does anyone know CPR?" Pamela shouted hysterically.

"I'm a nurse," a diner called out and joined Pamela on the floor and immediately began chest compressions. Five minutes later, the paramedics arrived, began the oxygen and IV bag and loaded Richard into the ambulance. Pamela left with them. Switching to French, Pamela told them who Richard was. The ambulance appeared to pick up speed. The driver called in a Code Blue. She watched the paramedic continue CPR so roughly she was alarmed. Pamela didn't realize she was crying. She focused on Richard whose head had turned toward her. Pamela felt another burst of hysteria and something worse. When she was extremely nervous, she felt a strong urge to laugh. She blamed the tic on her mother who had said that tears and laughter were first cousins. Pamela cupped her hand over her mouth to conceal the laughter rising from her throat.

For once, she couldn't read his expression. What was it? What was Richard trying to tell her? That he was scared, that he was in pain, that he was saying goodbye? What? Tears streamed down her cheeks, leaving dark streaks of blue eyeliner and mascara. Her hysteria increased. What if Richard died? What if she never understood what he was trying to tell her? Would he ever forgive her and understand the reason for her confusion? Her chief, felled by a spicy dinner! Pamela dashed that thought. Black humor was not something Richard ever appreciated. Pamela bent down and studied Richard's face.

Then she understood. He wasn't trying to speak. He was expressing bafflement. It was bafflement that caviar and catfish could take down the Chief of Major Crimes! Tears and laughter provoked a single roar that shook Pamela's whole body. Richard's stretcher bounced en route to the Lakeshore General Hospital. The next half-hour was a blur. On arrival, a triage nurse followed them into a small trauma room. Curtains closed around Richard, the ER physician and two nurses. Pamela found herself suddenly on the outside, steered back to the overcrowded waiting room and guided up to the triage nurse for information.

"I know you are very upset, but I do need to ask these questions."

Pamela looked at her hands. "Oh, my God, I've left my purse behind! I don't even know where. What will I do?" she shouted, weeping loudly. "I've lost everything and that's not like me! What am I going to do?"

A weary Good Samaritan, heard the frightened woman, left her seat and went over to Pamela. "Come and take my seat. You can use my phone. First of all, where were you tonight?"

"My purse might be in the ambulance or at the bistro or I might have dropped it. I just don't know!"

The woman helping Pamela asked. "May I call for you?"

Pamela grabbed the cell. "What's the number?"

"It's right there on the cell phone, but I should call. You're very nervous. Please let me try."

Pamela was stubborn and it took three tries to get it right. "Yes, hello, my husband fell ill. I've lost my purse and all the information in it!" Her voice rose to a shrill.

The hostess on the other end was young and calm. "We have your purse Madam – don't worry about that. How is …"

"Thank God!"

"How is your husband?"

"I don't know. How can I get the purse?" Pamela realized something else. "Our car is still there. I have to call my sons. I can't do this alone!"

"Both will be safe till you get here. We're open till one."

Pamela finally looked at her Good Samaritan and fell into her arms. "Thank you." Still holding onto the cell phone she tried to call her son Denis. The number escaped her, and she gave her forehead a few good raps. "I can't remember Denis's number. What's happening to me?"

"Look, sit down. Give me the phone and his last name, and I'll call him for you."

The woman found the number, called and handed the phone to Pamela. "Denis!"

"What's wrong, Mom?"

"Dad's had a coronary, I don't know. He collapsed. We're at the Lake-shore General – I've lost my purse – I don't have the car."

"Mom? What? Slow down. Dad had a heart attack? You lost your purse and the car is gone, too?"

"If you don't get here quickly, your father might die," Pamela sobbed.

"Mom!"

Pamela couldn't speak. The woman took the phone. "Denis, I'm trying to help your mother. She's left her purse and car at this Bistro Nolah on boulevard St-Jean. We've called; they have both there. Here's their number. Wait a sec – okay it's …"

"What about keys? Have you any news of my father?"

"Not yet." The woman turned and asked Pamela, "Is there an extra set of car keys in your purse?"

Pamela jumped to her feet once more and took the phone. "Yes! Thank God! The extras are in my purse, Denis. Hurry, I need you."

"I'll call Martin. Dad would want both his sons there. He'll go direct-ly to the hospital – I'll get the purse and car. I'll use Uber."

"What if your father …" Pamela could not utter the worst possibility.

"Then we'll both drive to the hospital and get the other stuff later. Just wait, Mom."

Pamela sat down and went quiet. She saw the evening in fast jerky motions, like in silent films. Pamela hated hospital waiting rooms where tired, worried people sat for hours, fragile and alone, thinking the worst, reminded of their mortality. A simmering anger rose and drained what color was left in her cheeks. It began with the catfish and found its source in Richard. *He should have retired three years ago.* She wrapped her arms around her chest and dropped her head. *If Richard survives, he's not ever, not ever going back to work.* She looked down at her yellow dress, smudged and crumpled.

Your detectives can hold down the fort for one weekend shift.

Chapter Two

Dylan Kane and Matthew Allen sat together on red stools in the legendary Montreal Pool Room behind the front window, people watching. Soon after, Dylan with rapt attention listened to Matthew's glacier story, head in his hand, never interrupting, while he picked at his hot dog steamé and fries. They were an odd couple that night. Matthew usually dressed down, and was pushing fifty. Dylan appeared younger than thirty, lean as a teenager. He wore tight black slacks, black sneakers with silver zippers on the side, topped by a luxury casual slim-fit shirt with epaulettes that gave it a military look. Dylan had a classic beauty that immediately prompted assumptions that he was gay. In fact, he was. Matthew was straight, a rock and glacier climber, a fearless adventurer, photographer and all-round idiosyncratic individual. Dylan had found a friend, a guy who wanted nothing from him and taught him about a different kind of life. Dylan learned to listen. He was in a bad place when he turned up at Café Cleo four months ago. His life had been on a downturn. His relationship had fallen apart. He wasn't looking for a hookup – he needed a refuge, and time to regroup. Matthew's hair-gripping stories, told with such detail, kept Dylan wide-eyed and far away from himself.

"Once I was doing an ice climb with my partner. We call it a mind-bender, about three hundred feet from the ground."

Dylan's mouth opened in awe.

"My friend had tied us to two massive icicles in a hanging belay, an anchor hook. I had to shift around a bit because my left leg was going numb. One of the icicles shattered. There's no time for nerves. With adrenaline pumping, I swung over to the remaining icicle that looked no more solid than the one that had just disintegrated. I didn't look down, and steadied my body. Fate was with us, and we got out of that one. Remember the ice axe that saved me when that ice bridge broke? I'd wandered off course in the storm and onto an ice bridge over a crevasse. When the bridge collapsed under me, I managed to lodge my ice axe into the far edge, which I clung to as I reached over and dug myself a hold in the snow. Laymen can't understand that high – the euphoria – you have to take those risks to feel it. You're on the edge, in the seconds between life and death. Ordinary life can't compare."

Dylan's awe bent into a *why*. "Do you have a death wish?"

"No, that's adventure. I don't scare like most friends I know. I have a high tolerance to pain. Once when I had surgery, the anesthesiologist had a hell of a time putting me out. Other days, like now, here I am eating a classic Montreal Pool Room hot dog. What's with you tonight? You bought the dogs for us. Looks like you found some cash." Matthew noticed the clothes. "You're what – up for a night as well?"

"Got'em on eBay. I kinda knew where I could find a few bucks. After Cleo's performance tonight, I just might have a second chance."

"Going back to an ex?"

"Maybe. But no more questions. You've really lived, Matthew."

"And you haven't?"

"No comparison. Gotta protect this face and body – it's what pays for me. I can't afford your kind of adventures."

"Really? That's not a life. I see other guys at Cleo's like you, going no-where."

Dylan's eyes hardened. "I'm not those other guys. I like older men, or maybe it's that they like me, and they take care of me. Gut honest – work has never appealed to me. Yeah, it's been quiet for the past two weeks, but if I play the game right tonight, I'm back."

"You're wasting your life, Dylan!"

"I'll have to buckle down at some point, but as long as this body works for me, I'm hanging on to that icicle. It's a different kind of high."

"Not funny. You staying for the show tonight?"

"Yeah, yeah, late date. If things work out, I might text you. I will." Dylan looked hopeful, camouflaging a hint of desperation.

Dylan and Matthew left the Montreal Pool Room and crossed the street to the Café and took in the performance in silence. The music was so loud you had to shout to be heard. Matthew took photos and videos of the acts for his blog. He had a ringside table that he shared with Dylan and two photographers. That night after their dogs and talk, Dylan sat lost, planning his own performance.

Café Cleopatra, in the center of what was once Montreal's red-light district, is one hundred and five years old, an institution situated on St-Laurent Boulevard below Ste-Catherine Street, known as the Lower Main, an entertainment landmark since the founding of Montreal. Developers wanted to tear down the building to 'revitalize' the area. Cleo put her foot down and boasted that she had been vitalizing the area for ten decades. Her clientele was francophones, anglophones, nationalities from all backgrounds, celebrities and the artistic crowd. People in the 'know' had been to the Café. Cleo's wasn't simply an aged strip joint. Still today, it produced reborn burlesque – festivals and burlesque shows of years gone by. The Café belonged on the Lower Main, and the city ultimately agreed. The owner fought the developers, campaigned against them and won.

A little after midnight the performers at Café Cleopatra, the stage kittens, makeup, sound technicians and the show's director surged onto the stage in a boisterous after-party for "The 30s Show" they had just concluded. The enthusiastic audience, some with face paint, one hundred and forty strong, six photographers, the doorman, and the candy box girl, all rushed to the edges of the stage to join the revelry. Music thumped, costume bits flew, cards littered the floor, and cameras flashed in the crowd. The commingling was virtually tribal in rhythm. At Cleo's, the Candyass Cabaret presented a show on the third Friday of every month. The audience who came back month after month, and the performers, were ferociously loyal. The nominal cachet the troupe received was not a factor – the performers worked for their love of expression, and perhaps for escape from the tedium of their lives.

No one noticed that Dylan had slipped away, or saw him climb the side stairs toward the dressing rooms. The performers were partying and had come down another staircase that opened onto the stage. Dylan reached the second floor and hurried into the dressing room on his right against the back wall. The closed doors to the roof were on the left side of the room. The person he was waiting for hadn't come. Well, maybe he wanted Dylan to wait for him. Dylan checked himself in a mirror. The inner door wasn't locked. He turned the door handle and gently opened it. He'd be barred from Cleo's if he was caught on the second floor, off limits to everyone but the performers. Matthew himself would have to answer to Velma for bringing him up to meet the actors in the first place. Dylan listened to the celebratory noise downstairs. It would smother the grinding sounds of the iron bar latches on the heavy steel safety door leading to the roof. He pulled the first bar back then, slowly, the second. He looked back into the dressing room, still hoping to see his friend appear. He'd forgotten to close the inside door and he ran back and pushed it shut.

When he was on the roof, he leaned in and carefully lifted and forced the steel door closed. The latched door could only be locked from the inside. They could easily sneak back into the dressing room and slip down the stairs without being noticed. The party usually went on till two in the morning. Dylan turned his attention to the roof. Even with the city lights, it was dark, but he could see the lazy graffiti on the walls and the rotting wood piled by the side wall, debris that must have been there for years. He walked over to a padlocked, spiked iron fence, a fire exit that overlooked a side street. No one was on the metal fire stairs, but they had been pulled down. He felt a twitch that he was alone in the darkness. His spirits fell. But that changed.

"I'm over here, Dylan."

Dylan walked around a second inner wall on the roof and smiled. "How the hell? Ah, the fire escape on the other side of the fence, right?" Dylan saw what he thought was an umbrella. "You used that to hook the bottom stairs and pull them down to the ground. You scoped the fire escape then. Cool!" Why hadn't he taken the stairs to the right of the stage as they had planned? Dylan felt a shiver of unease, but he had to discard it. He couldn't risk questioning. He needed the night to work out.

"It's more private back here. No one can see us."

"You're right. I'm glad you came. I thought maybe you wouldn't. Wow! You're in a hurry." Dylan turned to the wall and began to fumble with his pants.

"I swore I was finished with you, but it gets lonely." He was breathless and eager. "We're here now. That's all that matters."

Dylan relaxed, absorbing the whispers, the impatient need of him and the warmth and strength from the arm that went around his neck. He slapped both hands against the wall, waiting, but they collapsed with him when his windpipe snapped. He thrashed about for a few seconds, all in vain. Dylan died so quickly, he never had the chance to be surprised.

Chapter Three

Carmen DiMaggio was still on the service road of Highway 440 when she realized her mistake. All parking on Favreau was closed until the sewer and road work were completed. She'd have to find other spot to park, and her neighbors, tucked in for the night, had taken the closest spots. She wasn't crazy about walking alone on the dark streets to get to her place. She should have spent the night in Westmount at Caitlin's. "Get a grip," she said loudly to herself in the car. Carmen talked to herself when cooking, packing, even cleaning, when that last rare occasion occurred. She was a talker. The community where she lived was mostly Greek, hard-working families, who kept decent hours, except for their Christmas and Easter celebrations that always happened on a Sunday night. Then, they danced on heavy heels well into the early hours. Carmen knew this because her landlord and his family lived directly above her.

She finally found a spot one street from her home on Goyer, but a few blocks up the road. After locking the car, she looked around. It was dark and quiet. Her gang had clubbed too late. It would have been so much easier if she lived downtown. She quickened her pace catching her heel in a crack on the sidewalk. It didn't break. She thought of running. "I'm a klutz – I'd bet odds I'd trip in these shoes. That's all I need, a face plant. I'm thirty-four years old! Just chill! I'm not the first woman who stayed out late." The pep talk didn't work. Fear jumped into her legs and they stiffened and felt heavy. "I've lost nine pounds. I'm in pretty good shape. I should try to run." But she didn't. She'd read of the recent fatal shooting, not that far from where she was, and remembered the young woman stabbed to death on Curé Labelle years before in broad daylight. Nobody stopped to help. "Why am I doing this to myself? Just walk!"

Finally, it seemed forever, she reached the parking lot behind an apartment building that fronted boulevard St-Martin. She climbed the three feet of clay and small rocks and took a few steps onto the elevated parking lot. Without warning, or any sound, perhaps because she had been too much in her head, a runner streaked up the mound and knocked her down as he ran past her. She hit her knee when she fell between two parked cars, and bit hard into her tongue, tasting her salty blood. Dazed and gripped with fear, Carmen crawled back up to her knees in time to see a cop in hot pursuit. She didn't move or cry out. She couldn't. Even in the dark, she saw the cop's gun because he stopped only about five feet across from her on an angle from the runner. He held the gun in both hands, straight-armed, feet apart.

"Arrête!" he shouted. "Arrête, Jacques!"

An apartment still had its lights on and Carmen could see the runner's sweats and his long-sleeved cotton shirt. He began to turn around with arms raised towards the cop. Without warning, the cop shot three times – shot the runner three times. Carmen's ears exploded. She covered them with her hands and would never remember why she rose to her feet and stepped out. The cop turned, eyeballing her, and she him. He levelled the gun at her.

Lights in the building to their right snapped on, windows flew open, and shouting began. As the cop momentarily looked over at the lights and the voices. Carmen ran for her life. She never felt her knee or tripped, spitting blood as she ran while perspiration swept across her body. Carmen never looked back. She just ran and did not stumble on her heels.

When the cop looked up he had lost her. He rushed to the fallen body, bending over it. He reached into the side of his boot, extracted a plastic glove, put it on and dug out his throwaway gun. With his back as cover against the onlookers from the apartment, he pressed it into the victim's hand and made certain he'd left the victim's prints on the handle. He felt for a pulse. Then, clearing his throat, he swallowed and called in the incident. He was off duty and outside his own division. He'd have hell to pay for that. Vigilante, that's the word the media would latch onto. The only positive he could think of was that he'd worn his uniform. It suggested that he was acting as an officer. He had to get his story straight, the SQ, the Sûreté du Québec, might be looking to hang him up. The practice was *de rigueur* in the current political climate as a means of restoring public trust. The provincial police investigated all incidents of Montreal police interventions causing death.

Small cliques of curious tenants, phones held above their heads taking pictures, appeared at the back door of the building and began to edge towards the fallen man. The cop stood up rigidly and forced them back by shouting that this was a crime scene. He tried to inhale deeply, but his heart hammered. He heard the pulse in his neck. There was a witness. He had a wife and two children. He also had one count of excessive force a year ago. There was a witness. He had to get to her.

He'd seen her. She must live in the area. He'd find her. Had she heard him call out Jacques' name? Didn't matter, he couldn't take the chance that she hadn't. He had to find her.

Five police cars with lights and sirens screeched to a halt on rue Goyer. Ten officers jumped the embankment and ran up to the lone cop on the scene. Two began marking off the area with orange tape, waiting for the SPVM Crime van, the Poste de Commandement. Others kept the growing crowd from any clear view of the victim or the cop. The remaining officers packed the area with their presence. One officer knelt down beside the victim, then stood and checked out the cop he didn't know. The guy was a cop or he wouldn't have called it in. "Don't answer any questions without a union rep. Don't even talk to any of us. FYI, we know the vic. Deals crack and heroin. He's a sub-contractor. I saw he wasn't carrying a drop when you caught up with him."

The cop opened his mouth to speak.

"Forget that. Shut it down. Get your facts straight with the rep. I don't want to be called to testify. It's best for you to keep your account simple. I know what I'm talking about. Try to calm down. It's all I can offer."

Further north on Goyer, Carmen reached her car in full panic. Any idea of running down her street and locking herself inside her apartment was out. She had a hard time with the remote car key because it was wet with sweat. She froze inside the car. "He's seen me – he knows I can identify him. It was murder. I witnessed a murder!" Was that sirens already? She had to leave. It was a tight park. Pulling out, she grazed the left side of her bumper and the car in front of her. "Dammit!" Going to her mother's was out. She couldn't put her mother through the nightmare. "He's going to find me. I know it. He will. He has all the resources and he'll have to do it soon. Cops protect each other. I have no chance." Carmen didn't see the road or the passing streets, didn't realize she was speeding. Just drove and screamed, punching the steering wheel until her hand hurt. Every thought set up a blizzard of threats. "He'll canvass my area. He saw *me*. He knows what I look like. One of the neighbors will give me up, or my name. He will find me. How can anyone report another cop? He has to find me." Carmen blew her third stop and slammed on the brakes and pulled over to the side of the road. "I am so fucked!" Her knee throbbed and blood dripped out the side of her mouth. Her tongue was burning. She didn't feel either one.

"I have no clothes for work. Thank God, I have my bag. I'll call my landlord and beg him not to give my name to the police. I can't call him now, but early tomorrow morning. He can't offer my mother's name either. The cop never saw my car, but he can have a composite made of me. Some neighbor will remember me and my car – I've lived there for sixteen years." Carmen tried to bite some loose skin from her thumb, but her teeth were chattering, and her tongue began to hurt. The sobs began again when she pulled out and headed for Westmount, wiping her eyes to see the road. "WHY DID THIS HAVE TO HAPPEN TO ME?"

The traffic light turned red, but by the time she braked and slid, her car was halfway across Greene Avenue in Westmount. She drove through it with no flashing red lights behind her and took the next right. She hadn't caught a ticket and she found the last parking spot just past Caitlin's home. Her whole body ached as she climbed the few stairs to Caitlin's front porch. Darkness hid the lovely cosiness of the home. It was three-thirty in the morning when she rang the doorbell.

Caitlin Donovan didn't hear the first ring – it took four. She grabbed a terrycloth robe, barefooted it to the door and checked the peephole first. She threw the door open. "What the hell's happened to you?"

Chapter Four

Sometime before one, Sunday morning, Donat's sons drove to the Cajun bistro and collected Pamela's purse and car. Back at the hospital, the family was offered a cubicle that patients sat in for hours hoping to see the single ER physician on duty. Pamela was pacing the confined space. She'd kept the door open allowing her a few extra feet. "We still haven't heard one word! I have a mind to march up to the nursing station and demand information."

"Mom, why don't you sit down? They're probably still running tests. They know who Dad is, so we will hear something soon."

"You don't suppose your father has died?" Pamela whispered, trembling.

Martin stepped in front of his older brother. "No! Bad news comes quickly. If the worst had occurred, we'd have heard. Do we even know for certain that Dad's had a heart attack?"

Pamela looked disbelieving at Martin. "If it were a panic attack or indigestion, we'd know by now. It's been over five hours. I wish we were at the new hospital. Richard would have a private room, and we wouldn't be stuck in here like sardines. But there was no time. One minute we were eating, the next, your father had fallen to the floor."

"Mom, we're lucky to have this room. We could be sitting or standing out there with the other poor buggers."

"Language! I've become a curmudgeon – I'm just so worried."

Denis teased his mother. "You've always been a curmudgeon."

Pamela let out a guffaw, and her sons relaxed. "Your father fell on his fork."

Both boys were thinking the same thing. "Lucky he didn't stab himself. Try explaining that one at the division."

"Enough, we're becoming punch drunk. How long do we have to WAIT?" Pamela exclaimed loudly. No one spoke another word. They waited for two more hours.

A physician approached, and Pamela was the first to see him. The family retreated into the room, actually against the back wall.

"Good evening, I'm Doctor Lefebvre. We have your husband on the second floor in the ICU, and he's resting comfortably."

"May I see him?"

"Allow me to explain his condition thus far. We have more testing planned, but I have determined that Chief Donat, I'm told," the family nodded, glad this doctor knew who he was treating, "has suffered a coronary artery spasm. The blood flow to the heart was restricted and actually cut off. He suffered a heart attack. We will perform an angiogram tomorrow that might or might not indicate the source of the spasm. That's because these spasms can come and go. If things fall back into line, we medicate. There is always damage to the heart – we will determine the extent when all the tests are in. The Chief will survive. He'll need rest. Sometimes depression and anxiety are common in these cases."

"I have to see him!" Pamela pleaded.

"Just for a minute and just you, so we don't disturb the other patients."

"Will I be able to have my husband transferred to the new MUHC, the McGill University Health Center?"

"Actually, I work there, but here as well two days a week. I was called in tonight for your husband. I live in Beaconsfield. I will see to his care."

"Richard's in good hands then?"

"So I'm led to believe."

"May we go now?"

"Follow me."

The ICU was located on the second floor. Pamela did not look directly at the other patients – the sight would have overwhelmed her. She had never seen her husband so vulnerable. He lay, hooked to tubes, so still. He never got sick. He'd had only one cold in years! His eyes were closed. Pamela kissed his forehead and took his free hand in her own. Richard opened his eyes. "You're going to make it," she whispered. He squeezed her hand and closed his eyes. She held his hand until he was asleep.

Pamela and the doctor walked down the stairs together. "My husband is still critical for the next forty-eight hours, I believe?"

"That's correct. I can't rule out another spasm."

"We'll be here twenty-four-seven." The family booked a room at the Comfort Inn five minutes from the hospital.

"Mom, you and Martin go to the motel and get some rest. We can't all be here," Denis said.

"Martin and I will be back at ten in the morning. I can't stay away longer than that, Denis."

At the motel Martin lay on one bed, Pamela on the other. She couldn't sleep. Images of Richard falling to the floor flashed before her. What if Richard suffered another spasm and she wasn't there? Fortunately, the images faded and around five in the morning, and Pamela fell into a restless sleep. Her eyes flew open before nine. In the next bed, Martin was sound asleep. *Aren't you lucky!*

Pamela washed up in the sink and hated to put her soiled dress back on, but had no choice. A little makeup and the brush she always carried helped create some semblance of order. Martin was waiting for her when she emerged from the bathroom. "I'll be ready. I just have to use the bathroom."

Martin had parked on Seigniory Avenue just a few blocks from the hospital. "We need some fresh air and the walk will do us good."

"You're trying to save money on parking?"

"Hey, Dad taught us a few lessons."

They arrived at the hospital and found the room empty. They couldn't find Denis, not in the waiting room or the cubicle where they had spent the night. "Oh my God, Martin!"

"Mom! Don't stay here." He rushed over and spoke to the young triage nurse and hurried back to Pamela.

"Dad's been moved to Room 404 East. Denis is with him."

"Why was he moved so soon?" Pamela asked loudly. "Isn't that dangerous?" They walked quickly up the stairs to the fourth floor and found Richard and Denis in a room so small that it could have been a closet. Denis sat quietly on watch as Richard slept. They slipped quietly into the room. Pamela tapped Denis on the shoulder, startling him. He pointed to the hall and they followed.

"A nurse said she was told we'd want privacy, and this makeshift room was the best they could manage. Dad must be stable or they wouldn't have made the move."

"Just the same, they should have left your father alone."

"Mom, let's be grateful."

"Has your father been asleep the whole time?"

"No, I had a few words with him before he fell asleep again. He didn't say much but he's glad Martin and I are here."

"Give me a few minutes with him, boys." Pamela tiptoed into the room, bent over and kissed Richard on the cheek.

He stirred and opened his eyes. "What time is it?"

"A little after ten, Richard."

"At night?"

"Morning, Sunday morning."

"I'll get through this, Pamela."

"The doctor agrees, but you will need more tests and lots of rest. I'm going to see to that."

Richard lay quietly, thinking. "I need you to do something for me."

"Anything."

"Call Damiano at the station."

"Today?"

"Today. I don't want anyone knowing that I'm here."

"You've suffered a heart attack, Richard." Pamela could not hold back. "I never remember you taking time off work, except those half days when the boys were born. You need rest. Forget about work for once in your life. It's the reason you're here."

"I'm not done for, Pamela, not by a long shot. I trust Damiano. She can handle things at the station with subtlety."

"You've said she wants your job, and you trust her?" One good look at Richard told her that he wasn't going to change his mind. "Fine, Richard, I don't want to cause you more stress. I'll call tomorrow."

"It can't wait. Word will get out."

"I cannot believe you, Richard. Do you realize where you are?"

"Please, Pamela. Use my phone. Call now from the room. Make up a good story."

Pamela took the phone reluctantly, searched, found the number.

Lieutenant Detective Toni Damiano was out running on a leafy road on Mount Royal in the center of the city with her husband and son. "Hey! Stop for a minute, you guys!" She grabbed her cell phone from an arm band. "Chief?"

"It's Pamela. Richard's in the hospital, and he wants you to take care of things for a few days."

"What's happened?" she asked with alarm in her voice.

"It's …"

"Where is he?"

"At the Lakeshore General."

"I'll be there."

"I don't think that's wise, Lieutenant. It's not a good time."

"The Chief was there for me. I won't breathe a word to anyone, but I'm coming."

"What's up?" Richard asked.

"Stay calm, Damiano's on her way. I couldn't stop her. Something I never realized. You deserve each other. You're both as stubborn as mules and unreasonable, too."

Chapter Five

Caitlin Donovan jumped aside as Carmen DiMaggio bulldozed past her into the house. "Lock the door!" Carmen gasped through blood-smeared teeth. Her purse fell to the floor. She didn't move.

"What the hell happened to you? Come into the kitchen and sit down." Dazed, Carmen obeyed.

"Have you been in a car accident?" Caitlin went to the sink and brought a wet towel back with her.

"I bit my tongue." Carmen felt the pain for the first time, placing both hands over her mouth.

"You have to take your hand away. I'll be careful." Caitlin gingerly washed the blood from Carmen's face. Then she opened a kitchen cabinet and reached in for a bottle of Laphroaig.

"What are you doing, Caitlin? The last thing I need is a drink. I need the wits I have left."

"Come over to the sink. I want you to take a good swig from this glass, swirl it around in your mouth and spit it out. This is going to hurt. It's the best disinfectant you can use in your mouth. It's my single malt whisky and it will work. It stings. Be brave."

Carmen took a big pull, grimaced in discomfort, and spit into the sink. What came out was red. "Freakin' hurts!"

"Again!"

"Dammit." Carmen took a longer pull and swirled as long as she could, and spat. "Oooh!"

"Sit down and open. I want to see your tongue. I can see the marks your teeth made on your tongue. I'm not a doctor, but I think your tongue will heal. Chris fell off his bike once and bit his tongue and no stitches were needed. Any cut in the mouth bleeds a lot, but it heals quickly."

Caitlin noticed Carmen's swollen, bloody and gravelly knee and reached for the towel to clean it up. "You'll survive. Now, tell me what in the hell happened. Then, we can get you out of those clothes."

Shivering, Carmen cried out, "Where's that bottle? I need a double."

"Alright, now let's get you upstairs and changed. You'll feel better and then you can tell me what happened."

Upstairs, with tears running down her face and fists clenched, Carmen steadied herself on the side of the bed, trying to breathe normally.

"Promise me that you'll listen. Don't interrupt me and don't analyze! *I* have to figure this out. I am really freaked. Why did this have happen to me?"

"Carmen, you have to tell me what happened. If you don't need my help, why drive all the way here? Why not go home?"

"I can't go home! I can probably never go back there." Carmen sniffed loudly. "You'll see." She related what happened to her on the way home and finished without interruption. "One big night out, and I'll pay for it the rest of my life."

"This is terrible, Carm. I am so sorry for you."

"Me too."

"Don't jump all over me now. Are you certain you heard the name Jacques? I mean really sure? Could it have been something else? You'd taken quite a hit. Maybe you were disoriented for a few seconds. Are you sure you heard the name?"

"Before my ears exploded, I heard the name. Don't you think I wish I hadn't, but the cop was only about five feet from me. I heard him call the name Jacques. I still can't hear properly out of my right ear, but my hearing was fine when the cop called out the name *before* he shot."

"And the guy's hands were raised, you're absolutely sure? It was dark, right? Are you certain you saw his hands?"

"I know you're trying to help me, Caitlin, but you're making me feel like I'm being interrogated or something. On the top floor of the apartment building there was an apartment that had its lights on across from where the guy had stopped and turned. So, yes, I saw his hands in the air. The only thing I've just remembered is that his right hand was lower than the left, almost like he was about to point in my direction, but he never had the chance. He collapsed, kind of crumbling sideways to the ground."

"That's when you stood up?"

Carmen held her head in her palms. "I don't know why I stood up. It was just a reflex that I couldn't control. It all happened so fast. The cop shot the man three times – bam, bam, bam. I'd have thought it was a car backfiring if I hadn't seen the gun."

"The cop turned and you were eyeball to eyeball?"

"I thought he was going to shoot me. I couldn't move, or scream for help. It was as if I was out of my body observing. Lights went on immediately and I heard shouts. The cop, exposed, turned to see the commotion and then moved out of the light into the darkness. Adrenalin or whatever kicked in and I ran. I must have jumped the embankment, but I don't remember. I kept running, gasping for air, till I found my car. I heard sirens. I didn't dare go back, or attempt to run around to my place because the cop was still in the area." Carmen looked at her best friend. "Do you understand just how fucked I am?" she whispered.

Caitlin didn't answer, she nodded. She was about to suggest her father or that lawyer, Dino Mazzone, who'd once helped her.

"Don't. I know what you're thinking. How can lawyers help me? I don't trust cops investigating cops. Who does? The cop in the parking lot is a cold-blooded murderer. I'd need twenty-four-seven protection. Like I'd ever get that? Ha!"

Caitlin was trying to think and was coming up with nothing.

"The cop will be questioned for whatever they call it, a good shoot, right?"

"I think so. That's the movie phrase, but it's something like that."

Carmen lost all color. "I can't go to the police – but I can't hide either. He'll find me because he has to – to save himself. Remember he knows what I look like. Where can I go?"

"You can stay with me."

"For how long? Cops will canvass the neighborhood. I can call my landlord for help, to say I moved last month. But is it realistic to think that he will lie to the police for me? Neighbors know my car and a few are friendly. But how long will it take that cop to find me or where I work?"

"Maybe someone in the apartment complex witnessed the shooting. It's a hope, at least."

"But they don't have to admit what they saw. I wouldn't. The cop didn't see them. He saw me."

"Tomorrow, I'll drive to your place and pick up the clothes you need. Make me some kind of a list. You can borrow whatever I have. I'll drive over to your mother's. That cop doesn't know me."

"Don't tell my mother! She'll worry and call me every five minutes and then I'll have to worry about her. I don't have the energy for that."

Caitlin stood up and paced. "What are our chances of finding out the name of the cop? Mazzone could help with that. Maybe we could talk to the tenant in the apartment. See if someone saw the shooting. Before we start anything, let's make an effort to get some sleep."

"You mean reboot our sleuthing? Are you nuts? This is my life. I'd tell the cop right now that I didn't see anything. My life's at stake. I don't want to be scared every day I get into my car. At this moment, I don't care about the victim, or the cop. I don't know if my life is in more danger if I go to the police or hide out. Either way, I'm screwed."

Chapter Six

Hours earlier, the party at Cleopatra's had wound down some time after three. Most of the cast were hammered, giddy and sloppy. When Cleo had a full house, as they had that night, Tommy, the bartender passed out more drink tickets to the performers, who quickly exchanged them for drinks at the bar. Some of the performers felt lucky if they made it down the stairs without tripping before the performance. Velma, the producer, caught up in the thick of the show, didn't do much supervision. A party animal, she was busy playing the role she loved. After all, so was Cleo herself. Dionysus would have enjoyed the night with his penchant for wine and revelry, some of it dysfunctional. The café's customers loved the fun and abandon.

The cast staggered back up the stairs to the dressing rooms holding on to each other for support. The rooms smelled of stale air, powder, makeup, deodorant and skin. City clothes draped the backs of chairs; some had fallen on the floor, or remained in open suitcases. Jars without lids, makeup pencils and pods, pins, combs and aerosol cans of spray-glitz littered the counters in all four dressing rooms. Tipsy and happy, the performers peeled off their costumes and wiped makeup from their body parts. They'd pack the lot and take them home for another month. Velma climbed the stairs with the others to her own room, where she sorted the costumes and props. She opened the closet. Later, she'd stack and hang the costumes that would remain at Cleo's until the next show.

Pretty, plump Roxy Hardon had stripped down to her double-D bra and white panties. Balancing on one leg, leaning into a blurry vintage mirror, she successfully pulled off her long eyelashes. Smearing her cheeks with gobs of cream, she reached over for a handful of Kleenex and wiped off her freckles before she undid her pigtails. She propped up her heavy assets, smiling, remembering the delight of her fans. When she heard the first clang of the outer door, she shouted, "Someone's out on the roof for a snort or weed." The bluesy singer who shared the room with her shrugged as if to say it wasn't her problem.

"Well, I'm not going out on the roof almost naked." That comment drew a grunt from the singer.

"You're topless on stage."

"I'm dancing for an audience then! Besides, it's dark and spooky out there."

"Velma!" Roxy shouted loudly. "You better check the roof! At least she's dressed and she's the boss, right?"

Velma appeared at their door. "What's the problem – I'm bushed."

"You've gotta check the roof."

"I've told you guys not to go out on the roof after the show. Someone could fall over the side! Nobody listens."

Matthew Allen was behind Velma. The photographer was a fixture at the club. He always came upstairs with the cast, knew their names and sometimes took photos. He was interested in the whole show. The cast had gotten used to him being there.

"What's up?"

"The roof again, what else? Matthew, would you go out there for me? The roof creeps me out."

"No problem." Matthew opened the inside door just as the solid safety door swung his way. He caught it and stepped out into the cool night's blackness. He walked over to the back fence to the fire escape. He saw that the stairs had been lowered down to the street. He glanced down but saw no one. He turned back in the direction of the door. "Wherever you are, get back inside." Matthew called out one last time. "If you're there, get your butt inside."

No one answered.

Matthew hadn't checked out behind the cement pillar that had once been a chimney. Even if he had, Matthew still might not have seen Dylan lying face down in his black clothes. In the pitch, dark shadow of the old chimney, Dylan's silver zippers might as well have been black.

Dylan lay still and abandoned.

Matthew stepped back inside, pulled the heavy door closed and drew both bars across it. He shut the second door and walked down the hallway to Velma. "I looked around. No one! No smell of pot either."

"I'm sure someone went up on the roof during the show."

"How do you know, Velma?" Matthew asked.

"I was standing near the DJ, and I heard someone step on that high stair. You know, the third one from the top. Didn't hear anyone fall, but I'm positive there was someone on the stairs. There's no point trying to investigate tonight. Most of the gang are tanked. I'll warn the performers about the roof access again next month. I have to lock up. I don't even want to think about what might happen if some street trash got into Cleo's through that back door. I can't be the person responsible for a break-in. God!" Velma marched back out to the hall and shouted with hands cupped at the sides of her mouth. "Hurry and pack everyone, I want to get home.

Do I have a lift with you?"

"Sure," Matthew answered.

"I suppose I have to walk the three-and-a-half blocks to get to the car?" It never occurred to Velma to wonder why Matthew came to all the performances. He was a curious guy who took great photos. The other photographers appeared at every show for their blogs and it boosted her morale; she never queried their reasons either. Matthew was an undemanding friend with great stories. He was interesting. He also went out of his way to drive her home. What was there to question?

While waiting, Matthew thought momentarily of Dylan as he watched the performers spill out onto St-Laurent Boulevard to return to their private lives, and, for the fortunate, a steady paycheck. Vulnerable souls, perhaps like himself. *Am I one of them?* Matthew kicked that uneasy thought aside. Velma joined him and they took off together.

Chapter Seven

[2:55 a.m., Sunday morning]
Laval

The crime scene had been set up. It was a busy place. The police of the suburban city of Laval congregated just inside the taped-off area. The Crime van had arrived. The forensic team stepped into white Tyvek polyethylene suits that covered them from head to toe. The parking lot and the tented restricted area was lit by powerful lamps by the van's growling portable generator. The team was dropping markers on the ground, bagging the weapon and the victim's hands and finally, tabbing the bullet entries on the body. Using scissors for precision, they cut double-sided tape to size for marking hot spots on the ground. They had also shut down the area where the officer had stood and fired. The team recovered three shell casings and dropped them into labeled evidence bags and then meticulously examined the whole area with small UV flashlights. Photographers were flashing photo angles and close-ups. However, the pathologist was not on the scene. He did his work at the Montreal city morgue on rue Parthenais. After the autopsy, he would confer with forensics and the detectives handling the case.

Behind the cordoned-off area, a crowd of the curious had gathered. Neighbors from the triplexes on rue Favreau had either heard the commotion or called their neighbors and joined the folks from the apartment. A few police officers, wearing day-glo high-visibility vests, stepped out from the tape and tried unsuccessfully to prevent people from taking videos and photos. A few backed away, but rushed forward as soon as the officer turned his attention to another group.

No one from the apartment that had its lights on during the incident had come forward to admit witnessing the shooting.

Two Major Crimes detectives arrived and stood waiting to hand the case off to the SQ, the provincial police. They knew that the officer involved in the shooting was from the Crémazie Division. Not that that mattered much – they would support him because he was part of the brotherhood and sisterhood of Blue. His division had been alerted. Officer Daniel Boucher stood off by himself. He had answered few questions. He was focusing on the apartment crowd, willing their continued silence. Three feet behind him, it seemed that the officer who had spoken to him was there to protect him from any conversation that could get him in trouble. If he got through this, he owed that cop. His mouth was dry and he held himself so stiffly his body ached. He felt older than his thirty-four years, younger than a frightened four-year-old. He raised a fist to his mouth and began to bite hard on each of his fingers, a habit when he was upset.

A Laval cop spoke gruffly, "Stop that! Try to look composed. Eyes are on you."

Boucher squirmed as if ants were crawling up and down his legs. They had crawled into his stomach. They were eating his guts. Sweat rolled off his upper lip. His uniform was drenched and he could smell himself. There was so much to do. He had to find that woman and … and what … that didn't matter then. He needed to find her. He stood stiffly, his shoulders heaving up and down with each quick breath. Boucher was relieved that the Major Crimes detectives had not bothered him. He couldn't deal with both forces. When would the SQ arrive and set a date to interview him? Then he could leave and begin the work that would save him from prison. *I'm not going down for this! I'll do anything to save my ass!*

For the first time since the shooting, Boucher looked over at the victim. Jacques had fallen on his side. All Boucher could see were the Air Jordan trainers because the Crime techs were kneeling around him, still at work. Boucher remembered the shoes and the gray jeans when he forced the gun into Jacques hand. A tremor rushed up his legs to his shoulders. He had never killed a man, an unarmed man. *I just lost it. I told the bastard not to run his shit, probably Fentanyl as well, in Laval. I have kids. I warned him! You can't say I didn't warn you, Jacques. I'm not going to hold the bag for this one. You arrogant shit – you forced me to take you on. Now you've shut us both down.*

Two SQ detectives arrived at the crime scene. They walked over to the body; spoke with the techs in charge who pointed to Officer Daniel Boucher. He wiped his hands on his pants and tried to straighten up.

The cop whispered, "Don't give them anything – ask for an interview time."

Boucher turned slightly, asking as he put his hand up to his mouth, "Why are you helping me?"

"We're cops."

The detectives, stocky men in their late thirties – one balding, the other close cropped, were serious, focused. They introduced themselves.

Boucher did the same. "Officer, the vic had a weapon but he didn't get a shot off, not one discharge. You fired three times according to the techs." Detective Goulet, second on the case, struck quickly to take advantage of an obviously anxious officer who had fatally shot a man outside his jurisdiction.

Boucher cleared his throat. "I've, I've, the vic had … I can't answer questions right now. I've never shot anyone."

"You'd prefer to wait for a formal meeting at the Crémazie Division?"

"Yes, I never … I need a rep or something. I never shot anyone." Shock began to descend on Boucher. He had killed a man.

"That's procedure, of course. I had hoped we might have a head start. How about two Monday afternoon at Crémazie Division? But first, we'll need your gun." He produced an evidence bag. "Get yourself down to evidence. They'll need your clothes and will take photos of your hands for gunshot residue. Before the meeting, write up your sworn statement of this incident. Are we clear?"

Boucher nodded and handed his weapon to Detective Goulet. "I'll meet with you at two."

"Before you leave, the techs need the whereabouts of your car, and the vic's for that matter?"

"Up on Goyer." Boucher reached for his wallet and dug out his registration. The SQ detective snapped a photo of the information. "Mine's a gray Ford, and the vic's car is a black Audi, two cars in front of mine, one block up the street."

"How did they both get there?"

"I've never shot anyone … I …"

"I see, Officer Boucher. We are just trying to do our jobs. Take some time. Try to get some sleep."

Sleep! Sleep was the last thing on Boucher's mind. Once the SQ left him to talk again and make notes, Boucher lingered. He waited for what seemed an eternity for someone from the apartment to come forward. He wiped sweat from his eyebrow. If there was a second witness, he or she was no doubt waiting for him to leave. Boucher was wasting his time. He looked back at the cop behind him.

"I'll walk out with you. That's where it ends for me." When they were on the sidewalk, he added, "I was serious. Get the facts straight – don't give them shit that won't fly with cops. Give up the facts, period. Stories are nets. About the vic's gun – you know what you have to do."

"Why are …"

"I've been there."

"You came out clean then?" Boucher said hopefully.

"They broke me down to patrol. I was a detective. Ha, clean, right. Go set up your details."

"Then I owe you."

When Boucher was back in his car, he collapsed, exhaling noisily. His head rested on the steering wheel. His wife had told him that a woman in the neighborhood was frightened of drug deals being delivered at three in the morning next door on Goyer. The woman's car was vandalized. Laval police hadn't helped much. Boucher knew the dealer. Boucher had kids in Laval. He'd bust him down alone. What bumped in his head that night were 'facts' and 'gun.' He sat back up, turned on the ignition, took the wheel and noticed blood smears on his hands. When forensics finished up, a cleanup team arrived at the crime scene.

Chapter Eight

Lieutenant Detective Toni Damiano stood on Mount Royal – the mountain park in the center of the city – with her cell phone in hand, staring at the disappointed and judgemental faces of her husband Jeff and her son Luke.

"We planned this family day a month ago, Toni. Now you're doing your usual pull-out!"

Luke kept running in place, quiet and sullen.

"Jeff, I honestly thought the chief was calling me about the Laval shooting – I wouldn't have gone in. I swear."

"But … but what?"

"He's in the hospital, and Pamela sounded nervous."

"They have two sons, don't they? Why are *you* going?" Damiano shrugged distractedly. Jeff Shea could see his wife's mind was already back on her job, or a promotion, or whatever … She had already left them. How could he compel family values on a wife whose physical presence was all he had, and that not for much longer. It was a battle that had been lost long ago.

"Chief Donat was there for me." Jeff and Luke took off. "I need to take the car!" she shouted after them. "You'll have to cab it or walk home!" Jeff kept running, giving her a dismissive wave over his right shoulder. Damiano would not have seen their point of view six months ago, but that Sunday morning she was on their side. Still she turned and began her descent toward Montreal's imposing Sir George-Étienne Cartier Monument. "George-Étienne was honored *and* criticized, but he still managed to have himself memorialized with angels! There's hope for me," she said to console herself. She ran quickly by the tam tam drummers who were already in one of their jam sessions on the monument steps. Damiano was a tall and imposing figure herself. She was fit and strong, although one might not suspect she was also a top cop, a cop who breathed a sigh of relief that she had taken her car. Asking Jeff for his car keys, well, her eyebrows rose, "There'd be no justification, at least I can't think of one at the moment. Pamela doesn't even want me there!" When she found her car on Rachel Street East, she popped the trunk of her Audi and pulled out a rolled-up towel with a brush and eyeliner, the only makeup she had with her.

The renovation of the Turcot Interchange – Montreal's three-level freeway – and the many closures and detours had blown the fuses of most drivers. The city was in a virtual construction shutdown. Damiano was fortunate it was Sunday. Once she caught Côte-des-Neiges Road she wound her way out to the Trans-Canada Highway and exited on boulevard St-Jean in the West Island. From there, the route was simple, right on Hymus Boulevard, left on Stillview Avenue, left again on Seigniory Avenue where she parked. She knew a friend who lived at the Southwest One Complex, and Damiano cut through it and crossed over to the Lakeshore Hospital. At the information desk, she learned Chief Donat's room number. Damiano took the stairs and paused at the fourth landing. Would she be able to see the chief? She followed the posted directions and made her way to Room 404, just as an unsmiling, tired woman stepped out into the hall. She was as tall as Damiano and seemed to be capable of tearing a strip off the detective.

"I wish you hadn't come, Detective." There was little emotion in Pamela's voice and no interest. Her eyes were red from no sleep. She hadn't had any opportunity or chance to change her clothes or wash up. She looked as bad as she felt.

"You can't keep an Italian away from a sickbed, Pamela." The humor that Damiano had aimed for flattened. "The chief was there for me and he has helped me through my own recovery. I want to be here. I won't stay long. I promise." Damiano engaged Pamela, and behind the fatigue there was warmth, deep in Pamela's eyes.

Still Pamela stood her ground. "If any of this gets out …"

"Pamela, I'm here as a friend." The seriousness of the situation struck Damiano, and she felt extraordinarily out of place and intrusive. Color drained from her cheeks as she entered the room behind Pamela.

"Richard, are you awake? Detective Damiano is here," Pamela whispered as she kissed the chief on the forehead while herding the boys from the room with a turn of her head.

Damiano felt a stab of fear seeing Chief Donat so still, so fragile. She wanted to leave.

The chief opened his eyes, gently pushing Pamela away. He made no effort to sit up, but his eyes were alert with a fire Damiano welcomed. "Well, you're here," Chief Donat said. "Don't touch my files."

Damiano laughed loudly, and the chief knew she'd gotten the message.

"Or begin funeral arrangements."

Pamela, surprisingly, smiled too. "You are indeed hopeless, Richard."

"Whatever you want done, Chief, I will do. No one will learn about your condition. What about Head Office though?"

"No need to advise anyone yet. Don't be so anxious to take my chair. See where it's gotten me. Handle my affairs from your office and continue on with your own work."

"I understand. How are you, Chief?"

"How do I look, Detective?"

"I remember what you said in my hospital room with a bone protruding from my elbow. 'You're tough. Remember that, Damiano.' Well, Chief, I've seen you looking better. But you're every bit as tough as I am. How you look now doesn't matter."

Chief Donat smiled ruefully. "Now, get out of here. Leave me to my recovery." He appeared to be nodding off.

"Take care." Damiano said quietly.

Pamela followed Damiano out. "Detective, I see why Richard likes you. Thank you."

"He's an exacting boss, but he's a good man. I know it's a lot more serious than the chief wants to admit, probably his heart I'm guessing." His face was ashen, and Donat reminded her of her grandmother who looked much the same after her coronary. "Keep your spirits up, Pamela. You can trust me." Damiano left quickly. She thought of the chief's sentence. *See where it's gotten me!* She drove home, trying to come up with ideas for re-entry with Jeff and Luke. *Why is life so goddam tough?*

She left the car in the driveway and stood outside their home on Anwoth Road, in the affluent city of Westmount. A pressure began its usual rise, first in her stomach, then it rushed up her shoulders. *Why am I always apologizing, always wrong? What did Jeff tell me once? Oh yes, I am arrogantly selfish? The chief won't be back anytime soon, what do I do now?* Damiano braced herself and tried as best as a loud person could to open the front door and close it quietly. The air smelled of shampoo and cologne – of clean men, and comfort.

Damiano found Jeff on the back patio, engrossed with *The New York Times*. He heard the French doors opening, put down the paper and waited for her to speak. Jeff wore his indifferent look, she thought, as an irritation because it worked. An elbow on the table beside him, his thumb under his chin and two fingers crossed on his temple, like a professor, displeased with a student. "I think the chief has suffered a heart attack."

Down came the hand. Jeff collected the paper and put it on the table. "That's not good news." He didn't add anything.

Damiano felt awkward and continued to stand. "Pamela is very upset. You were right. She didn't want me there, but I think she was glad before I left."

"Were you able to speak to him?"

"For a minute. He looks awful, but he is alive and he survived the night. He says he'll be back." Damiano let that thought linger.

Jeff threw his head back and sighed wearily. Damiano took that opportunity to sit. He sighed again, shaking his head. "Donat won't be what, satisfied, until he drops dead at work and takes his wife with him. You've told me he could retire and live a good life. That's neither here nor there, I suppose. So," Jeff said knowingly, "I'm guessing that means you'll become interim chief – go down the same path, I mean."

"He told me to stay out of his office, handle what there is to do from my own office." Damiano knew her words sounded hollow.

Jeff laughed without commitment. "It'll appear that you are the interim chief reluctantly, but chief nonetheless."

"Jeff, stop with the barbs. You would have left us on the mountain today if one of your patients had taken ill. Stop the veiled accusations. These tired old fights destroy us and go nowhere. You've often said you'd be happier with me behind a desk, and not out on the street fracturing my arm and worse, risking my life. Well, now I might, or might not, end up behind a desk."

"Alright. You are a great cop, but you are politically naïve. Your colleagues, some still lust after you, I know that from parties I've been forced to attend. I'm aware of the way men look at you. Yet they will not accept you as their interim chief. They already envy you your cases. Men can be really deliberate and brutal. It'll be awful for you. As well, in all my experience, I have never heard of an interim anything being appointed to the permanent post. I don't want you hurt and used, Toni. In the end, they will appoint some male cop from Place Versailles. You'll be crushed."

"That's some reality check, but I sense you're still on my side, Jeff?" Damiano said. "I'm glad. Maybe I'm tougher than you think."

"I'm not finished."

"By all means go for it."

"To be honest, I don't want to be the one to pick up the pieces. Been there, done that. Jesus, Toni, I don't want to end up losing you to a coronary. You can't sleep as it is. When will you see who really needs you? Who's important, in for the long ride? Why the hell can't you recognize what matters in life?"

"Are you saying there's something wrong with me, something missing?"

"Just grow up, but I'm beginning to think you can't."

Damiano knew she had a mind for her job. She knew how it worked. She knew people. Most important, she had broken into a male-dominated world and had won the top cases and had been able to close them. She wasn't a numbers counter – she was a cop! *It's the best of me.* Still she was struck by Donat's warning. *See where it's gotten me.*

Luke appeared, looming by the French doors. "Dad, lay off! I could hear you from my bedroom. You've been on Mom's case for as long as I can remember. It's gotten old and I'm sick of it."

"Don't you speak to me like that, Luke!"

"Whatever!"

"No, not whatever. Apologize."

"Alright, sorry. It's just that you should have figured things out by now. Mom's a cop – the job comes first. Did you forget she won that medal?"

Damiano hadn't said a word. She stood off to the side, swamped by the division she had caused.

As Luke left the patio, he mumbled, "Mom, I don't mind you being a cop."

Jeff picked up his paper and went back to reading. *I wish that your mother's work or her absence wasn't the main focus of our lives.* He looked up as Luke left the patio and felt the sting of a familiar betrayal. Luke loved his mother unconditionally. The time *he* spent with Luke when Toni was absent, the love he felt for his son didn't seem to count. Somehow, it didn't seem fair. He was there for his son. Most times Toni wasn't. That injustice bothered Jeff. Life wasn't fair; but sometimes it ought to be, to keep a level playing field.

"Why don't you start your crossword?" Damiano suggested.

"I might win there, you mean?"

"You are a master of crossword, Jeff! The mother-and-child bond is a lock, even with a mother like me."

"There should be exceptions."

"I agree."

Damiano was rewarded with an open grin.

Chapter Nine

Officer Boucher pulled onto the driveway of his bungalow, a three-way-split, on 9th Street in Laval. He groaned when he saw the light in the kitchen. He sat in the car until the front door opened, and Manon stood waiting for him. It was almost six-thirty Sunday morning. Manon's father was a retired cop, so there was little his wife didn't know about the job. Manon was as tall as Daniel, five foot eight, and even with the pasta and pizza, they were fit, thanks to the running they did together, three times a week. Boucher didn't want a sit-down, he needed a shower; he needed to think. He had to call his partner. His plan was to go back to rue Goyer and do a house-to-house. He strode quickly past Manon.

"I should never have gotten you involved, Daniel." Manon said, following him.

"Too late. Anyway, I took this on for the boys, and not simply for some neighbor awakened at three in the morning for a drop-off. These street 'pumps' go to schools and nearby hangouts. Our kids find them. Not where I live, damn! Not on my turf. I freakin' warned Jacques off when I saw him months ago. I wanted to be a Good Samaritan. It all blew up in my face."

"What happened, Daniel?"

"Let's get into the kitchen. I don't want to wake the boys."

"They could sleep through an earthquake."

"Manon, I can't sit and talk. I have to shower and go back out there."

"What …"

Boucher threw his arms up in the air with his palms open. "I shot him alright! I wanted to arrest him. He didn't raise his right arm, not fully – he was pointing or something – I thought he had a weapon, and I shot him." Boucher's body was so tight that Manon thought her husband would shatter into sharp pieces.

Manon's eyes shut and she couldn't breathe.

"Did you hear me, Manon?"

"*Did* he have a weapon?" she asked, her mouth twisting with tension.

At that moment, Boucher hated his wife, hated her for knowing what to ask. He swiped some bread crumbs from the table and looked at her. "I told you I have to shower." As he got up to leave, Manon grabbed his arm.

"Can you cover yourself, Daniel?"

"That's what I'm trying to do. I've given my life to the force. Please let go of me, Manon!"

"Fine. Go up and shower, but I won't let you go back out without food. You haven't slept."

"I never intended to … I don't think I did … I just …"

"Go. I'll cook breakfast. I'm on your side. I should never have involved you. I don't even know this woman who needed help. She's a friend of a friend."

"None of that matters now. I shot a man and I have to find …" Boucher pulled away and ran up the five stairs, turned toward the bathroom, closed the door and stripped. The shower was scalding but Boucher stood under the spray with his head bowed. He dropped the soap and cursed, kicking the bar against the shower wall. He needed the second weapon hidden in the cabane in the backyard. Louis would help; he had to help. You stood by your partner. "No way I'm going down for this." He dressed quickly, slipped back downstairs, crept down to the basement, and went out into the yard and headed for the cabane. Inside, he dug out the second weapon buried in an old bag of fertilizer. He removed it from a Ziploc bag, dropped the bullets and the clip onto a picnic table, and reloaded the gun, leaving his prints on each bullet and the clip. He placed a brick on top of the fertilizer bag and pushed it back against the wall. Once he was back inside the house he checked and saw that the boys were still asleep. In the kitchen, he bent his head down and scarfed the eggs and cheese and toast. He drank three burning cups of coffee. "Manon, thanks for this. I have to call Louis."

Manon didn't argue. She knew the whole family was in danger. Daniel might go to prison, and she knew why. Fear gnawed at her stomach.

Officer Louis Doucette caught the call on the first ring. "I heard."

"One day you'll need my help, Louis. Today, I need yours." Boucher told his partner what he needed.

"Daniel, I won't be a party to a crime. That's where you're headed."

"I just need you to help find a witness. She saw the takedown. The rest I'll do alone. No harm, no foul for you. I have a family, Louis. You'd need one to understand why I have to do this. I just want to explain my side to her."

Louis sighed heavily. "Sure you do. What do you need me for?"

Boucher gave him the instructions. "In uniform, Louis."

"Fuck!"

"I agree. Park on rue Goyer close to St-Martin. See you in an hour, one hour, Louis. Our excuse is that we're trying to find a witness to corroborate the incident. What cop in my position wouldn't do the same thing?"

"It's not our patch, Daniel. If the Laval cops insist we leave, I'm leaving. For all you know, Crime might be back to work the site."

"I want to question the family in one apartment. That won't be a problem. The front door of the building is on boulevard St-Martin. Then, I say we do ten houses, they're triplexes, but that's it. She has to live in one of them, makes sense. If she lived in the apartment building, she'd have her own parking in the lot. There's no night parking on Favreau, so she parked on Goyer. You can't back away after this search. I need you with me."

"You were at the crime scene for a few hours. No one called in, right? Maybe she won't. Maybe she didn't see much in the dark. She was frightened. You're going off too soon!"

"We eyeballed! She saw!"

"The vic had a weapon?"

Boucher didn't answer.

"Ah shit!"

"I thought he did."

"Shit, shit, shit!"

Carmen DiMaggio had somehow managed to fall into a dead sleep. Caitlin left a note that Carmen couldn't miss: STAY PUT – BACK IN 90 MIN. By eight-fifteen, she was inside Carmen's basement apartment, hastily packing cosmetics, mousse, a hair dryer, clothes, shoes, underwear, and Carmen's work tote. That would have to do. Tempted to ring the landlord's bell, she thought better of it. She was about to scoop up the two bags when she heard men's voices. She edged cautiously over to the front window and gently pushed the vertical blind aside a few inches. Out on the sidewalk, she spotted three police officers in what appeared to be a heated discussion. Caitlin could hear them because Carmen's front window was slightly open. The iron bars gave her a sense of security.

"All we want to do is find a witness that might have seen something that could help me. We have a lead. I don't see a problem."

Carmen was right. That cop will find her. Caitlin inched the blinds back into place, but stood listening. How would she get the bags to her car?

"Let me, I mean us, canvass a few more homes and we're out of here."

"I gave what help I could last night. You're off your patch again, without authorization I'd bet. I told you last night I won't be caught up with your incident. You need to leave."

Officer Boucher squared his shoulders, tilted his chin up, but saw his partner had taken a step back. He had what he needed. The bitch lived close by. He'd be back, on his own, if it came to that. Boucher also wanted to talk to the tenants of that apartment again. He didn't believe them when they said they saw nothing, too pissed last night they said. He wanted to catch the couple awake and sober. "We'll leave. I don't want to botch my own case."

The voices faded. Caitlin stood very still. When she realized she was standing on Carmen's new carpet in her shoes, she hopped off. *Poor Carmen.* Caitlin could not leave with two bags and the tote without drawing attention. She kicked off her shoes, walked over the plush carpet and took out her cell phone, scrolling for the number she wanted, the lawyer who had helped her a few months ago.

Mazzone was already at a popular radio station prepping for his morning commentary. He had fourteen minutes, so he took the call when he saw the caller ID.

"I won't waste your time. I have a friend in serious trouble."

Mazzone interrupted. "Before you begin, send me a dollar by PayPal. Here's my account number." He waited. "Okay, your information is protected by lawyer-client privilege. You have five minutes." He listened. He thought before he spoke. "The situation is very tricky. The name of the officer won't be released, but the cops know who it is – the pipeline. This cop needs to find Carmen. If I pull strings and find out his name, the police will scrutinize my recent client list. That's a back trail to you, then Carmen. My suggestion is to go to the police – have the eyewitness publicized. The more people who learn of Carmen, the better protected she is, the less chance this cop will act."

"The police won't be fair with Carmen. They have enough trouble as it is with fatal shootings and unmarked cruisers killing innocent civilians. Who can we trust?"

"I have one person in mind – you met her."

"You mean Lieutenant Detective Damiano? She was arrogant as I remember."

"She was fair."

Chapter Ten

Caitlin waited for half an hour before she carried the suitcases out to her Volkswagen GTI on rue Goyer. She chose to cross the crime scene, lugging the bags up the embankment. Laboriously she made her way up Favreau and then halfway down Goyer. The walk wasn't easy with three bags in tow. The police tape was still evident, but other than that, Caitlin figured whatever blood was there had been washed away. No one on the street would mistake her for Carmen. She was a shaggy blonde with highlights; Carmen was a brunette with brown eyes, definitely Italian. Catlin passed a police cruiser parked on Goyer. The officer checked her out, but nothing more. The morning was already hot; blue sky smudged by a few lazy white clouds. It would have made a great cycling day, but such thoughts were off. Caitlin dropped the bags into the trunk and then made certain she kept within the speed limit. Cars sped past her, and she noticed one finger shoved out the window at her. She honked back. Classic Montreal!

Carmen was still in bed, but had gone to the kitchen to fetch yogurt and was spooning it gingerly into her mouth. That's where Caitlin found her when she got back. If possible, Carmen looked grimmer than she did at the door.

Carmen looked up at Caitlin. "My tongue is killing me."

"I have your things. I told you your tongue will heal. Be patient. You have more important things to deal with."

"I wish I could just stay here. I'm really scared." She looked at Caitlin with tears in her eyes. "Why did this have to happen to me?"

"Look Carmen, stop with the Italian pity party. This is bad, no question, but I can help you. When I was at your place I called Dino Mazzone and explained the situation. He said that the best thing to do for your protection was to go public."

Carmen jammed the spoon into the plastic yogurt cup and both fell to the floor. "You are so smart. Jesus! Can't you see the whole picture? I'm not just freaked about some trial. What happens to me *after* the trial? Every cop will know my name and can find out where I live. Don't you see that I will be hounded with tickets and threats and worse, forever? These guys don't forget. Who will help me then? I'll be out there on my own."

"Mazzone mentioned Lieutenant Detective Damiano, too."

"The same cop you called a bitch?"

"But remember, I reminded you that she was fair. You can trust her."

"Sure."

"You have to do something, Carmen."

"I have to think – I have to go to work tomorrow. And I have a ton of estimates to get through. I'm not on vacation like you."

Caitlin told Carmen about the heated conversation she overheard from the street in front of her place and the officer who was canvassing the neighborhood.

Carmen jumped to her feet. "I knew he'd find me – I just knew it."

"Carm, you have to call your landlord right now, and then your mother. Buy a little time."

"Will the media identify the cop shooter?" Carmen asked hopefully.

"They never do. The police will know who he is. We won't. He'll be protected."

"That's great! I'll be identified, but the shooter will be protected. I wish I could talk to him and say I don't know what I saw. I want to lie. What other option do I have? I'm caught. But I refuse to be snuffed out like garbage."

"We won't let that happen, but there is no simple fix out there. For now at least, the officer arguing with the shooter ordered him off the street. Call the landlord and your mother. Get going. We have to start somewhere, then figure out a plan."

"The only plan I can think of is lying. Morality is great in theory, but when my life is at stake, morals won't keep me alive. My whole body aches, and my ear is not fully back to normal. Do you have an Aleve or ibuprofen?"

"Just a sec." She headed for the bathroom.

Carmen kept on talking. She just raised her voice. "If I told the truth, that the victim did not have a gun and the officer shot him down in cold blood, imagine what they'd do to me in court? How many drinks did I have that night? Is there a possibility I was driving while intoxicated? Wasn't I dazed when I was knocked down between the cars? How could I have been certain of anything? Was I concussed? Did I actually see the victim clearly? Wasn't it too dark for me to see if he had a weapon? Couldn't I have missed seeing it? Is there a possibility I am mistaken?" She took the glass of water, downed the pill and carried on. "Would you believe my story?"

"You have a point. Are you sure the victim didn't have a gun? Do you have any doubt at all?"

"No. I know what I saw. He had no gun, but that cop never hesitated. He executed that man and he knew him."

"Okay, alright."

"I first thought the victim was trying to point at me to stop the cop from shooting him. Like you know, 'There's a witness. Don't shoot!' It just hit me now. He was exposing me. If the lights hadn't immediately come on in that apartment, the cop might have turned and shot me. Shit! The victim wasn't doing me any favors. I would have been as dead as he was. Later, I would have been seen as an innocent bystander fatally wounded during a police arrest. I remember the story of that cyclist who was accidently shot just going to work. He died at the scene. Nothing ever happened to that officer. Cops can get away with anything. That's how it seems to be. I still see that cop with his gun pointed right at me! The lights saved me, and the fact that I ran."

"I have to tell you something, Carmen."

"What?"

"When that officer was standing on the sidewalk, outside your apartment, I heard him say he had a lead. I think he pretty much knows where you live."

"Why the hell didn't you just tell me right off?"

"You looked so bad."

"What the hell am I going to do?" Carmen began to cry. She stood and cried.

Caitlin hugged her. "Call your mother. If he discovers your name, he might find her."

"From the outset, I told you I was fucked! I don't mean to be swearing so much. I am so scared." Carmen cried hysterically.

Chapter Eleven

On Monday morning Detective Damiano was the first detective to arrive on the sixth floor of the Crémazie Division, Major Crimes. Her plan was to check, unnoticed, Chief Donat's office for late-night emails and work he had not finished. Her thoughts jumped from one strategy to another about her future. She concluded she did not want to become interim chief. Such a move would abort her chance, she felt, of one day having that permanent position. Damiano believed she had earned a chance to be chief. After eleven years in Major Crimes, she deserved and wanted the challenge. It fed a drive that maintained her security, her sense of identity at something she did well. Stasis was capitulation, weakness. Damiano didn't see herself as a careerist. She never wanted to lose her drive.

Damiano sat down in the chief's chair, feeling uncomfortable. She took a minute before she reached for the last memo in his basket, the fatal shooting. Ordinarily, when the SQ were taking over a case, Chief Donat spoke with the officer involved to be certain he or she was well prepared, and that Chief Donat was informed and not caught by any surprises. She read the email and decided to meet with Officer Boucher in the main interrogation room on the first floor so as not to draw attention to the fact that Chief Donat was absent and that she was taking the lead.

Damiano printed the email, took two other files of work open on his desk and stopped in her tracks when she saw Donat's secretary standing like a statue watching her. The woman was devoted to her boss. She didn't say a word, but she gave Damiano a knowing nod. Pamela had called her. "I'm taking the work to my office," she said as she placed a warm hand on the secretary's shoulder. "He's tough – he'll be alright." Obviously upset, the secretary left without a word.

Damiano had taken greater care than usual when she dressed that day, and she walked back into the general office with a casual air of authority. Around the large room, fourteen detectives sat at their desks grouped in units of two, to provide a semblance of privacy in the open-space office environment. Some were on their computers, others working on notes and a few talking quietly. Damiano's office was in the far corner near the back elevator, glassed in on all sides. She was the only lieutenant detective in the room. She'd earned her office. At her own expense, she had added an electric blind that she rarely closed. For complex cases, there was a large erasable board on one wall. Premeditated murders, apart from contract killings committed by organized crime, were rare, perhaps two a year. Most of the city murders were 'stupid' senseless, lives lost to drunken fights in or out of the downtown bars. A fatal stabbing at one of the downtown bars had occurred over a bar stool.

Damiano was preparing her questions for Boucher when she looked up and saw that her partner Pierre Matte wasn't at his desk. That was unusual, so she went to investigate, but didn't find him. *Strange.* A few minutes later, Detective Pierre Matte walked into the office. Smiling, she pointed to her Cartier watch.

Matte had showered and dressed impeccably as was his style, but his drawn features suggested he hadn't slept and, if possible, had lost weight as well in the last two days.

"I was fighting a cold all weekend."

"It's June."

"And that means what? I can't catch a spring cold? I'm not up for jokes, Toni. Do we have something on?"

Damiano didn't comment, but asked him to close the door. "I have to interview Officer Boucher, the shooter involved in the Laval fatality. I thought it best if I handled the interview alone, but I realize I'd like to have you there. Boucher should be prepped, and we need the facts, before he meets with the SQ."

"Who appointed you to handle this?"

"That's the thing."

"C'mon, Toni, I don't have the energy for games!"

"You're definitely under the weather, Pierre. It's just that Donat's not in today. I was asked to take Boucher."

"Donat! He's never been off work since I came to the division."

"He's entitled then, right? He's the boss."

Matte's mind worked like a computer and a single fact led to links. He got to his feet. "Is this serious, Toni? The fact that we're doing this interview tells me you know what's going on with Donat."

"Look, Pierre, I can't tell you, orders. Why are you so bothered?"

"Why do you think?"

"Get over this cold. It's making you cranky. I'm your partner, Pierre. Nothing's changed about that."

Matte sat back down and blew his nose. "Let me see the questions."

"We'll interview downstairs so as not to draw attention to Donat's absence." Damiano reached for her phone and notes. Matte palmed his pad, and they took the elevator to the first floor. When Damiano looked down the hall, she saw that the officer was already waiting for them. As they approached, she realized he was older than she'd thought he'd be, mid-thirties. He was also tense. Damiano could smell fear. She kept the introductions formal and brief.

"Lieutenant Detective Damiano and Detective Matte." She led the way into a large rectangular room, sparsely furnished. They sat together at the top end of the table, Damiano and Matte on one side and Boucher on the other. Damiano put her phone on the table and laid her notes beside them. Matte was quick with his pen and pad. "This interview is prep for you, Officer Boucher, but we will record it to preserve the first account of the incident." Damiano pressed the record tab on her phone. She noted the time of the interview, the date, and the officers involved. Damiano lead the questioning. "In your own words, Officer Boucher, please relate the events as they occurred."

Boucher hesitated as though he didn't know where to begin. Damiano could feel his leg shaking under the table.

"Begin by telling us why you were in uniform, off duty, out of your jurisdiction, on surveillance in Laval at three in the morning. We're on your side, Officer, but we need the facts."

Officer Boucher wanted to give as little detail as possible, but he realized he had to reveal the background and the reason he pursued the drug dealer. He needed support.

"A friend of my wife told her that drugs were being dropped off a few streets from our home usually at three in the morning. The elderly woman who lived next door where this was happening couldn't sleep with the commotion. She called the police. They came, flashed the house. One week later she discovered her car vandalized. Later, garbage was thrown on her driveway, her reward for her civic duty.

"I thought that by making the arrest, nailing the adult pusher, I could protect my own kids. That night, like clockwork, he showed up promptly at three, but he saw me as he got out of his car. He ran and I took off in pursuit. He finally stopped and turned around on that parking lot because I had gained on him. He raised one arm; he pointed the other at me. I saw a weapon. I had no choice. It was a good shoot. I've never killed anyone before." Damiano did not interrupt. She continued her questioning when Officer Boucher finished.

"From the outset, did you have permission for this surveillance?"

"No," Boucher admitted. "The Laval cops sent one unit on a drive-by for a few nights. Did nothing. I felt I could help on my own time. Like I said, I have kids. Laval is my home."

"Why the uniform off duty?"

"I wanted him to know I was police. I wanted the arrest to be legit."

"This shooting did not occur in the line of duty, Officer. That's troublesome, but I'll leave the determination of this incident to the SQ."

Matte asked, "Are you certain you saw a weapon before you fired, Officer Boucher?"

Boucher rapped his knuckles on the table. Every impulse told him to stand and shout. And he did. "What the hell. You're supposed to take my word, not question it! I already told you he had his back to me. He turned slowly with one arm raised, the other pointing. I saw a weapon. I shot. That's what I'm trained to do, right? I wanted to take him in when he was getting out of his car, but he ran. I had no choice. I'm just repeating myself." He sat back down. "The vic did have a weapon. I never gave him the chance to use it."

It was Damiano's turn. "We learned just before ten that you were back there canvassing the area yesterday, again out of your jurisdiction. Why?"

"For a witness to verify my account – a witness who might have seen the vic's weapon. I could use support."

"You were way up the street – there were no witnesses in that location."

"It was a good shoot. Maybe someone was walking home and saw something. I'm not stupid. It was a good shoot! That's all I have. I have a right to protect my family, don't I?"

"Officer, we're here to gather the facts. Determination of the incident is out of our hands. Before I terminate the interview, I have to issue an order. Do not under any circumstances return to that area. You don't want to add insubordination to that other count in your file. When do you meet with the SQ?"

"At two, right here today."

"Good luck, Officer Boucher."

Boucher had to go back. He had a lead. He was very close to an address. He'd find the bitch alright, and have a word with the cop who'd reported him.

Walking back to the elevator, Damiano waited for Boucher to leave before she spoke. "Your take, Pierre?"

"Looking for witnesses halfway up the street …"

"That's the rub. Could be he's worried about that excessive force claim on his record and needs corroboration for this shooting. Could be something worse." Damiano stopped and read through the email. "No witnesses have come forward; no videos either."

"No surprise there. I read some early morning media on the shooting: 'The victim was known to the police.' The media doesn't usually follow these cases."

"I suppose. The last thing Chief Donat needs to hear is the possibility of a dirty cop. I'm not saying it is. The witness search is troubling."

Pierre Matte was reassured just hearing the chief's name. Maybe things wouldn't change. No other detective in Major Crimes wanted to partner with a gay cop. Damiano had never made an issue of it. They were a good team. He blew his nose and felt a sinus headache coming on. *Great!*

Chapter Twelve

Officer Boucher thought of returning to rue Favreau before his two o'clock meeting with the SQ, but he couldn't risk the chance of being spotted and reported. He blamed the betrayal on the cop who had helped him the night before. Boucher looked down at his left boot where he stowed the second throwaway. Some cops never admit they carry one. Those who did said they needed the weapon if theirs was forcibly taken in an altercation. No cop admits to using a throwaway to alibi himself. Generally, the weapon could not be traced back to the cop for a reason. There were rumors that cops nicked the guns from evidence rooms, although there was no proof. Boucher had spent a restless night trying to decide if he should take the weapon to the meeting. In the end, he felt the more truth he told, the better his chances. If the witness hadn't come forward, he still expected to be put on leave with pay or assigned desk duty. The SQ needed time to investigate. The force didn't want him back on the street. He'd read the news. The shooting was another black eye for the 'gun-happy Montreal police.' Retraining was suggested again by media vultures. Just a few weeks ago there had been another demonstration against police violence that had turned ugly, with nineteen arrests.

It was only June, but the day was already sticky and hot. Though the division was air conditioned, Boucher felt sweat sticking behind his knees as he waited for the second time that day outside the boardroom. If the witness called the police, he would be arrested. Boucher used the back of his hand to wipe the sweat from under his chin. When he saw the two SQ detectives approaching, he straightened up. They motioned for Boucher to enter first. They were well prepared and began questioning immediately after setting up the interview. Boucher summarized the events of the evening. He stressed that his elderly neighbor lived alone and in fear. She couldn't sleep most nights. She was seventy-five years old.

"What is this woman's address?"

"Could you call her instead? I have the number. They've keyed her car twice. She doesn't want to see cops. Here it is."

"The victim had no drugs. His vehicle was clean. No cash bag either." Lead Detective Pichon, SQ, was asking the questions.

"He ran. What more can I add?"

"From what you say, I assume he was a bag man who ran before the pickup. I was never Vice, but it's strange to me, two trips in lieu of one."

Boucher laid his palms down on the table before he answered. "Maybe there were two. He was the bag man; the other the dealer."

"Uh huh. Why run when he had nothing on him? He knew you had no grounds for an arrest. Makes no sense."

"You'd have to ask …" Boucher stopped abruptly.

"But we can't, can we?"

"No."

"Now, when you reached the parking lot, you called to him. That's why he stopped running and turned?"

"Yes, I shouted twice to stop!" Boucher's voice rose.

"When did you reach for your weapon?"

"When he stopped."

"And turned?"

"Yes."

"Think very clearly, Officer Boucher. Did you see a weapon before you used deadly force?"

"One hand was raised; he was pointing with the other. It was dark. I thought he had a weapon. He posed an immediate danger to me. I acted as I was trained to do. I discharged mine. He did have a weapon when I ran over to him, so I wasn't wrong."

"You are trained to use reasonable force. Was it necessary to discharge your weapon three times?"

"I discharged my weapon in rapid succession. He was still standing after the first discharge. His weapon was still aimed at me. I fired till he went down."

"Forensics is working on both weapons. Tell me, Officer Boucher, do you carry a throwaway?"

"Yes."

"Here today?"

"Yes."

"I'll need that as well, please."

Boucher scraped his chair back noisily and reached inside his jacket pocket and handed over the weapon.

"Our investigation is ongoing, Officer Boucher, but we do want to clear this file as soon as possible. This vigilante approach has earned you a one-week suspension without pay effective today. We do hope to conclude this within a week. We're not discussing further sanctions at this point. Please sign the report."

"I'm not a rogue cop. All I intended to do was to take him in, or run him out of Laval. I also have a family to protect. I've done nothing wrong!"

"Yes, you have. Still, we hope the facts will confirm your statement. We advise you to act accordingly. We know you were back at the scene. Do not interfere with this investigation again if you wish to continue with the SPVM." On that serious note, Detective Pichon ended the questioning.

Boucher left the room worried and depressed. The SQ was taking a hard line on the shooting. He felt shafted. Even his partner didn't want to go the extra mile. He found a washroom on the first floor, ran cold water, bent over and slapped some onto his face and neck. Leaning on the sink, he studied his reflection in the wall-mounted mirror. The veins on his arms stood out like cords, but his face sagged. *I should have admitted knowing Jacques, but they would have seen a motive for going after him, and killing him.* Boucher regretted his actions. The enquiry was just beginning. The witness was still out there. His suspension afforded him time to get to her, if she didn't come forward and beat him out. His determination to find her gave way to doubt. He could lose his job, but that bitch could put him away. Somehow, he had to find his way to those three addresses. His legs felt sluggish and heavy. Boucher left the division dull-eyed and confused. How had he become the target?

Chapter Thirteen

Mondays and Tuesdays were 'dead' evenings at the Cleopatra. Producer Velma took advantage of those days to hold auditions. By the time she had contacted the performers she wanted for her show, it was four in the afternoon on Tuesday. Matthew Allen had come through again for Velma. This time he wasn't asked to play one of the Roman soldiers carrying Cleopatra, ensconced on her sedan chair, up across the stage. This Tuesday she asked him to play a lecherous old man. He'd played many parts for her, but a lecherous old man, never. Velma explained that since most of the cast were in their thirties and early forties, he was the old man. His *Never!* converted to *Just this once!* because Matthew saw that his victim was beautiful and young.

Matthew rather enjoyed acting the lecher to the vacationing Concordia drama student who had joined the cast. His victim was scantily clad and as a dirty old man, Matthew delighted in the swells and valleys of firm young breasts. He wanted retakes to get it just right. In fact, when the cast took a break, Velma had to pull him away from the thespian. "But," Matthew toyed, "I'm just getting into character!"

"It's a part, Matthew," Velma scolded him. "In real time, you wouldn't get anywhere near her."

"Don't be mean, Velma, not if you need a ride home tonight."

Velma laughed as she climbed the stairs with her troupe. "Remember guys, if you take a break on the roof, lock both doors when you come back inside. Understood? Vagrants are more daring in the summer. I don't need problems."

Matthew and Velma sat together in her dressing room. Gary and Pyrometheus, the performer chose to mangle the spelling of the original Titan, made their way out to the roof, both waving smokes as their excuse. Matthew and Velma exchanged silent telepathy between friends. "I hope they use protection, but I'm not their mother. Fire boy is thirty-one. He's not a kid, though he still thinks he is. Still looks like one."

"When he's serious, Velma, or playing serious, I can see thin lines well defined around his eyes."

"He's still young, compared to us."

Roxy picked up her lunch bag, took a few steps towards the roof, and decided not to intrude.

The young men who both looked like they needed food more than they needed sex hurried over to their spot behind the chimney. Gary tripped over something and screamed, "OH, MY GOD!" They stared down at the body. "Velma! Roxy, Matthew! OH, MY GOD!" They leaned against one another, shaking.

"Is he dead?" Gary whispered to Pyrometheus.

"I dunno? Maybe he fell, hit his head, or OD'd? This is terrible. Velma!"

The cast came running out onto the roof. Gary was about to touch the body when Matthew shouted "Don't touch anything!" Matthew knew CPR and first-aid. He pushed to the front and stooped over the body. "Jesus," he whispered to nobody. "It's Dylan. Move back." Matthew knelt on one knee. "Move back!" He laid two fingers on the side of Dylan's neck. The neck was cold. Dylan lay face down on the cement floor like an exhausted toddler who had fallen asleep on a carpet. Except Dylan hadn't fallen asleep, and Matthew was aware Dylan was beginning to smell. Matthew remembered the smell and bloat from dead animals from back lanes when he was a kid. Still Matthew wanted to turn his friend over, lay him on his back, and re-store some kind of dignity. "Maybe a second chance," Matthew remembered Dylan saying. He had had no chance at all. Matthew didn't touch the body again. He rose, and spoke with sadness. "He's dead. Call 9-1-1 and an ambulance, I suppose." He backed the cast away from the body.

"Isn't that your friend?" Roxy asked. "The one who was with you Saturday night?"

Matthew nodded.

"Did he OD?"

"I don't know, Roxy. All you guys, go back inside. Velma, wait out here with me."

Looking back, all the cast could see as they reached the door was a black sneaker with the silver zipper.

"Matthew, you checked the roof Saturday night, so he must have come up by the stairs, maybe yesterday."

Matthew covered his face with both hands. "I was tired Saturday, Velma. I never thought to look back there. I don't usually miss things. I should have taken the time to search the whole roof, but it was late. He's probably been here for the past two-and-a-half days."

"You could be wrong. He was your friend, right?"

"Yeah, for the last four months he'd just show up, and he treated me to dogs and fries at the Pool Room before our last Saturday show."

"Was he more than a friend? Cause I saw you together a lot, talking and stuff."

"No! He was just another lost man-boy, like half the cast, looking for a friend. Maybe I was too. Dylan never saw himself as one of the 'boys.' He said he was above all the small stuff, but he ended up face down behind an old chimney on the roof. What a lonely place to die."

"He was 'thick' with you."

"He liked my stories. He said he had nothing going on weekends, except last Saturday."

"He had a date? But he was with you ... You?"

"No. Later, with someone else after the show. He wasn't a kid, Velma. He was thirty."

"Maybe he did OD. Maybe Roxy was right."

"He was never high with me, said he had to protect his body – his stock-in-trade. I don't even know his last name. Jesus!" Matthew stood looking down at his friend.

They heard a commotion below on the street. The police and paramedics had arrived. The paramedics were the first on the rooftop. Police advised the cast and permanent staff not to leave the building until police had their names and numbers and did some preliminary interviews. A uniformed officer came out onto the roof. He exchanged a look with one of the paramedics and realized he was dealing with a recovery. He pointed two fingers at Velma and Matthew indicating that they should stay put. Matthew kept his eyes on Dylan. The officer walked up to the body and called the Crime Unit and the Crémazie Division.

Chapter Fourteen

The call went to Chief Donat's office, and his secretary forwarded it to Detective Damiano. The rush was back! She listened carefully. "We'll allow Crime an hour for you to stage the scene and collect evidence. I'll send you more officers to slog through the cast and personnel for rudimentary information. No one leaves the building before I get there." She listened. "Good pickup. They know the vic. Keep them away from the body, but on the roof. I'll want to talk to both of them."

Before Damiano had a chance to call her partner, the phone rang again. It was the Chief's phone, as least it was his ID. "Lieutenant Detective Damiano."

"It's Pamela, Detective."

Damiano detected an impersonal note in Pamela's voice that Damiano understood, given the circumstances. "Pamela, I'm at my desk. Assure the chief, his chair is waiting for him." She half meant her words.

"We have most of the test results, Detective. Richard must rest for the next month, and the doctors will reassess."

Damiano was careful with her response. "That's good news, Pamela. Do you want me to contact Major Crimes at Place Versailles for them to appoint an interim chief?"

"You should know my husband by now. Richard made the call himself."

It was an awkward moment. "Fine then. They will see to things." Damiano felt off-balance, uncertain if her chance had just slipped away. She had wanted to decline the temporary position. How could she have declined, still suggesting she was definitely interested in the permanent post without coming off as power-hungry? Perhaps it was for the best, the decision was out of her hands. "Wish the chief well for me!"

"Detective, you surprise me. Richard is not about to allow anyone, including me, or Place Versailles, to make this decision for him. He was adamant that you act as interim chief. He also said to tell you he'll be back, so don't get comfortable. No one knows the seriousness of Richard's medical situation – please keep the news to a minimum. That's how Richard wants it for the next month."

"You have my word."

"If I had my way …"

"I can guess, Pamela." Damiano sat back in her chair satisfied and disappointed. *Will Donat be back?* She had no time for ruminations. She rose and walked over to Pierre's desk. "I need to see you." Matte followed his partner to her office and Damiano closed the door behind them. "Try not to cough. I don't need your cold."

Matte groaned. "I have a splitting headache."

"Alright. We have a case. Body on the roof of Café Cleopatra. Know the place?"

"A few years back, I went a couple of times."

"I'll give Crime time to do their work. I have other news."

A nervous charge passed between them.

"Donat?"

"He's out for a month."

"And you're in."

"I tried to send the decision to Place Versailles."

"The chief earmarked you."

"He says he's coming back."

"Huh. Where does that leave me?"

"Working this case with me. I'd bet he'll be back. If not, we'd be talking about an indeterminate leave."

"Maybe."

"Clear up whatever you're working on today. Be ready to leave in forty minutes."

The white Crime van had parked outside of Café Cleopatra. Orange cones were set up around it. The van parked on the wrong side of St-Laurent Boulevard, but road rules didn't apply in such cases. The techs were swathed in their whites, and they closed down the scene, including the stairs and sidewalk below. The van itself was well equipped to run tests on site. It had a 3D laser scanner for scene documentation and analysis. The rear cabin of the van had sufficient electric power, switches, UPS emergency lighting, shockproof and fireproof cabling.

On the roof, techs used digital cameras to capture fingerprints. A tech used a tracer laser on the walls and chimney to create an alternate light source to fluoresce chemically treated prints. Techs worked the stairs, dusted and photographed. They paid particular attention to the top of the spiked fence and the weighted fire escape behind it. The stairs had been pulled down to street level. Photos of the body were carefully recorded from all angles. Dylan's hands and feet were bagged in case they carried trace evidence. Crime would laser his clothes at the lab.

Marie Dumont, head of the Crime Unit, knelt beside the body with her kit. She did not turn the body. It wasn't only detectives who worried about botched investigations; Crime carefully preserved the scene as well. Dylan's head had turned to the side. "It wasn't a suicide," she thought. Dumont detected petechial hemorrhaging in the left eye, a sign of strangulation. She studied as much of the neck as she could see without disturbing the body. She covered her nose, just once, and went back to work. Dr. Michael Belmont, senior pathologist at the Montreal city morgue, insisted on receiving the body as it was found. Odd, she thought, there were no obvious marks on the side of the neck. Prelim: an attack from behind. The black slacks pulled down supported her idea. The pathologist would discover if sexual activity had occurred before or after the attack. The pants themselves showed no signs of semen. The condition of the body suggested death had occurred in the last forty-eight hours. She'd leave that for Belmont. Of course, she knew that even the best pathologist could never know the precise TOD.

Velma turned away from the scene upset and deeply saddened. She looked back at Matthew who was watching every move. "Are you some kind of ghoul?"

"It's very sad and surreal, but fascinating."

"He was your friend." *What's wrong with you?*

"He's receiving good attention. I'm glad of that." Matthew zoned in again. "This is real, not a show. It's amazing to watch the Crime crews at work."

"Have a sense of decency."

"I can't pull myself away. At least Dylan is being treated with care and close attention. I'm glad for him."

Chapter Fifteen

"We should have left earlier. No one can estimate travelling time when there are new street closures every other day in this city due to construction. The streets might as well be locked vaults. When we get to the club, park wherever you can. Leave the flashers on for ten minutes to dissuade a quota cop from issuing us a ticket on this unmarked car." Damiano radiated energy and intensity. Matte was a quiet PR master with a tech's eye for detail. He also hadn't said a word in the car.

"Look, Pierre, I can't deal with needless wrangling, I was appointed by the Chief. I tried to pass the job off." Silence. "Fine, would you stay on the first floor and check on the uniforms to see that they are gathering names, addresses, cells and any additional information? Weed out people who might be of help. I'll see what Marie can give me." Silence again. "Did you hear me?"

"Yes, Chief."

"You have more than a cold, partner."

"My head is about to explode."

Damiano was first out of the car. She wore a lightly tailored black suit with a pale peach camisole and a single string of pearls. Her dark hair was pulled back and tied with a matching peach clasp. She was tall, and strode briskly into Cleopatra's with Matte, who looked more like a professor than a cop. The uniforms didn't miss her entrance, and she acknowledged them. She found the stairs and followed the wires that the tech team had laid out on the roof. The techs stood and backed off to give Damiano time to assess the situation without intrusion. Damiano walked around the body while pulling on plastic gloves and taking out a pen. "ID, Marie?"

"Not on the body, but those two over by the door know him."

"No clue whatever to his identity anywhere on the body?" Damiano pressed.

"Nothing. I was thorough."

Damiano stooped over the body and used her pen to recheck the back pockets. She examined the hands inside the plastic bags and checked the semi-closed dead eye. She always felt some nausea at such times. The odor made her stomach turn. She breathed into her fist and closed her eyes for a second. The noise of the traffic below was a welcome distraction from the regret, close to grief. Another life lost, gone. "He's young. Such a waste. OD?"

"Strangulation. I don't have a lot of facts for you yet. This is one of your organized crimes, no shortcuts. I do know from those witnesses that he is thirty."

Damiano stood and addressed Dumont. "Your prelim guess?"

"Yes. I detected petechial hemorrhaging in his left eye. To the naked eye, there are no marks on the sides of the neck. No signs of a fight-back from the vic either. The scene is clean as a scalpel. It looks like the perp came at him from behind. Nothing is firmed up. I'll leave that to Dr. Belmont and the forensic team."

"Did you find evidence of sexual activity?"

"Belmont will be able to report to you with more accuracy than I have. If the perp used a condom, he didn't leave it behind. Our lasers detected no trace of semen on the body."

"But his pants are pulled down?"

"That was a blind, I guess to distract the kid. Might have been someone he knew, or a quickie."

"Silver zippers …"

"They struck me too."

Detective Matte noticed the witnesses and joined Detective Damiano and Marie Dumont. "Toni, I held four people for us and dismissed the others. The officers are taking them upstairs two at a time to collect their things. Some were able to leave without having to come up."

"Good."

Detective Matte took a step closer to the body. He knelt down and looked at the side of the face. Damiano saw him reach into a pocket for a handkerchief, the only person she knew who still used one. He crumpled the handkerchief into a ball in his fist.

"For God's sake, don't blow your nose near the body! Don't contaminate it any more than it already might be, Pierre."

Matte couldn't move.

"Pierre?" Damiano grabbed his shoulder. "Pierre."

The detective rose slowly and turned full-face to Damiano. "It's Dylan," he said, his voice breaking and raked his fingers through his hair.

Dumont backed off as Damiano moved towards Matte, both observing his shock.

"I'm sorry, Pierre. Do you want to leave?" Damiano wanted to extend further sympathy to Matte, but that was impossible with techs within earshot. It was Dylan who had been the love of his life and had broken his heart many times, nearly destroying him. But Damiano could not permit personal feelings to interfere with her job. She was interim chief and had to act accordingly. "I don't mean to be harsh, Pierre, but you can't work the case. You know you can't. You should be alone anyway. This is a hard blow."

Detective Matte stood with his head down, silent in his thoughts.

"Pierre?"

"I have to, Toni. You owe me from last year – you owe me for a lot of things. You worked your son's case. I haven't seen Dylan in eight months. There shouldn't be a conflict of interest. He has no one. He can't be just another toe-tag." His last words were garbled with pain.

"He was murdered, Pierre. You will be considered a person of interest. Interview these two with me. I'll decide what we do later. C'mon, wipe your face."

Matte used his fist and swiped at both eyes. He tried to breathe. He forced himself to be a cop. He didn't recognize his own voice when he spoke. It was someone else speaking for him. "Hmm. From his clothes, Dylan must have been on the hunt. Dylan was cavalier you know, even dismissive when he wanted to move on. Well, he finally had himself baked and dumped." Detective Matte stepped back and flinched. He made a bad attempt to appreciate the irony, but his face creased instead.

Detective Damiano pushed ahead, with some fear of losing Matte. "We need to do the interviews. I also want to wrap things up here and send Dylan's body to the morgue. We need more information."

Matthew Allen thought he might have picked up on something. He lost it when a tech walked in front of his field of vision, ignoring his and Velma's silent presence.

"Let's question the producer first, and her friend there with her. She'll give us a decent background of the place."

"I'd like to see the body out and deliver my usual ASAP to Dumont. Find a room and get her settled. If you're sure you can handle this, Pierre, take the prelims for me. Be sure to see her friend doesn't take a notion to leave."

It took fifteen minutes before Detective Damiano entered the room where Detective Matte introduced her with her new title as chief. Detective Matte had chosen the largest dressing room. The room reeked of powder, used clothes and grime. The producer sat up stiffly on the edge of her chair when she saw Damiano. "Chief, this is Christine Dawson, aka, Velma, the producer. She's an auditor for the provincial government."

Velma edged closer to Detective Damiano, perching then on four inches of chair. "Please keep my name from the media. I can't put my job at risk. I'll be as helpful as I can be. No one but Matthew knows my actual name. The production is my escape from numbers."

"How about we stay with Velma for now?"

Velma exhaled and sat back. "Thank you."

"Chief, I have the background. You can begin with what they know about the victim."

"Was he a regular at your shows?" Damiano asked.

"Matthew told me his name was Dylan. He began to show up one Friday night. He didn't notice him for a while. So many 'boys' come to the shows, but Matthew couldn't miss him a few months back because he always sat at his table with the other two photographers. He gave him a pass on the cover charge. Matthew says he never saw him with a drink. They talked a lot. They were friends."

"Did you meet Dylan?" Damiano asked the producer.

"I'm always very busy production night. Matthew brought him upstairs for the special tour, a month ago, I think, could have been longer. I recall waving at both of them."

"Was Dylan 'looking'?"

"No. I know my crew, when one of them hooks up, they're dramatic by nature and they announce it proudly. No one ever mentioned Dylan. I can't account for the fan base. Dylan was tight with Matthew. He was always with Matthew, but Matthew is straight. He's actually playing an old lecher, and I had to peel him off the young protégée in our cast. Matthew is quite the adventurer – his stories are hair-raising. He said Dylan liked listening."

"Do you know anything specific about the two of them last Saturday night?" Detective Damiano wanted a bone.

"Matthew told me that Dylan treated him to dogs and fries at the Montreal Pool Room. They came back here for the show. Oh, yes, Dylan had dressed up that night. They watched the whole show together. I mean as friends."

"What time does the show finish?"

"Around one-twenty in the morning, then we party."

"Thank you." Detective Damiano closed her notes. "Detective Matte will see that an officer drives you home. We might need to see you again."

"That's okay, I'll go home with Matthew. You'll remember about my name?"

"Yes, Velma."

"I forgot something. After the party, someone went out on the roof to smoke or make out, but never locked the doors. There are two doors.

Roxy, a performer, heard the outer door clanging against the inner door. I didn't want to go out there alone. It's pitch dark at night. Matthew went because I asked him to go. He didn't look behind the chimney. He said he was tired, but should have taken the time to look. We were all beat. Oh God, maybe Dylan was already there. Matthew felt bad that he missed the chimney."

"That is important. Thank you."

"No, it's not that important. I feel that I'm betraying a good friend. Matthew is straight. I sent him out on the roof. He was just being kind to Dylan, being his friend. The way I explained things didn't come off well for Matthew." Velma threw her head back her eyes welling with hot tears that wanted to fall down her face. "He can't be involved. He's one of the original good guys!"

"Alright then."

Matte led Velma downstairs to an officer. He made an attempt to calm her down.

Damiano sat and thought out loud. "Matthew, the adventurer, spent Saturday night with Dylan. Dylan dressed for an occasion, and he bought Matthew dinner. He was with Matthew till after one. From the odor of his body, I'd hazard that Dylan died some time after the show. How much time does that leave for a perp or a date to appear on the roof and strangle Dylan? Not much. Later, Matthew checked the roof, but never thought to look behind the chimney. The TOD time frame has definitely narrowed. That's a bone with some meat."

Chapter Sixteen

Detective Matte stood outside Cleopatra's. Cars and trucks of all sizes pitched their own battle along St-Laurent, indifferent to the body that lay on the roof. Matte's eyes burned. He hated the indifference that he met at every crime scene. He wanted to howl his anger at Dylan, at himself, at those idiots behind the wheels who went about living. Instead, he went back inside and adjusted his workface mask. He found the male suspect already in the changing room closest to the roof. Velma was frightened and nervous, but Matthew sat quietly with both hands comfortably on the powder bar as though he owned it.

Matte sat across from a six-foot, middle-aged male with thinning curly brown hair. Matthew wore a jacket that looked slept in, and a white rumpled shirt. To Matte, Matthew looked like an outdoor hick, strong, with muscles. What was he doing at Cleo's? Matte moved his chair closer, and asked the first question. "How did you meet the victim?"

Matthew was ready. "The table in the front of the stage is always reserved. There are two other photographers who join me. I take footage from the vantage point of the table and from different locales during the show. About four months ago, before the show started, I noticed Dylan leaning against the back wall of the club, alone. I motioned him over and told him the seat beside me was free. I always arrive early in case Velma needs my help, so we had an hour to kill and we talked, or rather I talked. He listened."

"About?"

"Rock climbing, caves, near-death experiences – stuff he wanted to hear. Stories about near-death experiences excited him. Dylan wouldn't take such risks. He said he had to watch his body. That was his ticket."

"There was no intimacy between you then?"

"Do I look gay to you, Detective?" Allen spoke deliberately, his tone level and flat. He kept his eyes on Matte. "Detective, I saw your reaction to Dylan's body. I thought that maybe you knew him, Detective." Allen sat back and watched.

"I have that reaction when I see a young life lost." Detective Matte didn't move a muscle; he perceived Allen as the enemy. Matte's eyes narrowed. How could Dylan have spent time with this jerk? Matte coughed into his sleeve and he leaned in closer. "Mr. Allen, we meet all sorts in our work. What drew *you* to Cleo's? Most people here are different. I'll leave it at that."

"Velma's a friend. I help out. Besides, I like quirky people. It's a break from the herd."

Detective Damiano took over to prevent a dust-up. "You were with the victim last Saturday?"

"I was." Allen looked squarely at Detective Matte when he answered. "I have to tell you that I never knew Dylan's last name. I feel sorry about that. He surprised me earlier that evening when he invited me to join him at the Pool Room across the street for a bite to eat. He never had any money. I asked where he got it, and he said he had his ways. He showed up in new clothes; said he had a date." Matthew smiled sympathetically at Detective Matte.

"Not with you?"

"No." Matthew punched the bar. "Velma thought the same thing, but NO! He seemed excited and desperate. I suppose frightened. He said he needed the date to work out."

"Did he say why?"

"He needed a place to stay – he needed somebody. He said he liked older men. They took care of him. He hinted about a second chance, but didn't explain it. He was secretive about his life."

Matte winced and rubbed his nose to hide it.

"Yet we are told he stayed with you till well after one."

"He said the date was after the show."

"Did you know he was going up to the roof for his date?"

"No. I had to have Velma's permission to show Dylan around a month ago. I had no idea he'd planned to meet on the roof, none at all."

"What do you do for a living, Mr. Allen?"

"I'm trained in carpentry, but I'm decent at most manual labor."

"Are you currently employed?"

"I'm a jobber. I was offered a permanent job at McGill University, starting next Thursday. I haven't accepted the work officially yet, because I enjoy free time."

"Back to the club, I find it curious you didn't do a complete search of the roof last Sunday morning. You appear to me to be a thorough man."

"You're right." Allen bowed his head. "I feel bad, very bad. I never thought Dylan would be up there. He would not have had my permission to use it. I left the ringside table to take some footage. When I got back, he was gone, just gone."

"How long were you away from the table?"

"Fifteen to twenty minutes at the most." Allen saw where the detectives were heading. "Hey, wait a minute … I had nothing …"

"We'll stop for now, but we will want to see you again, Mr. Allen."

"Listen, I was his friend. I know how cops work."

"Have you ever been arrested?" Detective Damiano asked casually.

"This is bullshit! Yeah, I have a sheet, but Dylan was my friend."

Allen stomped out of the room and out of Cleo's, where he found Velma waiting for him. "What the fuck did you tell them?"

Damiano approached Matte. "What do you think, Pierre?"

"He's in play. He's an arrogant snob who can't see he's one of the quirks."

"I'm glad you didn't mince words. I agree." Damiano brushed loose powder from the bar, hesitating. "About the case, you know I have to ask. Have you had any contact with Dylan in the last eight months?"

"Kane. Dylan's last name is Kane. I haven't seen Dylan since he came back looking for a place to stay. I sent him away."

"Look, Pierre, I can't play games with you. Any contact, phone, text, anything?"

"Dylan broke into my condo and stole three hundred dollars in the past week."

"What? How?"

"His last connection with me was to use the extra key I keep outside and grab three hundred dollars from a stash I hide in the condo. He could have stolen a thousand, but I'm guessing he knew I'd find him and nail his ass."

"What other further contact have you had with Dylan? Text or call. I have to know, Pierre."

"Yes, a few along the way that went nowhere."

"You will be a suspect. Someone will know that Dylan was seeing a cop. A second chance, that's what he told Allen – not good for you. The contact with Dylan is even worse."

"Toni, I know. I'm fully aware of my request and its implications."

"If I weren't acting chief, I'd take the chance, but I now represent Chief Donat. It's a conflict of interest. I'm really sorry, Pierre."

"I hate when anyone plays the debt card, but I want to nail Dylan's killer. I loved him, Toni. In some sad way, I still do. He's inside me, part of me. Don't forget that I could have had your ass if I had reported your drug use on the job, and the booze the last eighteen months. I didn't, but if you'd been found out, I'd have been out on my ass with you. Are you still using narcotics for that bad arm, Chief Damiano? Would you pass a drug test today?"

Damiano did a drum roll on the bar and wiped her hand. "Pierre, I have to ask …"

Pierre wanted to stab a finger into Damiano's chest and explode in anger, but he worked to keep it reined in. When he did respond, his tone was as cold as ice. "No, you don't. I would consider that question the ultimate insult." Pierre took a deep breath and swallowed. He laid a hand on his hip. "I've allowed you to shove the grunt work my way, but I'd never work with you again if you ask that question. I hope you are hearing me. I'd have to work alone probably, but so be it. Whether you know it or not, you need me on this case. I know where Dylan hung out, where he'd find another mark like me. You want to impress the brass with a quick solve. Remember, I make the murder notes legible. I cut your work in half. I'm gay. Dylan was gay." He winced at 'was.' "You need me. I'm not asking you for a favor. I'm telling you that you owe me." He stared Damiano down, daring her to pose the question, boosted by their past work together. His face appeared swollen with anger.

She shifted her feet, aware she was standing on a minefield.

Detective Matte understood her position, but he ignored it, and her title. "What about my subterfuge with your son to help you out on our last case. Wasn't that a blatant conflict of interest?" Detective Matte's phone buzzed. He let it ring four times. "Yes." He kept the phone to his ear and creased his forehead with the other hand. "Is *he* there?" He turned his back on Damiano. "I'll go when he's not there." He began to pace. "Alright! Of course, I promise. I love Mom just like you."

"Pierre?"

Matte placed his phone carefully into his breast pocket and rubbed his face with both hands. "My mother's had some kind of stroke. She's been taken to the McGill University Health Center."

"Just go."

"I can't right now. I can't deal with my father. I never could. Toni, I will see you tomorrow morning at eight at the morgue. You're not taking me off this investigation."

"Just go." The bluster of conflict of interest and rank had gone out of Damiano. She sat stunned and watched Matte leave. Maybe he *was* angry enough to expose her. In the last few minutes, he had become an unknown species, dangerous and unpredictable. Had they ever been friends? Her lungs emptied and she struggled to breathe, because Matte was right in what he said. Her cheeks flushed and tingled with anger. Why did everything have to change? Yesterday, her goals were clear. Close a case. Fight for the best ones. Move ahead. Pierre was a detective, her partner, but she was his superior. She'd been confident, able to live in the moment. Now, tomorrow's complications and Matte's threat gnawed at confidence she didn't feel. She rose to her feet and walked down the stairs and out to the street. The traffic was jammed up and noisy. "Yep! Chaos everywhere!" Damiano let loose with one of her full laughs. "Screw them all!"

Chapter Seventeen

Officer Boucher sat in his car outside a dépanneur on St-Martin Boulevard with a bag of groceries, weighing the risks of losing his career or going to prison. He didn't have a choice. He wore old summer clothes and sneakers without socks, trying not to be taken for a cop. Most cops had a way of walking that marked them as soon as they entered a room. He lit a cigarette and let it dangle from the side of his mouth. His hair was purposely unruly. He got out of his car and walked over to rue Favreau with his groceries. He walked casually up the street till the ninth triplex. No one seemed to notice him. He climbed the stairs slowly, put the bag down and rang the bell. He ran a hand through his hair.

A pleasant Greek woman, somewhere in her sixties, with a timid smile opened the door.

"Good evening. I'm a police officer."

Frightened eyes, and a step back into her home, told Boucher to be gentle.

"No trouble, ma'am. I just want to know if you and your family are okay?"

She nodded. The woman looked down the street. "Big trouble!"

"Yes. But you are safe." It didn't take Boucher long to realize her English was limited. "Everybody safe?" he asked, pointing to the three other apartments.

She pointed up to the apartment. "Yes, yes."

"Good." He pointed down.

She threw her arms out, palms open. "Carmen no come home last night."

"Tall, pretty, dark hair?"

"Yes, yes, Carmen."

"Let's hope she is with a friend."

"Her mother."

"Does she live in the area?" Boucher asked hoping for the information.

The woman hesitated. "Don't know. Come later, my husband talk to you."

"That's fine. I hope all is well." Boucher offered his genuine smile. "Lock your door!"

The door was already bolted before he finished. Boucher picked up the bag of groceries from the floor, having confirmed the apartment. It took great restraint not to toss the bag and run. He had her! He spotted a cop on the side of the parking lot. He turned and walked back up the street, hoping the Greek woman wasn't staring out her window. Boucher moved slowly, taking in the soccer field, trying to evade the patrol cop's scrutiny, not daring to look behind him. At the top of the street, he took a long right. He didn't try to reach his car by taking rue Goyer. He dumped the groceries in a container at the end of the soccer field. His excitement was dampened by the fear of being spotted. He walked two blocks before he felt safe to head back to rue St-Martin. Once there, he crossed the street and stopped often to divert attention. At the corner of Favreau and St-Martin, he bought a slice and a Coke from an old pizza joint that served students during the school year. His mouth was too dry to swallow the pizza. He could see his car, but he could also see the cop who had walked to St-Martin and was standing outside the dépanneur.

Had he seen him? It was light for at least another half-hour. What was the cop doing? Boucher regretted ditching the groceries. He could have used them as a cover when he went for his car. He was stuck, waiting for the cop to move. He did, he went into the store and stayed there for ten minutes. Had he seen him? Had he called for backup? Boucher bit into the thin pizza and tried to chew and washed it down with a gulp of Coke that nearly sent him into a coughing fit. Should he just take off and leave the car? He was the only patron, sitting on a rickety chair at a sticky table. There were two other cars besides his across the street. The cop didn't appear to be running the plates, but he might if he'd been warned to expect Boucher. Then again, Boucher couldn't afford to spend too much time staring over without drawing attention. When the cop finally appeared outside the store, he just stood there again. Boucher knew his face was known to Laval cops. The underground worked that way. Cops shared fatal shootings and they feared being snagged in one. Boucher couldn't walk to his car because the cop would recognize him. He took a bite from the cardboard pizza. Out of the corner of his eye, he saw the cop move and he looked over. The cop was talking into his shoulder phone as he left and walked briskly up Favreau. The woman must have called the police.

Boucher ran across the street, hopped into his car, backed out carefully, for St-Martin was a busy road. He never saw where the cop went. His nerves bucked and jerked. He drove slowly, trying to avoid treacherous potholes on St-Martin, and finally turned into a strip mall. He took his phone and found a C. DiMaggio on Favreau. He also found two other DiMaggios, one on 7th Street, Laval, and another in suburban Blainville. He fired the engine and drove onto Highway 13 and got off at the Ste-Dorothée Power Center. He took rue Samson to 100th Avenue, turned right on Ninth and drove down to 7th Street. He sat in the car a few houses away from the one that interested him. The home was in the middle of a block, a quiet little white-brick bungalow with an immaculate lawn. He grabbed the steering wheel when he realized all the curtains were drawn. If this was the mother, had she already been warned?

Boucher hadn't noticed that a neighbor had opened his front door, walked out unsteadily with a cane, staring at his car. "Neighborhood Watch! The old fart must be ninety!" The old man definitely had a bead on him. He took one last scan of the house. Had that curtain moved? Boucher saw that the old man's wife had joined him, walker and all. He wasn't going to sit and wait for a patrol car. He had what he wanted, to a degree. He had the phone number, but he couldn't use his phone to call. A visit had been the best route but that was lost. Boucher started the car. Surely the old man didn't have the eyes to pick up his plate. He wasn't going to take that chance. Boucher backed up on 7th and turned right out of harm's way.

Lena DiMaggio was eighty-eight years old. Although she might get flustered, she was a tough cookie with a quick mind. There were times Carmen admitted her mother had the better stamina. When old Anton alerted her about the car, she had already seen it. She had been on the lookout since Carmen's call. "I knew he was there, Anton. I have called the police, but I don't know what help they can offer. He didn't really do anything, but I'm very nervous for Carmen. You didn't happen to see the licence plate?"

"Lena, it's good for me that I even see the car."

"I have to go, Anton. I must call Carmen."

Carmen listened. "I told you, Mom, you should have come to stay with Caitlin and me."

"No. Leave my house and my things with my bad knees? I can't. I am so afraid, I never sleep now. I'm still in my nightie."

"I wish I could be with you, but I can't take the chance. Anthony will have to take over for me until I decide what I can do. I'll call him as soon as we are off the phone. He'll sleep at your house tonight."

"You're frightened, Carmen, just like me. You have to do something. What if that officer had come to my door?"

"I told you not to answer the door for anyone you don't know."

"I'm not young like I used to be. I have the years with me. I am very scared."

"Let Anthony sleep over tonight or go stay at his house."

"They'd drive me crazy in a day! Just a minute, please, I have another call. Let me get back to you Carmen."

"Mrs. DiMaggio, I am with the police. I need to speak with your daughter. I just want to talk to her …" Boucher slammed the one pay phone he'd found back into its cradle. "The woman hung up on me! Since when do people hang up on the police?"

"Oh my God! Carmen, that was the officer."

"Mom! Take some deep breaths. Watch your heart. I am so sorry. What did he say?"

"He said he wants to talk to you. He has a family, he said."

Carmen fought to keep the tears from her mother. She bit her index finger before she could answer. "I have a plan, Mom. Try to stay calm till Anthony arrives. I'm fine."

"Oh dear, the police car just pulled into my driveway."

"Mom, is it the same cop?"

"No, the car door says Laval police."

"Mom, before you answer the door, do not tell the police that the prowler was the cop after me. Just say your neighbors called you about a prowler. Do you get that, Mom? Me being a witness to the shooting cannot get out! Mom?"

"I hear you, Carmen. Just a prowler, just a prowler. My doorbell is ringing."

"Keep me on the line while you speak to him."

Any hope that her mother would get rid of the officer quickly evaporated when she began to tell the officer her age. He complimented her quick action. Then she complimented him for his efficiency. Carmen left teeth marks on her bottom lip, waiting for the call to end. She let go of her lip when she heard her mother wish the officer a good day. As soon as Carmen heard the door close, relieved, she shouted into the phone. "Good work!"

"A wonderful man. He has three sons."

"I heard, Mom." Carmen hid her exasperation. "Do not open the door for anyone but Anthony. I'll call you in an hour."

"I haven't been able to read my *Gazette* or do my WonderWords either."

"Go and lie down, Mom. Take it easy."

"How can I?"

"Try for me. I told you I have a plan."

"I'll use the sofa. I want to keep an eye out."

"Alright." Carmen nodded to Caitlin who had listened in. "I can't hide any longer. I can't think at work. I can't sleep. Now I have Mom to worry about. I have to call that detective. She was fair, you said."

"It's too late now. I'll make the call for you, tomorrow first thing. You take the phone and explain."

"I have to get to work."

"Half an hour late, Carmen. You have to come forward, before the worst happens."

Chapter Eighteen

In the kitchen, sitting across from one another, Damiano ate leftover barbeque with Jeff. Apparently their son Luke was busy studying for his last exam. "And you believed him?"

"It's chemistry. He's shooting for a perfect score."

"That's different. Luke has the head for math, like you. My whole day went south, and I don't want to talk about it." Her voice was almost a squawk, and Jeff knew when to back off. "I won't sleep tonight. I should sleep in the guest room because I want to be at the division early."

"I'd rather have you with me, but I understand. Toni ..."

"Not to worry about pills – I need my wits about me tomorrow."

Tuesday night, Damiano saw two-ten, three-nineteen, and three fifty-two. She gave up on sleep and stood under the shower at four thirty. At six, she was alone in her office ready to figure out the stalemate with Matte. Instead, Damiano stared at the fourteen files that Chief Donat's secretary had piled on her desk. She wasn't just the interim chief of Major Crimes; she was in charge of all six floors: Homicide, Narcotics and Domestic Violence, all of it. She sat down, lowering her chin and drawing out the lines in her neck. The full burden weighed down on her. She thought of the mountains of paperwork that would tie her to that desk, the stress of the work and the loss of her freedom. She hadn't worked for her lieutenancy to become a petty bureaucrat and old before her time. Damiano had intended to bring Matte along with her and dump some of the stress and most of the paperwork on him. Matte was a natural with notes, better than a computer because he had a good head.

Instead, he had become a threat. Damiano kept a book of quotes in her night table and remembered one she particularly liked: Lewis Carroll had said, "It's no use going back to yesterday, because I was a different person then." What Pierre had said to her, he couldn't take back. Had all his resentment been festering for years? How could she ever trust him? The bitter truth of his words struck her like a bullet. She had to figure something out because she feared Pierre as much as she needed him. She hurried through the files, noted what she felt should be done and left her comments on yellow notes affixed to each file. On her way out, she deposited the files with Donat's secretary and told her to make note of all calls, but hold them while she was at the morgue. She intended to turn off her phone. The crime scene was a sacred place. The victim deserved her full attention.

She arrived at Parthenais, the Montreal city morgue, before eight. Calling in favors from the senior pathologist wasn't something she wanted to do just yet. Instead, she filed in with the early birds through the scrutiny of metal detectors that Pierre Elliot Trudeau International Airport would envy. She called Pathology, and an assistant sent the chief coroner's private elevator up for her. The elevator was used by grieving families when they came in to identify bodies. On the way down, Damiano leaned against the elevator wall as a new surge of fear ran up her back. When she stepped out, she felt unsteady, wounded by Matte and the truth he had thrown in her face. She would lose her partner and perhaps her job if he filed a report. Lost, too, was what she'd thought of herself. She decided to wait for him at the elevator.

Four minutes later, he emerged in the clothes he'd worn yesterday. "I spent the night at the hospital." His stubble added strength to his face, but his eyes were stained red and heavy. He looked at the floor when he finally spoke. "The one kind thing I will remember my father doing was rushing my mother to the hospital. Her speech is affected; she's in and out of it, but the physician says she might make a good recovery."

"I'm glad for you, Pierre."

"Me too. My mother was always good to me. No matter what, she was on my side. I never get to see her much. My father dogs her side, even when she's watching television, or shopping. It's weird. He thinks he's so strong, but she's his rock. He hates being alone. And he thinks I'm the weak link in the family."

"About yesterday, Pierre, I have a plan. You have time coming to you. Take the time to be with your mother. You can work the case with me from the outside. Officially, I'll take on Stephen Galt. He's a decent cop."

"But he's a homophobe and already working the fatal stabbing on Ontario Street. This is my plan. My father wants to stay with my mother and sleep at the hospital. It might be guilt. It doesn't matter what it is. Mom's not alone. My sister and I will share the nights if he needs a break. I work the case. You've never met Dylan. My name may never come up. No harm, no foul. If and when it does, I will recuse myself and take the fallout."

"About yesterday …"

Matte raised his head and faced Damiano. "I was so angry with you, with Dylan, with all the shit I've done for you over the years that I struck out. I'm not a snitch. If I had been, I would have turned you in long ago for various irregularities. I felt, I feel you owe me a solid. Still do, but we are a team, just somewhat different now, porous I suppose. I don't have many friends. I always thought you were one of them, although it's irked me that you always believed you were the better cop. You're not, you know. We're good at different things. You earn the medals – I print the murder books. I figured out last night that you need me as much as I need you on this job."

Damiano parried. "I always believed you had my back, Pierre."

"I thought you trusted me. I remember reading that betrayal begins with trust. When I saw you waver, I lost it. Maybe it's good we fought. At least, we'll never be a comfortable cliché."

Damiano received the message. She said nothing, but offered her hand. "Let's go and see Belmont. By the way, you should see the files I have to work."

"And?"

"I'll need your help."

"Of course you will unless you take a printing class."

All talk stopped as they rounded the corner and stood outside the main examining room. The autopsy theatre was just behind it. An assistant pathologist appeared and ushered them into a small room used for lunch or breaks, with two tables and chairs. The only addition was a single sink. The assistant had no news. Damiano waited for her to leave before she spoke. "Pierre, did you ever meet any of Dylan's family?"

"No, but I know that his father lives in Richmond, British Columbia, and his mother, Mississauga, Ontario. He had a brother, but I have no clue about him. I'll do the search, but you should make the calls – that way I can stay off the radar."

"I'll make the calls after we have news from Belmont. I hope we have something soon. This place makes me uneasy." Damiano would never admit to squeamishness.. Still, nausea was not the only reason she stopped attending autopsies. A weariness had come over her as she observed the work of scalpels, saws and scales. In the end, a victim is reduced to nothing more than a clue. That idea saddened Damiano and reduced her energy. She was lost in thought and didn't see that Dr. Belmont had opened the examining room door, carrying his Thermos.

He was dressed in his usual spotless whites. The detectives knew he left his rubber apron behind when he came out to converse with them. He made a motion, from an old habit, to run his hand through his hair and settled on a temple scratch. What thinning hair he had on top of his head had been carefully combed. He didn't want to appear foolish, possibly leaving a few hairs standing on end. He was a tall man with a slight stoop. His hands were long and slender, like a pianist's. He must be sixty, Damiano thought. "Let's sit in the examining room. This room is for pathologists and their assistants." Since there were only two stools in that room, Matte stood. Belmont walked back to the theatre, and reached in for a plastic bag. "I thought you'd want these for the next of kin. I folded the clothes. The smaller items, a gold chain and a leather band, are in a smaller bag inside. You'll send these to forensics."

Instead, Matte took the items and held them for a second before he put the bag on the floor beside him. "Not much left at the end is there?"

"There never is," Belmont said. "You'll have a copy of my final notes tomorrow. We've sent off the tox panel. The liver tests indicate the victim died sometime Sunday morning. The June heat precipitated the body's breakdown, so I can't narrow the TOD more precisely than Sunday morning. The nail clippings, fibers, and skin cells found on the clothes have been sent to the lab. The manner of death is asphyxiation. I did find petechial hemorrhaging in the eyes. In clinical terms, the victim died from carotid restraint, anoxia, a type of chokehold in your terms. Such a fatal wound leaves few external markings. I removed the hyoid bone and examined the laryngeal skeleton. I have rarely seen such a clean fracture of the larynx. The victim had no chance. His airway was cut off. The angle of the fracture suggests the assailant was taller than the victim.

"Generally, in such cases, I'd find scratches on both sides of the neck, mostly from thumb scratches. The thumb is the strongest digit. These markings are made by the victim trying to fight for oxygen by loosening the hold. I find it curious there were none. There is a mustard bruise on the front of the victim's neck, the location of the attack. Usually, a victim thrashes during such an attack; the irony is that he or she kicks out, away from their assailant in a fruitless attempt to escape. As pathologists, we're left with very few injury clues that would assist us in our work.

"I'm not a detective, but I have to tell you this murder was committed with the precision of a scalpel. A hate crime normally involves a mass of injuries, an attempt to wipe out the victim. A jilted lover takes out his hurt with what we call steel-tipped vengeance. From what Dumont tells me, this crime does not have the earmarks of a random. From my examination, there was no evidence of sexual interference. If fact, there was no sexual activity in the last seventy-two hours preceding death. Most victims are murdered by people they know. This victim certainly appears to have known his killer. Otherwise, I'd have more to give you.

"In my medical opinion, the assailant knew how to kill. You might be looking at a cop, a fireman, a physician, a UFC fighter or a martial arts black belt. The list grows. You have a well-executed crime, detectives. The tox results will take a few days. I should get back to my work. Any questions?"

"Would you expect any bruising on the perp?"

"Perhaps on the inside of the forearm, but if this assailant is as smart as I believe he is, he'd have worn a jacket to protect his arm. In fact, you are dealing with a cold-blooded killer. This young man deserved a better fate. That's my medical opinion, with a personal note. Such a waste."

"Thank you."

"I wish I were of more help. I did test for HIV. I should have results in five days."

Damiano turned to Matte but saw no reaction, no sign of shock. When they were alone, she spoke up. "You'll have to be tested, for your own sake."

"Give me some credit. I have myself tested regularly."

"Good."

"I think you should commandeer a murder room. I'll set up the wall. I have a photo of Dylan. I'll begin the family search. We also have photos of the cast. It's a start. I'll have cast members I want to see at the division."

Once they were back at the division, Matte found a room and began the work. "We need a second interview with Matthew Allen. Find out if people saw him around the stage. We already know he knew his way around Cleo's. He appears for now to be the last person to see Dylan alive."

"I agree. I have to collect my calls from Donat's secretary. She didn't approve of me blocking my calls. She's a little martinet, that one! Such loyalty to Donat is admirable, but …. Doesn't matter."

"It's a pity you didn't take calls, Lieutenant. There was one very insistent caller, a Caitlin Donovan, a professor at Concordia."

"How did she get my private number?" Damiano ignored the tutorial. In the future, if push came to shove, she'd push. She was the interim chief after all!

"I have no idea, Lieutenant." Denise Roy, Donat's secretary, emphasized the title.

Damiano recalled giving it to Donovan, but months ago. "Thank you for the good work. I see you've taken care of the files, too." Damiano examined the office that was larger than the chief's. She saw that Madame Roy made copies of, it appeared, everything. The walls in the entire office were filled to the ceiling with paperwork. *The Green Party could build a solid case against wanton destruction of forestry.*

Madame Roy glowered at Damiano and her inspection, so she left the secretary with her files. Damiano wanted to get the call over as quickly as possible and tapped in the number.

Caitlin had stopped answering sixteen-digit numbers she didn't recognize and felt were scams. Nevertheless, she felt she knew the person behind this one. "Hello."

"Lieutenant Detective Damiano. You should have discarded my private number, Professor Donovan."

"I found it in my files."

"Well?"

"You are the only person we felt we could trust. I have an urgent matter."

Chapter Nineteen

"I must be honest with you, Professor Donovan, I'm interim chief and I am extremely busy. May I not pass your call on to someone I trust?"

"I'm not exaggerating when I say this is a matter of life and death, Detective. I would not have disturbed you otherwise."

"Go on then." Damiano felt obliged to listen.

"This concerns the fatal shooting involving a police officer in Laval."

Damiano exhaled. "The SQ are handling this case, but I can put you in touch with a good man."

"Detective, we may not have had a positive encounter last year, but I am a responsible woman, and I need your help. Don't pawn me off on someone else, please. Hear me out at least. I trust you to keep this conversation private."

Despite the umbrage Damiano took from Donovan's remarks, she was intrigued. "Go ahead, Professor."

"My friend of many years was a witness to the shooting. The victim knocked her between two cars in his attempt to escape the officer chasing him. She was on her knees when the officer called out to the victim by name and shot him three times. He shot the man outright. My friend, in shock, managed to get to her feet, but she then stood face to face with the officer. They were five feet apart. He saw her and she saw him. She was able to run away because illumination from lights emanating from an apartment building distracted the cop.

"My friend is staying with me. That officer has managed to find her address and the address of her mother, whom he has called. She fears for her life, and her mother's. Apart from her immediate fear, she is frightened about the retaliation that will follow, for God knows how long, if she comes forward. She has no choice – he knows who she is and where she lives. Today, he might discover where she works."

A goddam train wreck! Boucher is under my command.

"Are you there, Lieutenant Damiano?"

"I am. What was the name she heard the shooter call out?"

"Jacques."

Damiano's day got worse. "I see. When your friend says it was murder, is she aware that the victim was found with a weapon?"

"She knows that the man didn't have a weapon when he stopped and turned with his hands raised. He was pointing in her direction, she believes, to alert the officer that there was a witness. She is so frightened that she doesn't want to come forward. I've told her, she needs help. That officer is intent on confronting her."

"Was she injured when she was knocked to the ground? Is there a chance she is mistaken about the weapon?"

"Her knee was cut and she bit deeply into her tongue. She doesn't need glasses, so what she witnessed she saw clearly. If she *is* somehow wrong, why would the officer be tracking her down? His actions suggest she saw a murder. Can you protect her?"

"Has she consulted a lawyer?"

"I did for her. His advice was to go to the police and to alert as many responsible parties as possible, thereby making the situation difficult for the officer to retaliate."

Damiano couldn't argue with that advice, but it meant media and the great pleasure they'd enjoy cutting down the division. Worse, she had done a cursory prelim with Boucher. She should have done better. For a moment, she felt slightly lost. The parameters of her new position steered Damiano back on track. "I am first an officer of the law, Professor Donovan. I cannot withhold evidence in a criminal investigation. Before I do proceed ..."

Donovan held back a shouting match itching to erupt by clearing her throat and interrupting. "As an officer of the law, you are under another obligation, to serve and protect, Lieutenant Damiano. If you divulge this evidence when I have told you that this officer is out hunting down my friend, you are putting her in harm's way." Donovan continued without giving Damiano a chance to speak. "I have begun to record this conversation. If my friend is injured, you personally will have to answer because you know the present dangerous circumstances."

"Stop right there! Recording this conversation is completely inappropriate. Before I transmit any information to the officer handling this case, I will meet with this friend. You must know that eyewitness testimony is not highly regarded in the court." The fact that Donovan's friend had heard the name of the victim was strong evidence that Damiano kept to herself. "Can you both come to the Crémazie Division tonight at seven?"

"We've read that the officer works in that division. I would not feel safe going there."

Damiano pinched the roof of her nose. The professor was impossible! "Give me your address – make sure you are both there at seven. I haven't time to waste, so tell your friend that I said no embellishments. I need solid facts that the SQ will work, and her mother's address. I'll have a patrol sent out there tonight."

"I understand your position is difficult, Lieutenant, I do. My friend is in a precarious situation."

Damiano contacted the SQ and waited several minutes to be connected with the detective handling the shooting. She explained her new job and the need to be kept up on files. "Do you have the time for a brief analysis of your findings? Chief Donat wants to be alerted to the updates on his patch."

Detective Pichon was a fly fisherman, who knew about lures and casting techniques. "You have something for me, Chief Damiano? You know I have no obligation to discuss the case with you."

Damiano was a strong swimmer, but she had no time for games. "Nothing solid and it might be nothing at all."

"How about I decide that?"

"I hope to find something tonight, latest tomorrow morning. As soon as I do, I will promptly send it along. Can you give me anything on your progress?"

"I'm about to set up another interview with Officer Boucher. The vic's weapon was untraceable, but no fingerprints were found on the clip, or on the bullets for that matter." Pichon let that thought sit for a few seconds. "I wonder if our vic was some kind of hired security or knew a cop? Haven't found any evidence that he did. It's strange just the same, using a cop's trick for his throwaway."

"It is. Whatever I find, you'll have."

"That's the game, Chief Damiano."

"I know."

After the call, Damiano found Boucher's partner, Louis Doucette. She'd save him for an early morning interview. Something stank!

Damiano went off to find the room Pierre had chosen for the murder layout. He had found one beside the file room. She stood quietly, amazed at the amount of work he'd accomplished in such a short time, all of it as scrupulous as Matte himself. He had photos of the principal cast members with bios underneath and dates, times and numbers. On a separate wall, printed out were the four bits of information they had learned. He hadn't noticed her by the door. Damiano walked in and up to Matte's photo of Dylan. He was beautiful and boyish. Matte turned and said. "That's Dylan alright."

The strain on Matte's face was apparent. Dylan's death numbed him, hemmed him in by the loss and the pain of their failed relationship.

Damiano spoke quietly. "I was just wondering, Pierre, how do we explain this photo? We haven't even learned where Dylan lived."

"I'll have something tomorrow. A place, I hope. I intend to barhop tonight."

"As a cop?"

"Really, Chief? You should know better."

"Take care, Pierre."

Chapter Twenty

Back in her own office Damiano wondered if she should call Officer Doucette, or catch him off guard. She decided surprise was the better move. She checked the time and cursed that she had chosen seven o'clock for the interview on Wood Avenue. Montreal might as well be a city closed to any form of transit, walking included. The quickest route was prayers, and she had lost the knack. Rue St-Denis from Mount Royal south was shut down. She left the office in an unmarked car and drove or rather stalled on St-Urbain Street. She used flashers and siren bursts, but the drivers caught in the bottleneck couldn't move even if so inclined. Ten minutes later, she had travelled half a block. When she finally reached a red light, she saw a traffic officer and shouted "Thank God!" Her flashers and siren drew him running and ducking between cars to reach their vehicle. "Can you do something for me?" she pleaded, badge in her hand.

Damiano felt she was in the inlet, the Red Sea, and Moses had raised his staff, and God parted cars for her. The parting lasted until she turned right. Sherbrooke Street swallowed her up in another jam. She couldn't ride the sidewalks, a favorite mode. They were under siege as well. Damiano was ten minutes late for the interview on Wood Avenue. The twenty-minute drive had eaten up an hour and seventeen minutes of her life! She parked illegally and fumed up the stairs to the front door. She remembered she'd thought the house was expensive and greedily large for one person. She didn't bother with the bell; she hammered on a window pane.

The worried faces that greeted her at the door toned down Damiano's foul mood.

"Thank you for coming, Lieutenant. You can use the dining room. This is Carmen DiMaggio," Caitlin said, leading them both into a lovely room of yellows and whites. The oak table was only partially cleared of piles of papers. "Sorry, I'm sorting through things at the end of the year."

Damiano was quick to see, on the other side, the generous plate of salmon and egg salad sandwiches and a crystal pitcher of iced tea. She hadn't eaten since breakfast, and her stomach was grumbling. "I'm not here for tea and sandwiches!" Her eyes were glued to the food, and her declaration was feeble.

"Carmen hasn't eaten all day – you're both Italian, so I know what you can do with food. I'll leave you two."

Caitlin left the room and expected to hear hard questions from the lieutenant. Instead there was silence. She tiptoed to the door, maybe a shuffle or two, but that was it. Ten minutes later, she decided it was her home and she had a right to check to see if they were getting along. When she peeped in the room, the Italians, heads down, were putting the sandwiches away at alarming speed.

When Damiano spotted Caitlin, she wiped a linen napkin across her mouth and straightened up.

Carmen grabbed the last sandwich before she wiped her face. No one had touched the tea.

"I'm glad to see Carmen has finally eaten."

From that point on, it was all business. The recording began, followed by questioning.

Carmen reached down for her purse and pulled out a sketch. "I'm no artist, but I can do a simple sketch." She passed it across to Damiano who gave it an appreciative nod. "Come over here and show me exactly where you were when the incident occurred."

Carmen did.

As Damiano could see, Carmen was just shy of five feet from Boucher.

"Listen carefully, Ms. DiMaggio. When the victim stopped and turned, did you hear any noise that might indicate he dropped or tossed something?"

"No. He stopped dead and turned, raised his hands like I said, but pointed his right hand towards me. The officer just shot – it was over so quickly, but in some ways, it all seemed like slow motion. He called 'Jacques' as I've already said."

Damiano took out a selection of photos.

"Do you see the perpetrator here? Take your time."

"I don't want to appear in court – I'm not brave or stupid. I'm not risking my life and my mother's for some drug pusher. I'm sorry – I haven't slept – I'm scared all the time. Please don't tell me about civic duty! I want my life back."

Damiano drummed the table. "You don't have to point him out, just tell me if he's here."

"He is."

"If there is a second witness, would you be willing to ID him?"

"Let the second witness do the ID. What about me? What happens to me now? Do I wait for him to find me at work?"

"If you'd ID the officer, I'd give that information to the SQ who are handling this case. They'd make an arrest. But my hands are tied if you won't help. I can see you're frightened. I can put a patrol car on you for a week, but I can't do it forever, Ms. DiMaggio. We depend on citizens far more than we'd like to admit."

Carmen rubbed her face, smearing tears. "I'm totally fucked. Dammit to hell, he's number two. Now please leave and get me that car."

Damiano rose. "May I keep the sketch?"

Carmen didn't look up but nodded.

"If it means anything, you are brave. You were just in the wrong place at the wrong time. This is not my case, but I will help you every way I can."

Carmen buried her head into her arms on the table and wept. Caitlin saw Damiano out.

"Make certain she stays with you for at least a week. There will be a patrol car at her work tomorrow," Damiano said.

Driving back, Damiano knew she had to get the truth from Doucette early tomorrow morning. "It's a wonder Donat managed to stay sane. I have to check the other files – I can't get by with notes. Then there's my primary case, Dylan Kane." She knew she should have ordered Pierre off the case, but he had his screws into her. She felt his anger. He was blackmailing her. Home life was back on shaky ground. She gave the drivers ahead of her a loud horn that earned her a burst of honks and two fingers from bolder drivers. "I want *my* life back!"

Chapter Twenty-one

Detective Matte left Crémazie after seven and drove home to his apartment on Prince Arthur Street West in the La Cité complex. Like everything else in his life, Matte had taken time to choose an apartment. He had a view of Mount Royal Park, the old Royal Victoria Hospital and the Jacques Cartier Bridge. His home occupied the northeast quadrant of downtown Montreal in an area called Milton-Park. He liked the place with its large windows, closed in mid-summer with electric verticals, and quality wood floors that invited him to walk around in his bare feet. He had two pieces of abstract art, both by Michel Lafrance whose work was displayed in a gallery on rue Bonsecours in Old Montreal. In the master bedroom, above his chest of drawers, one on each side of the room, he had laminated posters from museum exhibitions that he rotated from time to time. The second bedroom displayed a wall of books: the architecture of the Greeks and Romans, the philosophers: Camus, Kierkegaard, Spinoza, Pascal and Watts. There was also a decent selection of memoirs. Young men who came to his apartment never asked if Matte had read the books. In fact, Matte had stalled after Camus and Kierkegaard, and the paradox of the absurd. There was no fiction, but he had read *Waiting for Godot*. There was no television. There was a sound system connected to an iPod. His kitchen had all the necessities for a good cook and someone who enjoyed fine wine. The wine rack was Matte's pride.

The predominant gray of the living room walls was highlighted by one white brick wall. One of Lafrance's sensual abstracts with its heavy blues, grays and yellows was elegantly displayed on that wall. Matte had met Lafrance, who had studied at the École des beaux arts. Matte was drawn to the painting's intense and seemingly spontaneous brush strokes. Dylan had feigned a grasp of the works. Both heavy throw rugs were gray tinged with splashes of blue. Furniture was sparse – two red leather sofas, no chairs, but good lighting. Matte recalled one young man who took a look around the room and asked, "Is this an Airbnb?" Matte assured the man he lived there. "How?" he asked. "This is unreal!" There was no point explaining his regard for minimalism. The kid was there for an hour at most before he'd gotten what he'd come for and left.

In the bedroom he checked the locked drawer beside his double bed, a precaution he took every day. He thought to himself, *I should have kept the cash here, and Dylan wouldn't have taken it. He might still be alive.* Matte ran a bath while he was undressing. He dropped his shirt and socks in a laundry bag in a hall cupboard, hung his pants and placed his shoes on a shoe rack. He stood naked before a full-length mirror. Matte thought he might see some change, some loss of bulk, but Dylan's death had brought only a heaviness to his eyes. When clouds of heat rose from the tub, he turned off the water and stepped in, sat and disappeared under the near-scalding water. He stayed under until he began to choke. He sat up for a second and dropped back under, allowing his thoughts a freedom he had not admitted to them. He wondered when he'd first begun to hate himself for loving Dylan. He had spent every emotion, money, care, time and lost sleep, everything he had, to win his love. In the four-and-a-half years of their fragile relationship, he knew he had shrunk as a man. His heart was exhausted. Its strength had trickled away. Wasn't that absurd, that love had cost him his heart?

He'd sometimes thought if Dylan moved out of the city, he could let go, perhaps make a new start. But Dylan's death, the unequivocal departure, didn't end his obsession and perhaps never would. Matte knew he'd still look in vain for Dylan in the men he met. Standing alone, Matte smiled sadly when he finally saw that Dylan was as weak as he was. Dylan had needed him, or men like him, for his survival. Matte reached for the bathrobe and wound its folds tightly around his body. He thought he smelled Dylan, but that wasn't possible. He'd bought the robe only last week. He dressed carefully. He wanted information. He needed the name of Dylan's last lover.

The bars never got going till just before midnight. Matte knew Jordan who worked the bar at Le Stud. He couldn't afford to wait for the bar to be jam-packed with ear-splitting dance music amid a cacophony of shouting voices. He'd linger by one of the pool tables until he saw Jordan was free. Matte figured that the tourists would crowd the terrace until the night heated up. He was at the bar before nine. Jordan was in his mid-thirties and wore a gray stubble beard. He was toned and friendly – perfect for the job. "What's up, Pierre?" he asked, wiping his hands on a wet towel and sticking it into his shorts. Tats ran up both arms.

"A glass of wine and a word."

Matte gave Jordan a twenty.

"That's way too generous!"

"I need some information."

"Ah man. You know the barkeep's bible: see no evil, hear no evil and speak no evil. That's how I keep my job."

"I have to trust someone." Matte looked around to be sure he wouldn't be heard. "Dylan's dead."

"Woah!" Jordan rubbed his balding head. "That's final."

"It is."

"Geez! Did he …?"

"No. No!" Matte leaned in and whispered "He was murdered."

Jordan was flustered and was relieved to see customers waiting on him. "Sec, I have to go."

Matte kept a close eye on Jordan. He was back in a few minutes. "You and Dylan, right?" Jordan asked, though he already knew the answer. He saw the dance of male lives from a good vantage point.

"Dylan and I were done."

"Kinda knew that. Sorry, the usual game with Dylan, he never ..."

"I need the name of his last mark." Matte answered, signalling a change of subject.

"That's rough language, Pierre."

"Just calling it as it was."

"I don't know, man."

"You know something. This was Dylan's favorite bar. He liked you."

"Why are you getting involved? You guys were done. Why do you want information now?" Jordan asked suspiciously, frightened for his job. "I know someone in the force. Dylan deserves your help. No one else will care."

"Sorry, gotta go. I'll be back – I have to think."

"Whatever you give me won't come back on you. You have my word."

"Customers! Be back."

Matte hadn't touched the wine. Jordan glanced back at him nervously as he handed drinks to a group of four. He reluctantly walked back. "This better not have throwback. Dylan's provider was, geez, sorry. I meant no disrespect to you, Pierre. His name was Nathaniel, his ortho man."

"Ortho man?"

"He was a doctor. Dylan might have boasted he was at the Jewish. I'm not sure."

"The hospital, you mean?"

"That's what I think he said. It's loud in here after eleven. I'm not sure."

"They were tight?"

"Like you and Dylan, I guess. You know what I mean. Dylan didn't change his MO. I guess none of us do. I have your word, right? If it gets around that I talk – I have no work. I mean, poor Dylan, but no way I'll testify. I did this for you and for Dylan. My mouth is a closed trap. Never broke that code till tonight. Don't screw me up!"

"I won't. Did you ever see this Nathaniel?"

"Tall, like you, but dark."

"Dark?"

"I mean hair."

"Nothing more?"

"Wasn't my type."

"I won't be back for anything else. Just one last question – was that his last mark? You know what I mean. That's how he saw us."

"Far as I know. It's crazy in here. You know that."

Mark, provider, Matte felt bruised. *Damn you, Dylan.* Matte left and drove to the Jewish General Hospital on Côte Ste-Catherine Road. He parked streets away and walked ten minutes back up the road to the hospital entrance. Once inside the hospital, he sought out the directory, found Orthopedics, and Nathaniel Goldberg! Nate! The information desk was closed, but Matte spotted a man in whites and hoped he was a doctor. He was in a hurried conversation with a couple. His shoulders and feet appeared to be pulling away from them.

Matte caught up with the fleeing doctor before he made good his escape. "Excuse me; I'm looking for Dr. Goldberg."

He checked his watch. "At this time? No surgeries are performed at night, but surgery is fifth floor," the doctor said, walking off.

Matte took the elevator to the fifth floor and approached the first nurses' station he saw.

"I'd like to speak with Dr. Goldberg."

"Are you family of a patient on the floor?"

"I'm Detective Matte of the Crémazie Division. I'm hoping Dr. Goldberg can help our investigation."

"Well," the nurse he was addressing looked back to colleagues for help. She was apparently not the head nurse. "I don't know if I'm authorized to give out such information."

"Perhaps not authorized, but obligated."

The nurse straightened up and checked a file on the desk under the counter. "There are no night surgeries, cutbacks! He wouldn't be in the hospital at this hour. Dr. Goldberg is slated for surgery at eight tomorrow morning."

"I need a home address."

"I can't give out private information, Detective. We never do that."

"As I've said, you are obliged to give me the information."

The nurse made a call, listened and said, "Alright then." She went back to a wall unit, searched for and located a file. She paused before she gave up the information. "Dr. Goldberg has a condo in Old Montreal, but the family home is in Rawdon. He must be at the condo because of tomorrow's surgery. I suppose you'll want that?" she asked reluctantly.

"Please. This is a police order – do not contact Dr. Goldberg. That would be obstruction. I hope I'm clear on that." The nurse was already flustered.

"I won't alert Dr. Goldberg."

Matte wrote down the address. *Family home!*

Chapter Twenty-two

Matte sat in his car deliberating whether or not he should impose on Goldberg. It was near eleven. Tomorrow's surgery could drag on, Goldberg might not be as easy to locate, and Matte had an opportunity that night. He thought about calling Damiano. He knew that only a small part of his brain was working, that he was hanging on. Still he decided against it. Goldberg was his find. When he popped the trunk, he smiled ruefully. *Always prepared!* He reached in for his badge and jacket. It was probably easier to walk down into Old Montreal, since he had no chance of finding parking. He got out of the car and fed the meter. The night was dry and hot. The dark sky didn't bother Matte. Old Montreal was still crawling with tourists and locals. He was so self-absorbed he didn't notice anyone as he walked down rue Gosford. Seeing himself as nothing more than a common mark in Dylan's MO was a low blow that hurt. Why had he been so blind and stupid? Matte had to meet with Goldberg, had to have a good look at the man to see if he was looking at himself.

Matte found the address on rue Notre-Dame, the south side of the street, in the middle of a block. The front face of the restored heritage building had been renovated with stone, in keeping with the character of the street. The outer door was not locked, and Matte walked into a tight lobby. The directory appeared inside the wall and lit up as soon as the door opened. Matte noticed the two bottom floors were legal offices. The doctor's name was printed in white block letters beneath them. Matte tapped a panel beside the name, giving him access to a programmed phone. He followed the prompt, and Goldberg, Matte assumed it was Goldberg, picked up with a strong tone of irritation. "Yes?"

"Detective Matte, Dr. Goldberg. I have a few questions I'm hoping you might help me with."

"At this time of night?" The tone was definitely condescending.

"Actually, Doctor, I am aware of the time. I thought you'd want to dispense with this quickly and avoid an interview at the Crémazie Division after your surgery tomorrow." Goldberg didn't answer immediately. Matte's dart found its mark, and the surgeon paused. "Doctor?"

"Come up. I'm the only occupant on the third floor."

Raw and angry, Matte opened the entrance door when he heard the click. He adjusted his jacket and stuck his badge to his vest pocket. When the elevator door opened, Goldberg was standing there. Matte noticed immediately the man had no shoulders, they sloped from the neck. With black jeans, he wore a red T-shirt with a black logo *EMPTY*, something a kid would wear, Matte thought. "Detective Matte, Doctor Goldberg."

Goldberg didn't move. "Ask away. No one will hear us in the hallway."

"I think you might feel more comfortable inside."

"I'm fine where I am." Goldberg rested one hand against a wall. He was as tall as Matte, middle forties, with a suggestion of buff, clean-shaven with a head of salt and pepper black hair intentionally curled. His dark eyes bore into Matte's.

Matte ignored their intended affront. "Is this your principal residence, Doctor?"

Goldberg took his hand from the wall, caught off guard by the question. He quickly surmised that the detective must know about both homes since he'd learned about his surgery. He'd make a point of finding out who doled out his personal information. He cleared his throat. "The family home is in Rawdon. I'm there on weekends. What exactly did you want to ask me about? It's late."

"Were you in Rawdon this past weekend?"

"My wife took the boys to celebrate her sister's birthday, big family event in Ottawa. I begged off and stuck around here." Goldberg looked down at the floor. "Perhaps you'd better come inside. We'd both be more comfortable."

Matte tried not to be impressed by the luxurious loft, but he was, especially by the black interior doors and the ultra-contemporary kitchen with red and stainless steel walls and hanging copper pots. As Goldberg walked towards a modern wide leather chair, he scooped up a sweater and tossed it into the bedroom. Matte couldn't believe his eyes. It had to be the Izod tennis sweater he'd bought for Dylan. He saw the wide 'V' and touch of purple inside it. Dylan had always folded it carefully. He loved that sweater. Matte ran his tongue across his teeth. His mouth was dry. "Doctor …" It was right then that Matte lost control of his interview. He was driven by a rage beyond his control.

Goldberg's face tightened. The attitude was gone.

"Do you know Dylan Kane?"

"Have you evidence that I do?"

"Yes, Doctor."

Goldberg felt a rush of agony through his whole body. He stepped back, trying to shield himself. "I, ah." He fought for sympathy. This cop had found him and connected him to Kane. Goldberg twice tried to clear his throat. "Before I say anything, I want you to know I have a family, Detective. I love them. I never meant – but I guess you've heard those words before." Goldberg covered his eyes with his hand.

Matt's pity was momentary. "You're not the first person to be in such a situation."

It was Goldberg's turn to blurt out information he should have kept to himself. Perhaps he was angry or scrambling to distance himself. "I'm not bailing him out of anything," he said, defiantly. "I have to protect myself and my family."

"That won't be necessary."

"This is a stupid shirt – Father's Day gift from my son." Goldberg tugged at the shirt and took a few deep breaths. "Why won't I have to bail him out? Why are you here in the first place?"

"Dylan Kane was murdered."

"What?"

"You heard me, Doctor Goldberg. Kane is dead, murdered."

This time Goldberg jumped to his own defence. "I'm not answering any further questions without counsel."

"I see. In that case, Doctor Goldberg, present yourself tomorrow at the Crémazie Division at four o'clock sharp. Here's my card. I will meet you and your lawyer at the front entrance." Matte turned to leave.

"Are you suggesting I'm a suspect?" he asked, stepping forward into Matte's space.

"From this point on, Doctor Goldberg, whatever you say can and will be used against you in a court of law. I'll see you tomorrow." Matte let himself out and shut the door behind him.

He exhaled once he'd stepped inside the privacy of the elevator. He remembered the Saturday afternoon he'd bought the sweater for Dylan at Ogilvy's. Dylan tried it on and checked himself out in every mirror he could find, drawing some admiring glances from the salesmen. "I always wanted a sweater like this – never had the money. Do I look like a Wimbledon star or what, Pierre? I'll keep it forever!" Matte sniffed and wiped his nose with a linen handkerchief. He owned a box of them. Goldberg had shown no emotion when he heard that Dylan was dead, not as much as a twitch. Matte was observant. Nothing! "What a waste, Dylan. What a bloody waste!"

Then the cost of a serious mistake struck him between his ribs. His heart raced. He had just given Goldberg time to clean up the condo and rid himself of any incriminating evidence, like the sweater. Jordan from Le Stud had clearly said he would not testify. Matte was the only other witness and he couldn't give testimony without incriminating himself. *Great work!* Damiano would not have made such a blunder. Once he'd found his car, Matte threw himself onto the seat, gripping the wheel. He sat alone for hours. "He didn't give a damn about you. I ... what does it matter now? Why did you have to steal from me – I gave you ... You wasted my life too, you fucker!" Matte finally realized a homeless man was staring through his side window at a rant he couldn't quite hear. Matte rifled through his glove box and found a bill. He fired up the engine, rolled down the window and handed the man the money. He received a salute that didn't quite reach the forehead before he took off. Matte's jaw was sore from grinding his teeth.

Chapter Twenty-three

Damiano wanted to pound her pillow, but she opted for yet another restless turn on her side.

"You still haven't fallen asleep, Toni?" a tired, irritated voice whispered.

"No, Jeff. I'm not asleep. I told you I want to be totally clean in this new job if it kills me. My elbow is throbbing. It's never going to heal. It's been two years since my accident."

"Stress always brings pain to the weakest area – ergo, to your elbow. You can't talk about the problems. Right, Toni? I'm assuming you have more than one. You can trust me, you know that. Plus, I'd like to manage a few hours of sleep."

"Jeff, I don't want this job, the chief part, I mean. I feel like I'm caught in a web. It's a minefield. New problems appear on a daily basis. I can't ruin the reputation of the division, but I'm heading in that direction. I can't handle it all and do a good job."

"What are you talking about?"

Toni needed help. She began with DiMaggio's plight and the meeting with Doucette first thing that morning. "There's the brotherhood, and officially it's not my case. I couldn't hand off DiMaggio right away. Her life is at risk."

"Toni, you are an officer paid by citizens to serve and protect them. DiMaggio is your first obligation. How would the division look if you held off or passed the work to the SQ, and she was injured or worse? I don't see the problem. You're a smart woman, work your way around the 'blue wall.' You have a sound skill set and you are a smart cop – use both to advantage!"

"You actually think that?"

"Toni, I'm your husband. You need straight talk from someone who knows you."

"Alright. I will. You met Pierre last year. I'm allowing him to work a murder investigation, knowing he has a conflict of interest. Dylan Kane and Pierre were involved in a tortuous relationship. Kane was murdered. Pierre's still obsessed with him even though they broke up eight months ago. Pierre reminded me that I owe him. He also says he'll take being busted down to a uniform, and that there is no evidence he ever knew Dylan.

He was out tonight trying to find Dylan's last lover. He'll find the man much faster than any other detective I have on the floor. Still, as I told you, there has been recent contact between them. Dylan stole from him the week before he was murdered."

It was going to be a long night. Jeff left the bed to get water for both of them. "Have any detectives worked cases where there was a conflict of interest?"

"Jeff, how can you forget Luke's situation last year? Luke might have been arrested in the girl's death. I stepped away in a manner of speaking, but I asked Matte to bend protocol to help us out and he did. He's not forgetting that. He covered for me, you know that. He's also covered for me on other occasions. He's always had my back."

"Why is Pierre so insistent on participating in the investigation? He could stand on the sidelines as you did. He's lost Dylan and he *will* lose his badge. You've always said he's calm and level-headed."

"He's obsessed. He loved Dylan, in spite of everything."

"He wouldn't be the first to sacrifice himself for love. Look at me."

"That's a low blow, Jeff."

"I didn't mean it as such. You're a hurricane. I fell for a bumpy ride."

"That's true, but you have a seatbelt."

"Funny. Think about this seriously. Is there a chance that Pierre is responsible for Dylan's death?"

Damiano was ahead of her husband. That thought had occurred to her. Dr. Belmont had said she might be looking for a cop, or a doctor, or a boxer, someone who knew what he was doing. She had dismissed the idea. Pierre was a gentle man, a partner she felt she knew.

"He could keep himself off your radar by investigating the case. Has using that tactic occurred to you?"

"Enough. I can't go there right now. I did broach the question, and Pierre actually threatened me. We've been partners for almost ten years, and let's face it, we know a lot about each other. But I can't see him murdering Dylan or anyone. Not now; maybe not ever. I trust him. I have to trust him."

"He really threatened you?"

"He was hurt – he had the goods, same ones you had last year, vodka and opiates. I'm sleep deprived now, but I'm clean."

Jeff wanted to have it out with his wife, point out ways the job was destroying her. When he opened his mouth to launch into his appeal and justification, he saw that she was about to cry. His timing was wrong. "Okay,

okay. Lie back down. Begin with that officer Doucette you meet tomorrow. The one involved in the shooting. The rest will find its way to you. Hurricanes always do. The first week of a new job is trying and tiring, but you'll learn quickly. One idea might be to delegate this case and stick to command operations."

Damiano had fallen asleep, and Jeff surrendered. They slept for three hours.

The next morning, he watched Damiano race around the kitchen with a piece of kimmel toast stuck in her mouth. "What's wrong with your eyes?"

"They feel dry. I don't know and I don't have the time to find out."

"Don't move!" Jeff ran to the bathroom and arrived with eye drops. "Tilt your head back. Good."

"Am I not too young for drops? I'm in my early forties."

"That's stretching it. Lack of sleep will dry out anybody's eyes. Take the bottle with you and come home at a decent hour! I'm serious."

"I will or I won't survive. Okay, I'm off. Say hi to Luke for me."

"Will do."

Driving to Crémazie, Damiano tried thinking clearly, but her mind was jumpy. She added depression when she saw the new pile of folders on her desk. She was able to walk around the main office with the folders because no one was in at six in the morning. She read carefully and commented or added suggestions. As chief, she should be meeting with the detectives who were on the cases, but she had no time as long as she stubbornly hung onto the Kane murder. Ninety minutes later she was still walking and annotating. Officer Doucette arrived and stood quietly inside the front door of the homicide room, waiting for her signal. Damiano wanted to rub her eyes, but rubbing would make them worse. When she finally saw Doucette, she waved him over and headed to her office.

She closed the door behind them, and lowered the shade. The Major Crimes Ds would be arriving shortly, and she didn't want the detectives to make anything further of this meeting. The detectives knew the shooter was in the division, but some might not recognize him or Doucette. She made a new pile of the completed work and parted them both to have a good look at Doucette. She had originally planned to contact Detective Pichon of the SQ, learn what they had and use it on Doucette. She shelved that idea because she simply did not have the time. She'd fake her way through the review. "Sit down, Officer Doucette. Move the chair to the middle so I can see you. Do you know why you're here?"

"Boucher."

"Exactly. How long have you been on the force?"

"Six years."

"Married?"

"Yes. My wife is expecting this month."

"Nervous time."

In spite of his discomfort, Doucette smiled, beamed. "Actually, I'm really excited. It'll be the first girl born to the Doucettes in twenty-one years!"

"How long have you partnered with Boucher?"

"Three years."

"We know that Officer Boucher contacted you."

Doucette didn't comment.

"I know you haven't a demerit on your record. I assume you do not want to be implicated in this shooting."

Doucette just nodded.

"Speak up, Officer Doucette."

"This is my career. From the time I was a kid I wanted to be a cop. Do something that counted."

Damiano quashed a smile, but she felt it. "Fine. I have two very important questions to ask you. Think about your career and your wife. You know the answer to both questions. Now, did the vic have a weapon?"

"He's my partner. I'm no rat."

"We traced your partner's calls. You are already implicated. We have a witness. At this point, anything you tell me is off the record. Boucher will never know you spoke. The witness is being threatened. Anything happens to this witness bleeds out on you."

Doucette's face lost color. He slumped visibly.

"I warn you, if this witness is harmed, I'm holding you as a co-conspirator. Then you can forget your career. Is Boucher worth your wife and imminent new daughter?"

"I'd put my life on the line for my partner. All cops do."

"Add your family's welfare and your own job. I haven't all day for you to recognize reality. Answer the question or face the consequences! You're mumbling Officer, speak up!"

"Boucher is a good cop." Doucette spoke with his head down.

"Did the vic have a weapon?" Damiano's voice rose, determined.

Doucette stood up. "I can't do this, Chief. What you're doing to me is not right."

"Boucher is out there and desperate." Damiano rose as well. "If you intentionally withhold information, I will nail your butt personally! I am the head of this division and I order you to answer the question!"

Visibly shaking, Doucette, spoke haltingly. "Boucher thought he had a weapon."

"Good. Did Boucher know the vic?"

"I don't know. Can I leave, please?"

"Boucher will never hear what you told me."

"I'll know."

Damiano rose, grabbed some empty folders and handed them to Doucette. "Carry these. We'll walk out together. I don't want you to draw any attention." They left together. "Officer, take these to Place Versailles."

Damiano met Pierre at the elevator.

"I have something," Pierre said.

"Follow me."

Chapter Twenty-four

Detective Matte knew to shut Damiano's office door. He sat down, wired but weary. He nervously worked his knuckles until Damiano's look conveyed her annoyance. "I have the name of Dylan's last mark."

"Mark?"

"That's what I was, what we all were. This guy's a well-heeled orthopedic surgeon. I went to his condo in Old Montreal last night. He's married and has a family in Rawdon – convenient don't you think?"

"That's fast, Pierre. How did you …"

"Knew a bartender at Le Stud, secured a name, drove to the Jewish General and tossed the law at a young nurse who gave me his name and address. That was it. Made my way to Old Montreal and went calling. The doctor is usually at the family home on weekends. It so happens, last weekend, he was in Montreal, so he has no alibi. I set up an interview here at four this afternoon."

"You were inside his condo?"

"Yes. I began with benign questions. He made the mistake of admitting he 'knew' Dylan, and I went for broke. Before you ask, I did reveal that Dylan was dead."

"By the time we have a warrant to search his condo …"

"I saw my error as he was closing his door shouting. 'Are you suggesting I'm a suspect?' I read him his rights. He then refused to talk further without a lawyer. He may come in today and have his lawyer quash what he said last night, but I saw a sweater I bought for Dylan on his couch."

"He might have disposed of it, Pierre."

"If I have to out myself as a witness, I will, but I hope it doesn't come to that. I hope our interview won't necessitate my divulgence."

"I have another matter I must discuss with you, Pierre, but let's stick with Dylan's murder for now. I can't see how you'll manage to evade discovery. We'll soon have his phone records, and you'll be there. This bartender knows you. Dylan might have mentioned your name to the surgeon. What's his name, by the way?"

"Nathaniel Goldberg."

"Oh no, I think I know that name. You said Jewish General?"

"Yes."

"He operated on one of my neighbors' sons who broke his hip in a hockey game. Pierre, are you really prepared to lose your badge? It's your livelihood for God's sake. Why can't you stand back and feed me information as I did with Luke's problem last year?"

"I have to be fully involved."

"You have to understand that I am chief now. I must follow protocol. I can't play with the rules. I didn't ask for the title. In fact, I've realized that I don't want to be chief. It's all paperwork and responsibility. I'm not giving the job the time it requires. I'd rather be in the field, working the case with you. That said, I need you on the sidelines. I have no other choice. Let's not argue about this. The situation is temporary. I'm interim chief. We're beginning our tenth year, warts and all!"

"Toni, I don't owe Dylan anything, but I can't stay away from the case either. Call it self-interest – you know something about that."

"Where's your mother in all this? How's she doing? Have you forgotten her?"

"No. I have seen Mom once. My sister keeps in touch. Mom's trying to talk. She was actually up with a walker for a few minutes. My father won't be at the hospital till nine. I'll be with her at six tonight for a good long visit."

"I'm glad to hear that."

"My mother has always been on my side. Apart from her, I have you – a support group of two."

Damiano smiled. "Will you set up an interview with Matthew Allen? How about three today? He's a viable suspect. We need to see that show producer as well."

"Velma. I'll see to that."

"We also have to discover if Goldberg was Dylan's last lover, and who else might have wanted him dead. If he and Goldberg had split, where was Dylan living? We don't even know that yet. Go work in the murder room. I'll join you. Before you go, listen to another problem."

Matte paid close attention as Damiano outlined the Boucher shooting. "What are you going to do?"

"What bothers me is that this DiMaggio is still at risk even if Pichon pulls Boucher in. He'll get bail. I can't have a patrol on her for longer than a week. If Boucher is remanded – he'll be released at some point. Boucher thought the perp had a gun – accidental, right. DiMaggio was right when she said she was at risk because she witnessed the incident. He won't forget her."

"She's not your responsibility. This is definitely the SQ's jurisdiction."

"In a sense, she is ours. She had to come forward. I told you Boucher knows where she lives. He called her mother for Christ's sake! DiMaggio doesn't want to testify. She's not stupid."

"She won't have to if they believe he thought he saw a gun."

"I think he dropped his throwaway on the perp."

"Stay out of that. It's their case. Call Pichon. He might have something that helps this witness. Let me get going on our case."

"Stay below the radar, Pierre!"

"I'm trying." Matte left Damiano in her office.

She stared into space, trying to figure out exactly what she'd tell Detective Pichon. His number was already on her phone and she tapped it.

"Chief, good to hear from you. I was hoping you'd call with some information that would move this case along."

"Would you first give me a quick rundown of what you have so far?"

There was a moment of male pride, an abhorrence of taking any order from a female. Damiano smiled. "Alright, Chief Damiano," Pichon answered, underscoring the title. "The weapon is unmarked, untraceable. Boucher's throwaway can be traced, so our feeling that Boucher dropped that gun on our vic is not a certainty, probable but not certain. When I interviewed him, he was angry, said it was a good shoot, the vic had a gun. He left with a week's suspension and a dire warning not to interfere with the investigation or face expulsion from the force. That's it in a nutshell. One more thing. Boucher caught a lucky week. With the Orlando massacre and the terrorist attacks, this shooting never had much coverage. The phrase, 'known to the police,' signals to reporters the story is a DOA. The floor is yours, Chief Damiano."

"He did interfere with the investigation, Detective. There was a witness to the shooting. Boucher tracked down her address, found her mother's home and actually called her, asking to speak with her daughter."

"That's a direct violation of a standing order. We should fire his ass. Your witness?"

Damiano recounted DiMaggio's account concisely. She omitted the information of Boucher knowing the name of the vic. She didn't know exactly why, but she hoped her action would help protect the witness. Her husband's words rang in her ears. *You're there to serve and protect.* "Boucher could have easily mistaken the pointing hand for a weapon. It was very dark."

Pichon was no fool. "What was the witness's take?"

"She echoed that possibility."

"By the way, the newly established bureau des enquêtes indépendantes, BEI, wants the case. I said we'd like to close it. What are your feelings? I need to meet with this witness."

"You handled it – you should see it through. Haul Boucher in. He's a real threat."

"We'll pick him up. Your witness?"

"She's frightened with good reason. I implore you not to reveal to Boucher that this witness has approached us, not yet! He knows of her existence. He doesn't know she has come forward. I want to keep it that way."

"Have her come into your office tomorrow morning, Chief Damiano! You did say I was handling this case. It's my prerogative to meet with her, isn't it?" Seniority was a sticky issue with a division chief. One neither of them wanted to argue.

Damiano didn't immediately respond.

"Chief?"

"As soon as I can, I'll have her meet with you."

"That's unfortunate," Pichon said piqued.

"I regret this."

Pichon hung up.

Chapter Twenty-five

Damiano sat in her office feeling somehow disconnected from the world she knew. Matte had placed a proprietorial arm around Dylan's murder, and that was after an initial order to back off, and stay off. She looked at the remaining files on her desk, sighed and began reading, this time with earnest attention. What she read caught her attention and moved her to further consideration. The work, especially the notes, was well prepared and presented. She continued with the next file. The work continued to impress Damiano and she decided she'd like to meet the officers who handled domestic violence. She missed lunch, reading.

Matte showed up at her door with sandwiches, egg and tomato, and two bags of her favorite chips – sour cream ripples. He also was carrying four coffees. "We need food. I've started prepping questions for all the interviews."

"What are you on, Pierre? You know kindness rattles me."

"This 'chief' thing has derailed you from eating. The title is doing you damage."

He was rewarded with a loud belly laugh from Damiano as she attacked the sandwiches. Matte on the other hand ate carefully, wiping his mouth with his serviette. With her mouth full and busy chewing, Damiano didn't notice anything or she'd have had a comeback for Matte's meticulous manners. When they finished, Damiano needed a bath, but settled for a sink. Matte stayed behind and cleaned up minutes before she returned, with just a hint of orange and lemon – from her freshly-applied Italian perfume.A whiff of freshness, he thought.

"Go back to the murder room, and I'll join you. I have to make a short visit to the DV, Domestic Violence, and deliver these files."

Matte didn't question the time she was losing. He was beginning to sense a change in his partner. "Alright."

Damiano descended one flight of stairs and walked into the large square room unannounced. By comparison to the Major Crimes room, it was choked with desks, boxed files and bodies. Detectives had their heads down, busy with files. Without warning, a detective at the far end of the room jumped to his feet.

"Chief Damiano!" All the detectives followed suit and stood at attention.

"No need. Sit back down. I just came down to say I'm impressed with these files. In fact, I am impressed with each report I've read."

A wave of relief and smiles met Damiano. The Ds sat back down, except for the detective who'd first noticed her. He was strikingly tall and young with a mop of the reddest curly hair she'd seen in quite some time. At first, Damiano was her cynical self and took him for the sanctimonious bullshitter who did the least amount of work and spent most of his time on PR. This unexpected welcome had switched Damiano back on. The overwhelming blanket she'd felt lost beneath lifted. She called the detectives up to retrieve their file from hers and offered congratulations. To her surprise, Carrot Head was the third detective she called. You learn something every day, she thought.

"I'd like to remind you that this squad, apart from the uniforms, handles life-threatening situations every day. From the alarming stack of files, I see it's a daily event. You've heard this all before, but take care of yourselves. Avoid risks, use vests. Lastly, don't try to be heroes. Most heroes are dead. Keep up the fine work." Damiano turned to leave.

Carrot Head was back on his feet. "Chief, this is the first visit we've ever had from a chief. We appreciate it."

Damiano tried to conceal a show of emotion that men often took for weakness and cursed quietly for blushing before she left. This buzz was different, but it was good! Damn good until she realized that not one detective on the sixth floor of Major Crimes had congratulated her. In fact, Matte had castigated her. Her husband had seen it as another betrayal of family. The irony was she didn't care because the job had begun to seem like a fit. Her goal now was to regain control of the Kane murder. She found Matte busy with notes.

"What do we want from Christine Dawson, the producer?"

"Take a look at the questions. Add whatever you think might be useful."

"What we want from the producer is the whereabouts of Allen around the time of the murder."

"Read on. She says she's 'one' with the cast and audience. Perhaps she saw Dylan hook up with someone any Friday night or that night in particular. It's almost two. Do you want me to fetch her?"

"Yes. I'll wait here." The boardroom used for questioning was a large, uncomfortable room. Suspects brought in there felt marooned, alone, hearing the echo of their words being recorded. And the room was intended to be intimidating. Velma arrived early and added nothing to her previous statement. Allen was friends with Dylan, nothing further.

Matte took the lead. "For a time, you did say you thought they were 'thick'?"

"Only because they were always talking, but I saw nothing suggestive between them."

"What do you think drew them together at his ringside table? Allen said the other two were there because they were photographers."

"I don't know. Matthew walked the floor recording. He probably saw Dylan alone and asked him to join the group. Ask him about this."

"It's an odd pairing, an older straight man with a very attractive young gay man. It wasn't just one Friday night. Dylan kept coming back and ended up inviting Matthew to the Pool Hall."

"Just about every single person who comes to Cleo's is lonely. Matthew is open to anything and he's good company. He didn't take Dylan to dinner. They were friends. I did remember something, though. Midway through the show, one of the cast members snuck up the back stairs for a bathroom break or a snort. I know because I heard our old stair creak. The oddity is that whoever it was decided against going and came back down, because I heard the stair creak again, a few seconds later I began to count the cast and I noticed that Matthew and Dylan were still at their table. Never figured it out, part of the show requires actors to walk the floor. Whoever it was doesn't matter, I suppose. That person changed his mind and came back down. More important, Dylan was alive at the time. As I saw, he was still at the table."

"Could Dylan's date have used those stairs?"

"No. The DJ is beside the stairs, they're not visible stage side and I'm around. There is really no access. His date would have used the main stairs. No one would have noticed him during the cast party."

"You said you were surprised that Matthew didn't do a thorough job that Saturday night when he checked the roof. A couple might have hidden behind that chimney and been locked out."

"Matthew called out that night – someone would have answered him. I did tell you the cast are drama queens. They'd be eager to come out from behind the chimney, smiling sheepishly. We were all trashed and wanted to go home."

"Did you notice anything different about Matthew on the ride home? Was he jumpy, irritated?"

"He was the same friend who drove me down. He's not a boozer. He was tired like the rest of us."

Ms. Dawson wore brown slacks, a pale blue blouse and a topaz birth-stone ring, a far cry from the busty, flamboyant producer they'd met at Cleo's. Matte gave Damiano a look she'd read before. He walked the producer out the gray steel front door. There was no time to waste. Dawson had no additional information to offer.

Damiano joined him, and they waited together for Matthew Allen. "That was a waste."

"I might get lucky and find some morsel in the notes. Toni, I hope I wasn't overstepping, but I called Dylan's father in Richmond this morning. You did tell me to work the case."

"I did. I hate making those calls, even if I manage to break the bad news quickly. They tear a piece from me. They always do."

"Stephen Kane wasn't destroyed when he heard his son Dylan was dead. He said he'd contact his ex in Mississauga. She'd see to things. He gave me her number, and I called her. Kane hadn't heard from or seen Dylan in years. He added, 'I never doubted life would turn out badly for Dylan. Wish I could be surprised, but I'm not. It was a tough life he chose. I don't mean his homosexuality. Dylan thought life was an adventure.'"

"That's a very cold reply to such a personal tragedy."

"His mother, Carolyn Davies, said she'd fly down when the body was released. She'd come earlier if she was needed for identification. I told her that wasn't necessary. She seemed relieved."

"Anything else?"

"I think she was crying. I'm not certain. She said, 'Dylan was too beautiful – he was frightened of being alone. On a roof, you said? How much more alone can one be?' I told her he didn't suffer. 'That's something.' She was crying then. I didn't know what else to say except that we'd be in touch. She'll have him cremated in Montreal. A bag of ashes – that's hard to compute."

Damiano and Matte were lost in thought and didn't see Matthew Allen approach. Allen was suddenly standing on the other side of the opened door. Damiano hadn't noticed how tall Allen was, nor had she expected to see he'd obviously showered and shaved. In fact, in tan jeans and matching shirt and decent work boots, he was presentable. He said nothing as they led him to the boardroom. He sat and laid one hand casually on the table. He listened intently to Matte setting up the recording with names, time and date.

Damiano decided to take over. Matte smiled sourly at being displaced. He wanted a go at Allen. "Mr. Allen, you were the last person to see Dylan Kane alive."

"Except for his murderer, you mean, yes, I was."

"You have no alibi."

"If you canvass the cast and guests, someone saw me on the floor. Can't the police be thorough in their investigation?"

"You told us you had a sheet, your jargon. Explain," Damiano said curtly. Allen perked up. "Nothing like murder." Allen's voice was smooth; the carpenter was articulate. "A year ago, I went down to Place Victoria, wearing a Canada T-shirt. A few separatists gather there on May twenty-fourth to harass us, but I'm the guy arrested. I ask why, and the cop answers, 'If we arrest one of them, we have a riot.' I've attended protests, many of them. Invariably, I encounter some idiot winding up to punch me in the head. I don't run. I clench my fists by my side and, at the right second, I butthead the guy first, grabbing his shoulders as leverage. He walks away screaming and dizzy with a bloody face. I've taught that defensive move to friends. You see, I have a military licence and training. Once on lower St-Laurent, near Cleo's, in fact, a street thief reached into my back pocket. I turned, grabbed his head with both hands and ran him into a wall. Then I left. That's my sheet, but, for the record, I do not invoke! That means I never start a fight. I have never used my fists. I act defensively." Allen was as calm as he had been at the outset.

"You do know the chokehold?"

"I wouldn't use it unless I was attacked. I repeat: I do not invoke."

"Why would Dylan seek you out, as a friend, let's say?

"I'm interesting; Dylan was lost, I suppose."

"What did you get from him?"

"Dogs, fries and a Coke. Dylan was decent, but afraid to live on his own. He adopted his lovers' lives, I'm guessing. He was passing time with me. Detective Matte, what do you think?" Allen asked pointedly.

Matte's eyes burned. He didn't answer. He looked over at Damiano, signalling her to go ahead with the questions.

"Did you kill him, Mr. Allen? For an adventure, I mean – to see death close up?"

"You have a vivid imagination, Detective Damiano. Dylan told me he had a date, a second chance. I asked if it was an ex, but he was secretive. Dylan needed someone to support him. I have a hard time supporting myself and my climbing."

"You're pumped by extremes, daring stunts."

"I'm not some freak. Why is murder your ride? Are you ever asked about that? I've had enough. I believe I can leave." Allen rose and pushed his chair back under the table.

"We should receive the forensic results this week. Stay available, Mr. Allen."

Allen took his time leaving the room. "I'll let myself out."

"He's a bastard!"

"He's just guessing, Pierre. He's playing you."

"He sees enough gays at Cleo's to recognize I'm gay."

"Ignore him."

Chapter Twenty-six

Earlier that morning, Doctor Nathaniel Goldberg nicked his cheek a second time while shaving. The irony of a surgeon who couldn't shave properly failed to strike a note. He tore off a corner of toilet paper, spit on it and pasted tiny pieces on the cuts to staunch the trickles of blood. He tried stretching to relieve the tension and heard his vertebrae creak. "'Flesh and apprehensive,' Shakespeare should have added bones to the measure of a man." He spoke aloud. Who'd hear him now?

Later that morning, Goldberg felt shaky as he washed up before surgery. In the OR, he sweated through the entire surgery. Twice during the vertebral fusion, he was asked if he could carry on. His fingers felt engorged and stiff. "Of course," he answered, "just a sleepless night. I'll be fine. We're almost through." He washed up quickly and drove to his lawyer's office on McGill College Avenue. They spent two hours in discussion and coaching. Aaron Spitzer had been recommended by a close colleague.

"Nate, you can't deny knowing the kid now. You admitted as much to that detective. The police knew about both of you. If they hadn't, you wouldn't have had a late night visit."

"He wasn't a kid. He was thirty years old," Goldberg snorted.

"Alright, calm down. Don't use an aggressive tone with me. Here, you're a client, not a medicine god."

Goldberg shrugged an apology. "If Rachel finds out, I am done for, Aaron. My boys, they're still kids, Gabriel is fourteen and Seth is ten. What the hell are you telling me? That I have to answer their questions? I thought at five hundred an hour you'd block everything! Make this nightmare disappear."

"The kid is dead, Nate."

"If the mouthy media get a hold of this, I'll lose everything." Goldberg pinched the bridge of his nose and shut his eyes.

"I'll do my best to see that they don't, but I have to say that public records are beyond my control. The trolls are out there. Maybe we can escape with this one interview."

"All I can think of is what Rachel said at our wedding. 'No cheating, no ifs, buts, or maybes about it. I will never stay with a cheater. I swear to be faithful to you.'"

"That's the brashness of youth talking. Rachel must know something of reality, sixteen years later. She has a family too, and everything you've given her. No one is perfect."

"She doesn't need my money. Her family's loaded, and she's their only child."

"How long were you involved with Dylan Kane?"

"Four months. I can see by your expression, that's more trouble for me."

"Did he live with you?"

"Monday to Friday."

"Where did he go weekends?"

Goldberg hesitated. "I set him up in a bachelor on rue Drolet."

"That's a paper trail. Was this relationship on-going?"

"Till two weeks ago."

"Go ahead."

"He promised to have regular testing. He lied. Don't ask me how I found out. It's humiliating. I put him out and cut the lease on the bachelor at the end of the month. I had myself tested. I don't have the results yet."

"Did you see or hear from him in the past two weeks?"

"He called."

"Often?"

"Enough. I can see that's a motive. Are you going to ask me if I …"

"No, not my job. When was he murdered?"

"This past weekend."

"Well, you were in Rawdon with the family."

"No, Rachel was away with the boys, so I stuck around here."

"Why?"

"Fear, test results. That's enough isn't it?"

"With anyone?"

"Just me, and Tony Soprano, Season Two."

"Doesn't help. Nate, listen carefully," Spitzer's tone was loaded with exasperation and warning. "Do not lie to the police. If you lie, they will find you out. You will be arrested. Don't lie. Keep your answers short – don't embellish."

"I thought you'd answer the questions. What's the point of this discussion?"

"You're not a kid, Nate. I can cut off the questions that I don't feel you are obliged to answer. Check with me before you speak. I'm a referee, but you have home advantage. This is some mess you got yourself into!"

"How much do I owe you for that?"

"It's on the house. We use my car. Walk on my right side. Keep your head down till you're inside the door."

"Do you expect reporters?"

"I want us to be prepared."

"You know me. I'm always prepared."

"Tell me, Nate. Was he worth it?"

"Whoever thinks he'll be caught?"

"You have a point. Let's head out. First, have some water. Have you eaten?"

"Coffee."

"You'll have to go on an empty stomach."

"Doesn't matter, I can't think of eating."

"We're all idiots, Nate."

"That's a real help."

"Nate, my clients mangle their lives; sometimes they inflict injury on others, and then they come to me to fix everything. I'm not a magician. I'll do my best working the legal angles. I'll defend your legal rights. Now, try to collect yourself."

Goldberg cowered, didn't move before he bent down to rub his knees.

"Nate, compose yourself, be strong. We have to appear at this interview."

Chapter Twenty-seven

Chief Damiano was sitting in the boardroom looking over Matte's notes when she heard voices out in the hall. "What the …!" She rose and walked out and found five officers loading boxes against the wall near the boardroom door. "What's happening here?"

The officers stopped in their tracks. The first answered. "Chief, these are old files we're sending to storage."

"Well, I have a suspect arriving any minute. I want the boxes gone."

"We'll move them around the corner, Chief Damiano."

"Good."

When she returned to the room, Matte was almost doubled over with his hands on his knees. "Pierre?"

He straightened up. "Haven't slept. What if Dylan told Goldberg my name?"

"Did he ever tell you about other lovers?"

"Once, maybe twice."

"Names?"

"First names."

"Shouldn't come up then, I hope. I'll wait here. We'll deal with any potentially dangerous issue for you when it comes up. Isn't that what you asked of me, Pierre?"

"Yes, but I'm beginning to see possible difficulties. I want to be on this case though. I have to see it through."

"Alright. Would you please go meet Goldberg and his mouthpiece? Proper protocol."

"Right, no problem." Matte walked to the front door of the Crémazie Division. He decided to wait outside and clear his lungs. The parking lot on the east side of the building held only ten cars. Matte saw three empty cars and didn't miss the late model Lexus that pulled into the front entrance and parked. He had a good view of the emerging twosome. He was shocked by Goldberg's appearance. The doctor didn't look at Matte. He tried to conceal himself beside his lawyer. Matte felt Goldberg was older than he was. The tan summer suit, white shirt and brown silk tie spotlighted the grayish skin of a terrified man. Matte saw no hint of the energy or confidence he had seen the night before. The black permed hair was unruly. Matte gauged him at five-eleven. He opened the door for them. "Follow me please."

No one spoke until they were ushered into the boardroom. Damiano rose. "Chief Damiano. This is Detective Matte. I believe you two met last night." Goldberg acknowledged the meeting with a tightening of thin lips.

"I'm Aaron Spitzer, Chief Damiano. We've met once a few years ago at court." Spitzer was fashionably attired. He was a short, stocky man with a ready smile and a mouthful of white teeth. He ran his cuffs before he sat down. Middle fifties, Damiano thought.

"I remember. And Doctor?"

"Nathaniel Goldberg."

"Let's get started, shall we." Detective Matte set the recording and entered the formal information. He closed with the date and the time.

Goldberg sat there wishing he had never married, never met Dylan and never snared himself in the quagmire of infidelity. In the end, it all rotted out. He was in no mood to be questioned or held accountable. He wanted to disappear.

In a commanding tone, Spitzer asked the first question. "For my record, what led you to believe my client knew this Dylan Kane?"

Goldberg looked up hopefully.

"You're not in court, Mr. Spitzer. This is an interview where I ask the questions. For the general record, I'll oblige. Most gay clubs have excellent surveillance video that is not erased every week."

Spitzer narrowed his eyes, trying to figure out what Damiano had. "I know of these establishments, but I would guess there are at least twenty such clubs. That's a mountain of footage to scan in a very short time, Chief Damiano."

"Let me get to the point then. Our detectives heard a phrase that helped to save us time, 'his ortho man at the Jewish.'"

Goldberg dropped his head, but not before he gave an angry signal to Spitzer to move along.

"Dr. Goldberg admitted to Detective Matte that he knew Kane."

Matte fixed his eyes on Goldberg. Matte was aware that suspects usually let loose when they were caught with "I wasn't his only lover, there were others." Ortho man, how had Dylan labelled him, badge man? Matte saw Goldberg shudder. The doctor knew there was no escape.

"How did you meet Dylan Kane, Doctor Goldberg?"

Goldberg looked at Spitzer, who gave him a nod.

Without embellishment, Goldberg's answer was confessional. Spitzer knew then that Goldberg was stubborn and would do precisely what *he* thought was best. He wasn't Spitzer's first client to disregard his advice. He sat back and listened. "I never sowed any oats, never went to bars. I studied. That was pretty much it. I married. My son was born eleven months later and that was my life. I went to Le Stud out of curiosity. I sat at the bar with a glass of wine. I didn't cruise anybody. A young man with blue eyes and blond hair he kept pushing behind his ears bought me a drink. I felt that someone had dropped me into a free zone. He didn't ask for anything. He didn't come on to me. He didn't even talk that much. He was just there in my space, and I let go. From there, I guess it's pretty stereotypical of most affairs: passion, sex, a storyline, guilt, fear and eventually, a fallout or betrayal. It's odd to become a cliché. Now the damage control," he smiled sadly.

Matte listened, curious and hurt.

"How long were you together?"

"A little over four months."

"Did Kane live with you?"

"Monday to Friday morning."

"Where did he go after that?"

"I set him up in an apartment, on Drolet." Goldberg reached for his wallet and found what he wanted. "It's 7813 rue Drolet. Here's the key."

"What happened?"

"Dylan betrayed me."

"I'm afraid you must explain."

"I kicked Dylan out and I cancelled his lease."

"Why, Doctor?"

He dropped his head into his hands. "Dylan swore he was clean, that he tested every month. He lied. I'm going to lose my family." Goldberg speaking through his fingers, "I trusted him." Goldberg's brain was functioning and he slumped visibly. He saw that he had just made himself a soft target.

Damiano tried unsuccessfully not to look at Matte. His expression had hardened. She did not pursue Goldberg immediately; she wanted to catch him off guard. "Detective Matte tells me that you were at your condo last weekend, Saturday night in particular."

Goldberg kept his face covered and nodded.

"Please answer so we can hear you, Doctor."

"Yes."

"With anyone?"

"Season Two of 'The Sopranos,' my fourth time." Goldberg sat back up.

"Did Dylan contact you that day?"

"Yes, he called. I told him to stay away from me."

"Dr. Goldberg, 'The Sopranos' don't offer you an alibi even if you can recite the dialogue. Will you consent to a search of your condo? We can have a warrant issued if you are unwilling."

"Go ahead. Give me a time in the evening."

"Tonight at seven. I'll contact the crime team. If you have had relations with your wife in the past, she too will have to be tested."

"I know! I had myself tested on Monday, didn't have the courage until then." Goldberg shouted, rising to his feet. "I know what I've done! I don't need pointers."

"Dylan Kane ruined your life." Damiano spoke softly. "He may have infected you with HIV, along with your wife, and damaged your practice. In your position, I can understand why you may have sought revenge. You have reason to want to hurt Kane."

Goldberg leaned forward again, planting his manicured hands on the table. "I wish I had." He thought a second before he leaned even more deeply across the table, cautioning Damiano. "I wasn't Dylan's only lover. There was … I've always been terrible with names. Give me time. I'll remember one, maybe two, first names and nicknames. That's how he labelled us. You'll have other suspects! I'm not alone." Goldberg heard himself whining like one of his patients. He loathed the sound of his voice.

Matte didn't move. The boardroom began to close in on him. Air escaped from his lungs, and he coughed into his hand.

Damiano remained focused. "Dr. Goldberg, expect an official interrogation once we have the forensic results." Her voice was dry and cutting.

"I didn't kill him," Goldberg whispered.

Matte formally terminated the interrogation and saw the men out with Goldberg looking glum. *What am I going to do? Rachel, I never meant to hurt you. I never thought …*

Did Matte know Dylan had lied about testing? Goldberg was desperate. He'd come up with names. Speaking aloud, "I've allowed Pierre to go too far. Why is he putting himself through this torture?" She peeked down the hall and saw Matte on his way back.

"I'll go now. I need to spend some real time with my mother, as much for her as for myself."

"Pierre."

"Can't right now."

Damiano's temper flared, but she kept it under control. Matte was suffering. "Have you brought Dylan's belongings to evidence?"

"They're locked in my desk. There's no risk of contamination if that's what you're thinking. I gave Dylan that gold chain. By all rights it's mine."

"It was a gift, Pierre. It belongs in evidence. Get it over there. That's a direct order."

"I won't touch it. You have my word. The bag is still sealed. Right now, I have to leave."

"We have to make a decision, Pierre."

"Not now!" Matte spun around to face Damiano, and came very close to actually accosting her. Instead, he turned back and walked off, desolate. *Why can't she just help me? She's my partner for God's sake.* Matte was revolted that he had come close to actually striking Damiano.

Damiano watched him go. A thought passed through her brain that left an ache in her heart. Pierre knew Dylan and his tricks – he'd lived with them. He hadn't killed for them, he hadn't. Pierre had suffered and borne the heartbreak of Dylan's cavalier rejections. He was not a violent man. Matte, the cop she knew, wouldn't murder Dylan; the kid was still a part of him. Goldberg's words rang in her ears. *I know what I've done!* He knew he may have passed the virus onto his wife, and his practice might be in jeopardy. Could surgeons who contracted HIV continue to operate? She'd have to check on that. He had no alibi – he stood to lose the honored identity he'd worked his life to achieve. He had a strong motive. *I wish I had.* Was Goldberg lying? Witnesses lied all the time. They were as bad as teenagers. Perhaps he wasn't just another fool who took a walk on the wild side and regretted the fallout. Damiano liked Allen. He was cold, deliberate, calculating. He smashed a man's head into a wall and walked away. Allen called it self-defence. *I do not invoke.* He enjoyed telling his tales. Damiano admitted she was creating her own theory that Allen would enjoy ending a life, just being there, being the man responsible. Taking a life for a daredevil was the ultimate trip. Dylan's murder was so clean that Matte and Goldberg and Allen were all capable of such a crime. Allen was the most heartless. What had Velma said? *Matthew is open to anything.*

Still, there were other lovers, other potential suspects.

Damiano walked back to her office and found new files piled on her desk from Donat's secretary. Five! "Goddamn, they're breeding like flies! The bitch wants me to fail." Donat was coming back, Denise believed. Damiano opened the first file. "Forget it for tonight. I need to eat and I want to see Goldberg's condo and Dylan's apartment." Since she hadn't time to grab something from a restaurant, she hoofed it down to the cells and the intake counter in the basement of the building.

Officer Robson was as dependable as crime. He was just opening his large Domino's pizza. Two Cokes were sitting on the surveillance desk, too. Damiano rifled through her purse, took thirty dollars and handed it to him.

"Quoi?" Robson spoke French on the job, unless addressed in English. When he was about ten, his mother had made certain he knew French, though she'd married an Irishman. Quebec was a French province, not a nation, she often reminded her son.

Damiano took the whole box and a Coke.

"Toute?"

"Je suis desolé." She handed Robson two hot pieces to hold him till he placed a second order. She turned and left with a smile he couldn't see. A chief should have perks!

Chapter Twenty-eight

Aaron Spitzer was so furious his mouth twitched. "Well, Nate, you made their day. I'm surprised you weren't arrested. I'm your lawyer, for Christ's sake, and you don't tell me about this HIV bombshell? What's wrong with you? I have heard over the years that you're an orthopedic surgeon." Spritzer dragged out each syllable of the last word. "Surgeons are carpenters, all saws and hammers. You certainly are not neurosurgeons. What were you thinking?"

Goldberg had elected to sit in the back seat to receive the tirade he knew was coming. "I thought things out. I am a doctor. The autopsy will reveal whether Dylan was positive. I chose to jump in first. You distinctly told me not to lie. I didn't."

"I know that you're the new kid on the block in an investigation room. First-timers are generally men who think they know best. Nate, did you have to exhibit your complete ignorance of the system?"

"The chief was civil ..."

"Nate, wake up! That's her MO and it worked on you. You handed her a strong motive. You're not just another gay man who has only himself to worry about. Dylan fucked up your life, Rachel's potentially, and your practice. You had every reason to kill him."

"Why didn't she arrest me?"

"She's collecting a few more nails for your coffin."

"Now, do you want to know if I killed the prick?"

"Not my garbage bag. I have to find a way to minimize the damage you've done – that's what I do. I'll stay with you until the crime team arrives. Right now, I want you to search your condo for any incriminating evidence."

"Toss it?"

"By law I can't tell you what to do with it. I can say from my experience the police will look at your garbage, most probably they have a warrant for your car, so ..."

"I'm not a magician."

"I'm placing my car keys on the mantel. I'd like to see Old Montreal from your roof."

"That way you'll have no knowledge of anything found in your trunk. No collusion, smart."

"Next, you have to come up with some names of past lovers. Otherwise, you are in the can. Think while you search. You need to shift the attention away from you. Understand, Nate?"

"Yes. I'm not telling Rachel until I have the results. There's no point in destroying her when there might not be the need."

"Finally, a decision! If I manage to cut you loose from this debacle, will you be able to practice? Do you know that much?"

"Yes, I do know medical procedure. I'd present myself to a confidential committee with my test results. If my viral count is low enough, with ample protection in the operating room, I would be permitted to perform invasive surgery. However, we both know what confidential means these days. Colleagues would learn of my condition. I'd hear whispers. I don't want to transfer. Gossip is a follower. At a new hospital, I'd still be forced to disclose. I'd rather stay put and work with colleagues, physicians and nurses, who'd choose to work with me."

"I am sorry, Nate."

"Thanks, but sorry doesn't come close to what I'm feeling. I join the legions of fools who lost everything for love. Thing is it wasn't love – it was an ejaculation. Pathetic really."

"You don't have to disclose, but this is not your first tryst. No freshman sets his lover up in a rental. That's experience."

"You know everything? By the way, don't you dare charge me for this conversation."

"I don't know everything, Nate. I'm not any better than you, or wiser for that matter. *My* wife caught me using a second phone when I mistakenly left for work, forgetting to take both. Sam still thinks it was my only infidelity because that's her way of being able to stay with me. I love my family, but life is short. I'd never leave her or my family, but I'm a man. Still, we haven't been the same. Trust is like youth, you remember it, but you can't have it back."

"You make us both sound like such shits."

"We are. How did you even manage to escape the family for the week?"

"Rachel decided she wanted to live in the country. She'd had her fill of traffic. I usually drove home Thursday night. It was like dating the first few months. She gave me a back rub and worked on my feet. She …"

"You are a shit!"

"I'm forty-five years old, but inside, Dylan made me feel I was a kid again. It began with Trevor, but guilt got the better of me and I ended it. There is so much baggage with married love. These guys freed me up."

"They're really prostitutes when you come down to it."

"I never paid them."

"You set them up, you fed them and what, bought clothes too, not prostitutes per se, but escorts."

"That's not how I saw them."

"That's how we lie to ourselves, Nate."

Nothing more was said until they were inside the condo. Goldberg heated up a frozen pizza while he looked for evidence and tried to think of a name. The police would be arriving in forty minutes. He saw the tennis sweater and realized he'd better leave it. Detective Matte had seen it. It surprised Goldberg to find so little of Dylan. Two shoe boxes and they weren't full. He left socks and a few shirts. Goldberg stopped looking and realized his second misstep, apart from his first. He'd given that detective or chief or whatever the hell she was everything she wanted. He'd given her a motive. What a fool he'd been!

Dylan's place was his second problem. Whatever Dylan had on him, the kid would hide at his apartment. Goldberg had stupidly handed over the key. He should have gone to the apartment first and given up the key after he'd scoured the place. All Goldberg could do was moan.

The only way Goldberg could redirect that cop's attention was to come up with the names of other lovers. "What was the name? Dylan did tell me a few. I almost have one. What? The professor! What the hell was his name though? Pete, no, Peter! There was another guy? Christ, the shield? Was he a fireman or a cop? I should have asked. I should have learned more." Nate sat down, forlornly depressed. "That's something though. Is that enough to get her off my back?"

That surge of youth he felt the night he met Dylan, the rise and fall of his body in reckless passion, dissolved and burned as though nothing had ever happened. Their ashes blackened every corner of his life. Nate Goldberg, who had not been afraid since childhood, shook with creeping self-pity.

"Nate! What the hell? Have you not brought that stuff to my trunk?"

"What's the point?"

"You have less than ten minutes – get down there. Stop thinking! Do it!"

Chapter Twenty-nine

Matte had decided not to pay the Montreal University Health Care Center twenty-five dollars for parking and was about to surrender and drive onto the Glen site when he spotted a car pulling out from a regular city meter. He slid into the space, got out, fed the machine and knew he'd been lucky. His phone rang. It was Damiano. "Toni, I told you I'd be at the hospital. I had no time to deliver the evidence."

"I know that, but Marie just called. She needs the Kane evidence bag tonight. I've made enough concessions, Pierre. You have to drive it over to Crime tonight after your visit. Tonight, understood? That's a direct order."

"Understood."

"I just heard from Detective Pichon. Boucher's taken off. Just what the Crémazie Division needed, a dangerous, armed cop on the loose!"

"I've told you, it's not your case. Let the SQ take the fallout."

"It's this division. I'm acting chief. Please don't let me down with the evidence."

"I won't."

"Is there anything I should look for at the condo?"

"I wasn't a welcome visitor. I tried to catch as much as I could, but Goldberg blocked my view. Look for the sweater. There was an antiseptic feel to the whole place, like it wasn't much lived in." Matte smiled awkwardly. His own condo was pretty much the same.

"Have a good visit."

"Thanks."

Matte was taken aback at the size and breadth of the new hospital complex. His mother was all he could think of on his first visit. He hadn't seen the hospital itself. The various buildings merged together like giant pieces of a game, resembling an airport more than a hospital. The different colored buildings, one red, two blue and one yellow were appealing. The colors reminded him of a gigantic Rubik's cube. He walked across the front length of the hospital until he found Hôpital Royal Victoria at the very end. The blue sign was clear. When he stepped through the doors, he was struck by the immensity and width of the halls and the emptiness. No one was around. If he shouted, he'd hear his echo. Matte knew his mother was in Room 825, but he was lost. He found one group of elevators on his right, but they didn't seem to be what he wanted. Another human appeared.

"I know the place. My mother's in the hospital, same pavilion. What room are you looking for?" Matte answered. "Follow me. This is what you want, elevators that reach the eighth floor. Your mother's in Room 25."

"Not 825?"

"No, eight is the floor. I'm here three times a week. You're on track."

Matte wasn't certain, but he took the elevator. The hospital wing was very quiet. He didn't see a single nurse or person. He followed the room signs, turned right and walked to the end of the hall. Room 25 was the last room on his left. The room was private – all rooms at the new hospital were private, spacious and clean. His mother was propped up by pillows and sleeping. There was a large window that brightened up the room. Matte made no noise as he sat in the chair right beside the bed. He gently laid his hand on hers. Matte looked up and saw his mother was trying to smile, a lovely slanted smile. Matte rose and kissed her. "It's so good to see you, Mom. You look just fine." Pierre's mother pinched his hand. "Well, maybe not fine, but good to me," he said. "I am so glad Dad was able to get you to the hospital in time. You know you'll make a good recovery." His mother gave him that wink of hope he knew. "How about a walk?" Matte had spied the walker. A nurse suddenly appeared, surprising Matte. He rose, "I'm her son, Pierre. I was wondering if I could take my mother for a walk."

"The best thing for her," the nurse said. "Make sure you stay on your mother's left side. Her knee might buckle. I don't think it will, but you want to be on the safe side. Do you need anything, Mrs. Hearn?" Matte's mother shook her head. "Good. I'll be back in an hour then."

Matte took the walker and moved the chair out of the way. He saw his mother's white sweater and took it from the bottom of the bed. "It's cold with the air conditioning. Let's get you ready for a real walk." Matte almost startled himself with the role reversal. His mother was always busy caring for others. It felt strange helping her into the sweater. "Let's put your bad arm in first." His mother followed all his instructions like a schoolgirl on her first day of class. Her innocence and the role change engulfed Matte with love. "Now, don't be afraid. Take your time. I'm right beside you."

"Okaaay."

"That's very good! Good pace."

"Thnnn yu."

"No need. I am so happy to be with you. Let's keep moving. Good. When you come through this, Mom, I want you to make me one promise.

You're only in your sixties, live your own life. Do what pleases *you*! We have only one life – you have one too. You used to sketch and you were talented. I've seen your work in the basement. Go back to that if you'd like, or anything that might interest you. Call up old friends. See them on your own. Dad has had a good life and he's fine. You've taken such good care of him, and you deserve your own fun. It's not too late. I want to know that you've lived, and not just lived for us."

His mother stopped walking. She was trying to smile again. Her eyes filled with excitement. "I wiii! I wiiil! You ra a goo soon!" Matte wrapped his arms around his mother and held on.

"I just want you happy, for yourself. Forget us. Let's keep walking." Once they were back in her room, Matte took off the sweater and lifted his mother back into bed. She was light in his arms. He felt if he squeezed, he might break a bone. He fluffed the pillows and wiped her forehead. "You're a trooper!"

"Yoou?"

"I'm okay."

"Happe?"

Tears welled in Matte's eyes. Happy to be here. His mother pinched his hand again. "Not much, Mom. Dad was right. He'd be glad to know that. I don't fit in."

"Hansoom."

Matte smiled weakly. "We look alike. I'm glad."

"Sooombudy?"

"Not for awhile."

"Dylan? Are you not togethe? You wer happy."

The jealousy Matte had been living with enveloped him, and his face twisted with rage. He turned away.

"Sooon?"

"It's okay, Mom. You're on my side and that's what counts. You know I love you, right?" His mother pinched his hand again. Matte saw himself in his mother. She was tall, small-boned, fine featured with long, delicate piano hands, like his. "Don't ever forget that I love you." Another pinch. An hour later, soothed by the warmth of her security, Matte fell asleep against his mother's hand, his first peaceful sleep in days. She watched over him.

Pierre Senior made a loud entrance. He was a muscular man with a wrestler's neck and a booming voice. "Well, Dorothy, my love!" When he saw Pierre, he was about to shout. Dorothy sent her husband a withering look. He was sulking when Pierre awoke, feeling awkward.

"Dad, I wasn't sleeping the whole time. It's been a tough week."

"You know that your mother's the patient, Pierre," he growled, leaning back on his heels.

"Mom, I better go. I have to deliver evidence tonight." He kissed her, nodded to his father and left.

Dorothy kept her eyes on her husband. "Whi?"

"Pierre gets under my skin – Jesus, he was sleeping!"

Dorothy closed her eyes.

"Alright, Do, I'm sorry, as usual. I'm always at fault in your eyes where Pierre's concerned. I'm sorry."

Dorothy shook her head, wishing she could say clearly, "He's your son." *You can be an insensitive bastard.*

Chapter Thirty

Officer Boucher had turned off his phone, although he checked his calls. The SQ had tried three times to reach him. He was on suspension without pay. The way he saw it, he didn't have to answer calls. Let them come to him. That Thursday night, he called Doucette. He parked outside Doucette's home. "Louis, I need to talk to you."

"I'm with my family, Daniel. We've said everything already. I'll tell you again I'm not getting involved."

"Five minutes – I'm your partner. I'm outside your house. If you don't come out, I'll come up."

"Is that a threat?"

"One partner needing another – get your ass out here! Five minutes."

"Marie-Claude, I have to go out to see Daniel."

"Why? Call the police. He's just making everything worse. You can't go, Louis."

"Call the cops on my partner? Are you crazy? You have no idea what shit would come down on me if I did. I'll be back in five." Louis told his wife to lock the doors. He walked up to the car and stopped by the passenger side. Louis leaned over. "What is it?"

"Hop in!"

"I can talk from here."

Boucher raised a weapon. "Get in the fucking car, in the front seat."

"You handed in your weapons. Where did you pick up this one?"

"I'm always prepared. Get in!"

Louis opened the door reluctantly and sat as close as he could to the door. "Why are you pulling this kind of crap on me? I don't deserve this ..."

"My ass is on the line. The SQ is looking for me." Boucher saw the dread pass across Doucette's face. "Damiano called you in, didn't she? Don't lie to me." Boucher pushed his weapon into Doucette's ribs.

It was clear that Boucher was wired. Doucette stalled, afraid to move. "Alright, she called me in, so what? It was bound to happen."

"What did you tell her, Louis? You're already sweating – you told her something, right?"

"You have a gun on me. That's why I'm sweating, dickhead!"

"I'm not going to ask you again, Louis."

"She knew we had gone back to the crime scene and ordered me to stay away or face suspension and a report. I don't want any part of this. This is your mess."

"Dammit, that's not what I asked you? What the fuck did you tell *her*? That's what I want to know. We're cops – you're my partner. She must know that you'd ask me if the perp had a weapon. Damiano's a cop who knows the game. That's what the SQ is checking. She must have fucking asked you that or else they wouldn't have an APB out on me!"

"I told her I didn't know. Is that good enough for you?"

"You're lying, you pussy. They want to arrest me!"

"I think they have a witness – I'm not sure. That was my gut feeling."

"Jesus. Did Damiano ask you if I discharged my weapon recklessly?"

"No."

"God dammit! You're still lying, Louis. Last chance."

Doucette felt his only chance of escape was charging Boucher. He body-slammed Boucher into the driver's door. The gun exploded inside the car. Doucette looked over at Boucher who was shocked as Louis collapsed against him. "I said you thought he ..." Doucette lost consciousness. Marie-Claude opened the front door screaming, but Boucher sped off, raising dust and leaving tire marks.

"Wake up you fucker. I would never have shot you, Louis. You're my partner! Don't die on me. Don't die on me!" He sped to Sacré-Coeur Hospital on boulevard Gouin with his hand on the horn, zigzagging through gridlock. He shook Doucette the whole way, trying to wake him up. Boucher's face swelled with fear. He tried to calm himself with the illusion that Doucette was responsible for the accident. "I would never have shot my partner!' he shouted. "Witness! It has to be that bitch or the idiots in the apartment. Now this!"

He drove to Emergency and honked. He jumped from the car, shouting, "Officer down! Officer down!" It didn't take long before nurses and a doctor came out running. Boucher knew the hospital had a trauma unit. In seconds, Doucette was lifted onto a gurney, and the nurses and doctor were running back inside the emergency corridor with the wounded officer. Boucher ran after them. "It's an accidental shooting. Is my partner alive?"

"Barely." The crew disappeared behind emergency doors. Boucher saw the blood on his shirt and pants. He hurried back to the car, popped the trunk and pulled out his football jersey. He tore off his shirt and pulled the jersey on over his head. He was stuck with the pants. He couldn't stay. Instead, he drove to an ATM and emptied the account. A hiding place was what he needed. His idea was risky, but he felt he had no choice. He drove to a Walmart parking lot. It took Boucher less than ten minutes to switch plates. In the Walmart he bought pants and a hoodie. He'd have to wait for darkness, so he sat in the vast parking lot. He did exit the car once to see what he had in his trunk, looking for tools. He found what he might need.

At nine-fifteen, he drove to rue Notre-Dame and parked. He walked to 7th Street, past the old woman's house, checking the height of a white wire fence. Not a problem, he thought. He stayed away from the old couple on the balcony across the street. That old fart probably called the cops. He'd jump the fence from the other side. He saw no patrol car – they must be finished for the day or changing shift. Seeing an open path, Boucher set about climbing the fence with new purpose. With one hand on top of the fence, he put a foot on the rail and hopped over. He felt a sharp stab in his hip and breathed air through his teeth. He crept around the back of the house and found a small door he wasn't expecting. A house directly behind had lights on, but the door he needed was located at the bottom of three steps shielding him from view. An air conditioner was attached to the side of the house making enough noise to muffle the sound of breaking glass. He couldn't take time picking the lock. He pulled his hoodie sleeve over his hand and broke the window, listening for an alarm. Nothing. In a flash, he was standing inside a dark basement. He heard loud talking.

"The police called. Just a second. I think I heard something. Don't speak." Seconds passed. "I guess I was wrong. Nerves. They're sending another patrol. I prefer staying in my own house. You both have to understand. I have my neighbors and I have the police. I'm fine here with my tea and almond cookies. I'm glad of your calls, too."

Boucher crept to the bottom of the stairs. He could see them because of the hall lights.

"I'll watch the end of the Blue Jays' game in the bedroom. I'll call to say good night."

He wondered if the old woman had an emergency bracelet. He'd have to surprise her, give her no time to press a call button or grab a phone. Boucher inched up the stairs to the living room on the first floor. He peeked around the carpeted stairs leading to the second floor. He saw items on the sides of the stairs and reminded himself not to trip over them. The television was playing in the room on his right. He crept up on all fours and scanned his target. From what he could see, the room was small. He didn't go farther. Boucher would wait for her to turn off the set and leave the room. He knew she had a phone with her. "I know where you are," Boucher whispered. "I can wait."

Chapter Thirty-one

Chief Damiano had heard from Goldberg's lawyer that the Crime team could change on the landing outside his condo, preventing an invitation to the media to swoop down on rue Notre- Dame like seagulls to garbage. Damiano had driven down alone because she had a favor to ask Marie Dumont of Crime. The crew arrived on time and carried their equipment up to the condo where they changed quickly and quietly under the scrutiny of Aaron Spitzer. Damiano had put on white booties and gloves.

"Don't touch anything, Toni."

Damiano wanted to fire back at Dumont that this wasn't her first time at the circus, but refrained. Goldberg's face was ashen, darker from the emerging stubble. He and Spitzer stood alone as the team invaded his condo like a creeping spread of ants, dusting, filling bags, lifting cushions, taking samples and pointing to jobs rather than talking. Damiano never liked watching the work. She motioned to Marie. "I'd like to go to Kane's apartment first. Will you do that favor for me? I'm not needed here."

"Toni, you know that's not protocol, even if you are the acting chief. Rules."

"You have my word that I won't touch anything. I'd like to get a feel for the place. I've been on the sidelines on this case. I never knew the extent of Donat's work. It's overwhelming. I want to be involved; I want this death to matter to me. I'm at my best when I feel outrage at the loss of a life. Do you understand?"

"I can't allow a detective to contaminate a scene related to murder. I'll go with you. My team will finish up and join us. That's the best I can offer. I'll lend you a cap. I don't want to be picking up your hair samples and wasting my time."

Aaron Spitzer approached them, leaving Goldberg alone in his anguish. "My client has come up with a few names, nicknames really, but they should help."

"You mean deflect attention from your client?"

"That too," Spitzer smiled smugly. "One is the 'Professor,' Pete or Peter, he thinks. The other is the 'Shield,' no first name. My client thinks maybe a fireman or a cop. I have to say the deceased had taste. He wasn't common."

Damiano was copying the names, but fell in silence without giving Spitzer the thanks he wanted. She waited until he left before she asked Dumont. "Do you know how many professors Concordia, McGill or UQAM has on staff?"

"A couple hundred?"

"Try four hundred professors at Concordia alone, from permanent staff, to associates, to visiting profs, to lecturers, to single courses and the list goes on. The campus is huge. This Peter may not even be a professor in reality, but we have to start somewhere."

"Still Pete or Peter. You're chief – delegate this grunt work."

"I will, Marie. I'd like to go to the apartment tonight."

"Remember what I said! Don't disturb anything."

"Girl Guide's honor."

"Were you ever a Guide?"

"Well, no."

"Thought not." Marie spoke to both techs and told them to follow her to Drolet when they were done here. She left them with the address.

Aaron Spitzer caught them before they left. "What about my client?"

"When we have the phone logs, the test results and forensics, I will personally contact Dr. Goldberg. What we've taken tonight will be returned when the case is closed if the items are not deemed evidence." Damiano and Dumont changed and left, taking two cars to rue Drolet.

It was almost nine-thirty. Both sides of Drolet were jammed with residential cars. They double parked and kept their flashers on. The ground-floor apartment was located directly under the left side of stairs that mounted to three floors. The curving stairs, treacherous in winter, were indigenous to the city. They stepped into gear in the darkness. Dumont led the way. "Just a second, I can't find the light switch." She spotted a switch on the right wall. It lit a single bare bulb. She walked to a toilet beside a shower stall surrounded by one plastic curtain and lit the second bulb. "A monk wouldn't find it easy living here."

Damiano saw a single, cheap rollaway, to her surprise, neatly made. No television, radio, photos, books or phone, two wooden chairs, one used bridge table and what was meant to be an open closet. Dumont opened an aged fridge. Inside she found two liters of IGA water, half a liter of milk and moldy brown bread. The freezer was empty. Kane owned three pairs of shoes, four pairs of pants, six casual shirts and one suit. He used cardboard boxes for drawers. She found socks, underpants and a handful of white T-shirts. Under the kitchen sink, she found Gain laundry detergent and rubber gloves draped on top. Before Dumont touched anything, Damiano felt sick with herself, felt like a maggot, picking through the fragments of a life that crashed.

Dumont didn't miss much. "What's wrong, Toni?"

"The kid had nothing, no life of his own. He assumed the life of his lovers, but he was always just this, nothing. Sex was the only wholeness he had. I wonder why he hung on, why he ran from one man to another."

"Why does anyone hang on? Incorrigible hope, I'd guess? What else does anyone have? You wanted to feel something for this vic. You have your wish. I have to get to work." Dumont opened the four drawers beside the sink, fingered items and bagged some of them. She found corn flakes in a cupboard. "He had a starvation diet for staying lanky." She went to the bed and scooped up the thin mattress. "Finally!" Dumont reached into her bag, found long tweezers and laid hold of the simple pad from the Dollar store. She also found a large photo of Dylan Kane.

"He was *beautiful*, flawless, and those blue eyes added a dash of flash." Dumont wasn't kidding. "Some package!" Damiano found herself staring and understood Matte loving him.

"And he lived in this hole and was strangled on a roof and abandoned. What a waste. It's hard to believe that this kid who had nothing held sway over so many lives," Damiano said with sadness. "Men ruined families, gay men suffered for an impulse of delight and passion."

"One of them grew to hate him and took his life."

Damiano wanted to grab the photo and pad. Instead, she stood beside Dumont as she carefully opened the pad on the table with her tweezers. The first page was neatly printed with Kane's name and family numbers. "Do you have these?"

"We have them."

On the second page three men were listed: Pierre Matte and his number, Peter Henley and his number and Nate Goldberg and his number. Dumont turned to face Damiano. "Did you know, Toni?" Dumont asked, aghast.

"I owe Pierre. He's devastated. He refused to stay away from the investigation."

"You owe him what?"

Damiano hesitated.

"I'm not asking as a friend; I'm asking as head of Crime. You're jeopardizing an investigation!"

"From one cop to another, Dumont, I worked in god-awful pain last year after my arm splintered on the job. I couldn't sleep, couldn't get through work without help."

"Advil and that stuff, that's nothing."

"I used prescribed meds with a boost of vodka. Is that enough for you? I'm clean now, but Matte worked with me and didn't turn me in. He also let me work the sidelines when Luke was involved in that student's death. So, I owe him."

Dumont asked warily, "Is that the reason you wanted to come alone to this apartment? To tamper with evidence? Toni, you're acting chief! You should have invoked the conflict of interest clause, debt or no debt. Have you even entertained the possibility that Pierre might have murdered this vic?"

"He loved Dylan. He was probably the only person who did."

"You've heard of jealousy, I hope."

"I can't think that Pierre would kill Dylan."

"Devastated, you said. You know the elemental motives for murder: love, jealousy, money and hate."

"He loved Dylan, Marie. Pierre accepted Dylan as he was. I know that first-hand."

"That's motive when you've been dumped. That's what happened to Pierre, right?"

Damiano didn't dare to reveal that Dylan had stolen money from Pierre. "He said he'd take the hit if he were discovered."

"I won't have my side of the investigation jeopardized. Is there anything else you're keeping from the investigation?"

Damiano clenched her teeth.

"What?"

Damiano thought of Donat who had entrusted her with the job of chief. She chose to be his cop. "Dylan stole three hundred dollars from Pierre the week before he died, but they hadn't seen one another in eight months. Dylan found the extra key and went into his condo. Matte said that Dylan knew enough not to take all his cash because he'd nail his ass. Dylan was already dead when Pierre told me about this." Damiano turned away from the glare of the light bulb.

Dumont's face was tense, concentrated. "Regarding you, what's past is done, no use analyzing it now."

"I want to add that it was Matte who found Goldberg. I needed his help."

"Where is he by the way?"

"He's at the hospital with his mother. She's suffered a stroke, but is expected to make a decent recovery he told me."

"Good. I like Matte. You make a good team. At the very least, tell me he has an alibi for the night of the murder."

"He was home with a cold."

"Fuck! I never use foul language the way you do. Sometimes, one word does say what you feel. You need to interrogate Matte! Do your job, Chief Damiano, and don't ever play me again. You should leave," she said stiffly.

Damiano was at the door when she heard Dumont shouting again.

"Hold up! The evidence, the gold chain! How do you know Matte hasn't changed the chain? God! That evidence is corrupted. It should have been sent to my department that night. Whatever skin cells from Kane and perhaps the perp might be fruit of the poisonous tree. How did Matte have the bag in the first place?"

"Dr. Belmont handed it to him in the examining room. He told Matte it should be sent to Evidence. He assumed Matte would follow through immediately."

"Well, fuck again! I can't go after Belmont – it's Matte! You have to do something."

"I'm sorry."

"Never mind sorry. Matte better have delivered the bag tonight. I'm going to call."

Damiano stood by.

"Finally!" She nodded to Damiano. "Put the envelope under a scope, check the seal and initials. Check the bag number and the bag itself, top and bottom. Be thorough. I'll be down tonight.

"It's there, Toni. If the seal hasn't been broken or the bag tampered with, we may have a chance. If this case goes to court, we have to disclose that the chain of custody has been broken. What evidence we find will be tossed. If Matte did this intentionally, that's obstruction, Toni."

"He gave that chain to Kane. The evidence was locked up for twenty-two hours."

"Matte's a detective! He knew the consequences of corrupting evidence. He's a prime suspect, in my opinion, or at least one of them."

"Marie, I get it, but Pierre is gutted. He can't think straight."

"I'll be in touch as soon as I have news."

Damiano felt she deserved the dressing down. When she was in her car, she sat and pounded the steering wheel with the heel of her fist and howled in pain. It had started to rain. Big, sloppy drops bounced off her windshield. A few people had begun running up the street to avoid being soaked. Her phone buzzed. It was Detective Pichon.

"According to Doucette's wife, Boucher shot Doucette in front of his home. She heard from the hospital that Boucher drove him to Sacré-Coeur Hospital. His condition is critical. I learned from the doctor in Emergency that Boucher claimed it was an accident. The wife is there now. Boucher took off. He's some scumbag. Continuing, BEI wants to take over the case."

"I thought they told you to finish it. You said they wanted you to close."

"Right, but that was before this shooting and my failure to bring Boucher in. They're afraid of a media cluster fuckup."

"Do you have a number for BEI?"

"I do."

"I want you on the case – I have that witness to protect. I won't further expose her. We serve the public, God dammit!" Damiano was still sitting in her car when she hung up. "I see now why Donat was always shouting." Suspects swirled in her head as she pulled out and drove home for fear some part of her would blow. She felt raw about Matte.

Chapter Thirty-two

Damiano preferred the house empty when she was stressed, but tonight she wanted to talk to Jeff. She needed him. She continued to use all her powers of persuasion to convince herself that Pierre had not murdered Dylan. That thought had a defeated sag to it. Still, they had viable suspects: Goldberg, Allen and perhaps this Peter Henley. She still had to contact Henley.

Dumont was taking her anger out on Matte because good evidence was corrupted. Matte hadn't taken the bag, Belmont had handed it to him. She parked on the street outside her home on Anwoth Road in Westmount because she knew she'd be back out driving to the hospital to check on Doucette. She saw the note when she turned on the kitchen light. "We have three Pokémon left to find. You're on your own." *My men!* She ate a peanut butter and honey sandwich that stuck to the roof of her mouth. She thought of vodka, and let it go. Instead, she drank milk to wash down the last cloying mouthful. One day she knew she'd end up choking, scarfing food as she did, but, not today!

Upstairs she stripped and showered and towelled off quickly. She wiped the mist from the mirror with her hand and was shocked to see the same strained eyes Donat usually had. As chief she'd become a hostage to her desk, stress, files and delegating. She'd lose the freedom of the road and the rush and work of a case. Damiano had no time to waste trying to figure out if she could multi-task and do both because so far she was batting a C+ average. She dressed and drove to Ahuntsic-Cartierville, the North End borough situated on the banks of Rivière-des- Prairies. The borough was created following the 2002 municipal reorganization of Montreal. Cartierville alone was annexed to the city of Montreal in 1916. It was a settlement established by the Sulpician Order in 1696. From the road, the hospital resembled a grand old Montreal cathedral constructed of brown brick and white trellises. Prominently displayed on a small balcony was a gold statue of the Sacred Heart. Completing the picture was the cross on the highest point of the hospital. All parking spaces were occupied by ten in the morning. Damiano drove into the entrance and bullied her way into a space. She left her card on the dash and dared anyone from security to ticket her. Wasting no time, she flashed her badge and asked for help often until she was led to a hall where she recognized Pichon and a distraught woman she took for Doucette's wife. Two men stood by, BEI, she guessed. It hadn't taken them long. The three men turned her way.

A stubborn streak took hold of Damiano. She went to Doucette's wife first, ignoring the others. She was chief of a division. She wasn't about to be turned away, or pushed back in line. "Mrs. Doucette, I'm Chief Damiano. I want to express the sympathy of the Division for this tragedy. Did you drive here tonight?"

Marie-Claude broke down. "A taxi," she wept. "I can't see straight. I begged Louis to stay in the house. Daniel spoke to Louis on the phone, and Louis went out to the car. He's fighting for his life! My husband had nothing to do with the shooting."

"Did you actually see Officer Boucher discharge his weapon?"

"All this police jargon is just bullshit! Did I see Daniel shoot my defenceless husband? No, I didn't, but I heard the shot. I watched Daniel pull out. Louis didn't have a weapon with him, so who do you think shot my husband?"

"I promise you we will find out exactly what happened."

"Louis's partner shot him. That's what happened. Leave me alone."

Damiano straightened up and walked over to Pichon. "Have you mentioned what we discussed?"

"No, not yet. These guys are very insistent."

The two BEI men stood impatiently, waiting to take over the conversation. The BEI was a separate team of investigators newly appointed to render independent analyses of cases involving police officers. The SQ would cease to handle such work. Damiano stood her ground. *Let them come to me.* Their patience spent, the BEI men approached Damiano and Pichon. They were both shorter than either of them, older, probably retired cops. Neither the SQ nor the public seemed impressed with their reports. Business as usual was the consensus.

"Chief, Jean Marchand, Louis Dionne. We are here to help contain what will soon be a front-page media blitz. As you know, we are lawfully appointed to provide an objective analysis of these cases. This is what Montreal citizens need and want. We would like to assume the responsibility for this file, although I understand from Detective Pichon you are reticent. "

"I understand your position, but I am dealing with a sensitive issue and before we hand over the case, I'd like to know exactly what happened in this shooting. The officer involved is part of my division. I'd like to hold on until we are better informed, one way or the other. I'm hoping for a complete factual account of the events that occurred the night of the shooting. If I discover a culpable fatality, or a shooting with cause, I will hand over the file. For the time being, I don't wish to make a decision on wild speculation. Can you wait?"

"Reluctantly, we will."

"Thank you both."

A physician in scrubs finally made an appearance two hours later after the surgery. Doucette's wife jumped to her feet and stood waiting to hear if this surgeon had saved her husband's life. He took her aside and spoke with her. The detectives positioned themselves within earshot.

"Your husband is a lucky man. The bullet entered his chest at an angle. He suffered two broken ribs and a collapsed lung. One centimetre to the right and he would not be alive. He's breathing with both lungs and is out of danger. He'll be out of recovery in fifteen minutes."

"Thank you, Doctor, thank you so much. When can I see him?"

"In half an hour. The nurses need time to set him up in a room. One of them will take you to him."

"Doctor, I'm Chief Damiano. Will I be able to ask Officer Doucette a few questions?"

"Yes, after he has some time with his wife, but two minutes, no more."

"Thank you."

Time dragged, and the five of them sat uncomfortably with one another. When a nurse walked through a set of doors, Marie-Claude bounded to her feet and rushed from the room. Doucette was in a semi-private room with the curtains pulled around him. He was awake and raised his hand to take hers. "Thank God, Louis," she wept. "I thought we'd lost you. Next time, listen to me, please." She wept loudly and kissed Doucette's forehead. "The doctor said you were lucky."

Doucette smiled, still visibly shaken, and held his wife's hand. He had four draining tubes attached to collection sacks and bottles. Doucette bore that euphoric glow of one who has survived. The weight of the pain would start the second day. "I ..."

"Don't talk, Louis. I love you and the kids do too. Just rest. I'm so happy I didn't lose you. You'll find a new partner. We'll be okay."

Tears, unbidden, trickled down the sides of Doucette's face, but he kept smiling at Marie-Claude. He had survived!

Marie-Claude kissed her husband on the lips. "Rest." Reluctantly, she rose. "I'll be back in a few minutes. I'm just outside and I'm not going anywhere. Don't try to talk much. Save your energy. We need you at home. I love you, Louis."

She brushed by Damiano who was waiting by the door. "No more than two minutes!"

Damiano walked quietly into the room. Doucette appeared relieved and frightened. "Officer Doucette, I'm very pleased to know you will make a full recovery. I don't wish to tire you. I have only one question. Did Boucher intentionally fire on you?"

Doucette whispered because his throat was chafed and sore. "Boucher was wired driving with a weapon in his hand, and shit scared, so I charged him, and the weapon fired. I didn't know what else to do. Daniel kept me awake on the way to the hospital."

"You are a brave officer."

"Did you tell him that I ratted?"

"No. I gave you my word," Damiano said.

Doucette nodded knowingly.

"Take good care." Damiano left and joined the three men in the hall. She recounted Doucette's response verbatim.

"You are still looking at reckless endangerment with a firearm and a wounded officer. We'd like the file. It's in the best interest of the Crémazie Division. It's also the law, Chief Damiano."

"It's an untidy situation. Can you not see your way clear to giving Detective Pichon twenty-four hours to apprehend Boucher? Then, I'll give you the case and the evidence. I have good reason for this delay."

"I'll want to know what that is. One day, no more," he said in a querulous tone. Damiano was pulling rank she felt. Jean Marchand of the BEI was miffed. He wanted and deserved the case, but his position was awkward. He did not wish to incite an argument with the chief of a division. He'd need her cooperation on future cases. He turned and stomped off.

Chapter Thirty-three

Boucher crouched on the stairs, ready to take the old woman as soon as she left the room. The Jays played on – then they went into extra innings. Her phone rang. "No, no, I'll watch till the end, at least two innings. I'm fine. What did you have for dinner? That sounds dee-licious! I finished up the pasta we made. I love you too. You have a good night, Carmen. I'm fine I said. Don't worry about me." He wished the old bitch would turn off the Jays and go to bed. He was hungry, tense and now achy. Visualizing a cop lying in wait to pounce on an old woman sent a dull chill of shame deep in his veins. The house, the quiet life this woman led alone he saw as accusations of his intentions. The shame didn't last long, replaced by frustration and anger. *Go to bed!*

He wasn't about to injure the woman, but he quickly recalled he hadn't intended to hurt Doucette. If Doucette was dead, he'd be the target of a take-down. Armed and dangerous, that's what he had become. All of this had begun with trying to help a woman he didn't even know. Eating his gun was not an option. He wasn't a wimp. If the worst occurred, he'd choose a cop suicide – run out brandishing his gun, and be shot down like Butch Cassidy and the Sundance Kid. Yeah, if the worst happened, he wanted a splash.

Shit! She was watching the post-game show! He couldn't move. She had a phone and perhaps a safety button. *Go to bed!* Ten minutes later, his patience spent, Boucher was about to rush into the room when he heard movement. The TV went off; the sound of someone moving awkwardly in the room had him crouching back against the wall. He heard the drag of a walker coming out of the room and heading his way along the landing. He tried to melt into the shadows of the wall. The woman, at least the side of her he could see, had a rugged determination he admired. He read pain in the side of her cheek, but she pushed along. She didn't look his way. He figured she didn't want to fall. Boucher waited until she was almost at her bedroom door before he made his move.

He crept up behind her, but the old woman had good ears and she turned. All she said was, "Oh!"

"Don't scream. Keep your hands on the walker. I'm not going to hurt you." Boucher reached around her and took the phone from a pocket attached to the walker. There was nothing on her wrists, no emergency button. "Is the curtain open in your bedroom?"

The woman nodded.

"Do you close it at night?"

"Yes, it's too sunny too early."

"I'll stay against this wall until you close it. I have a weapon – don't do anything stupid. I promise I will not hurt you if you listen to me. Do you understand?" He watched as she pushed the walker to the window and pulled down a blind. "Now, come back and sit on your bed. Do you have an alarm system?"

"Yes."

"Why wasn't it activated?"

"I never forget, but I thought my son might come by. Time just passed, and this is the first time I've made such a mistake."

"I want the truth. Your well-being depends on telling me the truth. Where can the system be activated from? What rooms in the house?"

"The hallway downstairs, the TV room, and the basement."

Boucher thanked the fates that he hadn't rushed into the TV room. "Not from this bedroom?" Boucher began to check.

"I don't lie."

"What's your name?"

"Lena." Lena's heart pounded and the back of her neck was wet, but she did her best not to allow this man to see how frightened she was.

"Lena, I'm not a bad cop. This incident occurred because I was trying to help someone."

"Tell me how." Lena wanted him far away from her daughter. She listened to stall him.

"The woman couldn't sleep nights, her car was vandalized, and they threw trash on her driveway, so I wasted three nights on Goyer, waiting to arrest the pusher. I caught up with him on the fourth night. I tried to arrest him, but he ran, see, and I took off after him. I called for him to stop. He did, but he turned and pointed what I thought was a gun at me. I feared for my life – as an officer I have the right to use deadly force. I did. All I tried to do was help. Now, I've lost a career, my pension, and I'll probably be sent to prison. Is that right? It was a good shoot. I was acting above and beyond and all that crap. Yet, see where I ended up?" Boucher saw the end, knew he was finished, but he wanted to tell his story. He had a desperate need to be heard. "So you see, I need to speak with your daughter."

"That can wait. Right now, I can't go on sitting on the side of the bed with no back support. You look hungry and tired. Italians make the best food, at least that's what we believe. No one matches my meat balls or lasagna. What's your name?"

"Look Lena, I need to talk to your daughter." Boucher was exasperated, but he found he could not be angry with this woman who managed to smile, even with him in her home.

"You need food more and I need a chair! I know you won't hurt me."

"Daniel. My name is Daniel." Boucher was ready to keel over. He was starving and bone tired. He helped Lena to a chair and stood shifting from one foot to another. "I can't just leave you alone. Shit!" He searched the room, tore the top sheet from the bed and ripped it into strips.

Lena wanted to give Daniel a good kick, but that wasn't possible anymore. Twenty years ago, she would have lashed out. But she admitted the years, all eighty-eight, leaned heavily on her.

"I have to secure you, Lena. You're feisty. I don't think I can trust you. You're playing me, but I'm starved, so you win Round One." Daniel tied Lena's wrists and ankles tightly and Lena winced. "That's so you won't move. Are you going to scream?"

"What good would that do?"

"That's just it – good!"

Boucher flew down the stairs, met with open kitchen curtains and remembered the nosy neighbors. He crept into the kitchen, used his small flashlight, found bread, opened the fridge three inches and pulled out cold cuts and mustard. He grabbed a Coke, slapped a sandwich together and ran back upstairs and began chomping.

"They're better with mayo."

"What is it with you, Lena? You have to have the last word. Is that it?"

"I was just saying."

"No, I was saying I have to speak with your daughter."

"No, you don't. I can tell you what you want to know. My daughter says she is frightened of what will happen to her after you are arrested, I guess. She has no intention of testifying in any court. If compelled, she will say all she heard were the shots. Her hearing is still not fully back. The victim knocked her between two cars and she was injured. Other than hearing the three shots, she doesn't remember anything."

"My partner said the cops have a witness."

"It's not my daughter."

"I don't believe you. Get her on the phone."

"If I do, the police will be here shortly. You should sleep."

"Fuck! They have a witness … unless it's that apartment, or Doucette was lying. Get your daughter on the phone: do it!"

"Finish your sandwich first."

"Do you want me to hurt you?"

"You're not a bad man, Daniel. Eat and I will call."

"Fuck. What am I going to do with you?"

"I know bad people when I meet them. I raised three children. Do you have children?"

"Yes. That's the reason why I got involved in this in the first place. You don't know anything, Lena. I shot my partner. He might be dead. Get your daughter on the phone!"

"Another accident?"

"As a matter of fact … oh, fuck this. Get your daughter on the phone!" Boucher pulled out his weapon so fast that Lena almost missed seeing it. She didn't move. Boucher himself seemed surprised by his action because a thought struck him like a knife in the stomach. He'd lost control. He was dog tired and he had no place to sleep. "Your daughter can wait. I need some sleep." His forehead creased in thought as he tried to figure out a plan that would safely allow him to sleep there for a few hours. "Do you take meds or whatever before bed?"

"I have to go to the bathroom. I will not wet myself." She might be powerless, but Lena refused to be defeated.

"I saw the bathroom. It's at the other end of the house."

"My pills are there, in the medicine cabinet."

"Why do you have to be so difficult?"

"I have my dignity."

"Don't you dare scream when I leave." Boucher crept across the carpet, closing two doors and lowering the blind in the bathroom. He went back, untied Lena, helped her to the bathroom and watched her take some pills.

"Well, Daniel?"

"I'm not shutting the door. I'll turn my head. Work with that." When she was finished, Boucher helped Lena to her feet and led her, leaning on him, back to the side of the bed. "I'm sorry." He tied both hands to the headboard, not as tightly as before, but secure. He pulled up a cover. "I'm right here on the floor. I'll need that pillow."

"That was my husband's."

"I'm not going to shoot it. Lena, go to sleep. Don't make a sound. I don't want to hurt you. Remember that." Despite his wildly pumping adrenalin, Boucher dropped off in minutes. He hadn't slept in two days.

Lena lay wide-eyed, unafraid in the night's stillness, trying to work the knot in the sheet. Boucher's steady rhythmic breathing brought a kind of peace into the room and a whiff of envy. *To be young!* In time, Lena felt her hands were stone cold. Panic set in. She thought of a blood clot and her breathing became erratic, so erratic she felt she couldn't breathe. "Daniel!" she screamed. "Daniel!"

Boucher heard his name the second time and got to his feet. He couldn't see Lena but he heard her struggling to breathe. "Jesus!" He lit a lamp on the night table. He reached up and cut the sheet ties. "Try to relax." He began to rub both her hands. "It's the circulation – you'll be fine. I know CPR. Listen to me, Lena. I'm going to put my hand over your mouth. Breathe slowly and deeply through your nose. Try! Try! You can do this. Come on. Dammit, breathe!"

Lena was too frightened not to listen. She breathed through her nose, once, then again.

Boucher watched her. "That's good, Lena. I'll take my hand away, and try to keep breathing through your nose." Sweat from Boucher's hair dripped onto the back of his neck. "Don't stop or try to talk, just breathe. Good! I shouldn't be here! I should be home with my family. It was a good shoot."

"I need water and I have to go to the bathroom."

Boucher and Lena repeated a journey they knew, except that Boucher closed the door to the bathroom for Lena. He helped her back to bed. There was a moment of silence between them, something shared, a trust they understood. Boucher reached into his pocket and took out some bills. "I'll leave you fifty dollars for the window. I have to go. Please, give me a half hour before you call the police."

"Why don't you stay and call the police yourself?"

"I might have killed Louis."

"You don't know that. I won't press charges – you have my word, Daniel."

Boucher's features twisted in grief, in truth, mostly for himself and what he had lost. Boucher was shocked at how quickly his life had unraveled. He wished he had the courage to stay and turn himself in, save what was left of his dignity. Accosting this old woman shamed him deeply. She was braver that he was. "I don't have your faith." He left quietly. Lena reached for her watch and gave him forty minutes. She wasn't shaking, she was deeply saddened.

It was three-fifteen Friday morning.

Chapter Thirty-four

Earlier Thursday night, Damiano was in the kitchen nursing a double vodka. She had to think. She saw both cases falling away from her. What were Pichon's chances of apprehending Boucher in what, twenty hours? BEI would take over and she'd have to give DiMaggio to them. Jeff and Luke were still not home, so she poured herself another double. Dumont was right, but she was Chief Damiano and she would call the shots in the Kane investigation. Her phone rang twice before she heard it.

"Toni, I came down pretty hard on you. I understand, when I calmed down, how tight you and Matte have become." Dumont was sincere. She dealt with facts that didn't shift like people. She hadn't taken into account Damiano was conducting an investigation with a partner she trusted who was a suspect in a murder. She'd been thinking of her job.

"I have to handle the case my way, my mistakes." Damiano realized she was trying too hard to pronounce her words.

Dumont's quiet censure on the other end of the line didn't need words.

"One double. I deserve it. This is a bitch of a job, being chief."

"Stop boozing. I do have something. First, the HIV and other forensics should be out Monday or Tuesday latest. Here's what I do have. We took the video footage from Cleopatra's. I have a dark, mediocre visual of Goldberg entering the club. We cleaned up the video as best we could, and it's Goldberg. I guess he put 'The Sopranos' on pause."

"That's great, Marie."

"Do you want a suggestion?"

"Maybe."

"Wait for results – then you may have him dead to rights."

"I'll consider that, but fear tears things open, too. It's a good setup. I want to find this Henley, question him and have another go at Allen and Goldberg, before I turn my eyes on Matte. If Goldberg or Allen killed Dylan, I don't want to have lost a friend and a great partner. I don't want to destroy Matte."

"I agree, just don't blind yourself to the possibility that …"

"I won't and I can't. Question."

"Shoot."

"What's the plural of Pokémon?"

"It's a singular and plural noun."

"Aren't you the smart one!"

"From time to time. You'll have the video tomorrow."

"Thanks. Oh shit, I heard Jeff's car."

"Dump the vodka."

Damiano did. And she ran up and bushed her teeth twice before she came back down.

"We found all the Pokémon, Mom!" Luke said, jumping like a kid. "Did we walk; well, just across the city! Wow! We're probably one of the first people to finish the game, and we didn't run into any poles."

"Is there some kind of trophy?" Damiano asked sarcastically.

"Don't be mean, Toni. We walked for hours and we got it done!" Jeff shot back. "How was your day, I dare to ask?"

"I wish I had been with you guys."

"Wanna talk, wife?"

"I could use some wisdom."

"I may not be the man for wisdom."

"Most days, you are to me."

"You guys can be nuts!" Luke made his escape down the hall.

Jeff pulled his wife into his arms. "I think you need some coffee."

"One double – my first break."

"You're not going to jail. Why don't we get changed and talk in bed?"

"Sounds very good to me." Before conversation, the couple who often disagreed reached for one another in a familiar embrace that was the miracle of their seventeen years. In seconds, the love was passion, gripping, intense and loud.

Down the hall, Luke heard his mother in his free ear. The other held his earbud. He covered that ear with his hand. He smiled recalling the first love of his life and the noise and passion she had brought to him, the power he'd felt when she was with him. His smile darkened. She had lost her life, and he had been linked to the tragedy. He put the buds in both ears and blasted Coldplay's 'Up&Up' to smother his thoughts and his parents' noise. At sixteen, Luke swore he'd never love again. Eight months later, he was keeping his promise, the debt he felt he owed her.

Jeff and Toni lay together quietly. "How can you still be that wild girl that I first saw seventeen years ago?"

"Believe me, I never pre-plan. We're just lucky. Who the hell knows why? Until now, I've felt utterly alone this past week. I'm trying to hold on to so many reins, but I have no control on any of them. I'm gutted by the possibility of Pierre might have killed Dylan."

"Let me talk – you listen this time."

"For how long?"

"I don't know, just things I've learned. Who knows, might help. First, a new job with more responsibility is never a good fit in that first week. Everyone feels lost. It takes a good year for the fusion to take hold. What you're feeling is normal. Second, Donat had no active case work. He oversaw, dealt with administration and press and was stuck to his desk. If he can't return to work, ask yourself if you want that path. You can't hang on to cases, Toni. You're looking at desk work and stress. Third, in this case, be yourself, follow leads, don't shrink and doubt. Move forward. Follow leads, all of them."

"I have another person of interest. I want to question him. I mean to interrogate four people when the forensics and autopsy results are in."

"What's wrong with that approach?"

"I have new evidence on one of the suspects. I don't want to touch Matte until I'm certain the first three are off my radar."

"I don't see a problem."

"I should drop him from the case."

"Do it!"

"He covered for me and he let me work the sidelines with Luke involved. I already told you that."

"I remember. Fine. Direct him to the sidelines. They worked for you."

"Easier said than done."

"You feel guilty for the years that you were rather harsh and abrupt with him. This is the first time I can recall you working with less confidence, unsteady really. That's how most of us live. Few achieve what they might think they deserve. It's good to see you wobbly and a kinder person. Right now though, take the risks you always took. Pierre is hurting his career and yours."

"He knows that, but he's as stubborn as I am and …" Jeff's arm dropped off her own. "Have you fallen asleep on me?"

A mumble confirmed he had. Damiano curled into her husband's back and tried to let go, but thoughts continued to thump in her head. *When you're really lost, you are alone. Matte became a part of me. Losing him is worse than losing a partner; it's losing a friend. I used his skills. Most of the time, I was a shit. I don't want to be the cop who takes him down.* Damiano heard the quiet level breathing of her husband and she envied him. Jeff was a good man, an optimist, a gentle man. Everything about her was jagged and uneven, tortured. What sleep she snagged didn't help.

Chapter Thirty-five

Damiano was in early Friday morning to tackle the new files. It was difficult to believe she'd been chief for less than a week. It seemed like months. Halfway through the second file, her phone rang. She read the ID and picked up.

The voice was rushed and anxious. "He broke into my mother's house!"

"Officer Boucher?"

"Yes! He spent the night there!"

"Is he still there? Has she been taken hostage?"

Carmen took two long breaths and tried to lower the range of her voice. "I don't believe what I have to tell you."

"Is Boucher still there?"

"He left about forty minutes ago and he gave my mother money for the window he broke."

"He didn't hurt her?"

"Let me finish. He was kind to her, they talked, he helped her to the bathroom, and he told my mother his story. She vows that he's a good man, but very frightened. What caught me off-guard was that my mother, apart from being frightened, actually enjoyed the break-in. It brought some excitement into her life. She's a brave woman who might well have been in the hospital being treated for shock. Instead, she has a story to tell her neighbors. She's some character. She told him to turn himself in."

"Did he tell her where he was heading?"

"My mother said he was very tired and frightened and hungry."

"Officer Boucher is not a bad officer, but he was involved in a shooting. Things escalated from there."

He shot a man in cold blood, a man he knew, a victim who had no weapon, Carmen wanted to scream, but she valued her life and her mother's safety more. "I'm nervous about going in to see you today."

"Stay put for the time being." With that, Damiano hung up and called Pichon.

"I just heard. The woman called the cops, and her call was redirected to me. Have you any ideas where he'd go?"

"Nothing solid, but my gut tells me Boucher might go home. The elderly woman whose home he broke into told her daughter he was tired and

155

frightened. He made a point of telling her his story," Damiano added. "In his condition, home is his best bet."

"I have his house staked out already. I also have unmarked cars on the roads around his place. He's not about to walk in through his front door. The area is secured."

"Half a day is already past. BEI said twenty-four hours."

"Thanks, I needed that."

"Just saying. Keep me updated."

"Yep."

Damiano got back to the file.

Matte was the first Major Crimes detective to arrive and he went directly to her office. "I brought Dylan's bag to Evidence last night as directed, Chief."

"Dumont dressed me down for this technical problem."

"Seeing Dylan's body that night alone and discarded on the roof knocked me off balance. That image is all I see in my head. My complete attention to detail that drives you crazy abandoned me Tuesday night. The evidence *was* locked in my desk. I never touched it, but I know the mix-up is my fault. I'm sorry. I also understand the implications of my lapse."

"Well then, you know it's a chain of custody problem if the case goes to court. You're also aware that the whole case could be tossed. The judge will demand to see Dumont and me, to say nothing of the Crown prosecutor."

"Make me the fall guy. I'll accept the consequences."

"How's your mother? I know she's on your mind, too."

"She's all there, but I thought she might be speaking more clearly. The prognosis is still good, but I guess there are no miracles. Her recovery will take time. She's a fighter."

"Your father?"

"He caught me sleeping. I left immediately. He …. There's no point. He called strike three many years ago."

"Dumont sent us new information. We have Goldberg on a grainy video entering Cleopatra's. We also have a new suspect, somebody called Peter Henley, 'the professor.' Before I haul Goldberg in for interrogation, I want forensics and autopsy results. That should be Monday or Tuesday." Damiano made a show of closing the file. "Sit down, Pierre."

Matte did not take his eyes off Damiano when he sat.

"I have to put you on the sidelines. Dumont found Henley's name, but she also found yours at Dylan's apartment. This is my case. I will interrogate the suspects first and I sincerely hope I won't have to subject you to that damn room. You are implicated, you had contact and then we have the evidence fuckup."

"Nicely put, Chief Damiano."

Matte examined his nails and ran his fingers up and down one palm and then the other. He finished up by cracking his knuckles. "What about my work in the murder room? I can find this Henley for you. I don't want Galt anywhere near my personal life."

Damiano's phone rang and she took the call to break the tension between them. She listened and then asked, "Why?"

"Matthew Allen said Dylan deserved some vigil. The media, the press really, had Dylan's murder on page four."

"Allen is behind the idea?"

"Yes," Velma answered petulantly, "but I fully support the idea. We've called the press and LGBT groups. They will attend."

"When is this event?"

"Saturday night at ten."

"I suppose I'll see you there then." She turned to Matte. "Allen has set up a memorial for Dylan this Saturday with the media and the LGBT folks. That prick just wants the attention back on him. I can't wait for the results. He smells to me."

"Henley?"

"You work it."

"What about this memorial?"

Damiano rubbed her nose. "Truth is, I need your eyes, and I don't want to be there with Galt either. It's at ten o'clock tomorrow."

"Do you want me to pick you up?" Matte fastened intelligent eyes on Damiano when he posed the question.

"I think we should go separately," Damiano answered, turning away.

Before he left, Matte got to his feet and leaned against the wall. "Something broke, right?"

"There's Krazy Glue," she said hopefully, looking over at Matte. Her sense of loss and hope froze in a frame.

He smiled wretchedly and left.

Damiano slumped, staring after him.

Chapter Thirty-six

Earlier that Friday morning, the streets were dark and still. The sky appeared shadowy, blocked by tall trees in full leaf. Boucher hurried to the vicinity of his car, believing cops were in wait for him. The car was there. He walked warily past it to the end of the block before retreating and running to his car. Once he was safely inside the car, he bent forward, resting his forehead on the steering wheel, allowing both arms to drop. He reeked of dried sweat and the stench of fear and dirt he'd smelled on men he had pulled in. He wasn't shaking, but his nose was running. He wiped it on the side of his hoodie. He clung to a thread of hope. What had Lena said about Doucette when he told her he had shot him and perhaps killed him? *You don't know that.*

Boucher started the car up. He wasn't going to be shot in his own car, stinking like some alley rat. In that condition, he couldn't pursue the apartment witnesses. Doucette may have betrayed him, and he'd be easy pickings for patrol cops. He believed Lena. He'd met liars and she wasn't one of them. He drove close to home. Boucher knew how to reach the house from the street behind his home. The house was dark and he was glad of that cover. What if a cop was in the house? He had no other choice but to take the chance his family was alone. Once he'd rolled over the fence, he crawled to a basement window no one ever locked. The family called it their secret. He pulled out a row of bars and slid the window aside. He went through head first. He landed on his hands and left shoulder and winced. *Damn! What a great move, crashing my shoulder in my own house?*

A scurrying of feet brought Boucher to his feet. "Daniel?" Manon whispered in the dark.

"It's me."

"Thank God! The police are out front. I don't dare turn any lights on. I'll come down." Manon was light on her feet and could find her way in the dark better than anyone in the family. She ran to Daniel.

"Careful. I fucked up my shoulder coming through the window."

"Other than that?"

"I'm fine. I need a shower."

"You don't have to tell me. You can shower down here. I have a pen light, but we don't dare use more than that. Wash up and I'll go and make some food. Then we can talk. You have no idea how sorry I am for getting you involved."

For the first time in forty-eight hours, Daniel felt safe. The steaming spray felt good. Soap felt good. If only he could hide forever. The shower ended. His shoulder still ached, but he was at peace, a peace he'd never felt in his life. Manon was waiting on the old brown couch with tuna sandwiches and coffee made in the microwave. He ate hungrily, and Manon waited in silence. "I really did a number on my shoulder." Manon got up and went behind Daniel and massaged it. "Mmm, better."

"Daniel, the police make a house search every five hours. They will be here at seven."

"Do they have warrants?"

"What do you think?"

"Are the kids awake?"

"They're escaping through sleep."

"I thought of going out gun blazing."

Manon paused. "I'll be standing beside you – are you choosing for me?"

"I'm just fucking tired. I can't believe this is happening to me, to us."

"You have an hour and a half – why don't you sleep."

"With you – you can set the alarm."

"I think you're safer down here."

"I can share the couch."

"Two people on that old, stinky couch?"

"We made children on this old thing. Come on …"

Manon scrunched in beside Daniel. "Watch the shoulder. What about the alarm?"

"Do you think I can sleep?"

Manon fought to stay awake and lost.

Just as early that morning, Carmen DiMaggio had driven out to her mother's home and the two were sitting on a brushed pink velvet couch. Carmen, as Carmen would, was in the middle of a speech about the values of alarm systems. Lena was listening patiently. "Mom, I know you are not paying attention, but what if something … how could I ever forgive myself?"

"Look, Carm, fifty dollars for the window. He wasn't a bad man. I wasn't afraid at the end. He was kind and scared. He was never rough with me, never!"

"He shot a man in cold blood."

"That's what you think, Carm. Stories have many sides."

"Oh, for God's sake! Are you telling me you don't believe *me*?"

"I believe you and I believe him – that's not impossible. You read the victim was a drug pusher. I hope you won't change your mind and testify against this officer."

"The man had his hands up. Know what, I give up. You're impossible."

"Life is not black and white. I learned that once more today."

"That's how I see it."

"If memory serves, not always, Carm."

"I hate when I'm wrong. I'm just happy we are both okay. I've missed you."

"Me too. No one can change the world, Carm. He wasn't a bad man. I should know."

The banging on the door woke Daniel and his wife with a start. "Get out of those clothes. We have some down here. I'll go to the door. I'm going to tell them you will turn yourself in peacefully, but no cuffs."

"What about what I want?"

"You have a family who love and need you – your wants are superseded by our needs. Now, change and join me upstairs. You are a brave man, Daniel. Don't choose to be a coward!"

Boucher was shaking when he met the police at the door, but he left without hand cuffs and he looked back at Manon. She knew he was grateful the choice was made for him.

Chapter Thirty-seven

Chief Damiano, as requested, joined the SQ detectives in the board-room on the first floor of the Crémazie Division awaiting the arrival of Officer Boucher. They had decided to question him and outline the charges he was facing before escorting him to intake. Damiano filled them in with the facts of the B&E. She repeated, "The woman is adamant that she will not press charges."

"Does she know Boucher?"

"No, but she liked him. He opened up to her. Go figure. He also left money to fix the window." Damiano thought about connecting mother and daughter, but protected DiMaggio. She was the chief. Her word meant something. Besides, the mother was not about to press charges.

"This is some weird shit."

"Such is the stuff of life."

"BEI has backed off. Now, what about this witness you have on the shooting?"

"From the outset, she swore she would never testify. She was knocked between two cars by the victim and hurt, perhaps even concussed. What she saw, were she willing, might not hold up in court."

"Well, what did she see? Don't play me, Chief Damiano," Detective Pichon expressed forcefully.

"She heard Boucher call for the perp to stop. He did and turned, rais-ing one arm and pointing with the other."

"A weapon?"

"She thought the perp was pointing, but she'd struck her head, so she might not have seen the weapon."

"Did she think he had one?"

"At first, she thought it was his finger, but she's repeated that every-thing happened so quickly ... "

"That she could be mistaken?"

Damiano did not want to put DiMaggio at risk. She paused.

Pichon broke in. "We can compel her."

"Or, you can play Boucher. We do that. He doesn't know what she saw. He also doesn't know if Doucette divulged anything."

"That's a tactic. I'll work to break him down. He must be fried by now.

I'd invite you to sit in, Chief Damiano, but this is my investigation. I'll need to contact this witness if we can't crack Boucher. I know you are trying to shield the witness, but civilians have obligations. We should work together."

"They are also real people with legitimate fears."

Pichon ignored that last statement and began to lay out sheets of notes. He was prepped.

The patrol car with Boucher in the back seat made its way slowly through the traffic on Highway 13. Boucher tried to compose his thoughts, but the weight of his actions and the taste of humiliation bore down on him like a man buried under twelve feet of sand. He labored to breathe, and the passing cars upset his stomach. His eyes settled on the door handle and then remembered the doors were locked. The job was his life, and he had just blown it. He could taste his stomach bile in his mouth and he shoved his hand over his mouth and swallowed hard. He tried to steady his knees, but he choked and shifted on the seat.

"Are you alright back there? Do you want water?"

Boucher waved off the question, did his best to lie back until they pulled into the bowels of the division, and he was led to the first floor. When Chief Damiano opened the door, she thought Boucher looked stunned. He probably was, she thought. He stiffened his spine and followed her inside the room.

Detective Pichon hadn't bothered to stand and his partner took his lead. "Sit on the other side of the table, Officer Boucher." He began to read his notes. "I would advise you not to say anything. I will tell you what we have. You should get hold of a union rep and a lawyer. When we first spoke with you the night of the shooting, I ordered you not to interfere in the investigation if you wished to continue working for the SPVM. We know now, with ample evidence, that you disregarded that order. You did so with rather clumsy and dangerous attempts to direct the investigation yourself." Pichon stopped and read his notes. "While we are still looking for a lockdown on the weapon found on the victim, the primary conclusion leads us to believe that the weapon was yours."

Boucher stopped himself from speaking up and fought back tears. He shook his head.

"We do have proof of reckless endangerment with a firearm resulting in the wounding of a fellow officer, your own partner. That action carries with it a felony charge. You must be aware that we cannot solve this problem in-house."

Boucher could not contain himself. "But Doucette ..."

"Are you about to say charged you?"

Boucher nodded firmly.

"Officer Boucher," Pichon said icily, "Officer Doucette charged you in an attempt to save his life. While he blames himself for the wound, to protect you I would say, you threatened a fellow officer with a weapon! I distinctly recall you telling us you were not a rogue cop. You cannot make that assumption today."

Boucher leaned back as though he had been struck.

"We also have evidence of a B&E, although the victim refuses to press charges. You appeared to have made a friend there."

Lena wasn't lying.

"Finally, we have witnesses to the shooting. There will be no bail. You have shown yourself to be a flight risk."

Witnesses, plural! Boucher couldn't stop himself. "I thought he had a weapon. I was trying to take him in, trying to help a terrified woman."

Boucher was startled by the door opening. Two officers appeared in the doorway. The detectives rose. Pichon spoke. "Please escort Daniel Boucher to intake." Pichon had decided not to try breaking Boucher. Cutting him down was simpler. He methodically shut down Boucher's life. He deliberately omitted Boucher's service on the force in his report. Pichon had no use for reckless officers.

Boucher sat, forlorn and almost invisible. He stared at Chief Damiano in a desperate plea for help. "I'll go down with him," she said to Pichon whose shoulder shrug suggested he didn't care. In the next seconds, Boucher was hustled from the room. He walked as though he were timing his steps, degraded and vulnerable. The one thought he held onto was that Doucette had betrayed him. He was the only person who knew the perp he'd shot was unarmed. He wished at that moment that he had killed Doucette.

In minutes, like the frames of a film, he was taken to the control desk, walked to the side wall, printed, mugged, searched and jailed in cell twelve. He faced the back wall of the cell, trying to hide from the hovering presence of fellow cops. There was a cot, no blanket or pillow, a toilet bowl and a single roll of toilet paper. He looked through the cells and saw one suspect four cells down pacing. He felt the heat from the lights and the scrutiny of eyes. Prison pipeline is second to the blue line. Every cop knew he had turned on his own.

Damiano stood at the control desk and told the duty officer, "Strict suicide watch." She wanted to say something to Boucher, but decided not to interfere.

Boucher didn't move a muscle. Thoughts roared through his head. No one had mentioned he knew the perp. The cops didn't know that Jacques Fillion had run for his life. Boucher had warned him out of Laval. "If I ever find you dealing, I'll bust your balls." Well, he had. What had he sworn at the crime scene? *I'm not going down for this! I'll do anything it takes.* Boucher was crushed. *I was only half right. I'll die before I go to gen pop, the rat cage.*

He couldn't end up another common criminal. He wouldn't allow that to happen. He curled up on the cot and pulled an arm over his eyes. He had to think. *I won't go out this way.*

Chapter Thirty-eight

Damiano went back up to the sixth floor office in time to see Denise Roy happily carrying more files to her office. "Let me take those from you, Denise." Damiano could have sworn the secretary was smirking. "Have you been in touch with the chief?"

"Of course, Pamela and I have spoken." Insulted to have been asked the question. "We've always had a close working relationship and friendship."

Damiano wanted to say, "Well, Donat is not working, he's recovering, so you had better try being more cordial with me. I can be very unpleasant." She'd deal with Roy another day. Damiano took the files into her office. She thought of checking on Matte, but she had no doubt that he was working. They needed their own space for the time being. It was only Friday afternoon. The test results seemed a way off. Damiano thought she'd caught a break when her phone rang.

"Chief Damiano."

"Perhaps I have been improperly connected. I was hoping to speak with the detective investigating the murder of Dylan Kane. I'm sorry for the inconvenience."

"You are?"

"I apologize. I'm Marcel Beaubien, president of Montreal's major LGBT association. Many of us will be attending the vigil at Cleopatra's for Dylan Kane on Saturday. Till now, there has been little publicity. I was wondering if you have made an arrest."

"M. Beaubien, we are in the early stages of the investigation. We hope to close as soon as possible."

"I have to say I am very pleased to know you are handling the case, Chief Damiano. Sometimes still, we have to fight alone."

"Rest assured the murder of Dylan Kane is receiving the utmost attention."

"Thank you for this special assistance in this tragedy."

Damiano was about to feel good about the call when her phone began to ring and didn't stop. The media! She had experience with the hordes and delivered her stock response. Next, she called for three patrol cars to work the Kane event. Her objective was a close look at Matthew Allen who had set the wheels in motion for the vigil. She recalled Allen didn't know

Dylan's last name or where he lived, or so he said. For the remainder of the afternoon she paid close attention to the paperwork and was saddened once more by the assaults and battery on women. She took a sip of cold coffee, hoping to prevent a spiral into depression. Her case, in a sense, was going nowhere till she had the lab work. It had plateaued and then lost ground to a customary dip that triggered the threat of a possible unsolved. She hoped Pierre located Peter Henley. He was batting a thousand.

She grew tired of the files because she had no involvement, a comment and a push here and there didn't provide her with any enthusiasm. Damiano decided to check up on Matte's progress. To her surprise, he'd left the door open and hadn't heard her approach. It wasn't spying, she told herself; she was surveying her partner, a man she'd rarely noticed in action. He was sitting up straight, like a young student, though he was just a year younger than she at forty-three. Even from behind, she saw his notes set out in an orderly fashion, his pen in hand, the phone in the other. He was calling universities looking for Henley. The bottle of water hadn't been opened. He was still in his jacket, and Damiano realized she'd never seen Matte in shirtsleeves. Whatever image he'd constructed of himself, he protected. He was cleverly effective in his thoughts and work.

She was about to stop watching and enter the room when she saw that Pierre had dropped his head into his hand, his shoulders shaking. Damiano wanted to comfort him but knew she couldn't. He was so alone, not close to his family, no friends he ever mentioned, dismissed or barely tolerated by colleagues and often bullied into work by her. She tiptoed back a few steps and made some noise before she walked into the room. Pierre turned away as he rose, trying to hide in front of her. He recovered himself and arranged the image Damiano saw every day.

"I'd like it if you'd pick me up for the vigil. It's all over social media, so we are looking at a circus."

"What time?" he asked, relieved. "When you say a circus, you mean a Mardi Gras. Expect masks and costumes and flags. It'll be wild! It's funny, Dylan was a quiet person. He would never have gone to something like this. He liked attention, one on one, because he needed it all focused on him. I know and agree that we all prepare a persona to meet the faces that come into our lives, but most perceptions are partials. Does anyone ever see the whole person?"

"Ten o'clock. Did *you* know Dylan?" Damiano asked.

"Hmm, I think I saw more of him than Goldberg did – then again I'm not certain. Dylan was a beautiful schemer. He could make you believe he loved you. For a while he carried you along that ride. I see now it was all the same shtick. I loved the face he showed me and most of the flaws. Funny thing is I wanted a life with him. I never felt that way with anyone. I live day to day and didn't see the next chapter. I never gave any thought to ending up alone. But I suppose we all deceive ourselves. I wanted something that wasn't real. No matter, I loved Dylan. He's still inside me."

"Is there a chance some guys at Cleopatra's might know you?" Damiano asked, changing the intimacy of their exchange back to work.

"I'll deal with that. I'll see you tomorrow at nine, an hour travel time."

"I'll be ready. Let's call it a day. Saturday will be a long night."

"I'd like to keep at Henley. He may have taught at Concordia University. Dylan had some actual work, editing essays a year ago. Henley wasn't the name I recall. I'm dealing with Fort Knox – 'we cannot give out private information, no, not even a name.' I'm in the midst of checking each faculty member. Henley might be a full-time professor. In that case, he'd be listed in the faculty directory that Concordia posts online."

"I wonder if Caitlin Donovan ever heard the name. It's worth a try. I'll do that before I leave. Take some down time before tomorrow. The vigil won't be an hour." Damiano made the call, but as expected, Donovan was of no help with Henley. She drove home past orange cones and detours, using her horn. By the time she arrived, Damiano was in no mood to cook. Her first smile of the day broke when she smelled the grill and found Jeff with trout and corn. In addition, he always made the best salads. Damiano stood taking note of her good fortune, to be loved and fed. A combo hard to beat. Before work enveloped her thoughts, Damiano walked out to the deck and caught Jeff off guard. "Thank you for you! I am so lucky."

"About time you realized that," he said, smiling. "About time! What brought this on?"

"Pierre has nobody, and I haven't helped him much." Damiano said, teary-eyed. "We're partners, even friends. I never thought much about his personal life. I hope he's not involved."

"I do, too."

Friday night passed quietly, but Damiano was back talking shop twenty-four hours later.

"I don't want to be chief. I like working cases. I'll make more time for you and Luke. By the way, where is he?"

"Out with friends. Don't get carried away with sympathy promises. Nobody changes. You're still in that vulnerable stage. It doesn't last. The old girl I know will be back. Still, I'm glad to hear them. You haven't been in the job a week, don't make rash decisions."

"I feel out of touch with everybody, you guys, Matte, Dumont. The detectives on my shift barely say anything. They used to tease me, just stuff. I miss the chief. So much has changed. Donat might not be back; Matte is in limbo till I close the case. I don't even feel like my old self. Maybe sober with no sleep is not good for the cop I used to know. I'm most afraid of losing Matte, and worse, having to take him in."

A repeat performance with trout and corn seemed appropriate to Jeff since Damiano was back on the same subject. He wondered why talking didn't appear to tire his wife. It fortified her. Standing at the grill, he turned the cobs, and Damiano went on. It didn't seem possible a whole day had passed. When she finished, he put the food on the deck table he had already set up. The blue and white umbrella offered a welcome sense of privacy as it had the night before. Their neighbor's home wasn't especially close, but he did spot the man at the window a few times over the course of every summer season. "Sit. I never have to tell you to eat." He watched Damiano dig in with gusto. "Every detective wanted the chief's job, so they are envious. It'll take time for them to accept you. Get over the pity party. I've always respected your arrogant 'tear-'em-down, take-'em-in' style. It's what made you a good cop, perhaps not a nice person."

Damiano was halfway through her second cob, with a few kernels sticking to her bottom lip, but she was listening. She got rid of the kernels with a flick of her middle finger. "I'm not as tough as you think I am."

"Ha! Well, get a grip, Toni, tackle this case, be thorough, don't stall, question Matte when you are forced to, and close. People's lives are complex and love, in whatever form, especially love's decay, is at the base of most heinous acts. Matte is not your only suspect. Remember that."

Damiano wiped her mouth with a few napkins. She'd demolished the dinner and her fingers were sticky. "I should listen to you more often. That's good advice."

"Sometimes, I manage to hit it out of the park."

"Thanks. Gotta run. Matte's picking me up for Cleopatra's gala."

"Why? I thought …" Jeff asked, throwing his arms in the air.

"I had a weak moment."

"It happens to the best of us."

An hour later, Damiano appeared in a very modern navy blue midi dress. Around her neck, she wore a gold pendant. Tan heels and a simple gold bracelet complemented the style. She wore clothes well.

"Trendy and alluring!" Jeff gave her two thumbs up and a swat on the bum.

Damiano heard a car and went to the front window. "He's already outside, early as usual."

"You better hustle. Remember, stay the course."

Chapter Thirty-nine

Matte actually got out of the car, ran around the back of his Volvo and opened the passenger door for Damiano. "Chief!" He, too, was nicely dressed in tan pants and a blue blazer over a white shirt and navy tie. He looked improved, younger. That was Matte's aim, Damiano thought.

"Enough with the 'chief!' I should have figured you for a Volvo. It's unadventurous and secure for a man or woman who doesn't want to take unnecessary chances. Yet, there's Dylan and risk. You're right. Who knows anyone? We humans are a puzzle."

"Mostly true, but I like the drive, and it's a little different."

"I won't touch that one."

"Just not part of a repetitive assembly line." Matte dropped south from Peel onto Ste-Catherine and turned left.

"Why do we want to take Ste-Catherine? It's jammed. Nothing moves."

"You'll see," Matte hoped. They drove or edged forward two feet at a time. Matte knew Damiano would soon begin to hum and fidget. They stalled and he felt growing heat from his passenger. Twenty minutes later, Matte shouted. "The answer!" A car was pulling out, and Matte used his hazards and left signal, satisfied. "I use my scheme like the old Chicago 'Policy Game' – put up a buck a chance and see if you win. And, this time I did."

"This isn't the corner of St-Laurent."

"It's a four-block walk. This way, we'll avoid the jam-up now and later."

"How do you know each block? You're reminding me of a directions guide! How do you find the time to learn this stuff? Do you ever sleep?"

"I extend my skills to other tasks." Their conversation was banter undercut by what wasn't said. One block from Cleopatra's, they ran into the gay crowds and a blend of curious Montrealers. "Stay behind me. I'll lead you safely inside. Cleo's should have hired crowd control." The costumed group were in high spirits, ready for a bash, something very different from a vigil. *Dylan would have hated this mock show,* Matte thought.

Velma made it a point to be on the lookout for Chief Damiano. She, too, had dressed for the evening in solemn black that highlighted her mane of auburn hair. Nervous and excited, she spoke too quickly and almost hopped from one foot to another. "I'm very happy you came, and thanks for the patrol outside. There are so many more people than we expected. We had no photo of Dylan, so I contacted an artist I knew, and Matthew coached her with the details. You'll see the results. You can stand with me. That way you won't be pushed around. I may have a problem. There's this man, in costume, of course, who has been drinking heavily, so I thought …. He hasn't been a bother, but he might become one."

"We're Homicide. You have bouncers for that sort of thing, don't you?"

"The problem is he's paying for his drinks and all, but when I walk past him, I feel he's angry. Matthew thinks the guy could be a jilted lover."

Damiano and Matte exchanged a thought. "Where is he?"

"It's become so crowded so quickly, but he's over there at a ringside table. I see others have joined him. Just as I'm talking, people have crowded behind him."

"Can you guess his age? You must have gotten a decent look at him."

"I purposely brought him a drink to see if we had to get rid of him, so I'd guess mid-forties. I told him we were having a vigil and he might not want to be present. He took the drink and didn't say anything."

"Keep the bouncer on alert," Damiano said. She and Matte hoped they'd spot the man at some point.

People kept pouring into Cleo's, completely obscuring all the ringside tables. Velma and both detectives were bumped twice by the incoming crowds, jockeying for positions. "I have to go." Velma's face brightened. "I'm opening! This is so sad and exciting. It's almost unbearable." With Velma's signal and her flight up the back stairs, the music directly behind Damiano and Matte blasted and thumped. Matte cupped both hands and shouted into Damiano's ear, "We'll be deaf if we don't move."

Damiano shouted in Matte's ear. "Let's push our way to the right." They elbowed past the DJ's speakers. The room began to vibrate with sound. Cleo's spread like a balloon ready to burst. Finally, the front doors were shut and kicked by patrons on the street wanting in. A few minutes later, the music stopped. It restarted with Mary Hopkin's haunting 'Those Were the Days' and although the room grew silent for a moment, everyone began to sing and band together until Cleo's rang out with the special lyrics 'we thought they'd never end,' and at the end of that song, the music died. Lights shone on the dark stage. Velma descended the back stairs. A spotlight followed her to a portrait covered with a black sheet. The silence was eerie. As Velma drew the sheet off the portrait, a second spotlight illuminated a decent portrait of Dylan Kane. Damiano was awed by the silence. Velma raised the mic and began. "I didn't know Dylan well, but he came to Cleo's, like most of us do to get away from the chaos of life. He found us. He was one of us. Tonight we celebrate the loners – we're a big bunch. A quiet thought for Dylan Kane, please!" You could have heard a pin drop. It reminded Damiano of the silence at the Bell Center the night the fans paid silent tribute to the great Canadiens hockey player Jean Béliveau. A minute later, the music blasted 'Cabaret' and the show was on.

A performer brought out the rainbow flag, and, one by one, the performers, body painted with a color of the flag, acted out each theme: red – life, orange – healing, yellow – sunlight, green – nature, blue – serenity, violet – spirit. The first actor introduced its creator, Gilbert Baker. The crowd was wild, music bounced off the walls. Dylan Kane's image was highlighted throughout the show. Two hours in, the music stopped, the performers melted from the stage and a lone figure held the mic and introduced himself as Al Packham, in homage to journalist Al Palmer, who chronicled the gritty and gossipy side of Montreal's night life in the fifties. Damiano and Matte recognized the performer as Matthew Allen, aglow with the attention. He was familiar with Mark Antony's iconic rebuttal because he used its scheme and form. "Dylan was my friend. He was a quiet listener, a lost soul, I thought, a peaceful guy, but someone thought differently. The night he died he bought me dinner. And yet somebody... Dylan is not here today because someone took his life."

A lone voice howled, "Dylan was a slime ball who got what he deserved." The shouter rose and pushed his way towards the front doors. Matte and Damiano shoved and elbowed their way trying to follow the man out of Cleo's. They had the disadvantage of being on the other side of the room and lost precious time sandwiched inside a human mass reluctant or unable to move. Cleo's was filled well beyond capacity. What they hadn't seen was Matthew Allen fly from the stage and tear after the runner. Velma had signalled for the DJ to pump out music. "Play 'Cheap Thrills' and turn it up!"

Allen ran and jumped over chairs, knocking patrons back against one another by bracing his elbows and opening a path for himself. He plowed his way past them and out onto the street.

The intersection of St-Laurent and Ste-Catherine was still crowded and rowdy. Neither Damiano nor Matte could see Allen or the runner. When they finally hit the streets, they found themselves stuck in another crowd. Matte shouted, "What do you want to do?"

Damiano looked in all directions and then shouted back, "I have no clue." Then she heard screams coming from across the street and saw people running in that direction. They flashed their badges, zigzagged between honking cars on Ste-Catherine and ran to the commotion farther down the street. A crowd had already gathered, and people were visibly disturbed by what they were seeing.

"Don't! He's already hurt! You'll kill him!" Men had grabbed some assailant and were trying to pin him to the ground. The fallen man lay unconscious, his face a mask of blood. "Is he dead?" A woman fell to her knees and felt for a pulse.

Matte reached the mêlées before Damiano, but not by much. He pushed his way to the front of the crowd and confronted Allen. "What did you do?"

Allen yanked himself free of four men, got to his feet and shrugged. "He had no right to malign the dead."

Damiano was kneeling down with the injured man. "Has someone called for an ambulance?"

"Yes," a male bystander answered, "two minutes ago."

"Did you find a pulse?" Damiano asked the woman with the wounded man.

"He's alive but unconscious." She wiped some of the blood from the man's mouth to allow him to breathe more easily.

Damiano got to her feet and confronted Allen. "Why did you do this? Aren't you the man who does not engage?"

No one moved; every person wanted to hear what Allen was about to say. He was unruffled. "My intention, Chief Damiano, was to hold this man until you got here. That's what I told him very clearly. He yelled that he had a right to exercise his freedom of speech. He pulled away from me, and I grabbed him again. Next thing I knew, the bastard nailed me with a solid shin kick. I'm sure I'll be able to show you the bruise. Quite simply, I head-butted him and he went down. Legally, I had the right to do just that."

One of the four men who'd held Allen said, "He smashed the guy's nose. He coulda killed him! The guy might have hit his head."

"A nose," Allen scoffed, "mine's been busted three times. Teenage boxing did a number on my nose." With that he knelt down beside the man, felt the damage and, holding the bone between his thumb and forefinger, he snapped the nose back into place. "He has his nose back," Allen said smugly. "No big deal."

They could hear the ambulance. In minutes it arrived, the man was attended to, lifted onto a stretcher and rolled into the ambulance. Matte said, "I'll go with him." He asked a paramedic where they were taking the man. "Here are my keys. MUHC. I'll call you."

Damiano knew Matte wanted to know the identity of the victim and his link to Kane.

Allen approached Damiano with his hands held together for the cuffs. "I'll go peacefully, Chief. I was just trying to help."

"The rest of you clear out, please." People moved away, as slowly as slugs. They hoped the action wasn't finished.

"Well?" Allen asked, raising his hands. "He maligned the dead. That's low."

Damiano was thinking of the paperwork and Matte's car. Where would she put Allen? She wanted to be at the MUHC. "Stop performing! We may charge you with assault. I want to hear what the victim says."

"I bet my bruise is quite visible as we speak."

"We will be seeing you. Go back to Cleo's."

"I'll walk you back. One never knows."

"I'm in no mood for games."

"What? No thank you? You know I'll be around when you want me again. I'm not going anywhere."

Damiano fumed and took off, hoping she remembered the whereabouts of Matte's car.

Matte sat beside the victim who was coming to. "You'll be alright," Matte said reassuringly, placing his hand on the victim's shoulder.

The man was in a foul mood and disoriented. "Get your hands off me. You have no right to touch me!" Despite his protestation, the man ran a nervous hand through his brown hair. When he looked up at Matte, he was seeing the detective through milky brown eyes, stained bloody.

"You're in an ambulance, and you are safe. I'm Detective Matte. Why did you run from the club?"

"I didn't want to be mauled by idiots who didn't even know Saint Kane," he said, scowling. "Look at all this blood!" He touched his face, and his hand came away bloody. "I'll be okay?" he asked, frightened.

"You will be. What's your name?"

Suspicion creased his forehead. "I don't have to tell you," he shot back. "I didn't commit a crime. Why is a detective with me in the first place? Did you arrest the asshole who broke my nose?"

"Tell me what happened."

"I got out of Cleo's. Two blocks down, this guy jumps out in front of me, blocking my way. He says you guys want to talk to me. I didn't break any law, so I try to go on my way. He jumps in front of me again. Twice more, so I let go with a kick and next thing I know I'm lifted into an ambulance. Look what he did to me!"

"You laid hands on him first. He could press charges."

"A little bruise for a smashed face?"

"That's the law."

"I already asked you why a detective is here with me."

"I'm investigating the murder of Dylan Kane. I was at the club tonight. How are you connected to Dylan Kane, Sir?"

He was about to protest again, but the alcohol and the face butt had taken their toll. "He left me a changed man. That's all I'm prepared to say."

"I'd like your name, please, in the interest of justice, Sir."

"I'd like my life back," he whined. "Justice for whom? Where is my justice?"

"You must have realized there would be a police presence at Cleo's. You wanted to be heard. You must have known you'd just made yourself a suspect."

"I set the record straight – that's all I intended. Now, back off. I have nothing more to say."

"Except your name, Sir."

Their new suspect didn't say another word. The ambulance drove onto MUHC grounds, and seconds later, a paramedic opened the back doors. Matte stayed with the suspect in Emergency and called Damiano.

"Use your badge at the triage desk to get his name."

Matte tried to smile in sympathy as he walked past ailing, helpless patients on stretchers back to his suspect.

Chapter Forty

Boucher stood sullenly as he watched the only other prisoner taken from his cell and led out the back door to a van. If he couldn't think of something, he, too, would follow another cop out to a waiting van. He knew the desk cop casually, so he'd have to work some blue sympathy. "Officer Robson, I haven't had my phone call. May I make it from the cell? My wife will be frantic. I have kids, like you probably."

Robson didn't answer. He poured himself another coffee and pretended to be busy with a file.

"I'm not asking for a favor. It's my right, isn't it?"

Robson put down his mug, closed the file, opened the wooden door behind him and walked around it over to Boucher's cell. "I'm two years past my pension, done with favors" he said. He looked around to be certain they were alone. "My friend in Laval tried to help your sorry ass, told you how to proceed and walk away from the shoot. You chose to fuck up."

Boucher saw a short, paunchy cop, heavy on his feet with gray skin from too much work in the bowels of the division. Skin creases around his mouth and eyes stood out starkly when he spoke. "It was more complex than he thought. I still owe him."

"More complex than it is now?" Robson tried not to scoff. "You're not hungry?" The spaghetti and milk carton hadn't been touched.

"Can I have a freakin' fork?"

"You're on suicide watch. Use your fingers."

"The call – come on, I'm owed that. I can't be processed to gen pop."

Robson saw the terror in Boucher's eyes. "I'll put in a call – get permission."

"The phone's right there. All I want to tell my wife is that we need a lawyer. Give me the phone. I'll be off in seconds."

"That's how quickly I can lose my pension. You forgetting you shot your partner?"

"I know. The truth is he charged me because he thought I would."

"What does that change, Boucher? Your partner is lying in a hospital."

Boucher squeezed his eyes shut to keep from screaming. "I know that. I still need that call."

Boucher was still a cop. Robson padded back behind the desk and made a call.

Boucher wiped the sweat from his face and waited, cracking his knuckles. He exhaled when he saw Robson heading his way with a phone. "Thanks, man. I mean that."

Boucher knew immediately that Manon was crying. "Listen carefully. We need a lawyer. Stop crying. We haven't time for tears. They're charging me with a felony count for Doucette. A rep's of no use to me. I need a good lawyer."

"We have fourteen thousand in savings – that's all we have. We'll have to take out a second mortgage on the house."

Boucher cut in. "We can't."

"What? When did you do that, Daniel? Of course, that's that car of yours. Why didn't you tell me that's how you managed to buy it?"

"I made yet another selfish mistake. Doesn't matter now, does it? You'll have to go to your parents. We need money. They can mortgage their house. What now, Manon?"

"What about your parents, Daniel?"

"My father has never helped me out of a scrape in my life. Believe me, he wouldn't help now. Whenever we needed him, he disowned us. He's some operator. His money is locked up."

"I have my job."

"And I have no salary. We need help. You got me into this, Manon."

"I had nothing to do with you shooting Louis – you know that."

"I know. I know, but I'm desperate. We're desperate. We need the best lawyer to get me off, or I'm done. Did you hear me? I'm done. I'm not a criminal! I'm still a cop! I still don't get why all this happened. Do you understand any of this? Do you?"

"What kind of money are you talking about?"

"Fifty thousand."

Manon wept. "I can't ask Dad for that kind of money."

"Did you hear me? I can't be transferred from Crémazie. Your family loves you. You have to find some way to work this. I'm only thirty-four. I can't be done. I wish I had never heard of this woman. I'd be home now. We didn't even know her, Manon."

You had to be a cowboy! "I'll go tonight," Manon wept. Her body began to shake as soon as she hung up the phone. Nerves stung every part of her back. She left a note for the kids. Dinner was in the fridge and they could reach her at their grandparents. The kids already knew which ones to contact. She changed quickly, wiped her face, applied sparse makeup and drove to Dollard-des-Ormeaux on the West Island. She sat in the car for ten minutes before she had the courage to walk up the short cobbled path and ring the bell. Her parents had owned the semi-detached together for forty years. It was a simple brown brick with siding and a single garage. The house, her mother had boasted, was paid off fourteen years ago. The inheritance from the house her parents had proudly promised would be divided among the three children. Her mother planted red and white begonias every year that were meticulously watered and dead-headed to encourage growth. By the end of the summer, they would have the fullest flowers on the street. Her father cut the grass and was often on his hands and knees picking out weeds. It was a proud home.

Manon bit her bottom lip as she rang the bell. After she married, she always used the bell. Her parents deserved their privacy. As usual, her mother answered the door.

"What a lovely surprise!" That emotion evaporated when Nicole saw her daughter's face. "I don't know how that just slipped my mind – I was just so happy to see my little girl. Come on in. We're in the kitchen." Nicole gave her daughter a quick hug and led the way.

Her father's antennae sensed the reason for the visit. "Sit. How bad is it? Nicole, sit down. We don't need coffee, honey. We need to listen. Tears won't help. Now, start at the beginning. Omit nothing."

Manon looked around the room and saw that nothing much had changed in the kitchen since she was there as a child. The placemats she and Daniel had bought in Miami were still on the table. It must be fifteen years! The patterned wallpaper with its pictures of kitchen appliances had yellowed over the years but it was clean. Her mother washed the walls every year. She wondered how long her father had the mug he was holding. They had supported and raised three children. She saw for the first time that her parents had begun to look alike. Tall, gray-haired, tanned, simple people with kind faces. How could she ask her parents for fifty thousand dollars?

"Take a deep breath and talk to me," her father said with authority. "Dial back the tears."

Manon took every second of twelve minutes without a break. Her mother reached over and held her arm.

"I can see where they have a felony count. Daniel's still at Crémazie?"

"Yes, but he's really scared of being transferred, processed to …"

"He's made himself a flight risk. That's serious." Her father scratched his forehead, shaking his head. "He'll need a lawyer alright, a good one."

Manon dropped her head and pressed her palms against the table until her fingernails turned red. "That's why I've come here, Dad. We need money. I'm so ashamed to have to ask."

Marcel looked at his wife. "What kind of money are you talking about?"

"We have fourteen thousand in savings. Daniel says we need fifty." Manon could not go on. Her voice rang hollow in her ears.

"We don't have that kind of money," Marcel said. Nicole was crying. "Your mother and I are not old enough to collect the Canada pension. We live on my one pension. We've planned our first Florida trip in three years, sharing a condo with friends."

"Daniel was thinking you might take out a second mortgage for us."

"What about your own?"

"Daniel took out a second mortgage for his car."

"Well, honey, sell the car first." Marcel raised his hand to Nicole. "I will write you a cheque for one thousand dollars. That will give you fifteen thousand. Sell the car. You should get twenty. I'll reluctantly take out fifteen thousand against the house. I can't believe I'll have house payments again. It's very distressing. You do understand, honey, that this fifteen thousand will eventually be deducted from your inheritance. What about Daniel's parents? You will probably need more than fifty. Can you support the family on your salary?"

"I don't know, Dad. Daniel says his parents have never come across for him, ever. We have no chance there. Thank you so much."

"I'll go with you for the car. I'll get that twenty. Daniel will still take a loss, but he needs to be accountable."

"Daniel loves that car."

"The last thing Daniel needs right now is that car. He's looking at prison time. If this lawyer can work magic and he walks with community service, he still has no job, and I don't see that he'll ever work security. He has a felony on his record now. He's cut himself off from both opportunities. He's off the force forever. Don't blame yourself for this. Daniel made this mess. What the hell was he thinking, pulling a weapon on his partner? Go home and have the car washed. First thing tomorrow morning, we sell it."

"Dad and Mom, I don't know what to say."

"Get some rest. I still have some connections on the force. I'll hunt for this lawyer. You need one who knows how to work dirty cops and find glitches in technicalities."

Manon flinched at her father's description and then hugged them both and hurried back to her car.

Chapter Forty-one

Detective Matte waited for Chief Damiano beside the triage cubicle. He didn't have long to wait. "Hey! It *is* Peter Henley. Sometimes we do get lucky. He lives on Monkland Avenue."

Damiano looked at her phone. "It's eleven forty-three. It's late. Let me have a crack at him, and I'll decide what we do tonight."

"And I'll go check on my mother."

"Pierre, it's a little late for that. You're probably not permitted on the floors."

"Trust me. There's no one around during the day. It'll be deserted at night. I'll do a sneak run. I want to be certain she's asleep."

"Don't use your badge to gain access. I don't want this coming back on me."

"Yes, Chief Damiano," Matte growled.

"You know what I mean." Damiano saw a nurse nearby and approached her, asking if there was any place she might interview a suspect. She didn't need more than twenty minutes, a half-hour at the most.

The nurse was on the bad side of forty and was no amateur. "Who are you?" she enquired, taking stock of Damiano's dress and shoes. "It's a hell house tonight. Patients are packed in here like Millionaire sardines."

"I'm Chief Damiano from the Crémazie Division. This is a murder investigation, and Mr. Henley is a suspect. To respect his privacy I can't interview him in a hallway, but I have to question him tonight."

"Well, we all work for Joe Public. The floors are out and the cubies are full. Let me see if I can displace a patient for twenty minutes. I can't give you more time than that. This is a hospital after all."

"Thank you, Nurse. I'll wait right here." Minutes later, she saw Henley being wheeled into a room. The nurse walked back to her. "Cubie seven – twenty minutes!" Then she disappeared among the patients. Cubie was an apt description for the white claustrophobic cubicle with no window, a stationary examining table and a chair. The walls were completely bare. Once Damiano closed the door she knew the room would be sweltering in five minutes. She was right, and she hoped the conditions would work for her.

Henley's spirits rose and fell when he realized she wasn't a doctor. "I thought they were bumping me up. I've already told your partner I have nothing to say without a lawyer."

The fellow was pitiful. Blood had caked outside his nose and seemed to have blocked his nostrils. It had dried on his mouth and cheek. Henley was breathing through his mouth. He was a slight man with intelligent, clear eyes, but Damiano noticed dried blood on both hands.

Henley followed her scrutiny and said, "I'm a mess. I can see that. Anyway, it's not the first time in my life I have been beaten up. I'll survive. I haven't changed my mind about answering questions."

"You can listen. You told my detective that Dylan Kane had taken some part of your life. I can only assume Dylan harmed you in some way. I don't think you are referring to the time spent or love lost in the relationship. We all take those chances and bear the scars of lost love. I have a very good idea of what you've lost. I have to know where you were this time last Saturday, with or without a lawyer. A lawyer won't change that answer. You'll have to verify your alibi if you have one. You're very angry, probably with cause; but that anger gives you a reason to harm Dylan Kane. Now, you can change your mind and speak to me or you can come down to the division Monday at nine sharp. Here's my card. That's the address. Is there anything you want to say?"

"All the bullshit of how gays are coming together as a family, marching as one for the victims of the Orlando massacre and all other victims, is a crock. I suppose it's not much different in the straight world. No one cares. You're on your own. When I was a kid, I always felt if I ran to a group of kids, I'd be protected from the taunts of the schoolyard bully. Even that was never true. Kids just stood around watching, cheering him on."

"And?" Damiano said, steering the flow to the present. Henley wanted to be heard. That was the reason he went to Cleo's, the reason he howled his anger.

"I'm not pretending I have it more difficult than anyone else, but I have to take medication. Coming to terms with epilepsy by admitting the illness was difficult. For years, I chose to fall, pass out and injure myself, risk my life and the lives of others. I hid my illness because I had to work. I needed to drive. I'm not the only person to have taken these risks. My story isn't new. When I totalled my new car last August, I finally surrendered, saw a neurologist and now take the meds. I felt good about myself. I'm a healthier person today, a better person. People hide for all sorts of reasons, being a gay kid was just another."

He paused, and Damiano waited in silence.

Henley started to bury his face in his hands but pulled back and winced. The surface of his face was raw. "I always practice safe sex. I have no illusions about partners. The truth is not something I often find in the men I have known. That's probably a universal fact. Dylan had said he was tested for HIV every month. That one night, I took a chance. I didn't bother with protection," he said bitterly. "Well, I paid the price all right, and I will for the rest of my life."

Damiano whispered, leading, "Dylan was different."

Henley tried to smile, but pain twisted the attempt into a grimace. "I thought so."

Damiano watched Henley closely. She had never known betrayal until she thought of Matte threatening to expose her. She could only imagine the deep ache when a broken trust threatened your life. She waited again for Henley, checking her phone for the time.

"I wasn't in love with Dylan. It seems like yesterday that I was the young boy old fags sought out. It still rankles at how quickly roles change. I took Dylan for what he was, a beautiful boy who needed fathering and a home in exchange for intimacy. He was a natural, and easy to live with. It took a week for me to realize he didn't work. Odd, really, he had nothing. He was Peter Pan. I played it safe with him, until he finally convinced me he was tested monthly just as I am, to avoid a life-long cocktail of pills."

Damiano couldn't stop herself. "Why not see someone your own age?"

"They have too much baggage. Sometimes young men can be more trustworthy – the young have hope and youth. But I suppose I've just proven my theory false. Yet, look at the guy who butted me. If you hadn't shown up, I'm sure he would have stomped me."

Damiano had been given a twenty-minute window for questioning. She had only one minute left of that time. "Everything I've said should be proof to you that I can't trust anyone ever again. I'll see you Monday at your office, but, for the record, it took every bit of courage to go to the vigil and shout that diatribe. Murder? Detective, suicide is like murder in the sense that they both require courage. Do I look like someone who has the courage to commit murder?"

"You have motive. You might not need courage if you want revenge." Damiano opened the door and watched Henley wheel himself out. Damiano wanted to thank the nurse, but she was nowhere to be seen. She waited for Pierre at triage.

While Damiano waited at triage, Matte was standing in the doorway of his mother's room. From the street light that splintered through the trees, he could make out his father asleep in a chair beside her bed, his head back, slightly to the side and snoring. His legs splayed, like a man who took up a lot of space. Matte tiptoed inside and stood at the end of his mother's bed. She had turned on her side away from her husband and had pulled her pillow across her head to block out his noise. Matte crept over to that side and very gently knelt and kissed her hand and held it. He couldn't see that she was awake until she gently squeezed his hand. Neither spoke. He rested his palm against his mother's cheek. He knelt there and smiled at her before he rose and kissed his mother and left as quietly as he had entered the room. *I'm sorry, Mom. I wish ... I'm just who I am.*

Matte made it to the elevator and was surprised to see a nurse as the doors opened. "You shouldn't be here," she said.

"No problem. I'm leaving." The elevator door closed.

Damiano was pacing with her phone in her hand when he arrived.

"Anything?" Matte asked.

"His life story."

"Anything in the epic we can use?"

"Just as I hoped he would tell me his whereabouts, he announced he'd meet with us on Monday at nine with a lawyer."

"Any gut thoughts?"

"Nothing I can cuff. Your mother?"

"Holding on. My father was asleep in a chair. I crept around to her side, and she knew I was there. Mom knows I haven't forgotten her and she's a fighter."

"I just thought of this. Henley did say that if the crowd hadn't arrived, he felt that Allen would have stomped him."

"We can't do anything with that. He felt – he might have been wrong."

"Agreed," Damiano said, "but I believe him."

"Same problem. Let's head home. It's been a long day." Matte took off his jacket, folded it and opened the back door of the Volvo and laid the jacket across the seat. When he slid into the driver's seat, he started to roll his sleeves. "Oops, I better remain presentable for you, Chief Damiano."

"You can be annoying, Pierre." *Despite your wisecracks, I haven't forgotten that you are a suspect.* The mood on the ride home turned quiet but uneventful. Damiano slept through the night, a rarity. The next morning she went running with Jeff and Luke. At noon, she made lunch. Sunday afternoon, Damiano snuck off to the office to work on files. That afternoon, Damiano left her guys without the usual guilt load that dogged every weekend departure.

Chapter Forty-two

Matthew Allen wasn't ready to sleep. He wished he'd cornered that jerk on a side street. He should have waited, allowed the asshole to make a turn. He ran his palms against his thighs as he walked back to Cleo's early Sunday morning. The party would be revving up. He was in no hurry. When he was across the street from the club, Allen was surprised to see streams of gays leaving, evaporating, like fans emptying a ballpark when the game was lost. *What happened?* Allen ran across St-Laurent on a red.

The dark club was empty, except for stragglers and Velma who sat mid-stage, crying. Allen jumped up onto the stage in a single leap. "What the hell happened, Velma?"

"You ruined everything!" She dragged the portrait of Kane around from behind her. "Look! You knocked it over and stepped on it as you ran out. I now have to pay the artist who lent it to me eighty dollars. Why didn't you let the police handle that man?"

"That asshole ruined the vigil!"

"He was running out of the club. It was a single tirade and then it was over."

"Those detectives would have lost him because they were on the other side of the room. He defamed Dylan. What's worse than that? Dylan is not here to defend himself, so I defended him. He was my friend. Can't you understand, Velma?"

"Matthew, let's just clean up. I need some help."

"Then you don't understand, right?"

"I'm tired. It's been a long night that ended badly. Let's pack up and call it a day. I'm tired and down."

"I'll help you. Of course I'll help." Mathew jumped off the stage and started straightening tables and chairs. He watched Velma climb the back stairs to change. Still in a slow burn he shoved the chairs under the tables, loaded trays with dirty glasses and brought them to the bar. Velma walked back down soon and joined him to finish up in silence. The cleanup took well over an hour. Fatigue had aggravated both of them. "Answer my question, Velma. Do you understand why I went after that guy?"

Velma knew she was making matters worse, but common sense lost out, too. "What was it between you and Dylan?"

"What are you talking about? Are you accusing me of being a fag?"

"Calm down, Matthew, I'm just asking, because honestly, I don't understand anything about that relationship."

"Relationship? So, you don't get me at all. We've known each other, and you still don't get me. Dylan was a friend, like I thought you were."

"Were? That's good." Bristling, Velma shot back. "He was some friend. You talk to him for hours – he takes you to dinner, even though you said he never had a dime. You don't see something weird there? I bloody well do!"

"You bitch. What, were you jealous of Dylan? Is that why you pretend not to understand?"

"Matthew, I wasn't jealous of this kid. I like weird people, but if you can't see that there was something off the rails between you and Dylan Kane, well …." Velma went on, "He hung on to your every word and you kept talking like you desperately needed his attention."

"You noticed all this. You had the time between your busy low-grade productions to track my stories? I'm the one off the rails? You're hallucinating, you are mental!"

"If my productions are that bad, why take part in them? Why do you come here? You with all your daredevil accounts, how do you end up in a B-joint working with me?"

"That's what a mental case does, veer off course – confuse the opponent."

The hairs rose on Velma's arms and she backed away. "I'm tired. I just want to go home. Please leave. I'd like to lock up."

"I'm not leaving till we settle things."

"Settle what, Matthew? I didn't even know what I was saying. I was pissed at you for ruining the evening. Let's call it a day. I may be mental – the shows may be lackluster. Right now, I want sleep and a good drink to knock me out."

"What if I don't allow you to leave? I want you to understand that Dylan was a friend."

"Alright," Velma said, capitulating.

"That's all you have to say?"

"Matthew, it's late. We're both fried. Please let it go." Velma pointed to the door.

Matthew ignored her. "I liked Dylan. That's all. And I would have busted up that drunken foul-mouth if we'd been alone. He busted up our vigil didn't he?"

Velma said nothing. Her nerves were on edge.

"Did you hear me, Velma?" he hissed.

Velma nervously twisted a few strands of hair. "Yes."

"That's all you have to say."

"I didn't mean to suggest anything." Fear crept into Velma's voice.

"Didn't mean what?" Matthew took a few steps closer to Velma.

"To suggest anything more."

"Finally!" Matthew said, relieved. "Let's go."

"Matthew, I may be to blame, but I am really upset. I should go home alone."

"You already owe money for the portrait. Come with me. Look at my hands – see how steady they are?"

Velma squeezed her eyes shut, but tears fell anyway.

"You're crying now? I'm not going to touch you. I'll take you home. Lock up and let's go."

Velma thought of running when she was on the sidewalk.

Matthew stood beside her, smiling. Once Velma was inside the car, she didn't say another word on the drive home. Matthew drove at break-neck speed, braking hard at stops, running others. Velma kept her hand on the door handle, hoping to see a patrol car. That didn't happen. When Matthew stopped abruptly in front of her apartment, Velma's body jerked forward even with the seatbelt. "Don't be a tight ass. I was kidding. Dylan was a friend – that's it. I'll be there next week. You'll need me to set up and make contacts. We're a team."

"Thanks for the ride," Velma said quietly, edging out of the car. Matthew burned rubber for effect as he took off. Velma reached the front door shaking. In the elevator she started to cry. She struggled to insert the key into the lock of her unit. Finally, inside her place, she turned on all the lights, headed for the kitchen table where she dumped the contents of her bag. "That detective gave us her card. I hope I kept it." Her hands were still shaking. As usual, she finally found the card as she was about to give up the search. It was wedged in with other bag paraphernalia. She held it with both hands, breathing hard. "I don't want Matthew at Cleo's ever again. He could have hurt me. He's a nutcase." She fingered the card. "If he finds out I called …. Oh God, what am I going to do?"

Velma tossed and turned all night. The card lay on the night table. Twice she turned on a light to be sure it was still there, and twice she padded to the front door to check the double bolt.

Chapter Forty-three

After Spitzer had left his condo, Nate sat alone in the dark with his third double scotch. The phone rang just after midnight, Sunday morning. He was slow and clumsy searching for it in the darkness. When he recognized the number, he fumbled for a light and shook his head violently, trying to sober up. "Rachel!"

"Are you alright?"

"Of course, a little lonely maybe."

"You're drunk."

"That too. Why the late call?" he mumbled.

"We drove back early. I had enough family. I love them dearly, but three days, whoa!"

"Gotcha." Nate was quite pleased he managed to get that word out in his condition.

"I know I'm calling late, but I just listened to a voicemail for you, asking if you were okay, with the police and all. Diane was worried about you because the nurses said you didn't seem well during a surgery. Police, what does she mean?"

What a busybody! Always has her nose into everything. "I'm a little drunk and missing you and the kids. It's been one of those weeks." He was sobering up better than he thought he could. Nate could not confess then. He wanted the test results. Besides, it was too late, and he wasn't brave enough to lose his family when he didn't have solid control of his faculties. He was scared shitless. He didn't want to shatter Rachel – to hurt her so badly that she might not recover emotionally. He realized he hadn't thought of her. He had zeroed in on his loss. At that muddy moment, he knew he'd hear Rachel break. No, not till he knew. He couldn't wound her until he knew for certain. That was fair, he told himself.

"What about the police? What did a detective want with you?"

"A patient of mine suffered multiple fractures to his right arm. Apparently, there was an issue of domestic abuse. The police asked me if the patient had confided in me when I spoke with him before we put him under." Nate was amazed at how easily he lied and fabricated.

"Really? I mean did he, tell you, ?"

"No, but I knew he didn't injure his arm falling down stairs. There was no other bruising on his body. He beat his wife so badly, she's critical. I heard that from the police."

"What did you tell them?"

"I couldn't say anything. He didn't open up to me."

"Yes, but you knew his story stank."

"Patient confidentiality."

"Really, Nate!"

"I might have been wrong – I didn't want to implicate myself, I guess."

"I'm disappointed with you."

"I'm disappointed in myself. This week I have no set surgery for Thursday. I was thinking I'd drive up Thursday morning, barring emergency surgery."

"Sure, you wuss. I thought you wanted a little freedom from the usual humdrum."

"Freedom is not what it's cracked up to be."

"A cliché from my genius. Why are you drinking, Nate? That's not like you. Unsteady in surgery? That's not you either."

"I had trouble sleeping and then this guy who hurt his wife – it all just got to me. They have a five-year-old. I wonder what I'm doing sometimes. I spend my days cutting when all's said and done."

"Stop with the clichés, Nate."

"Blame the scotch."

"Do you want me to drive in to see you today?"

Nate sat up. "No, no. Take care of yourself and the kids. I'll see you Thursday, four days from now. I love you, Rachel."

"I love you back, a lot of years back. Please don't even contemplate a mid-life crisis. I'm stuck with two teenagers and their moods!"

"I'll sober up. I'm really glad you called. You're still the neat woman, girl really, that I ran after and caught up to on Mount Royal."

"Go to bed, Nate."

"You too."

"I'll make poached salmon and creamed potatoes for Thursday. Right now, stop drinking, shower, don't fall, and then go to bed. That's an order."

"Night, Rachel." He'd make the call tomorrow – he never heard of anyone rushing to the endgame. Monday he'd have his answer. Monday was time enough to do that. He was also due in surgery at nine. Work first, clear the decks. He'd wait till the afternoon. He didn't want to rush. Nate needed to think, plan. How would he begin to explain himself to Rachel? He needed the right words. He knew the power of words to hurt. Panic began to set in. He tried to stand, wanted to clean up. Instead, Nate flopped back onto the couch and drank until he passed out, until the sting of all his actions eased. The crystal glass fell from his hand and rolled a few inches on the carpet.

Chapter Forty-four

Chief Damiano was in the office at her desk before seven making notes about all the suspects: Matthew Allen, Nathaniel Goldberg, Peter Henley and even Pierre Matte. She was printing on index cards using bullet points. Her phone rang. *"Dammit, can't I catch a break? I don't start till eight!"* She reached across her desk for the phone. "Chief Damiano." A terrified voice on the other end of the phone tried to speak coherently. Damiano couldn't understand a word. "Who is this please?"

The sobs continued amidst wheezing.

"Who is this?"

"Velma. I'm sorry, but I have asthma," she finally muttered. "I had to wait a whole day to call you."

"Take some deep breaths and try again. I have a very busy day."

"I'm scared. I have been for twenty-four hours."

The words clicked. "Of Matthew?"

"Yes."

"Tell me what happened."

It took Velma six and a half minutes to recount the events. Damiano was counting.

"You're not back at the club till Friday."

"That's right."

"Go to your regular job. Do not contact Mr. Allen." Damiano wondered if she should reveal that she'd be calling Allen in for an interrogation and decided against disclosure.

"What do I do if he calls me?"

"You don't want to further antagonize him, so speak as though things are back to normal. I have recorded this conversation."

"That's okay. I want you to know. I never knew this side of Matthew. I heard of his exploits, but I didn't know how angry he is or how violent. I was afraid he was going to hurt me."

"I was going to suggest another officer. I'm Homicide, but call me if he just shows up or threatens you. Are you okay with that?"

Tears again. "Thank you, Chief Damiano. I really mean that. I'll do exactly as you say."

"Stay away from him. Don't walk home alone. Check your apartment before you enter to be certain Allen hasn't found his way inside," Damiano warned Ms. Dawson, aka, Velma.

"I was right. This is serious," Velma said, more frightened.

"Let's say you are using necessary precautions." Damiano hung up, played the recording and made notes that she added to Allen's index card. She saw Matte and two detectives arriving for duty. All three gave a curt acknowledgment of her presence, a first on the floor. Her phone rang again. Damiano saw that it was Dumont. "Marie, how are things going?"

"We're ready to meet with you at Crime. Belmont has agreed to be present with his results."

"That's good news."

"Well, not all. I conferred with a Crown prosecutor regarding Kane's belongings. Forensics has some results, but they are still working with them. Unfortunately, whatever evidence we have recovered and continue to recover is corrupted. None of the findings would stand up in court. I'll discuss this when we meet, but ..."

"But what?"

"For the meeting, I do not feel it appropriate to have Detective Matte present. It's my belief that he knew the full consequences of his actions."

"Not that he was emotionally devastated?"

"Maybe both, but he is a servant of the law first. He should never have been on this case. I'm not attempting to ride a white horse here. I've made my share of errors. This fallback hurts us both. I don't want the protocol minefield he created here at Crime. Simply, until Detective Matte is no longer a viable suspect, he should not be privy to forensic information."

Damiano fumed and wanted to point out to Dumont that she was chief of Major Crimes, and, in a sense, Crime worked for her. On the other hand, she recognized the validity of Dumont's position. "I'll see to it that Matte won't be present."

"I gather that nothing has changed regarding Matte's status."

"He is a suspect, and I will conduct his interrogation, but last. We have two strong suspects and perhaps a third. Matte is the fourth. I have an interview with the third suspect at nine. When would you both be available to meet?"

"How about one this afternoon?"

"I'll be there."

Dumont knew her friend. "Would you like to have another detective with you for notes?"

"Know what? I've had to work on so many files this week that I can actually read my notes. I'm using index cards. Can you beat that?"

"They still make those things?"

"I don't know. I had a drawer full of them, intending to use them. I just got lazy when Pierre came to work with me. He has a hold on detail and he can print flawlessly. He could print Hallmark cards. He's that good. The mother lode is that he enjoys charting and note-taking! Did I luck out or what?"

"I do hope he comes up clean, Toni."

"Me too. See you at one. Just a second!" Damiano had a small brainstorm. "Would you mind if I brought a detective from Domestic Violence with me to set up the recording? That way I won't miss anything, and Pierre wouldn't be Major Crimes' gossip. If Pierre is our killer, they will know soon enough. If not, I don't want him to endure further stress. He's had enough in his life."

"I have no problem with that plan."

Damiano called Matte into her office. He stood waiting as she finished a last scan at her questions for Henley. "Sit, for God's sake. Crime wants to meet with me this afternoon. Dr. Belmont will be there."

"What I'm hearing is that I'm excluded. Is that correct?"

"It is, Pierre. Once you broke the chain of custody holding onto Dylan's belongings, you gave Marie good reason to be angry."

"She thinks it was intentional then?"

"Afraid so."

"And you?"

"I know how gutted you are. We all make mistakes. It's just that you generally don't."

"You're on the fence, then?"

"Where would you be in my position?"

"Sitting up there beside you."

"Thanks, Pierre."

"Will you share any of their findings with me?"

"When I see what they have, I'll decide. Do you mind if I take Henley, protocol that's all. You shouldn't be openly involved. You understand, right, Pierre."

Matte was about to object, but changed his mind. "Go ahead. I'll be in the murder room."

Damiano checked her phone, took a file and elected to walk down to the fifth floor. Carrot head wasn't hard to spot, and he saw her at the door because his desk was in its line of vision. She waved him out and explained what she needed of him. Excitement lit up his face though he made every effort to appear controlled and serious.

"Detective Gilles Biron, Chief. I'll get what we'll need and meet you at the back door at twelve-thirty. We're not going far, but there are orange everywhere." He turned and left. Damiano swore he walked back with shoulders raised, thrilled. She was also impressed that Biron wasn't inquisitive. He reminded her of a young Matte.

She decided to walk down the five flights to the entrance to wait for Henley. He and his lawyer were early, already standing outside the front door. In the last twenty-four hours, Henley's bruised and swollen face had become more pronounced than she'd have expected. She opened the doors and forced herself not to stare at his face. "Follow me please." Once they were seated across from her in the interview room, Damiano felt alone and twice looked over to where Pierre would have sat. The lawyer introduced himself.

"Paul Ashford, Chief Damiano."

Damiano acknowledged him and recorded the time, date and names and the file number of the Dylan Kane case. "Are you feeling well enough to proceed, Mr. Henley?" His eyes were slits; his nose swollen and purple. "It looks worse than I feel."

"Then we can proceed. How long were you involved with Dylan Kane?"

"Five and a half weeks."

"What happened?"

"He promised to prove to me he was clean on a Tuesday night. I was having doubts. He didn't show that night and never came back. I knew I might be in trouble. Turns out I am. Had myself tested and the end result is that I have to take an NRTI cocktail for the rest of my life. I discovered that four hundred people are infected every year."

"I'm sorry," Damiano said. "The HIV infection was the reason you attended the vigil and spoke your piece, wasn't it?"

Henley looked at his lawyer and back to Damiano.

"Yes."

"Mr. Henley, where were you on Saturday night, June seventeenth?"

Henley's lawyer gave him the go-ahead. "I was in Emergency at the Jewish General Hospital, complications with the meds."

"The whole night?"

"I called my sister, and she picked me up just before eleven. As soon as I was home, I went straight to bed."

"Did your sister stay with you?"

"She has a family, three kids, so I told her to go home."

"Crime has video of the club, inside and out, of that night. Is there a chance they will see you there? Do you have a photo of yourself with you?"

"No."

"To both questions?"

"Yes."

"Are you on Facebook?"

"Isn't everyone?"

"Open your page, please."

Henley complied. Damiano reached for Henley's phone and sent herself a photo.

"Can she just do this?" Henley snapped at his lawyer.

"Facebook is a public site. You didn't refuse."

"Damn, man, you should have told me to!"

"Mr. Henley, you have no alibi for the time of the murder. I'll have Detective Biron contact the hospital to verify your statement. Mr. Henley, we will be in touch."

"Why?" Henley asked, shocked and infuriated. "I can verify that I was ill and spent four hours in Emergency. I lost electrolytes with all that vomiting. I was in no condition to murder anyone!"

Damiano knew something of low electrolyte counts. "Did they administer an IV saline solution to bump up your count?"

Henley's face looked even worse angry. "The nurse gave me a glass of orange juice, and they told me to drink a lot of fluids, not coffee."

"You weren't in peril then."

"I thought I was. I vomited five times."

"At the hospital or in front of your sister?"

Henley's lawyer tapped his client on the shoulder and whispered.

"You think I was setting myself up with an alibi?"

"I look for possibilities. Dylan Kane was murdered later than eleven. You had the time to get to Cleo's, sir."

"If I *had* murdered the little shit, why would I attend the vigil and draw attention to myself?"

"Arrogance. All murderers are arrogant. I've learned that over the years."

"I may plead to arrogance, but I am a professor of Renaissance literature. My weapons are words. You should have learned that over the years. Paul, I'd like to leave. I don't think I'm under arrest. I have had enough."

Damiano's interview terminated at nine thirty-one.

Henley and his lawyer left in a huff.

Damiano stopped the elevator at the fifth floor. Biron rushed over. She told him what she needed. He took her phone and sent himself Henley's photo. "I'll have his story checked before we leave for Crime." Walking up to the sixth floor, Damiano thought of Matte alone in the murder room and felt like a traitor.

Chapter Forty-five

Detective Biron drove past orange cones and stalled traffic, typical of Montreal urban chaos in spring and summer. "Chief, I just wanted to know what exactly you want me to do, apart from recording their findings." Before Damiano had a chance to answer, he continued, "It's a few years ago, but I had a decent system of note-taking at McGill. I even sold copies to friends who wanted to be lazy and use mine. May I take notes? I'd feel more involved."

Damiano knew a good thing. "Well, with our recording, my notes and yours, I think we will do very well together."

Detective Biron wanted to know what had happened to Damiano's partner, but knew not to ask. He was in a good place. They reached their appointed meeting on time. The forensic review room was located at 1701 rue Parthenais, SQ-1, on the second floor, in Montreal's East End. Dr. Belmont, in his standard whites, had already arrived and had the time to set up his documentation in neat piles on the table. Beside him, Marie Dumont was thumbing through hers. A tech wheeled in a video screen at the end of the room. The team was ready and, Damiano could see, prepared.

"Chief Damiano. And you are?" Dumont enquired as she sat down beside Damiano.

"Detective Gilles Biron."

"Chief and Detective Biron, I think I'll let Dr. Belmont begin with the autopsy results. I'll follow. Doctor, you have our attention."

"Thank you. I'd like to begin with an apology. I originally promised to send the full report days ago, but the victim, a thirty-year-old male, became a case study. I'll explain why later. The COD is unchanged, asphyxiation. As I said, the victim died from a carotid restraint, anoxia, a chokehold in your terms. The TOD has been narrowed down with an examination of the stomach contents. The closest I can estimate the TOD is between one and two-thirty Sunday morning. I did recover matter from the index and middle fingers. Dumont has those results. I maintain again with assurance, from the angle of the fracture, that the assailant was taller than the victim. There was no semen on any of the clothing or on the victim. I repeat that the sure hand of the assailant precludes a random hate crime or a lover's argument. I'd have much more information if this young male had met his death at the hands of cases I've just named. I tend to repeat myself, but I still maintain that the assailant knew his victim, and that you are investigating a premeditated murder.

"The victim did bite his assailant on the arm. Initially I believed on the forearm. I now include any part of the arm. No blood was drawn, but we detected clothing fabric caught between his front teeth.

"The victim himself has become a case study. He is infected with HIV. His tox panel came up clean. I found no evidence of the HIV cocktail, a combination of Integrase Inhibitors that I would have expected from an infected male. Further surprisingly, his tox panel was clear of any drugs, even counter drugs. The early and continuing symptoms of the virus detected in an autopsy should be swollen glands, rash, irritated throat. If he were alive, the list would include fever, stiff joints, digestive problems and weight loss. This victim could have infected others, but he himself, though infected, continued to enjoy good health. He very well may not have known he was infected. These discoveries brought me to Massachusetts General Hospital and Harvard University. They have found that one in every three hundred men infected with HIV carry the protein HLA-B. That protein works with the immune system to, and I quote, 'grab pieces of the virus and drag them to kill cells.' This protein will, they hope, translate into a cure for the virus. I suggest that you ask the next of kin to donate the remains of Dylan Kane to science. His death was solitary and vile, but his body might play a significant role in saving lives. His family will be recognized for their gift to science."

Damiano, Dumont and Biron listened attentively. Damiano wrote a note to herself to get the mother's number. Kane's mother needed to know these results.

"The body of Dylan Kane is ready to be released to the next of kin. My hope is that it will be donated to science. The mother will receive thanks from the department and a testimony to her son that might be of some solace at this difficult time."

Damiano had a question. "If the victim had been tested, would the HIV have been detected?"

"Yes, it would have, just as I traced it."

Damiano thought of Pierre and wondered if he knew Dylan had never been tested. This threat gave Pierre another motive to kill Dylan. Pierre took great care of his health and his appearance. In addition to the heartbreak and theft, now there was the possibility of an HIV infection. Damiano closed those thoughts down. In time, she would have to confront these motives. Damiano wasn't deliberately sleeping on solid leads. She simply wasn't ready to destroy a partner she still trusted.

"Thank you Dr. Belmont. I know you are a busy man, so you can leave if you wish," Dumont said.

"I can stay for a while."

"I'm glad to have you. I start with the video from Cleo's, but before we show the video, I'll brief you on what we found. The screens in the club are stationary, so we cannot control or readjust what we are about to see. That Saturday night, we were able to locate the ringside table and see Dylan Kane talking to Matthew Allen. Two other photographers are seated with them. Run the segment now please, David."

Damiano saw Kane leaning across the table to hear what Allen was saying. As Dumont pointed with her finger, Damiano caught the side of his face. He was young and animated, and appeared slighter than the photo she had seen of him. He was dressed in black, a color that made anyone appear slimmer than they actually were. She felt a pang of sorrow for Kane, something she had felt the night he was found on the roof and when she saw the dive Goldberg had rented for him. Kane never knew how vulnerable he was. Damiano tried to block out Kane as she studied Allen's face in the video, intense and dominating. What was it between these two?

The video ended. "Any questions?" Dumont asked. "Fine. Let me tell you about some interesting things we noticed in the video. First, regarding one suspect, there is a time of great interest to us. It was twelve thirty. David, roll till I tell you to pause."

Damiano and Biron paid close attention.

"Pause, David. There's Goldberg! He's just standing by the front door of the nightclub, trying to find Kane, I expect. David, give me a close-up. Good."

"That's the surgeon who was not at home with *The Sopranos*," Damiano said.

"Right." Dumont continued. "I tried to keep tabs on Goldberg, but he disappears from the screens. Maybe he intentionally evaded them because the cameras are fixed, and a person can avoid them. I have one shot of the stairs that lead to the second floor. Apart from people standing on them, I can't spot Goldberg. We did find an exit on the first floor, past the bar and the women's washroom. That short hallway is very dark, and there was no camera setup. Goldberg might have left that way if he knew there was no surveillance. At least you know that Goldberg was at Cleo's the night of the murder."

Damiano and Biron stood and walked closer to the screen. "You're right, Marie," Damiano said. "He could also have slipped up the stairs and not be caught on camera."

"I have two last segments and both are interesting. David, please. Because of the crowd, the visual is not clear, but you can make out the ringside table. Allen is not there. You can see Kane rise and head toward the camera, and it's only a partial of Kane as he heads for the stairs. Pause, David."

"He looks happy," Biron said. "It's not often we see a victim minutes before he dies."

No one added anything to that comment.

"David, show our last segment. It's a scan of the club with the video from three cameras. We could not locate Allen anywhere on the floor."

"He told me he was in a bathroom," Damiano said.

"He knew the cameras' blind spots, but we clearly see the two washrooms. Even after an hour he never comes out of either one of them."

"Could he have been on the stairs taking photos?"

"I don't see how we missed him, but that's possible I suppose due to the limited video camera range."

Damiano asked her favor very carefully. "I have another suspect. Could you possibly see if you can find him?"

Dumont grunted and took the photo. "For the record, no other pickups."

Damiano nodded acknowledgment of her thanks. Matte had not been caught on camera. "Remember Marie, we think the perp may have come up the outside steel fire escape stairs. They're weighted and make a hell of a sound coming down. And they were down that night. Pre-prep from the killer who knew of them beforehand. He had a plan."

"I haven't forgotten. David, we're done. Thanks. I have some results, but not all of the forensic testing I was hoping to have. Ready?"

Damiano was pleased to see that Biron was ready to take notes on his laptop.

"I'll begin with the fabric found lodged in the front teeth of the victim. We tested Kane's clothing; the evidence did not come from the victim's clothing. Considering its location, we have grounds to believe the fabric belongs to the perpetrator. The material is also black, good quality, and better for our perusal. I sent the specimen to Toronto for further testing: thin-layer chromatography, which examines the color combinations and ID infrared spectroscopy. If lucky, what I hope to receive from that lab is the brand, manufacturer and, at very best, a list of the sales and locations. If this shirt was custom made – we're in! If the brand is high quality, not as good, we begin a further search.

"From the roof, we have seventeen palm prints varying in quality. We found a lone print on the spike fence. I found nothing on the side railing. I was surprised. Some of the prints are smudged, others are better. None are excellent. Like fingerprints, palm prints are based on the aggregate of formation we find in the friction ridge impression. We study flow of the friction, the presence or absence of detail on the ridge and the intricate detail of a single ridge."

"In layman's words – do you have a palm print I can use?" Damiano asked.

"What would expedite this process is a palm print from the suspects," Dumont added.

"I'll need search warrants or voluntary prints," Damiano said with little hope. "Most suspects have been advised by legal counsel not to accept drinks during the interrogation, so that we don't get prints. Dumont struck abruptly and pointedly. "Warrants for *all* suspects!"

"If you're right, Dr. Belmont, the killer is intelligent and smart enough to have gotten rid of the shirt he wore that night."

"You know, as I do, Toni, that killers, even the high IQ set, sometimes keep trophies, tokens they can later revisit," Belmont reminded Damiano. "It's a common failing."

"Let's hope for a sentimental killer."

Chapter Forty-six

Chief Damiano was trying to decide who best to approach with her warrant requests. What if the judge said he had already issued a warrant for Goldberg and was not inclined to issue a second? She remembered another judge who might give weight to her new title. The thought of serving Pierre with a warrant sent blood rushing to her cheeks. "Are you alright, Chief?" Biron asked. "You haven't said a word, and we've been driving or stalled in construction tie-ups for fifteen minutes."

Damiano hated to have her thoughts interrupted. Pierre knew enough to wait. "Fine. When the warrants are issued, I want you to pick them up ASAP. Understood?"

"I stay on with you then, Chief?"

"For the time being."

Her phone rang. Damiano was just about to swear at Apple for inventing the cell phone, but caught herself. Biron didn't know her, or she him. Her foibles did a quick retreat. "What? Slow down! Call 9-1-1!" Matthew Allen was a suspect. "He's outside your apartment door?"

"That's what I'm saying!" Velma whispered, trying not to alert Matthew.

"Give me your address and internal door code. Got it. Call 9-1-1 immediately. Do not open your door. Do not tell him you have called the police. Stay away from the door."

"Detective, break every speed limit, don't kill anyone, but rush, and I mean rush." The car took off like a bomb. Damiano held onto the side door handle and was pleased. She'd have handed off the call, but Damiano might profit by going herself. She'd like to have Allen inside a cell and ready for an interrogation Tuesday morning. Let him stew overnight. By the time they reached the suburban city of Pierrefonds and found the apartment on Gouin Boulevard West, Damiano was surprised not to see a patrol car out front. They ran up the front stairs, and Damiano ran her finger up the glossary of names, found 'C. Dawson' and punched in the code. As soon as they heard the buzzer, they rushed to the elevator and got off at the fourth floor. Allen must have heard Velma make the call because he was saying goodbye calmly through the door and walking their way.

He had a smirk on his face. "Are you here to arrest Velma for Dylan's murder? I think she was jealous of my friend Dylan."

"Mr. Allen, accompany Detective Biron to the car, please."

"Why? I haven't done anything. Please explain."

"Detective Biron, cuff him and take him down to the car." Expecting Allen to retaliate Damiano stepped back. He didn't, but he stared her down before he allowed Biron to cuff him.

Damiano walked past Allen and knocked on Dawson's door. "It's Chief Damiano."

The lock clicked, and Velma opened the door. "I didn't call 9-1-1 because Matthew threatened to kick down the door."

Damiano raised an eyebrow.

"He heard me talking to you. I'm guessing he didn't think you'd come. What am I going to do?"

"Do you want to press charges?"

"God, no! He'd get back at me for sure. I know guys are released a few hours later on the same day. What do you think happens to me then? Can't you just take him out of here? I am really frightened. I never saw this side of him and I've known him for years."

"Does Mr. Allen live nearby?"

"Seven blocks away."

"You should file a restraining order. I have to return to the city. Don't have any further contact with him. From now on, if a problem with Mr. Allen arises, call 9-1-1. And you must call."

Velma held the door, reluctant to let Damiano leave. "I have to tell you something – something I promised never to reveal. I never have, but I am truly frightened. My hands are sweaty because I am so stressed. But I must tell you that despite his talk Matthew has never rock climbed or hiked in dangerous places. He reads about extreme sports, and he pretends he's one of those men."

"How did you find this out?"

"His partner and I are friends. We went to high school together. Two years ago, it must be, I was asking her how she felt when Matthew went on those dangerous treks? Dinka swore me to secrecy and explained how Allen was adopted and had a terrible childhood. Dinka feels that Matthew's contrived stories give him stature, even confidence. Matthew has no idea that Dinka told me his story. Dylan was captivated by his supposed exploits. I guess we all were at one time or another."

"He has a partner?"

"Dinka and Matthew have been together it must be twelve years. She's a lovely person."

"What's he doing at the club?"

"Pretending, escaping and creating like the rest of us."

"Does his partner Dinka attend?"

"Used to, but she has a good job and works hard. Dinka has her own circle of friends."

"Why was Mr. Allen suggesting you were jealous of his friendship with Kane?"

"He flew off the handle when I said their friendship was somewhat odd. I thought it was. The age difference, one gay, one straight, but I shouldn't have said anything. I was angry with Matthew because he ruined the vigil and the portrait, which I now have to pay for. I just blew up, and he came after me. I have never seen his anger explode."

Damiano didn`t say anything. Was everybody lying? "Look, stay away from him. Protect yourself. I have to go."

"You cannot reveal what I've just confided. You'd ruin two lives, mine and Dinka's." Velma said with tears welling in her eyes as Damiano closed the door.

Damiano left. She wished she could discuss Allen with Pierre, but how could she? Dumont had been adamant about excluding Pierre from further involvement in the Kane investigation. She found Biron and Allen eyeing one another on the sidewalk. Biron was standing straight, feet set well apart and firmly planted on the sidewalk. Allen was swaying from one side to another.

"Release him, Detective Biron." Damiano turned, glaring at Allen. "Mr. Allen, leave Velma alone. That means no contact, text or phone. Stay away from this apartment. Expect a call from my office to set up an interview." Allen stopped swaying. He rubbed his wrists and was about to say something. Instead, he turned and left.

Driving back to the division, the car was quiet. Biron was driving. Damiano was prepping for the warrants in her head. Her muscles were in knots around her shoulders, the result of the issue with Matte, Dumont's demands, and the constant files of other cases that pulled her off course. Damiano took a deep breath – she felt disconnected. She gave both temples a good rub and worked on her notes once she was back inside her office. She closed the door and pulled down her blind. With her bullet points highlighted on each suspect, Damiano picked up the phone to call the judge. She hung up when she saw Pierre at her door.

He didn't bother to knock first. "Who booted me from the investigation this time, chief? Never mind. I can guess," he said, rubbing his palms together. "Dumont, of course. She has me in her sights now. Look, Toni, I have some time coming. I'll take Tuesday off and see my mother, help her walk. At least she wants to see me."

"I feel as badly as you do, and I miss you, miss your work."

"Everything's changed. You don't even sound like yourself. I miss the work I do well and all the things that have crashed." Matte gave Damiano half a smile and left.

Damiano swept imaginary dust from her desk with her arm, got up once more and closed her office door. Then she sat back at her desk and picked up the phone. The call felt like a betrayal of Pierre. *I never thought I would be forced to sideline Pierre from an investigation or need a warrant on my partner. If Pierre is innocent, this warrant will tear him apart.* Damiano began to remember all the times Pierre could have turned on her, but he never did. She stared at the phone for a few minutes before she made the call.

Chapter Forty-seven

Officer Boucher was trying, with difficulty, to scrub himself clean in the small sink beside the toilet inside his cell. He was waiting on an electric razor. Robson walked over and handed the razor through the bars. He stood with Boucher until he finished shaving. Robson took suicide watch seriously. Boucher's wife Manon had left a message with the front desk that his lawyer would be meeting with him that day. Boucher had no way to ask Manon for fresh clothes. His shirt stank. The underarms were stained. He could still smell himself after he washed. He needed a shower, but he couldn't complain. He hadn't been transferred to Bordeaux Prison. That was one piece of luck. He took off his shirt and thought of washing it with what was left of the small bar of soap, but gave up on that idea. He didn't want to meet his lawyer shirtless. Boucher walked to the front of his cell and shouted at Robson. "Did they get a time for my lawyer?" he called to the desk.

Officer Robson checked his ledger. "It says four o'clock Monday. It's almost five."

"What the hell? He's being paid a shitload of money. He should be here on time."

"It's probably the traffic." Robson was working past his retirement for money his three daughters needed for university. It wasn't easy. He had a booming voice, a cop face that had seen too much destruction humans bring down on one another and enough belly to be Santa. He walked slowly on bad knees. Hockey had wasted them both. When he was forty, a doctor had told him he had the knees of an eighty-year-old. Both ached every day. According to his doctor he was lucky he could still work.

Boucher sat on the cot, working on his nails. He was numb, caught up listing every problem he was facing. He didn't see or hear the desk officer on the phone. "You ready? He's in the building." He took one look at Boucher and said, "I have an extra shirt, not a good fit. I have forty pounds on you."

"Please! I don't care." Boucher jumped to his feet. He ripped off his own shirt and waited. "Thanks, this means a lot."

Robson was about to open the cell, when he had second thoughts. He handed Boucher the shirt through the bars. "I should cuff you." He went back to the desk to fetch them.

"Dammit, man, the interrogation room is less than fifty feet on the other side of the cells."

"Let's both be on the safe side. Turn around and lean your hands out the bars. I'm doing my job."

"Not so damn tight." Boucher was furious when the officer opened the cell door and led him by an arm to the interrogation room where he undid the cuffs.

"For the record, my name is Officer Robson, and you're welcome."

Miffed about the cuffs, Boucher dismissed him with a snort and turned in the claustrophobic room to meet his lawyer.

"Georges Pichette. Sit down, Daniel. You're paying big bucks for me – let's not waste a minute. If you had taken the trouble to learn Robson's name, he wouldn't have cuffed you. Manners 101. The BEI is handling the street shooting and insubordination. You were suspended when you wounded your own partner. Your union wants nothing to do with a vigilante. That's why you're paying for me."

"It was a good shoot."

"You're wasting time. We are not working with the shooting of the pusher. We are dealing with reckless endangerment causing injury. You know already that's a felony, made worse by the fact that you are a police officer. I hope you realize the gravity of your action."

"Don't waste my time. I've already figured that out. I never meant to discharge my weapon. Doucette is my partner. I needed to know if he'd screwed me."

"Never mind didn't, wasn't, wouldn't. I've spoken with the Crown prosecutor. I have all the information from the file and your wife. What I am trying to accomplish is release on bond with electronic monitoring pending trial."

"An ankle bracelet?"

"Don't interrupt me again. It won't be easy."

"But Doucette charged *me!*"

"You pulled a weapon on your partner!"

Boucher slumped back. He wanted to stand and kick the chair into the wall, but the room wasn't large enough. He knew where the cameras were even though all the recorders were turned off due to client-attorney privilege. He laid both hands on the half-diamond table and sat up. "What are my chances?"

"I have Doucette's statement. Your partner blames himself. He could have baked you like a Thanksgiving turkey. He didn't. That's a good sign for us. I should have an answer tomorrow. I'm hoping to see Doucette. If he doesn't press charges, my ultimate goal is not to have a jury drawn. We need a settlement; a fine and weighty community service would be a huge win. Otherwise, you are looking at time."

Boucher shielded his eyes with his hand. "It all started out with trying to help."

"Didn't finish that way though, did it?"

"I'm not a flight risk, I was trying to find …"

"Stop! I've heard from your wife what you were out doing – we don't go there."

"Yeah, I get it. My job?"

"You know the answer to that."

"I can't believe this – it's like it's someone else's story. I'm not a bad cop! The job is my life. I made sacrifices – Manon as well." Boucher folded in two. "My freakin' life – gone."

"Daniel, this is your story today, and I'm going to try to give it the best spin possible. Believe that. Remember you have a family. Be a man. Own your actions."

"I need some decent clothes."

"I'll have them for you in short order."

"What about the B&E?"

Pichette checked his notes. "You made a friend. The woman will not press charges. Lucky you."

"Can I speak to my wife and my kids? I can't just be cut off like a perp."

"You've had your one call – nothing now until I hear from the Crown prosecutor."

"None of this is right. It's not right. All those years I put in, fuck!"

"How about lying in a hospital bed in a hot room recovering from a bullet wound?"

"At least Louis can eventually leave the hospital and have his badge. I know, I know, I'm acting like a selfish shit. One good deed ruined my whole life."

"Be real, Daniel. You went off the rails, and not just once."

"Enough, I know. None of this seems real. That's not me."

Pichette ignored him. "If I succeed in having you released with monitoring, you are not to contact Doucette or anyone involved in the case. If you contravene my orders, I'll walk and your family will be out fifteen to twenty thousand dollars before I've even begun the file. You don't want to toss that much money. I argue to win. I have to warn you, it's a long shot."

"I'm just supposed to rot in here in the meantime?"

"Daniel, grow some balls! Begin the fight." Pichette called for Robson.

Chapter Forty-eight

An hour later, Damiano had managed all four warrants. She contacted Detective Biron and he was on his way to pick up originals. She could have used faxed copies, but Damiano determined to follow the letter of the law. In particular, with Dr. Goldberg and his lawyer Spitzer, Damiano didn't want to be sidelined by delaying tactics. In all probability, Goldberg had surgery in the morning, but she planned to execute the warrant for one-thirty Tuesday afternoon. That was a time she felt Goldberg would be free to come to the division. First on her list was Matthew Allen. When her phone rang, this time she cursed until she read the ID.

"Pamela."

"No, it's Donat."

A wave of relief swept through Damiano. "It's so good to hear from you, Chief. I've missed you. We've all missed you," she said effusively before she realized she sounded like a schoolgirl, or simply desperate.

"Well," Donat answered, "I should collapse more often. Denise has kept Pamela and me up to date. I have to say, she's managed to discover a new-found respect for you."

Damiano sat back, finally relaxed. "That's because I haven't used your office, which Denise has guarded like a fortress."

Donat offered his signature half laugh. "True, but she tells me that you're hard at work with the files. I made a good choice. That makes me feel good. I'm on the mend."

"Good, then you'll be back!"

"Not so fast, I have Pamela and doctors to contend with now. It seems I have lost some strength. I won't be back for a few more months."

Damiano's spirits fell.

"Are you there?"

"I was hoping for sooner."

"Really, I thought you were on the hunt for my job. Was I wrong? Aren't you a fast-track D?"

Matte and Dumont were both out of reach because the Kane investigation and the screw-up had strained relations on both sides. Damiano, being the Italian she was, talked too much, revealing personal anxieties. Once she began, there was no stopping Damiano. "Chief, most times, I feel lost in No

Man's land. I can't devote my full attention to anything. I miss being my own person. I miss the freedom of field work. You ran a good ship. Other times, I think I'm changing and I fit in."

"You don't think that's normal, Detective Damiano? I admit I am surprised at you. Are you suggesting you want to be replaced?"

"No, I couldn't handle the embarrassment of stepping down. You had a structure I found compatible with my work methods. Everything feels unsteady."

"It's Matte you miss. Your partnership. You were secure. No one is immune to change. I'm a good example."

"Dumont. She shouldn't have interfered," Damiano chirped.

"She was calling about my health. She has every right to be angry. Matte broke the chain of custody. The mitigating factors don't change that. Dumont's case work is affected. You should appreciate her position," Donat said firmly.

"What about loyalty, keeping division business in the division?" Damiano was angry.

"She's worried about you, not Matte. Putting things in my perspective, a partner is a partner. I never ran into the kind of problem you're facing. Do you believe Matte's negligence was accidental? That's the issue."

"I was with Pierre the night we found the body. He broke, crumpled in front of me. He couldn't talk."

"And later?"

"That's the crux. He bought the chain for Dylan and he hung onto it. Somewhere, outside the case, I understand him. That chain was all he had left of Dylan."

"You are the chief in the investigation. Was his action motivated by emotion or expedience?"

"I don't know."

"You don't have to be Hercule Poirot. This is a murder investigation; stick to the facts and keep a clear head. That's your prime level of consideration. Don't make the investigation personal. You know better, Detective."

"I know you should be resting, but may I ask you one question?"

"Shoot! Pamela is still downstairs. Go ahead."

"Matte found two of our suspects – he's done great work as always. I'd need him in the interrogations. If I find I am compelled to interrogate him, I will, as the fourth suspect. Can I make use of him for the others?"

"No. While you think he will be of help, he may also be helping himself and using you in that process. You ought to consider another point.

You have doubts about Matte. Have you asked yourself why?"

Damiano narrowed her eyes and rubbed her brows. "I know Pierre. I also believe driven to extremes, we are all capable of murder."

"Richard! Finish the call." Pamela had entered the room. "You're not to get yourself worked up, not about the job. Just a second, give me the phone. Detective Damiano I presume."

"Guilty."

Pamela left the bedroom, closing the door behind her. She made a bee-line for her computer room on the first floor. "Detective, I know Richard called you, but please, don't bring up work issues. He can't let go of them. He's up there now trying to plot out your conversation. I don't want to lose him. He's very vulnerable. I also know Richard's at fault. The man is a cop, and he cannot or will not separate the man from the job. What bothers me most," Pamela laughed heartily, "is that my little bugger is happy as punch upstairs now. He's had his fix."

"Look, Pamela, I'll follow the rules. I hear you."

"You two are two peas in a pod," Pamela said. "That's exactly what Richard will tell me when I go back up and scold him for his own good. What's worse, you'll both believe what you're saying. What is it with cops?"

"The truth is I don't know. I'm still trying to answer that question myself. My husband's on your side if that's any help."

"What's wrong with a smoothly paved road? An ordinary peaceful life?"

"It has no bumps?"

"Go back to your bumps then."

Damiano hung up and sat thinking for a minute before she made her next call.

Detective Matte picked up immediately. "What's up?"

"I have the warrants and I'll begin to serve them early tomorrow. I need you at the interrogations with me, but that . . ." she paused.

And Matte finished for her. "That won't be possible." He made no attempt to hide his irritation. "I'm officially off the case then."

"Not quite."

"Right," he snapped, "as a cop, but not as a suspect."

"I'm deeply sorry, Pierre."

"I have more vacation time I can use."

"I won't call you in unless it's necessary. You have my promise."

"I lied for you, Toni. Well, not lied exactly, I spun the truth for your son. In other words, I supported you and put myself at risk in the process."

Damiano's temper flared. "Pierre, I'm not responsible for the leak."

"Dumont?" he guessed.

"She was talking to the chief."

"Bitch," he hissed, smoldering.

"She called about his health. You know Donat. I have no doubt he wormed it out of her."

Matte fought for the right words. "We were colleagues," he reminded Damiano. "I'll be around. Dumont can't see anything but her case, her reputation really. She is 'La Belle Dame sans Merci.'" He hung up.

Damiano grabbed a stack of files and threw them on a table beside her. She took a sip of cold coffee and felt like throwing the rest at the door. Instead, she called Marie Dumont and discussed her plan for Matthew Allen. "Early surprise is the best way not to endanger innocent people and discover he's lying about pretty much everything. I want to break him. Expose him and we'll see a different person."

"You said seven, right?"

"Yes, keep the Crime vehicle out of sight until Biron and I are inside the domicile. You know what you're looking for."

"Clothes, gear and skin cells."

"See you there at seven."

How could I have better dealt with you, Pierre? You think I betrayed you. I had you on the case for as long as I could. Why the hell didn't you hand in that evidence? You're a stickler for detail. That's on you. For most of their time together, they'd made a good team. They understood one another. It was never for her at least, a question of tolerance. She was the leader, but he was a close second. She scored at one end – he took care of the net. They worked. Now, something between them was broken. If Pierre was not involved in Kane's death, the fissure would remain, like a fracture that never healed.

Damiano walked out to the main room and headed for the water cooler. The few detectives present acknowledged her, dropped their heads and went back to work. They could smell something was amiss. Matte's absence from the room and from a murder investigation was on their minds. On her way back to her office, Damiano addressed them. "Pierre's mother is in the hospital," and left it at that.

She closed her office door and made a second call.

"Yes?" The voice was abrupt, irritated.

"Detective Damiano, Doctor Goldberg. You are to present yourself here at Crémazie for a one o'clock interrogation." She could be just as brusque.

"As opposed to an interview."

"That's correct."

"Would one-thirty work? I have surgery and I'll need to shower and change."

"One-thirty it is."

"We will be there," the doctor replied as bristly as he had been summoned.

"Of course you will. An interrogation is not an elective procedure."

Chapter Forty-nine

D r. Nathaniel Goldberg put down the phone and stared at beads of sweat already apparent on the top of his hand. He picked the phone up again to call the hospital for the results. He spoke with a lab physician he knew. "I didn't want to do this at work, Josh. He's a friend and understandably upset. Please keep this between you and me."

"I appreciate that. I'll call up the results for you right now. Well, your friend …"

"Thanks, Josh." Goldberg cut the line and picked up the list of calls he'd been prepared to make. He crossed off Rachel's name. He sat down in his favorite chair, raised both arms, stretched and exhaled. Most of the tension was released. How small and insignificant everything suddenly felt. The sweats, the cold fear, the pledges, the prayers, the impending loss of everything he'd worked for, all closed down, ended, by a single word. Goldberg was shocked by the power of a word, no sharp scalpels, a word. A decree. He recalled months ago saying to a patient, "You have now begun a new phase in your life." Cancer had decreed the man had three months at best. Goldberg saw the patient shrink, but the patient then said. "At least I know where I stand. I'm free of doubt. That's better than not knowing." The patient walked unsteadily from the office, bearing the judgment of a death sentence. He was courageous, Goldberg thought, and he remembered that the man actually turned and thanked him.

Goldberg looked over at the phone, still awed by the power of a single word. He'd never seen himself as a patient waiting to hear that word, but that's exactly what he had been, a captive for seven days. One of the common herd, one member of the human race, nobody important. He was a surgeon, stalled in his tracks. That Monday night, he, too, was free of doubt.

He reached for the phone and tapped in Spitzer. "Aaron. I've been called in for an interrogation tomorrow at one-thirty. Clear that time for me, will you."

"This is serious, Nate."

"We'll get through it."

"Did you get the test results?"

"I don't have to call Rachel."

"That's great! Nate. An interrogation. I still have to say an interrogation is far more serious than an interview. My guess is that the forensic results are in, and they have something further on you. They will record everything and warn you that anything you say can …. You know the rest."

"I'm not worried yet. Can you pick me up at my place at twelve-thirty tomorrow?"

"I'm not a taxi, Nate, but I will and I'll bill the time."

"That's fine."

"Is there anything else you can think of that they might have discovered? I don't want either one of us to be blindsided. I have to know what they have to prepare you for your protection. Can you think of anything else? Try, Nate. This is important for you. I can't stress that enough."

"I have one thing."

"Go."

"I was at Cleo's the night Dylan died."

Spitzer bit his bottom lip. "That's problematic. Dammit to hell! Why weren't you up front with me? First, you lied about your alibi. Second, they have you at the scene."

"They have other suspects. Remember that, too, Aaron. I'm not worried."

"You should be."

"Prep for the interrogation. We'll be fine. I'll be outside the condo waiting for you tomorrow."

"Pack a toothbrush in case."

"Funny."

"I'm not trying to be." Spitzer pounded his desk after he hung up the phone. "What a stupid, arrogant idiot!"

Goldberg stripped and showered. He also took out a brand new toothbrush, brought it into the living room and laid it on top of his wallet. His condo was fresh thanks to his cleaning woman. He wore a plush blue robe and poured himself a double. That night was his. His mind was clear. It was odd he thought how fear can wilt a man, how its departure can release and quiet the soul. He walked out onto the balcony and breathed deeply, resting one hand against the railing for assurance. The air was heavy with the humidity of a Montreal summer. Inside his head, he railed at the life he felt had been pushed on him, how he stumbled forward, often relentlessly. *I suppose I'm not much different from anyone else.* Below him, he heard Montrealers and tourists talking as they walked the streets, easygoing banter that was music in itself. He smiled, surveying the Old Port and Bonsecours Market. *Charming, elegant, historical, and I've never enjoyed them till now.*

Nate coughed and coughed again. He placed his fingers against the bottom of his neck. His throat felt raw, and the spell broke. "Don't tell me I've caught a summer cold." He had one call to a colleague and friend. As he walked reluctantly back into the condo, he closed the patio doors and locked them. He stood while he made his call. The call done, the evening was his, and he poured himself another generous double. Goldberg tried to remember a time in his life when he'd felt this release, the peace. One surgery following another, the family, travelling back and forth, the staff meetings, the politics and, he thought, the other side of his life and its gamble. Was all of it a staged show, a rush through the years, a fevered passion not to miss out on anything? Goldberg hadn't grown tired of life; he had found himself tangled up in the web he'd made.

From his McGill days, he had never forgotten the villain Iago from *Othello*. His professor had demanded the students memorize his words. Iago had said reputation was "an idle and most false imposition: oft got without merit and lost without deserving." Goldberg held the glass of scotch up to a lamp, watching the scotch slide from one side of the glass to the other. "Tis not so, Iago," Goldberg shouted loudly, toasting the villain. "I earned my disgrace. I sought it out."

Goldberg sat back in his favorite chair. "Finally," he whispered, "I can be honest." He drank the rest of the scotch slowly, savoring the taste, allowing its warmth to linger at the back of his throat. He looked over at his toothbrush and laughed.

Chapter Fifty

Tuesday morning, Damiano and Biron drove down boulevard St-Jean on the West Island and turned right when they reached boulevard Gouin. They located the side street, found the semi-detached five houses up and parked one home past their target. Damiano was surprised; she had expected an apartment. The semi-detached was a red brick with ivory acrylic siding. River rocks bordered a flower garden and shrubs. The windows in the front of the house had blue shutters. There was no car in the shared driveway. It was, no doubt, in the single garage. The house was not in sync with her image of Allen. It had a gentle, inviting character. The Crime van drove slowly up the street and past her car. Damiano's phone rang.

"We're ready. We couldn't find Peter Henley on the club video. We might have missed him. He's not a definite no-show. How long do you want us to wait, Chief Damiano?"

"As soon as I have Allen in the car with Detective Biron, you come knocking."

"Got it."

Damiano turned to Biron who hadn't said a word since they left the division. "Detective, you can talk if you have something to say."

"On a call, I like to collect my thoughts. I figured you might be doing that and I didn't want to disturb you."

"You aren't one of those perfect people are you?"

"Far from it."

"Alright. We go up together. I want you to take Allen to the car and stay with him. He won't be pleased to see us. He's a tough, unpredictable suspect. Be on your guard."

They walked up the five stairs, and Damiano gave the door a good knock. A woman in her mid-forties answered, a gentle soul, slight and dressed for a business day. Her eyes were intelligent and alert.

"Oui."

"Chief Damiano, Madame."

"Dinka." She smiled.

"I must speak to Matthew Allen." Damiano was intrigued with her name.

"Do come in," Dinka said nervously. "Matthew, please come down," she called, standing at the bottom of the stairs.

Damiano and Biron held their ground just inside the door. Allen came bounding down the carpeted stairs. "What the hell are you doing here?" His bluster stopped at the bottom of the stairs. He stood awkwardly, wearing only in a T-shirt, briefs and large bare feet. "Shouldn't you have called?" he growled, scratching his head and shielding whatever privacy he could salvage with his hand.

"Get dressed and come back down," Damiano ordered.

Allen stomped up the stairs, "This is wrong and damn rude." Still he reappeared in minutes, still buttoning his shirt. "Why are you here?" Dinka gave him a look, and he didn't say anything else.

"Please accompany Detective Biron out to the car."

"Are you arresting me? What about my rights?"

"Mr. Allen, I need you down at the division for an interrogation. You may call a lawyer. That's your right."

Dinka was about to offer help. "Never mind spending anymore of your hard-earned money on me. I can handle myself. I always have before. Is this because of Velma?" The veins on Allen's neck popped.

"What? No, this is an official interrogation. Now follow Detective Biron to the car."

"Matthew, please. Just go. I will be alright. I will call a lawyer."

In a much subdued voice, Allen put his hand on her shoulder. "Please, don't. I know my rights. Let me handle this myself." Allen nodded to Biron. "Let's go." The humble walk he had assumed for Dinka's sake exploded when he looked over and watched the Crime van turn into his driveway. "I'm being set up by the cops!" He began pounding the side window of Damiano's unmarked car and kicked the door twice.

"If you don't calm down, or, if you vandalize this car, you will be arrested, Mr. Allen. This is just an interrogation. Keep it that way," Detective Biron advised Allen without shouting.

"Who the fuck are you?"

"A detective with cuffs."

Allen began to bounce against the back seat. Biron ignored him.

Dumont had alerted her Crime crew to first seek out the clothes and the sports equipment. All else was secondary. Damiano stood in a bright yellow and blue kitchen that reminded her of Greece. Dinka stood by the kitchen sink. She was without fear and spoke with confidence. "Matthew is a good man, Detective Damiano. He's a loving partner. He is not a murderer."

"Is he bipolar, Dinka? His actions lead me to believe he may suffer from that illness." Damiano wanted to be gentle with the woman. "We have been together for almost eleven years, and I have never seen a violent side of Matthew."

"He's been arrested. He told us that. He has injured people, badly. He told us that too."

"His childhood was wretched, brutal. His mother, whom he finally located a year ago, had been just a girl when she was violently beaten, and her son was taken from her. Matthew was bumped from one foster home to another, finally adopted and poorly treated. The military taught him structure and defence. He has trust issues. I do believe he does not start altercations, but he does engage. I am the only person who cares about him and I love him. He is a good man and I know him."

"Anger issues?"

"Yes, but never with me."

Dumont stood by the door and waved Damiano over. She listened and walked back to Dinka. "This is a murder investigation and perjury is a crime. Think well before you answer. We have searched Cleo's," Damiano was gambling on that point, "and the crew has searched the house and garage. We have found no sports equipment. Is Matthew a rock climber?"

Dinka's eyes were watery. She appeared forlorn. "Matthew trusts me."

"That's not an answer, Ma'am. You are the special person in his life. What nationality are you?"

"I'm Croatian, but born in Canada. I immediately felt an affinity with Matthew. My father did not live an easy life either. He was a merchant marine who jumped ship in Naples, claimed asylum and received it. He was sent to a refugee camp where he finally learned that Canada was offering free refugee status. He didn't know where Canada was but he left for this country. He fought for his family for two years, and they eventually joined him. He had nothing when he came to this country. A struggling life is not new to me."

"I need an answer. Is your husband a rock climber?"

"Matthew is quite the reader. He created a life he wished he'd had, a life that gave him standing. He believes people respect him more with his stories. He has trouble with steady work, but I don't mind being the principal breadwinner. The garden at the back is his," she said proudly.

"No children?"

"I already have a child, Detective Damiano," Dinka smiled. "Matthew is not a murderer."

"You don't know the other side, Ma'am." Damiano left and joined Biron in the car with Allen, and they drove to the division. Allen had grown sullen and quiet. That mood changed as he sat alone in the claustrophobic interrogation room. Damiano and Biron watched him from the video room immediately behind. He clenched his fists and sat with them in front of him, one beating on the diamond desk. The cameras hadn't escaped his eyes. He looked under the table and saw the mic. Damiano decided to take him on alone, but had Biron in the video room on the ready if Allen became threatening.

Damiano entered the room and officially began the interrogation, interrupted immediately by Allen. "You think I'm some maniac. Take a look at my shin where that drunk at Cleo's kicked me." He pulled up his pant leg. Damiano saw a pronounced hematoma below a palm-sized bruise.

"His eyes are slits they're so swollen. You broke his nose. He's thinking of suing you."

"Let him try. He struck first."

"If you wish, put your hands on the table – cut out the fists or I'll have you cuffed." Allen complied, and Damiano saw she had her palm print. The table had been swabbed first.

Damiano took out her phone and set up the video. "Crime made video copies of Cleo's the night of the murder. We have you and Dylan talking together. We see Dylan leaving and slipping up the stairs. What caught our attention is that when the video catches the table again, you aren't there either."

"I told you I always roam around taking photos and I used the washroom."

"See, I know you told me that, but the cameras don't pick you up anywhere. Here, look for yourself." Damiano handed him the phone. Allen thumbed through the video twice.

"That's not possible. I was there! I must have been out of range."

"This is a selection from two hours of scanning."

"I was out of range, that's all."

"For two hours? Did you change clothes for the cast party, Mr. Allen?" Allen rubbed the back of his neck, then his forehead. "No!"

"We have a problem then, don't we? Do you have some kind of locker there and any clothes?"

"No. Even for major parts, performers have to take their clothes home after the show."

"That means you could have had clothes there that Saturday."

"I wasn't performing."

"Did you use the back stairs to go up to the second floor, the ones behind the stage? Velma said she heard that loose stair squeak."

Allen slammed the table. "She said she heard that stair during the performance, not after."

"Did Dylan ever tell you he had a cousin who rock climbed?"

"No."

"You said he liked your stories and …"

"He did. He listened all the time! Never interrupted me like you just did."

"Do you think it's possible he realized you were fabricating, lying really, about your exploits? I mean that you never rock climbed? The closest you ever got to that sport was a printed page in a book."

Allen narrowed his mouth, his face scarlet, but said nothing.

"I think he told you he was going up on the roof. He knew your secret, that you were a fraud. You thought he might ruin you at the club, ruin your rep. You know how to kill – you've told us that. See, I think you followed him up to the roof, or you were already there, and you killed him, quickly, even painlessly, because you liked him. No head butt or smash up, something quick that knocked out the threat of disclosure. If you didn't get rid of Dylan, you'd just be another loser when the performers discovered your big stories were lies. You had to save the Matthew they knew."

Allen sprang across the table and grabbed Damiano by both shoulders, hoisting her from the chair and pushing her against the wall. "I never hurt Dylan, and he never knew about me! Never!" Spittle was flying from his mouth. Biron rushed in, grabbed Allen off Damiano, threw him to the floor and pounced on him, trapping his arms with his knees.

Damiano steadied herself, shaking. "Lock him up for the night. Charge him with assaulting an officer."

Biron had hold of Allen. He opened the door on the back wall and pushed Allen through it towards the cells. Allen shouted back at Damiano. "I'd never hurt Dylan, Detective Damiano. You accused me of murder. You purposely baited me! You're trying to set me up. Dylan was my friend." Like the eerie calm after lightning, Allen flattened. He cowed as though he had been struck. "He was my friend. He was an innocent, like Dinka."

"Mr. Allen, would you volunteer a DNA swab and a couple of root hairs?"

Allen tilted his head to one side, trying to figure out if this was another trap. "Yes. I didn't kill Dylan."

"Detective Biron, get those tests done for me."

Damiano turned away, dispirited. She had prided herself on clarity and goals in her work if not in her personal life. She saw things other detectives missed. Pierre's implication in the investigation had muddied her thoughts. She knew then that Allen would continue to barge into people, but he wasn't a killer. She had wanted him to be the killer to free Pierre, to reunite their team and salvage their broken trust. Damiano needed to feel she was back on track. Allen was part savage, but he *was* another innocent, a lost soul. She was caught seeing what she'd wanted to see. Damiano had been wrong about Allen and she felt the bite of her error because she had put her personal feelings ahead of the department.

Still, the tests had to be run, and Allen could surprise her. He was a liar. He'd created his own world. The story she'd just heard might be another creation. She wouldn't step on him and discard him just yet. He stayed on the list.

Chapter Fifty-one

Damiano sighed deeply when she found nine new files on her desk. Her stomach rumbled and felt out of sorts. She had a little over an hour before the Goldberg interrogation. Jeff had an early meeting with the MDs in their group, and she had no lunch. She thought of ordering in but changed her mind. She left the files, rode the elevator down, darted across the service road, walked down rue St-Denis and stopped at the first Vietnamese restaurant she found. She began with boiling noodle soup that burned her tongue and finished off with four spring rolls. Her green tea was the best part of the meal until she remembered that she hadn't called Peter Henley in for his interrogation. As soon as she was back in her office, easing herself behind her desk, she called Henley for Wednesday at nine.

"It's not convenient for me," Henley scowled. "My face is sore and it's a mess. I'm considering suing. The guy is a nutcase."

"Mr. Henley, it's imperative that you present yourself tomorrow at nine. Secondly, I've seen the results of the kick you gave Mr. Allen. I'd think twice about suing. You laid hands on him first."

"My word against his."

"Do what you will. I expect you tomorrow." Henley didn't argue.

Damiano made a beeline for her locker and freshened up for her one-thirty. She had an urge to call Pierre, but she didn't pick up the phone. She wasn't lost without him. Mostly, she missed him. An important part of her job wasn't there, and she felt the void. She rested a hand on her stomach, now a puddle of salt, courtesy of the soup and spring rolls. She wondered what had happened to Boucher. She learned from Officer Robson that Boucher had secured a lawyer and that he was spending his last day in their cells. The lawyer was trying to work out a plea deal with the Crown prosecutor. If his spin failed, Boucher would be transferred to Centre de détention de Montréal – Bordeaux Prison, which held prisoners until their court date. It was located on boulevard Gouin in the Ahuntsic-Cartierville district. It was not a place for bad cops.

"How's he doing?" Damiano asked.

"Never stops pacing. Lost a few pounds, I figure. Doesn't eat much either. He's imploding. Apart from his personal mess, he's put his family in some big debt. I've seen this lawyer. He doesn't come cheap."

"They probably mortgaged their house," Damiano said.

"I feel for the guy, but he pulled a weapon on his partner. I mean, man!"

"Can he hear you?"

Officer Robson looked over. "No, I think he's mumbling to himself."

"Matthew Allen?"

"As quiet as an empty church. He's sitting on the edge of his bunk watching Boucher."

"I should have guessed that. He likes shows. Thanks."

"Anytime, Chief Damiano."

Damiano took out her review notes on Goldberg. Two of his sentences stuck in her head: *I know what I've done! I wish I had.* Damiano wondered why Goldberg had not named Kane. He couldn't, or he hadn't murdered the kid. He simply wished he had. She reached into her desk for a card. Goldberg had multiple motives. He knew about the HIV testing lie. Kane had put Goldberg's wife at risk. Goldberg would lay the blame on Kane and see himself as his victim. He had been in contact with Kane the day of the murder. Now, Damiano had evidence that Goldberg was at the club the night of the murder. He was a surgeon. He knew about chokeholds. The murder had been clean, almost without clutter, as clean as a scalpel. Her mood picked up. She had solid evidence against the surgeon.

She called Detective Biron and asked him to meet Goldberg and Spitzer and escort them to the interrogation room. Damiano wanted to be in the room when they arrived. Her presence, she hoped, might further unsettle Goldberg.

Earlier that morning, Aaron Spitzer was finishing his four-minute egg and dry pumpernickel toast, washing them down with black coffee. "I just wish Nate had told me. That lie changes everything," he told his wife.

"Clients lie to you all the time. Why's Nate any different?"

Spitzer tried to calm his anger. "His lie puts him at Cleo's the night of the murder. That's why."

"You'll find a spin – you always do."

"You make my work sound simple and corrupt."

His wife didn't comment.

Spitzer tried to laugh. "You have a point. Well, I'd better give myself plenty of time to reach Notre-Dame. I need some prep time." Spitzer grabbed his case and brushed his wife's cheek with a kiss. "Wish me luck. I'll need it." Spitzer had given himself forty minutes for a usual nine-minute drive. Any of the three thoroughfares – Ste-Catherine Street, Sherbrooke and de

Maisonneuve – were usually jammed with cars, obstructed by roadwork and hampered by unsynchronized traffic lights. There were cops, paid upwards of sixty dollars an hour directing traffic. He stayed with Sherbrooke Street and regretted his choice. Stalled, he drummed the wheel with his finger and turned off the classical music that always calmed him.

That Tuesday the music was an irritant. The exhaust fumes, the frequent stops and starts creased his face with stress and rage, provocations familiar to Montrealers every summer and fall. His right front wheel hit a deep pothole, and Spitzer swore, wondering how much damage it had caused the right front bumper of his Lexus. He'd heard the crack. It was a definite crack. He'd bill Nate for it. They should have made plans to meet at Crémazie.

Spitzer found a rare parking space because he was very close to a driver edging his way out. He parked there and decided to walk the rest of the way. He bent down to see the scrape and hairline crack in his front bumper. "It'll be the whole goddamn bumper that will have to be replaced." He hurried down rue Gosford, the same route Matte had taken, and hurriedly dodging tourists and Montrealers alike, made it to the condo building. "Damn, where the hell is Nate?" Spitzer elbowed his way to the front door of the condo, stepped inside and buzzed Nate on the intercom. He waited and hoped. Nothing. Spitzer stepped back outside, looking up and down Notre-Dame from the vantage of the steps. He headed back inside and buzzed again. Still nothing. "That prick! He's never once been on time. This is his career and his life in jeopardy. What the hell is wrong with him?"

He took out his phone and called up. No one answered. "Maybe his surgery was delayed." He searched and found the MUHC and called the hospital. He was handed off to another receptionist, then another till he finally found the right person. "I need to speak with Dr. Goldberg immediately."

"And you are?"

Spitzer was furious. "His legal counsel. We have a meeting."

"Just a minute please."

"What the …"

"Thank you for waiting. Dr. Goldberg called in ill last night and rescheduled his surgery for Wednesday."

"So he wasn't in at all today?"

"No, not today."

"You're certain?"

"Yes. Have you tried his home?"

"I'm standing in front of it now. I have no answer to my calls. Thank you."

Spitzer spotted a tenant opening the door, and he shouldered by him. He tapped the panel beside Goldberg's name and picked up the phone and waited for a prompt from Nate. There was no response. He dialed again. Nothing. "Has that fucker pulled a runner?"

Chapter Fifty-two

Georges Pichette rang the bell located on the right of the single elevator in the lobby of the Crémazie Division minutes before one o'clock. He waited patiently for a response. An officer escorted him to the second interrogation room and then carefully searched the bag he was carrying. He waited in the room for his client, Officer Daniel Boucher, to arrive.

Officer Robson received the information. He called over to Boucher. "Your lawyer's here to see you."

Boucher sensed the news might not be what he wanted, what he needed to hear, and recoiled. Five days in a cell had drained his hope and energy.

Robson walked over to him. "Just wash your face. You don't have time for anything else."

Boucher slapped water on his face and used what passed for a facecloth to wipe it. Robson went back to his desk for cuffs.

"You don't need the cuffs. I've been in the same clothes for days. I have three-day stubble and I can smell myself. I'd never pass for a cop. I'd never make it out of the building."

Robson returned to his desk again for the electric razor. "Hurry up with this." He handed the razor to Boucher through the bars.

"Thanks." He pushed the razor over his skin like a saw. Then he went to the sink, ran hot water over the cloth and wiped his armpits. "I guess I'm ready." He passed both hands through the cell bars for the cuffs. and then followed Robson for the short walk to the interrogation room. The first thing he noticed was a bag and his spirits fell. Was he being transferred to Bordeaux? Robson uncuffed him.

"Officer, these clothes have been searched," Pichette told Robson.

"Alright by me." Robson closed the door and left them.

"Sit down, Daniel. I have a change of clothes for you." Pichette handed him the large paper bag. "There's a bar of soap in there, to wash your hair."

"In a sink?"

"Look, Daniel, the compromise we made was staying at Crémazie to avoid the transfer to Bordeaux as long as possible. You'll have to make do."

Boucher exhaled but quickly jumped to other concerns. "What about my bail, my release, the stuff that matters?"

"I've met twice for long periods with the Crown prosecutor."

"And?"

"She's still deliberating."

"Why? This is my life! I'm a cop! Doucette's injury was accidental. I haven't spoken to my wife or my kids in days. What's going on?"

"Daniel, try to get a realistic grasp of your situation."

He dropped his head. "Right, I'm not a cop anymore; I'm just a felon."

"Look, the Crown prosecutor could have refused outright, but my gut tells me she might be going to take a hard line on this file. You know what the political climate is out there about police tactics. You shot your partner, Daniel. No matter how many times I explain that your partner had blamed himself, she comes back to you pulling your weapon out in the first place."

Boucher's eyes closed to slits. Tilting his head, he took Pichette on. "What are we paying you for this magic?"

"Settle down. It's not over."

"It all began with me trying to help." Boucher knew he had nothing to bargain with, other than his good intention. His actions flashed in his head. He looked at the floor and dug his fingers into his knees.

"I've reminded the prosecutor of that many times. But I have some tough news that can't wait."

"What the hell now?" Boucher got up on his feet to hear the news and stretch his spine.

"If we don't hear about bail and monitoring today, you will be transferred to the Centre de détention de Montréal tomorrow morning."

Boucher took a blistering swipe at the table that startled Pichette who jumped to his feet.

The lawyer backed against the wall and waited a few seconds for Boucher to sit down. These sudden outbursts were nothing new to Pichette. "You'll have to await your court appearance there. That's why I brought the clothes. I also gained permission for you to call your wife. You can use my phone. It has to be a short call. I'm doing the best I can."

Boucher had stopped listening. His face and neck glistened with sweat. He braced himself with both arms. "You know what they do to cops in prison." He began rocking from one side to another. "They'll tear me apart. I have a long list of perps who hate me," he said unblinking. Boucher's face was washed out. He bore the terror of a kid lost in a park. "You gotta find something solid. Don't just run your mouth and charge us," Boucher shouted.

Pichette scowled but controlled himself. "Do you want to talk to your wife?"

"What?"

"You can call your wife for a few minutes. Use my phone."

Boucher smiled forlornly. "Manon said I was a brave man. She should see me now. I should have run."

"Where to?"

"Any place would have been better than this," he laughed. "I wanted to go out like a blaze of glory."

"That's fiction, Daniel. There are no blazes and no glory, just bloody, mangled bodies with half-open, milky dead eyes."

Boucher didn't answer. He reached for the phone and tapped in his number. Pichette had made certain that Boucher's wife would be home to take the call.

"Hey!"

"It's so good to hear your voice, Daniel. How are you holding up?" Her voice trembled.

"Is it tough for the kids at school, Manon?"

"They're managing, like me. I found a job. Don't get depressed. I'm still hopeful. I love you. Take care of yourself. I'll make do at home, but remember, we need you, Daniel."

"This busted out our finances, I know." Boucher couldn't hold in his fear. "You should have let me run, Manon. They're transferring me to-morrow. I'll do time. Do you hear me, I'll do time!"

"I still have hope, Daniel. You have to be brave. I have to count on that. I know you are."

"I'm not, Manon. I've told you what inmates do to cops. I didn't start out to hurt anyone. It was a good shoot. I just lost it with Doucette. I swore I'd never go to prison."

"It's not a done deal yet, Daniel. We are with you."

"I fucked up, Manon. I really fucked up. This can't be happening to me."

Chapter Fifty-three

Spitzer began to feel uneasy. *Nate wouldn't have committed suicide. Jews and Catholics don't commit suicide.* That thought didn't last long. He remembered a Jewish friend who had hanged himself in his bathroom. "No, Nate! No!" He was shaking when he called the hospital. He had no intention of waiting for the various options and dialed 0. "This is a dire emergency. My name is Aaron Spitzer. I need Dr. Goldberg's Rawdon number. The doctor's life may already be in danger."

"Are you family?"

"If Dr. Goldberg dies because you're wasting precious time, I will sue your ass off. Connect me, now!" He tapped his right foot as he waited, drumming the cell against his ear.

"Yes."

"I need Rachel's number. It's a dire emergency. Understand that, please."

"I have to know who you are, sir."

"I'm his lawyer. We had an important meeting this afternoon. He's not answering at his condo. I need help immediately. Every second counts."

There was a pause.

"Good goddammit, are you there?"

"The number is …"

Spitzer wrote the number on his palm and tapped it in.

"Hello?"

"Rachel, this is Aaron Spitzer, Nate's lawyer."

"Why does Nate need a lawyer?"

"Rachel, listen carefully. I had a very serious meeting scheduled with Nate this afternoon. I'm at his condo. He's not answering."

"He had morning surgery. It's probably gone late. Try the hospital."

"Nate called in sick last night. Rachel, I need to get access to his condo. I'm frightened for his safety."

"What? What are you talking about? I spoke to Nate a day ago."

"I'll answer all the *whats* later. Right now I need his door code. I think you should come into the city. If you give me the code, and he's not there, I'll call you right back. Don't move till you hear from me."

"I don't know you. How can I just give you access to my husband's condo? This could be a scam. I wasn't born yesterday," she said with uncertainty creeping into her voice.

"I'm calling the police and an ambulance as soon as we get off the phone. Unless you want them to break the door down, I need the code."

"Is Nate in some kind of trouble?" Rachel's voice shook. "I need to know."

"He believes he is. I can't say more, except that this isn't a scam. Nate needs help."

"The code is 789345. I'm leaving now. Here's my cell. I wish I were there."

No, you don't. "Thank you, Rachel. I will call you."

"Please don't. I'll be there as soon as I can. I don't want bad news on the phone. I couldn't bear that. I'd drive my car off the road."

"I understand. Be safe."

Rachel burst into tears as she ran for her keys and screamed for the boys.

"What's up?" Gabriel asked.

"I have to go into the city immediately. I'll call Geraldine. You're to stay with her."

"Why can't we go with you?"

"You can't, that's all. I haven't got time to explain."

"But you're crying, Mom."

"Please, Gabe, I don't have time. I need to depend on you right now. Get your brother out of the water. It's freezing. I don't want either one of you in the water. Got it?"

"I don't understand."

"Do what I'm telling you. For once, just listen to me!" she shouted.

Rachel picked up the phone. "Go down and get your brother. Get out of here. Geraldine, Rachel. I have an emergency in Montreal."

"I'm on the boys. You go. They're safe with me."

"Thank you." Rachel knew without doubt that was true. Geraldine and she were great friends. In fact, the property they now enjoyed was once Geraldine's great-grandfather's farmland. The whole community of Masonville was named after him. Geraldine's heritage was a golden piece of Rawdon. Nate was her worry.

"Good luck!"

Spitzer tapped in the code. Nate's front door opened. He took two steps inside and stopped. He reached into his pocket for his cell and called Chief Damiano.

"Chief Damiano."

"Aaron Spitzer, Chief Damiano. I have an emergency. I was forced to call Nate's wife because he was not answering. I'm standing at the doorway of his condo. I fear the worst. What do you want me to do?"

Damiano stepped out from behind her desk. "If he's breathing, he needs help quickly. Apart from the door handle, do not touch anything in the condo. Go inside now."

Spitzer walked falteringly to the bedroom and gasped. He continued cautiously to the bed. "He's here. His eyes are half-open."

"Lay two fingers on the side of his neck."

You idiot, Nate! "His body is cold. I touched his cheek too."

"Is there a note?"

Spitzer saw it on the night table and two small bottles with the remains of a milky liquid. He bent over and read the label, Propofol. He read the envelope and backed out of the room. "Yes, to his wife. There are two near-empty bottles of Propofol on the table, too."

"Mr. Spitzer, leave the condo. Stay in the lobby, please. We need to talk to you. I'll have the crews, ambulance included, on their way. Allow them entry, but close the door for now. I'm on my way. I don't want to contaminate the scene." Damiano made the calls. She wanted to call Pierre. She knew she couldn't. Biron drove them down with a jockeying, daring speed that rivaled hers. She liked Biron, but she didn't think of him as her partner. Matte was her partner.

Spitzer stood in a daze. He cupped his hands together. He was cold and shaky. *You stupid fool. You threw your life away! You didn't even put up a fight! What a despicable legacy you've left for your family, scarring each of them for the rest of their lives. Why, Nate?* Hot waves rushed up his back. Spitzer covered his face and shivered. Nate was a man whose behavior he knew because he was as guilty as Nate of lies and infidelity. He was fortunate he'd never been tested to the extreme. He had an urge to run back into the bedroom and scream at Nate. He wanted to read his note, but he didn't move. He felt safer, trying to distance himself from his client. *You jellyfish! You're a selfish coward.*

Weeping, Spitzer leaned on the wall to steady himself, afraid he might keel over. "Oh, Nate."

Chapter Fifty-four

The ambulance was the first to reach the condo. Spitzer stepped back inside and buzzed them up. When the elevator door opened, two paramedics rushed to the door. Spitzer raised his hand, stopping them. "This is a potential crime scene. Major Crimes should arrive any minute. I was ordered out of the condo and told, except to check the body, not to touch anything else. One of you should go on in and verify the death. Then, we wait for the police."

The paramedic was hesitant to follow orders from a civilian.

"Listen, I'll call the chief for you, but one of you should go in and verify the death." Spitzer called Damiano and handed the phone to the paramedic. He identified himself, listened and ended the call. He told his partner to stand back while he walked inside with his equipment.

Spitzer waited. He felt better in the presence of the men, distracted from his thoughts and inner fear. His phone rang. He answered quickly, thinking it was Damiano. "Yes."

"Are you in the condo?" The voice of Nate's wife Rachel was almost unrecognizable. Her five words carried such dread.

"I was briefly. A paramedic is with him, and I'm waiting for the police."

"Police?" The woman broke. "Why are the police there? Is Nate hurt?"

Spitzer didn't know what to say. "How close are you?"

"Forty minutes away. I asked you, is Nate hurt? Is he …?" The word that ended a life and tore hers apart wouldn't come out.

Spitzer heard the condo buzzer. "Rachel, the police have arrived. I think you should speak to Chief Damiano, not me. Be careful on the road." Spitzer stepped back inside the condo and opened the entrance door, hoping to see Damiano who'd take over. "I'll have her call you. Is that alright?"

"Nate is dead, isn't he?" The voice had lost its energy.

"Just a minute, the chief is coming off the elevator."

"It's Nate's wife, Chief Damiano." He handed her the phone.

"Chief Damiano."

"I want to know if my husband is dead." The word was out, and it would be repeated. "I should be there soon. I have to see Nate. I have to see him."

Damiano saw the paramedic at the door. Without a word, he conveyed the fatality. Spitzer whispered Rachel's name. Damiano loathed conveying such news by phone because whatever she would say would sound cold and brutal. It was the swing from life to death, an end that could not be reversed. "Rachel, I regret to inform you that we have confirmed the death of Nathaniel Goldberg."

"How?" Rachel wailed. "Don't touch him. I have to see Nate. Do you hear me? I should get to the condo in forty minutes. I just spoke to him. How? How can this be? I won't believe any of this till I see Nate. This could be some terrible mistake!"

"I will wait for you. We can talk then. Drive safely."

The buzzer sounded again. Dumont had arrived. Damiano and Biron booted up and slipped on white plastic gloves. The paramedics stood by. "Crime techs are arriving. Dumont will advise you." She approached Spitzer. "You handled this situation well."

Spitzer's face fell. "I never suspected. I should have perhaps. I should have guessed somehow."

"No one ever really does."

"May I stay here to talk to Rachel – and to find out what happened? It's quite a blow."

"I'll decide when I've seen the body, but you cannot stay long." Damiano, with Biron behind her, entered the condo and walked into the bedroom. Damiano had seen her share of dead bodies, but she still felt that each one would open his eyes and … say it was all a mistake. But the dead stayed dead, quiet, smaller and gone from their bodies. Goldberg was no different. He didn't look peaceful. His eyes and mouth were half open. His arms were under the sheets. It was a pose that appeared unnatural. Damiano took out a pen and turned down the cover and sheet. A syringe was stuck in one arm, and Damiano saw the small puncture in the other. "He was determined." She saw the bottles and read the labels. "You know what this stuff is, right?"

Biron leaned on his side and read. "Yes, the Michael Jackson death drug."

Damiano saw the note addressed to 'Rachel.' She also saw that it wasn't sealed. "Do you think he left the note unsealed purposely?"

"I don't know. Most physicians write carelessly. You can't read what they've written. Not sealing the envelope might have been carelessness, but he may also have wanted you to see the contents. The doctor appears to have planned what we see here."

"Fetch Dumont. We will follow protocol."

Dumont was quick. "The victim made no attempt to keep the contents personal. We have a right to them." She was suited up in white. Dumont held the envelope by its tip, pulled back the flap and slid the note onto the night table, careful not to hit the Propofol bottles. She opened the note with tweezers she took from a kit.

They leaned over together and read the note:

Rache,
Always remember that I love you. I lost my way and I couldn't come back.
For all the damage I have done – I surrendered my life.
In time, I hope you can forgive me.
Nate
Rache, you have to be tested. I couldn't tell you. In that, I suppose I am a coward as well.

Damiano read the note again. "Do you agree I have a confession, Marie?" Marie reread the note. "The 'all' suggests that's exactly what you have."

"Put the note back, Marie. I wouldn't want to be his wife." The paramedics backed against the far wall. Damiano walked out to the lobby and motioned for Spitzer to follow her into the condo. "Did you know that Goldberg was infected with HIV?" She kept her voice to a whisper. Goldberg couldn't hear her, but she felt the dead deserved respect.

"No, I didn't. In fact, I thought the exact opposite. We spoke Sunday night. I told him to prep for Tuesday. He seemed relaxed. He said not to worry. He didn't have to call Rachel. I figured that meant he *wasn't* infected. He was off the hook. I was relieved for him. God knows, no one is perfect. Nate did drop the bombshell that he was at the club the night Kane was murdered. I was puzzled that he wasn't stressed to have lied to the police and to have placed himself at the murder scene. I stupidly put it all down to the fact that he'd escaped HIV and his dread of infecting his wife." Spitzer brought his fingers to his mouth and shook his head. "All the while, he was planning to commit suicide that night. That's why he was at peace. He was, Detective Damiano. From the moment we met, he was stressed and afraid. Last night, he wasn't afraid. I think his decision had set him free. He was beyond the investigation, he was preparing his leave-taking. But he was a Jew, life is so precious. I don't understand.

"I've always thought people who commit suicide are cowards, but I think Nate gave up his life in atonement. There's something noble in that."

Chapter Fifty-five

Damiano directed Spitzer back to the lobby. She told him he could stay and talk to Goldberg's wife after she had spoken with the woman. She had her conviction, her solve, but it felt … She couldn't put a word to what she felt. Sudden, that's what it felt like, sudden, like Goldberg's suicide.

Dumont saw the work ahead of her. "I'll still run all the tests on the body: a palm print, a swab and hairs to be certain. I can't afford another gap in my log book. We should have the results from the chain. You have your close, but I want a swab from Matte. That evidence is useless because Matte corrupted that part of my investigation. I have to see things through. I hope you do as well. I have to tell you something. I'm angry with Matte, but I'm just as angry with myself. Kane had so little. I should have seen the evidence bag was missing that very night, and I didn't. My omission will stick with me."

"Thanks for that," Damiano said to Dumont. The chief seemed momentarily shaken.

"We all mess up at one time or another. Still Goldberg was a surgeon! You know the years of study he spent, and he threw it all away and left the burden of his suicide with his family."

"I remember he was most worried about his wife. In spite of his trysts, he loved her," Damiano felt she had to add.

"That or he couldn't face her. Not my kind of love," Dumont said dismissively.

"Just the same, look at what he lost."

"I'll probably never understand us humans. That's why I stick to facts. They make sense."

Minutes later, the buzzer sounded. "Marie, pull the covers back up. I think that's his wife. It's godawful for her. She's the only innocent victim and she may be paying for her husband's boy toy for the rest of her life. She thinks the only 'damage' is Goldberg's death. I'm truly sorry for her." Damiano walked out to the elevator to meet Goldberg's wife.

Rachel Meyer was a confident, attractive woman with deep brown eyes, a woman with a quick wit and a hearty laugh. But the widow who walked out of the elevator was desperate and frightened, a shadow of the woman in Rawdon. Rachel brushed by Damiano. "I want to see Nate now. I can't believe any of you. You don't know Nate."

Damiano caught her shoulder. "Please, hold up. Take a few breaths before we go inside. You can see him, but I can't let you touch him. The crew has not begun their investigation."

"What do you mean I can't touch Nate – he's my husband!"

"Rachel."

"Meyer." Rachel did not want to conduct a personal exchange with this chief or detective, or whatever she was. She wanted to see her husband.

"Fine, I cannot permit you inside the room until you agree to my order. Aaron Spitzer told me your name. I see how devastated you are. Do you understand? The bedroom area cannot be contaminated. Follow me if you fully appreciate the boundaries. I'm sorry, but that is the law."

"I have to see Nate. None of what you're telling me makes any sense until I see him." She stopped, cupped her hand over her eyes and slumped. "I just spoke to Nate. I just spoke ... we made plans for the weekend!"

"Would you like to wait out here and talk to me first?"

"No, you have nothing to say that will give Nate back to me. I have to see him."

Damiano had reached into her pocket for another pair of rubber gloves and gave them to Meyer. She followed behind, using the taller Damiano as a shield. Meyer's legs wobbled as Damiano stepped aside.

Meyer took two steps out from behind Damiano and stopped at the end of the bed, tilted her head to the left and stared, till she couldn't see through her tears. "Oh, Nate. You said not to come into town because you'd see me on Thursday. You told me you missed me. What happened?" She took a few steps closer to the body, reached out to touch Goldberg's cheek.

"You can't, Ms. Meyer." Damiano saw Meyer's dark-wash blue jeans, the blue patent leather designer sneakers without socks, and a white pinpoint Oxford shirt, the same clothes she must have worn that morning. She hadn't taken the time to change in her rush to reach the condo.

"How?" she whispered as though she'd wake Goldberg. Before Damiano could answer, Rachel saw the note. "Oh no! But Nate wouldn't – we have a family. We don't believe in suicide. Don't you see Nate wouldn't ... he ..." Rachel saw her name. "That's my note. I can have that. It's personal and it's mine! It's all I'll ever have."

"You can read it here, Rachel, but it's part of the investigation. You can't take it with you."

Meyer wasn't listening. She was pulling the note from the envelope. Damiano was grateful that she had remembered the gloves. Meyer's face hardened. Her lips thinned. The envelope fell to the floor.

"Don't destroy the note, Ms. Meyer. We have to talk to you about it."

"You've read it?" she accused Damiano. "How could you?"

"It wasn't sealed. I believe Dr. Goldberg wanted me to explain things to you."

Meyer turned her anger on Damiano. "Know what? We can use the chairs right here in the bedroom. I want Nate to hear what you have to say." Meyer plopped herself down in a chair, gripped its sides, crossed her legs and began jiggling her foot. "Before you *tell me* anything, I can guess that Nate had an affair." She looked over at the body. "And, I can surmise he got himself infected with an STD that he might have callously passed on to me." She made a fist and drummed her forehead before she could speak again. "How am I doing, Nate? You couldn't face me, you coward!"

Damiano's heart went out to Goldberg's wife and she wished everything had been said. But sadly, that wasn't the case. "Rachel, may I switch to first names?"

"What does it matter now?"

"I'll do my best to be brief. You are correct about the affair. Dr. Goldberg did …"

"First names for him, too," Rachel shot back impatiently.

"Nate had an affair with a young man who …" Damiano was cut short.

Rachel broke. "What? A man? Nate wasn't gay! You're making no sense, no sense at all. I knew Nate." Then she stopped abruptly. Rachel had begun to see what was coming and she cringed, forcing her body farther against the back of the chair, waiting for the blow.

"That young man infected Nate with HIV. He was murdered over a week ago. The note you read is Nate's confession to that murder and to the damage he has caused you. We will not close the file until our investigation is complete. I'm truly sorry, Rachel."

Meyer's whole body shook. Damiano rose and tried to comfort Rachel. "Leave me alone!" She shook her head violently and rose. "Saving face meant everything to Nate. He could cut into patients, but he didn't have the balls to tell me." She dropped her head. Still focused on the floor, she said, "I will have myself tested. I have children who'll need me. If you have any consideration for me and my family, keep this from the media when you close the file. I'll hold you responsible for that, Chief Damiano. Nate has scarred us for life – don't add to it."

"I can't keep the file from the public domain, but I'll do my best with the media. Your influence will help in that as well. For all his flaws, he did love you."

Meyer hadn't heard a word Damiano said. She turned to the body. "At this moment, I hate you, Nate. I loathe you." Damiano didn't move fast enough, and Meyer stepped closer to the body and spat on Goldberg's face. She grabbed her purse and ran from the room. Spitzer ran after her.

Chapter Fifty-six

Damiano and Dumont had followed Rachel Meyer to the door. A thought struck Damiano, and she went back into the bedroom. "Marie, would you check both arms. Dr. Belmont said we might see some mark." Marie pulled down the sheet. The body was in full rigor. She bent down close to each arm. "I can't see anything. Belmont might. The blood has pooled under his back. I can't see well without better equipment."

"Belmont said the killer likely wore a long-sleeved shirt or jacket to prevent marking. He's probably right."

"You have motive, opportunity, a confession and a suicide, how much better can you score, Toni?"

"What we have is Goldberg's statement 'all the damage.'"

"Toni, he was writing to his wife. He couldn't bear to tell her he had murdered someone and that he might have infected her. He left that to us."

"If he hadn't been infected, we'd still be investigating, and Goldberg would be alive. I have an interrogation slated for Peter Henley tomorrow morning. Is there a point for you? He wasn't a strong suspect."

"You're the chief."

"I'm thinking of your log book. Do you want his tests?"

"There's no need to bust a gut on him. There is no point now."

"Why Matte's then?"

"You know why."

"You're vindictive, Marie."

"I'm still angry. He's a fine cop who screwed up my investigation and yours, too, I might add."

"I have to get back to the office and release Matthew Allen. He's dangerous, but he's not our killer. I'll call Matte." Damiano scanned the condo. "This is all pretty grim."

Rachel Mayer's fear, rage and disgust momentarily paralyzed her. She stood without moving. Seconds later, Spitzer walked out of the elevator. "Rachel, would you like to go for coffee to talk? You can't drive back to Rawdon in this condition."

"Who are you?"

"Nate's lawyer. Nate paid me well. I'm not an ambulance chaser, I …"

Meyer laughed hard, interrupting him. "No, Nate went first class, right to the end. No bullet or jump for him, he had the means and chose a well cushioned exit." Then she seemed lost. "He murdered somebody? I can't … it's too horrible to try to comprehend."

"Let's get out of the building. We can walk if you want. I can fill in the facts for you, help you understand."

Meyer followed like a lost child.

Spitzer tried to bring her around, with kind words. "I spoke to Nate last night. What he most cared about, I'm not exaggerating, was what he might have done to you. He had to wait for the test results. The first thing he said last night was 'I don't have to call Rachel.'" They walked down to the Old Port. It was cooler down by the water. They passed Bonsecours Market without seeing it and continued on. "I thought he meant he hadn't been infected and hadn't infected you. He was at peace. I didn't realize why he wasn't stressed. He had an interrogation today. Whatever he did, I saw that he was deeply wounded because he had hurt you and ruined his marriage. He repeated twice in the first police interview 'I know what I have done to my family.' In time, with family support, you will be able to put the grief and the loss behind you."

"He murdered this kid!" Meyer had burrowed into that devastating thought.

Spitzer had no answer.

She aimed her anger and disdain at Spitzer. "Do you think you knew Nate from a couple of talks?"

"Rachel, he was human and flawed. He was decent. For whatever he did, he paid the ultimate price, didn't he?"

"You don't know Nate. We were just kids when we married. We promised one another the night of our honeymoon, that we would be faithful. It was a sacred pledge," she smiled woefully, her mood shifting back to pain. "At least to me it was."

"He told me about that."

"Ah, so you know something. Nate was intelligent, loving, a good father, a very good surgeon, not the best, but very good. He was also spoiled and arrogant. I think pride goes with being a surgeon, having these superior feelings about oneself. Nate got everything he ever wanted, a good family, a loving wife, work, status. But really, deep down, he was a coward. He never could stand up to his father, although he was far more successful than his father ever was. He was a risk taker, even in surgery.

Now, I see he was a risk taker in his private life. You think he took his life because he hurt me. Ha! He took his life because he couldn't face his colleagues and reveal his HIV status. The catalyst, the final one, is easy for me to understand. Nate, the man I loved, took his life because he was a coward. He couldn't face me.

"I don't ever want to see you again. I have a family and they need me. Nate also murdered my love for him. I feel nothing for him now, not even pity." Meyer turned away from Spitzer, straightened her back and walked off alone.

Spitzer wanted to call after her, "Remember to be tested." Instead, he stood and watched her go and he envied her strength. *Nate didn't have everything, Rachel. He didn't have your strength.*

Chapter Fifty-seven

It was almost four o'clock by the time Damiano was behind her desk writing up the closing notes for the murder book. The precise work was new to her because Pierre had taken care of notes, closures as well. Thoughts spun in her head, and she was doing her best to dial them down. She felt no familiar rush. Some part of her was reeling. She saw she'd just misspelled Goldberg's name. Damiano stopped writing. The notes would have to wait. She remembered Matthew Allen was still in a cell.

He gave her an excuse to move, settle her nerves. She didn't have to wait on the elevator. She spoke to Officer Robson. "Allen's been quiet. It's Boucher who's been having a bad time."

"Good, I'm releasing Allen on his own recognisance. Get the papers out please."

Release papers were far simpler than transfer papers. Robson was finished in four minutes. Damiano and Robson signed them. Allen got to his feet when he realized they were coming for him. "Mr. Allen, I'm releasing you today without further charge."

Allen looked skeptical, but pleased. "What about the assault?"

"I dropped it."

Allen cut the jocular remark in time to say, "Thank you."

Robson unlocked the cell, and Allen stepped out. "Apart from dropping the assault charge, what about Dylan?"

"We're closing the case."

Relief slid across his face. "I'm glad. He was the only male friend I had. I would never have hurt him."

"I had no option but to investigate everyone who knew Dylan."

"I know. Was that detective somehow, you know, connected to Dylan?" Allen wished he could take back those words, when he saw Damiano's face darken.

"I didn't mean anything. He just … It's not important, doesn't matter."

"His mother suffered a stroke."

"I'm sorry again. I better just clear out."

"You do that."

Boucher had sprung to his feet, listening to the release of the suspect next to him. He gripped the bars of his cell, sweating, waiting his turn. "Chief, they're transferring me today if my bail doesn't come through. Is there any way you can keep me here? I can't end up in Bordeaux."

Damiano's face was creased with concern when she answered Boucher. "I have heard about Doucette," she said sternly. "I've been blocked since BEI took over your file." She turned to Robson. "Aren't the transfers earlier than four o'clock in the afternoon?"

"There are two a day, if need be. One takes place at one o'clock and the other at five."

"Officer Boucher, I wish you luck." Damiano left frowning. *Allen didn't forget Matte. The case is closed. Pierre made a mistake. I've made them. We all do!* Once she was inside her office with her door closed, she called Pierre. Perhaps it was the lack of contact or Marie's frustration that was causing her unease. She was wired when she made the call. Matte picked up immediately. "I have news," she announced.

"As do I. Dylan's mother called me. I had left my number with her. I told her about donating Dylan's body. She went for it, either because she believed Dylan might redeem himself posthumously, or she'd save a trip to Montreal. I hope it was the former, and I believe it was.

"My mother came home today. I drove her. My father is worn out and he actually thanked me. It's been a decent day for me. I'm planning to have sautéed calf's liver tonight, join me and bring your news. You've never been to my place and I could use a friend."

Damiano was caught off guard.

"If you can't make it, it's okay."

"I'll bring the wine."

"Just bring your company."

"Deal. Where do you live? Can I park?"

Damiano tapped in the address.

"Parking? Toni, since when has parking been a problem for you? Seven?"

"Works for me." Damiano closed the paperwork. It wasn't going anywhere, and Dumont still wanted to give her final results. The other files waited accusingly, but Damiano closed the office and drove home. She needed a shower and she needed time to think of her approach, the theory she'd run by Pierre. She began to gather her thoughts when Jeff arrived home early. *Damn! I needed some alone time.*

"Wow! My chief is home. What a great surprise."

"For me, too."

"How do I take that, Toni?"

"I could use some loving. My nerves are shot. You are the magic maker in this house, Jeff. I should have seen a long time ago that I am lucky."

"Hold those thoughts. After a shower. I don't smell good, lady."

"Time was that didn't …"

"Take a whiff."

"Hurry then."

"You, too!"

After they were sated, they lay quietly in one another's arms, Damiano was breathing easily. "You're a good man, Jeff Shea."

"That I am!"

"I'm seeing Pierre for dinner at his condo." She told Jeff about Goldberg.

He lay there analysing the news. "Is this confession a first in your work?"

"Yes. I pity his family."

"Do you think you and Pierre can work together again? Do you have lingering doubts about him and Dylan?"

"I'm tense about both questions. I have to see Pierre because I have to know."

Chapter Fifty-eight

D amiano was absent-mindedly drumming the door handle.
"That bad?"

"Yep. There's a lot at risk."

"I'm glad I'm driving you. The best cop in Montreal couldn't find parking around Prince Arthur. If you want, I'll pick you up. I assume you'll have a few glasses of wine."

"You're being too good, Jeff. I'll cab it home. I'll need some time to gather my thoughts."

"You look wonderful as you always do to me, and I gave you our best wine – that should start a conversation at least. Why not save the investigative work for the office tomorrow? Try to renew a working friendship." Jeff looked over at his wife, and his tone was serious. "Toni, I hope you haven't brought your weapon. I don't want you in danger. If you ask me, this theory you want to test on Pierre is an ambush and a costly venture that could blow up in your face."

"I didn't."

"I'm doing my best to look out for you."

"What I'll promise is that I'll see how the dinner plays out before I act."

"I suppose that's my best offer."

"It is." Jeff turned north on rue St-Denis. "I can get out here. I'd like to walk the rest of the way. It's not far." Jeff stopped the car, briefly double-parking. Damiano blew him a kiss. The driver behind Jeff honked, and he drove off.

As she approached Pierre's condo, Damiano saw that he was on the sidewalk, full smile, waiting to greet her. He, too, had dressed for their dinner. Damiano tried to recall him ever smiling and couldn't. He was quite cute, not handsome, but boyishly cute. She wore a soft floral dress, and Matte, tan pants and a crisp, white shirt, the sleeves rolled mid-arm.

"Welcome, Toni. I'm glad you're here. Follow me." The first sour note occurred in the foyer of his apartment. "I ask my guests to leave their bags and phones here. Mine's on that ledge. A dinner should be phone free. I know you're chief. If you have a call, I'll leave it to you if you choose to take it. Fair enough?"

Damiano tried to hide her irritation. "Yep. If you don't mind, I'll take out my phone and leave it on top of my bag, so I can get to the call quickly if need be." She reached into the bag and turned off the recorder.

Pierre walked into his condo, pleased. He stood by the window, waiting on Damiano. "Your place is lovely, Pierre. Is that Diana Krall I hear?"

He nodded.

"Thought so. I like her."

"I've only had one piece of toast all day and I'm famished. May we begin now and save the talk till after dinner?"

"Smells good. It's fine with me. I'm always ready to eat and happy to help." Damiano noticed a memoir on the kitchen table and checked the title and author, *Almost There*, Nuala O'Faolain.

"After dinner discussion," Matte said. They worked like hungry people, and thirty minutes later, they were both comfortable at the table with a glass of wine. Pierre raised his glass. "I toast a friendship strong enough to field a few bruises, to my partner, and my friend."

"To its continuance!"

"This is good wine!"

"Jeff would love to have your recipe. Best liver I've ever had."

"You don't cook?"

"I do my best to avoid it, but sandwiches I like to do." Without warning, Damiano felt a crushing wariness to the effort given to circling one another, avoiding minefields. Damiano scanned the room. "Your condo is an apt reflection of you, with its precision and taste, Pierre." Stevie Ray Vaughan was singing, 'The Sky is Crying.'

"I don't know if that's a good thing."

"It is." Once they had finished the dinner, Pierre told her he had no dessert.

"Leave the dishes on the table. Let's go to the living room." He slid his hands into his pockets, relaxed. "You have your close. Tell me."

Damiano didn't miss a detail in her summary of the case.

Pierre sat back. "I'd thought Allen was good for it. Goldberg gave you the keys to a close: motive, opportunity, a confession and his suicide. The close was as keen as a scalpel. He had a family. That was reason enough, I suppose."

"Me too. The HIV infection added to Goldberg's motive for suicide. Dylan left a trail of damage. I saw a photo of him – he was beautiful, but … He didn't infect you?"

Pierre appeared to have gained a new confidence over dinner that approached smugness. "I had an *amour fou* with Dylan, but I never trusted him, so I'm safe. I've lived my life alone. I don't have many friends, so I took care of myself. Have you closed the murder book?"

"Didn't have time, and Dumont still has results coming in."

"I'll take care of the notes if you want."

"Of course I want!"

"Toni, I know, or sense you have something to drop on me. I have some questions for you. I'd like to start."

"Go ahead."

"In this memoir, O'Faolain says, 'I don't know of any other event that causes as much pain and destruction, and that is as little understood, as the destruction of love.' She goes on to ask, 'If love was an illusion in the first place, why should its absence be so devastating?' Her last pointed question is 'Where does that love go when it's over?' When I saw Dylan lying on that roof, my first thought was that I was finally free of him. But, I'm not. My obsession, that's what it is, was battered, I can't think of a better word, with each suspect. I thought Dylan loved me. I thought it was the job that ruined us. You know what our hours do to our partners. But I learned that I was just a trick, a shabby affair, diluted to loving an escort. Dylan didn't love any of us. Goldberg didn't love him. Dylan was a boy toy to the surgeon. I don't know about Henley. Jesus, Toni, I loved him." Matte turned away from her.

"I know you did."

When he turned back, Pierre appeared forlorn. "Have you ever lost your control, your soul, to love, or what passes for love?"

Damiano realized then the depth of Pierre's loneliness. He needed a listener. She smiled sadly. "I was a teenager. The high was fantastic, but I was scared. I broke it up and ran, and I never lost myself again. You're in free fall. I save ten percent for myself now."

"You have what you need. I never had that for more than a few weeks on and off with Dylan or anyone else. But, I was happy and miserable, I was alive. You're the best friend I have. At times, that wasn't saying much. I never knew how lost I was until Dylan died on that roof. I was invisible. At least, you saved yourself when you ran away."

"I'm not so sure. I still think of him from time to time and wonder."

"Huh. I dove in heart first, and I surrendered. I don't have HIV, but Dylan broke me and my trust. Now, I'm nowhere, but alone."

Pierre was leading Damiano to the reason she'd gone to his dinner. Inwardly, she began to mourn a friendship that might be lost. An abject sense of failure fell on Damiano, as Pierre continued.

"When my father said thanks today, I was almost elated, but that simple recognition had come too late. I disappointed him early on and I don't feel anything for him now, but pity. I don't have the desire to connect with him. You've been lucky, Toni."

"I have, but Jeff is loving and kind like you, Pierre. I've shortchanged him and he knows it. I'm not lying to myself, but I am a good cop. You know I'm not the greatest wife or mother."

"At least you're honest. I've dropped my load. It's your turn, Toni. I believe that I'm about to hear a theory even though you have a confession."

Damiano nodded, as blood drained from her face.

Pierre's expression hardened.

"This whole case got away from me. I think you believe me when I said I refused the acting chief temporary job. I don't want it now. What I miss is the field work, the freedom of it, and you. Donat's secretary piles my desk up with new files every day. I've kept up with Donat's wife, and I'm making an effort to be better at home. From the night we found Dylan's body on that roof, I lost my footing. There was so little violence on Dylan's body that the murder seemed to have a gentleness that I'd not seen before. From the start, I believed Dylan's killer was someone who loved him, and I didn't want that person to be you, Pierre.

"Allen is a twisted bombshell, trained to kill. He did look good for a time, but he's a smash and grab, in reverse. He likes to leave his victim bloodied. That's his trademark. He's too rough to have murdered Dylan. He didn't fit. When you located Peter Henley, I wanted him to be our perp. He'd want to kill Dylan, but he's a whiner, a name-caller who runs away like a kid. He's not a killer. Further, he never loved Dylan, he used him.

"Nate Goldberg has given me what I need to close the case as we've already said. As Dr. Belmont told us, 'Your killer is intelligent.' Goldberg was. He was at Cleo's the night of the murder and he had motive. I still want to use his confession, it's a firm close." Damiano paused, thinking.

Pierre braced his arms across his chest, giving Damiano a hard stare. A coldness had entered the room.

"Yet I remember the hole that Goldberg rented for Dylan. He had nothing, I was appalled, and sad for Dylan. When his father took off, Dylan was on his own at seventeen. What could he know of love? He thought he'd learned about survival. Here's Goldberg with all his money, toying with Dylan and tossing him out every night. He felt nothing for Dylan. At the very first interview, near the end when he rose to his feet he shouted, 'I know what I've done.' Referring to killing Dylan he shouted, 'I wish I had.' I don't think Goldberg did kill Dylan. He didn't know he was infected then. I weighed the odds. He wasn't stupid. He may have said that in the event he hadn't been infected. Spitzer, he felt, would have found some loophole to get him off if we charged him. I'm not forgetting that point.

"Allen also said something interesting when we first talked to him. Dylan had told him that he was meeting someone for a second chance."

Pierre dropped an arm in an attempt at laxity. Damiano didn't miss the movement.

"Allen wasn't certain, but he thought Dylan had hinted at a second chance. I was there. You weren't. Let's say Dylan did say that. Allen wouldn't have given Dylan a second chance. That leaves you and Goldberg. Dylan had just seen Goldberg. The statement suggests someone he hadn't seen for some time. You." Her voice had dropped to a whisper. "We thought initially, or I did, that our perp was a coward, coming up on Dylan from behind. I think the killer loved Dylan and couldn't bear to have Dylan know he was about to die. He wanted it to be almost painless."

Pierre made an attempt to shrug the last sentences aside. "How?"

"You used the back stairs, arrived before Dylan and surprised him. Whatever you said to him, he turned around for you, trusting you …"

They sat across from one another for an uncomfortable silence until Pierre smiled. "Why?"

"I'm still theorizing. It was the theft, and the humiliation of it. The trigger was Dylan's arrogance, believing he could call you and you'd come running. You killed Dylan to save yourself. To protect yourself, you deliberately corrupted evidence that couldn't be used against you. There might be skin cells that Marie will find, but can't use, unless …"

"I confess! Your theories sound like well-plotted ravings. You've been scrambling and still are, Toni." Pierre sat up. His body stiffened. His face drained of color.

"Pierre, you are a suspect. I'm the lead cop."

"You have a confession, Toni. I don't know why you're ignoring it. I thought tonight's dinner was a makeup of sorts. I'll finish up the murder book tomorrow. My father can't leave my mother alone. The house is a mess. I'll do the cleanup and the groceries for them. I'll be at work by two and I'll stay late to finish up."

Toni got to her feet and walked stiffly to the foyer.

"The only thing you've proven tonight is that I can't sustain a relationship."

Damiano had her hand on the door handle. Her heart raced. "I know what you did, Pierre."

"No," Pierre said dejectedly, "you'll always think you know. What if you're wrong? What if from the time you lost your footing, you were wrong in your assumption about me. Your whole theory is faulty at its core. I remember warning you way back – don't go there. If you had kept an open mind, you might have zoned in on Goldberg sooner and saved his life.

"Now, leave before we hurl insults that we can never take back. In the end, theories are suppositions. I stood by you and your son without question."

Damiano snatched up her bag and phone. She hurried down the front stairs. All she left with was failure and doubt.

Epilogue

It was a mistake,' you said. But the cruel thing was, it felt
like the mistake was mine, for trusting you.
—DAVID LEVITHAN

Matte locked his front door. The dirty dishes and wine glasses lay on the dining room table. He picked up the plates and glasses, rinsed them, loaded the dishwasher and turned it on. He went back to the living room and sat reviewing Damiano's theory. He wondered why the relationships in his life had soured, leaving a trail of bitterness. He had lied for Damiano, covered for her, all for what in the end? Matte laughed forlornly, "It's a small wonder she didn't read me my rights." That night, no matter the outcome, Matte knew that Damiano's theory had forever changed their relationship.

As soon as she was at a safe distance, Damiano called Jeff. "I have to stop off at work. It might be another hour."

"What happened, Toni?"

"I can't talk about it now. I have work that needs doing."

"At this time of night?"

"Please, Jeff."

"Call me when you're finished. I'll pick you up. Don't you dare call Uber."

"Thank you." She reached Crémazie in good time. Damiano grabbed some pens from her desk and headed for the murder room. She found what she needed on page nine. She had begun to print up the notes on the corrupted evidence, but she hadn't finished. Initially, she had decided to make short shrift of it. That was no longer the case. Pierre would see this work tomorrow. Damiano fanned the pens across the desk in front of her. On a blank sheet of paper she wrote one word, trying to match the pen with the one she had used. None matched. *Damn! Where's the bloody pen?* She dumped the contents of her bag on the desk. *Ah ha!*

Damiano began to print that her partner Detective Matte was overwrought with the death of his friend. He wanted a memento, the gold chain he had bought for him. Uncharacteristically, Matte had locked the bag in his desk drawer. As soon as the lapse came to light, Matte personally delivered the contents to Crime. Although it was determined no tampering of said evidence had occurred, the chain of custody had been broken.

Damiano wrote up the next two paragraphs as camouflage. Matte would believe she'd written the notes yesterday. She left the book as she had found it, and returned the pens. If it worked, the snare was set. Damiano had the proof. She'd read Dumont's email before Matte's dinner. A half hour later, she was safely in the car with Jeff. "I laid out my theory." Jeff shook his head. "You're right – he gave me nothing, except a reminder of his loyalty to me. You know how I feel."

"Serves you right. I told you to conduct that questioning at the office."

"I know, I know, but I have to cover all the bases. That's my job."

"You could be wrong, Toni."

"I know that, too."

Earlier that afternoon, Daniel Boucher was counting down the minutes to five o'clock. "Are they ever late for a transfer, Robson?"

"With all the construction, what do you think?"

Boucher flicked sweat from his forehead. He thought of himself bending over naked with his legs spread. *I'm not a freakin' dog!* His legs jellied and he sat on the bunk, grinding the sides with his palms. When Robson's phone rang, Boucher flew to his feet and stopped breathing.

"He's ready," was all Robson said.

Pichette walked in with a police escort, carrying a cardboard box. Robson understood and dug out his keys to the cell door. "You'll be under house arrest with monitoring until your court date."

Boucher's shoulders relaxed. God! "Wow! That's the best thing since this whole mess-up began."

Pichette walked inside the cell. "Sit down so the officer can attach the ankle monitor. House arrest is mandatory. Any violation and you'll be sent to Bordeaux. Clear?"

"Yes. Oh, man, thank you."

Boucher was driven home in a patrol car. Manon ran out the door when the car pulled into the driveway. The officer walked into the house with them. He turned on the monitor in the kitchen.

When the officer left, Daniel made a beeline to the door leading to the garage. "What the hell! Where's my car?" he shouted in rage. "What the fuck happened to it?"

Manon hadn't followed him because she knew he'd be back. Boucher slammed the door and marched into the kitchen to confront her. "You're wearing it on your ankle."

Boucher bit his thumb. "That car was my handle." He couldn't say another word.

At seven thirty Wednesday morning, Carmen DiMaggio was driving to work in St-Eustache in her new lease, a black Mazda 3 Sport, blaring her favorite eighties music. When she was pulled over, she wasn't surprised. "That bloody cop. My car's not even a day old!" She rolled down the window, waiting on the officer who approached pad in hand. DiMaggio took out her own pad, prepared to ask for his badge number. "Officer, I wasn't even doing a hundred. It's a new car, so I was being careful."

"*Dans un zone de cinquante kilometres, madame!*"

She hadn't seen the marker for the construction zone ahead. Carmen threw her pad across the seat and the ticket with it. "Shit, shit, shit. There goes another three points!"

Velma hesitated when she saw the call display. At least it was better to deal with Allen by phone. "Yes?"

"It's Dinka, Velma. The police have closed the case. Of course, Matthew wasn't involved. I never thought he would be. He's sorry for the fight. Do you still need an old lecher for Friday's show at Cleo's? Before you answer, I will go down with both of you. Let's not end a friendship on a misunderstanding where both parties were hurt."

"Well, I don't know if I want to risk it."

"For me Velma, and the great fun in our high school years."

"Truth is I've tried but I can't find a lecher as convincing as Matthew."

"Good! We'll pick you up at seven Friday night."

Damiano hadn't slept much and struggled with the files Denise had left for her the next morning. Rubbing her eyes and blinking didn't help. She didn't feel right about the ambush. By nine fifteen, she had already snapped at Detective Galt for his early morning gab fest, waving him back to his desk. The room was almost cold with the a/c. Still her taupe shirt stuck to her back and she leaned in and pulled it out. She had made a comfort lunch, a peanut butter and jam sandwich which she devoured by ten with three cups of coffee. From time to time, she found her Ds looking up at her. Cops had good noses.

Thankfully, Dumont arrived an hour early, and they studied her results in the murder room and spoke in whispers. "You're absolutely positive, Marie?"

Dumont produced the receipt. "Henley? I'm surprised." Damiano studied the receipt. "You're thinking Matte's skin cells are on the chain. You discover that with the swab and hair sample? If they are, Matte deliberately broke the chain of custody so that evidence could not be used against him in court.

Matte reads my notes today indicating he bought the chain. He signs below my signature, and we have his testimony of the lie. You make the arrest."

"I'm sorry."

Damiano pinched the bridge of her nose. "What if we're wrong? What does it amount to if they were intimate? I already have a confession."

"And I have a job to do and I want it done thoroughly."

"It stinks! Here we are lying in wait to ambush a colleague. I need more coffee." Dumont produced her old Thermos and poured a plastic cup. "You can't leave, Toni."

Damiano read the test results of the chain. Dylan Kane had been a busy boy who never thought to clean the chain. There were two names: Goldberg's and Henley's and two unknowns. Dumont was counting on Matte's to be one of them. With Matte as a murder suspect, the corrupted evidence was then admissible.

Matte arrived fifteen minutes early, haggard and hesitant. He stopped at the door when he saw Dumont. He walked to the empty seat, eyes fixed on Damiano. "Company I didn't expect, Marie." He said nothing more to her. "Toni, do you want me to read your notes, is that the lead here?" Matte took the book calmly though his cheeks burned.

"Read what I've done so far; make changes if they're warranted. We'll sign my notes, and I'll officially hand the rest over to you." The emotion in the room was as cold as the ambush. Matte read, tracing the words with his finger. "Well, everything looks fine. By the way, I was able to fish out the receipt for the gold chain. Thought you might want that, Marie."

Damiano's relief was short-lived. Her phone rang. She looked at Dumont. "I have to take this."

Dumont studied the receipt. Kane must have been gifted two chains then, and probably lost the first. Her face fell.

"Rachel Meyer, I did not expect to hear from you."

"I have no time to waste. I was tested for the virus this morning. I'm at the condo now with men who are packing up all the furniture. I'm donating everything to the Jewish Community Foundation of Montreal. There is something here you must see. I'm at the breaking point. Get here quickly. I cannot spend an extra second of my life in a place that revolts me. I never want to see this condo again."

"There was a search warrant, Ms. Meyer."

"I am not a vindictive or stupid woman. Nate cut into the side of the mattress and then sutured it. I thought I was seeing a zipper until I recognized his work. He used to practice his sutures at home, a long time ago.

He's hidden something in there that your *experts* missed."

"You are anything but stupid. We are on our way!" Damiano shut the murder book. "Pierre, I need you on this. You too, Marie. You'll need your equipment."

Dumont took her own car. "Pierre, I need you to speed to Old Montreal," Damiano said.

"I've been there. Did you forget?"

"Dumont and her log book. Her techs missed something. She's not perfect."

"Is this some contest?" Matte asked curtly.

"Let's just beat her to the condo."

They arrived together. Meyer buzzed them up. She was standing in the lobby, edgy and visibly tense like the three who had just arrived. Two men huddled quietly against the far wall. "Thank you for calling me, Rachel. I can't imagine how difficult this time is for you."

"Then don't try. Look, I'm sorry – I never knew what shock was. I can't sit still, I can't cry. I don't understand anything anymore."

"Just show us and we will work as quickly as possible."

Meyer didn't seem to hear Damiano. "I made a point of ignoring everything in that rat hole, but I couldn't keep my eyes from the bed and what went on there. I tore off the sheets and tossed them down the chute. I wanted to burn them. The men were turning the Tempur-Pedic mattress because it's awkward and heavy. That's when I saw the sutures. I can't go back inside. You'll see them."

The three detectives entered the near empty condo and walked directly into the bedroom.

"I don't know how we missed this," Dumont said apologetically to both detectives.

The sutures were at the top of the mattress, midway down its side. They did resemble a zipper or trademark. Dumont put on her gloves and took scissors from a kit. She saved the suture bits in an evidence bag. Next, she put her gloved hand into the tight cavity and slowly extracted a black shirt that had been folded flat. She laid it on a larger evidence bag. All three zeroed in on a sleeve. Dumont had a magnifying glass and a fluid. "That's saliva." She looked closely. "I have to handle the shirt with great care. I think we can make out slight indentations of the chain on that sleeve. I'll work with Belmont for teeth marks. We have the palm prints. Give us twenty-four hours for complete confirmation. The confession, with these results, will be as precise as the surgeon who committed the murder." Dumont turned to the detectives. She felt she was on the outside of the team and in the way. She packed up and left Damiano and Matte alone.

"Let's talk to Meyer first, Pierre."

Meyer had stopped moving. "Nate killed that kid, didn't he?"

Damiano nodded and Meyer broke down. Damiano laid her hands on Meyer's shoulders. "How does this happen? Nate was a husband, a father, a healer; I loved him. How could he take a life? Commit suicide?" Her breath was ragged. "I have to leave. I can't be here. I just can't. I never knew this man." Damiano didn't try to stop her. What could she say that would change anything?

The men went quietly back into the condo.

Damiano herself felt unsteady. She abhorred women who cried and now she was one of them. "Pierre, I messed up." She sniffed and swiped at the tears as if they were black flies. Their partnership was branded now. A layer of trust gone. "I am sorry to the core."

"You should be," Matte said, standing in Damiano's face. His eyes locked on hers, with an inexorable sadness that Damiano would never forget. He turned and walked away.

He got as far as the door. "Let's get out of here."

Perhaps their accounts might never be settled. In police work they were far into their careers. Both detectives knew what was at stake and understood the work of change. Some residual rancor diminished in importance as they drove away from the condo on rue Notre-Dame.

Silence was not a comfortable fit for Damiano. She barged ahead. "Pierre, would you have gone to Cleopatra's if Dylan had called you?"

Matte sighed deeply. He didn't look over at Damiano. "Yes," he whispered raggedly, "but he didn't call."

The car was silent again.

Damiano could not let go. She continued with an anxious hope of mending the divide. "That was some detective work to come up with the receipt."

Matte looked at the wheel before he gave up a nod. He wasn't sure whether he wanted to work again with Damiano. She had ambushed him, and worse, she hadn't trusted him. He allowed seconds to pass, then a minute. Yet, he could not resist uttering the perfect sequitur. "And the timing?"

"Legendary!"

One month later, Chief Richard Donat announced he would be back at Crémazie in September.

ACKNOWLEDGEMENTS

It's quite the experience to be invited into a different world. We have all attended plays and shows, generally at our common venues, particularly in Montreal: Place des Arts, the Bell Center, Théâtre Saint-Denis, Club Soda, the Centaur and the Segal Center. We know what to expect. Robert Idsinga, who has become a good friend and a marvelous resource, invited me to a show at Café Cleopatra on St-Laurent Boulevard. Over the years, I must have unwittingly passed Café Cleopatra without ever really noticing or inquiring about the Grande Dame of the Montreal Main.

The night's experience was unique. Robert guided me up the stairs to the dressing rooms and the cubby holes and finally to the roof past the solid steel door. The Café's construction – the wooden floors, walls and even the cupboards are a testament to the enduring quality of a craftsmanship that we don't see today. The performers' exuberance, the powdery rooms and the costumes were all a delight.

The surprises kept coming. At first, Robert and I were alone at our ringside table, and I wondered who would attend such a show. Our table filled up with photographers, and then all varieties of Montrealers appeared, some in costume, others made up. From the minute the show started, the audience turned on, clapping, dancing, singing along, and cheering each performer as though they were friends. It was a raucous festival! I learned from Robert that most performers returned every month and to my surprise so did their fans. Everyday people with drama in their hearts perform for the thrill of the show. What an evening for 'Cleo' and me!

I am deeply indebted to Robert Idsinga for his willingness to share his knowledge of Montreal's secrets and the time he offers to take me to this city's sites. There doesn't seem to be a corner of the city he hasn't explored. His photos are a great help, his conversations always interesting and his generosity gracious and ready.

A grateful shout out to 'Velma' the producer of the monthly shows at Cleopatra's; her enthusiasm and ideas set the show on its monthly roll. I thank her for her time and information about the makeup and the love that goes into each presentation.

I continue to be grateful for my time at the Crémazie Division, Place Versailles and Parthenais. In my books, these places feel like home. The simple and spare reality of these venues have lost their 'otherness' and have emerged as ordinary places, part of our city. What wonderful friends I have: Louise Morin, patient, generous and technically adept, my sister Mary Kindellan Tellett (she's my Toronto sales rep who finds time and enthusiasm to personally deliver books hither and yon for me), Kathy Panet, Claire Coleman, Noreen Barrett, Hamid and Maryam Afshari, my brothers and sisters who generously support each and every new book, and Dick Irvin whose continuing optimism and enthusiasm are appreciated. Thanks to all!

I offer a final salute and thank you to Irene Pingitore, a proof reader, invitational helper, book counter and second greeter at each and every signing. To Cynthia Iorio, half of the sales team that Chapters wants to hire for their stores. Cynthia has a busy life, yet she has never missed working an event. Her charm with people is fun to watch. I'm lucky to say, she is a friend of mine.

I give a huge shout-out to Brenda O'Farrell. Thank you for the generous offer of your time and your excellent long-standing editing skills. I hold your friendship very dear and close to my heart. Margaret Goldik has accompanied me from the day the journey began. She is a friend I respect and admire. Her editing and word skill are second only to the support she has always offered to my betterment. Thank you, Margaret.

Gina Pingitore was the first person who heard "Saddle Shoes & Lilac" from *Sheila's Take* and the first person to read the opening chapter of *In The Shadows*. Gina has read and proofed each book more than once, she has attended every presentation and she is the other half of my great team. I am forever grateful to her.

Simon Dardick, my intrepid publisher maintains his joyful approach to books and keeps authors on course with his expertise and flawless judgment. He is a trusted and respected gentleman in the literary world. It is my privilege to work with him and learn from him.